Inside Lindsey's Handbag

Adrian Dalton

WITH THANKS TO

Gareth Ellis, Rick Morgan, Sophie Ramsden
and Danny Diedrick

DISCLAIMER

CONTENTS

Prologue

Si Fraser and Gypsy Wright are relaxing in the garden. It's an unseasonably balmy spring afternoon. Si is lying on the grass watching an airplane's progress as it inches across the azure sky. Gypsy is trying to read a copy of QX; the wind rustling the pages infuriatingly. She basks in the rays, face tilted heavenwards before rummaging through her bag for some Factor fifteen.

"Isn't it just gorgeous out here babe?" She stretches, blissfully relaxed.

He nods his agreement.

"Fabulous. It reminds me of this lodger Mam had when I was a kid. Lindsey."

"Oh? Why?" She begins massaging the cream liberally into her pink shoulders.

"Well, you see the line that airplane's made across the sky?" He screws up his eyes and looks towards the sun again. "She used to tell me that the whole world and its entire population are living in her handbag, and that line is the zip."

She raises her eyebrows and pushes her sunglasses up onto her head. "So, we're all inside Lindsey's Handbag are we then, darling? Well, I suppose it's as good a theology as any other."

"Yes, I quite like it." He closes his eyes. "Could you pass me *my* handbag please, sweetie? I don't know about you, but I'm dying for a fag."

Chapter 1: No. 69

It was late afternoon before Gypsy laid down her paint-brush. Finally she was satisfied the walls looked an even shade of magnolia. From upstairs came the sounds of Si getting ready for work and taking a shower, which put the time at around six o'clock. It'd taken most of the day but now, as she'd envisioned, her sitting room was transformed into a light, airy haven. The smell of paint hung headache-inducingly in the air.

She uttered a weary but satisfied sigh and slid open the French windows leading out onto the garden. Jezebel, a marmalade tabby hurtled in, nearly knocking her off her feet and yowling reproachfully at having been so rudely banished. Gypsy knelt down; tenderly stroking her under the chin until rumbling purrs informed her that all was forgiven.

Good. She thought to herself, trudging upstairs to change. If there was one thing she really couldn't be doing with today it was a fecking mardy cat.

The smart, semi-detached that was to be her new home boasted three bedrooms. Gypsy had chosen the medium sized one overlooking Kershalton Street. After all she didn't need as much space as Si, who'd be sharing with his boyfriend. Curiously she peered round the door of the smallest room. It was empty. The only sign of George, their new lodger (and the sole applicant to their vacancy ad) was a Louis Vuitton suitcase and several packed crates stacked neatly on a mattress.

Having been unavoidably detained at a casting on the day of his interview she'd not had the opportunity of meeting him. This was a shame as when they'd first decided on getting another housemate she and Si had planned to do an amusing "Shallow Grave" style series of interviews. On second thoughts, she conceded, perhaps things had worked out for the best. It wouldn't have been so hilarious to put off their only candidate. Although she trusted Si's judgement, his description of George had done little to satisfy her natural curiosity. She was dying to get a good gander at him herself.

Grateful that it was Saturday and the rest of the weekend stretched enticingly ahead of her, she stripped off her paint splattered jeans and jumper; dumped them in the clothes bin and stood in front of the mirror, eyeing herself critically. She was aware that thanks to strong features, a slightly square jaw and an overbite, most people would describe her as striking rather than conventionally pretty. Despite trying every diet going she still had a naturally curvaceous figure. If she had it her way, she'd be whippet thin. Rubbing a smudge of mascara from under her eye she smoothed her hair away from her face before covering herself with a towel.

Stretching her arms tentatively, she grimaced, discovering aching muscles. Although her body had been put to good use, in this case as a painter and decorator extraordinaire, her mind had remained firmly fixed on a calamitous audition she'd given earlier on in the week.

Gypsy cringed at the memory. The part she'd gone for had been in an advert for an invigorating (and highly caffeinated) alcopop. She'd been required to dance free-style, whilst lip-synching to the 'Blueberry Vodkatini' jingle. Unfortunately an overly spirited high kick combined with tights and a laminate floor had resulted in fiasco. She'd whacked herself in the face with her foot before landing on her rear with a painful, undignified thud. Literally adding insult to injury, her nose had proceeded to bleed copiously. The Producer, a loud, shouty woman, had spent the next twenty minutes nervously plying her with tissues before paying for her cab home. Heinous.

Every time she thought about it she froze with mortification. Not only had she not received a call back, unsurprising as it may have been, she'd also managed to cover herself in blood and ruin one of her favourite tops. Not to mention the fact that from a certain angle she was convinced, yes *convinced* that her nose was slightly crooked now. But what really got her goat was that it had started off so promisingly! It'd nearly been a triumph, the part had been hers for the taking – she'd been bang on top of her game. That is before she was sabotaged by her own treacherous feet.

Ruefully, she prodded her nose before searching for some tweezers. She frowned at the dark hairs sprouting above the offending appendage. Bitter experience had taught her that unless she attacked these on a regular basis they persistently regrouped into a monobrow. Whilst plucking, she ruminated on some of the close-calls to success she'd seen in her career to date.

After finishing her degree at Putney School of Dance & Drama she'd managed to secure a small part in a certain well known West End musical. She'd been confident this would be the perfect launch pad for her career, but then the show had ended and she'd found herself struggling to find work ever since. Last October her hopes had been riding particularly high after she was cast in a series to be filmed on location in Spain, only to be dashed when the production company went bust. As for a singing career she'd been to countless auditions to little avail.

She exhaled noisily, letting her hand drop to her side. A lesser person might've been discouraged. But, she decided, it was far better to have almost done something than not to have even come close. Why, with the right attitude, she'd practically done it all!

Just then her mobile sprang to life. Seeing her friend's name flash up on the screen she swore to herself and slapped her hand to her forehead. Somehow in all the DIY upheaval she'd completely forgotten she was expected in Hounslow for dinner.

"Babe! You're still coming round aren't you?" Kate's voice demanded as soon as she picked up. "I hope you realise I'm cooking for us. Tell me you're on the way."

"Shit! Give me fifty minutes, okay?"

Hanging up she rapped loudly on the bathroom door so as to be heard above the sounds of running water. Si was not going to be getting the lengthy shower he'd expected.

She never heard the phone ringing downstairs.

X

It was nearly two hours later when Gypsy finally arrived at Si's mother, Cathy Fraser's home, where Kate was currently living.

"Hey," Gypsy gasped bending over and clutching her side whilst making an apologetic face and trying to catch her breath. "Sorry I'm late, I came as fast as I could. How're things chez Cathy?"

Kate finished fixing them both a coffee and turned around with a wide welcoming smile. Dressed casually in tracksuit bottoms and a vest top, she flicked her honey coloured hair behind her shoulders and gave her a hug.

"I love it. It'll be perfect until I can find somewhere nearer work. You're a doll for introducing us." She carried the mugs carefully over to the table. "Cathy's out walking the dogs by the way, but she sends kisses and left some of her home-made chocolate fudge for you in the fridge."

"Oooh, go on then, twist my arm. How much stuff does she put in it anyway? Enough to get a small elephant stoned I reckon. I have to stay with it this evening you know."

But she opened the fridge anyway, quickly locating the small, tissue-covered square between the live yoghurt and some yams. She unpeeled it and dropped it daintily into her mouth.

"It tastes gorge," she conceded, eyes closing as she chewing appreciatively.

4

"I know, I think she really overdid it this time. I swear I got high from my room with the fumes of it cooking last night." Kate offered her the sugar. "You were right though, she's dead nice; not at all starry. Who'd have thought Si's mum would be such a laugh as well as a celeb? She's so much fun. I'm going to miss her when I go."

Gypsy licked the chocolate off her fingers. "I'm sure she'll miss you too. It must get lonely here when she's not entertaining. I know she doesn't see as much of Si as she'd like. Poor baby's always working; unlike me."

"How about that waitressing job you were going to try?" Kate asked doubtfully. She wasn't convinced that working in a busy restaurant would be the absolute best job for her friend. Gypsy had her heart in the right place, but as well as being forgetful and terminally disorganised she could also be tactless to the point of rude.

"I've agreed to do a trial tonight, but I'm positive I'm going to hate it. What a cliché it'd be if we were in Hollywood, eh? Wannabe actor gets waitress job. How depressing, but I need to pay the rent. Oh hell, I'll probably get all the orders mixed up." She shrugged. A laissez faire attitude that did not bode well for a job valuing customer service, Kate couldn't help but think.

They took their mugs and a plate of hob-nobs and migrated next door, parking themselves onto an old and comfy velvet sofa. Wincing, Gypsy kicked off her painful (but to die for) Christian Louboutins. Rubbing her blisters she looked round the walls at photos of Si in various stages of kid-hood.

"So," Kate took a sip of her tea and lit up a cigarette, looking apologetically at Gypsy who was trying to give up. "Hope you're hungry? Food will be ready soon."

"I'm starving! Bring it on, I've lost the will to care that I've got a huge, fat arse. Oh, and talking of dinner I was thinking of inviting Dario and Mark round soon, we haven't got together in ages. Would you like to come?"

"Mmm, that sounds nice. Are you going to cook?"

Gypsy laughed hysterically. "That'll be a no."

"Well, in that case I will." Kate smirked. "FYI your arse isn't huge."

"Whatever. Just telling it like it is."

"What you've got is a J-Lo butt. Do you realise how many women would pay good money to have a bum like yours?"

As the evening progressed, they moved back into the kitchen and chatted about work and mutual friends over a couple of bottles of Chardonnay while waiting for Kate's lasagna to cook. It grew dark outside and started to spit with rain, eventually bringing in Cathy Fraser, a few dead leaves and an assortment of large, wet Poodles.

By nine o'clock feeling slightly stoned and a little pissed, Gypsy finally got up, announcing she'd have to go or risk missing her first shift at work.

"The bus-stop's just up the road; you'll be there in no time." Kate squeezed her goodbye.

It wasn't until she was halfway up the road that she realised she had no idea which bus she needed to get her to the restaurant.

Sod it, something told her this job wasn't going to be a keeper.

Chapter 2: The Black Cock

"You're late." Lisa snapped as Si entered the deserted pub, dripping water and apologies.

"I know." He took off his coat and flung it over a stool. "Gypsy has been painting the sitting room."

She looked at him, one eyebrow raised like a dagger.

"So..."

"So, she left all the windows open didn't she? I had to rush around like a maniac shutting them all before everything got drenched."

"Hmm, just don't do it again, okay? I've got a million things on my mind right now without my staff disappearing on me."

"Fine, fine just get off my back will you. I'm here now."

He was one of the few people who could get away with talking back to Lisa Carson, the new Bar Manager. Weaker souls had been known to cringe away in terror from the prospect of Her Wrath. Si knew better, she was a cherub at heart.

"Where's Dario tonight?" He asked starting to unload the dish washer.

"Stock taking."

"And Marina?"

Lisa took a sip of coffee from the Wonder Woman mug he'd bought her for Christmas. "Upstairs painting I think. But it's her night off so she'll probably be down later. By the way Dario and Mark broke up."

Si blinked. "You're kidding? What happened?"

"No idea. You can ask Dario yourself when he resurfaces."

She started on the next task in hand, arranging cranberry fcuk bottles in a display at the back of the bar.

"It's going to be mental tonight Si and we open in less than half an hour. Can I trust you guys to get things set up while I take care of some phone calls?"

"Fine," he said distractedly, "I just have to text Tony and ask him exactly when he's coming back down."

"Are you still thinking about going on holiday this summer?"

"Hmm." He frowned. "Yeah, Tony's desperate to go. I just don't have the funds right now."

"I'm sure you'll work something out." She was already on her way to the office running through a mental checklist of things to be done before opening time.

He stared at his mobile and tried to think of a witty, funny message to send.

Boyfriend aside, everything else, particularly financially, had been stressing him out lately. Si shook his head deciding that he probably needed therapy. He wondered if retail therapy counted.

X

By the time Tony received Si's message he'd showered, changed into a fresh shirt and jeans and was already on his way out to meet Stella for dinner.

Born and bred in Scotland Tony had moved to London to pursue a job in advertising at the age of twenty-five. Six years later, he now had a large group of friends in both London and Glasgow. He enjoyed visiting his home city as often as work would allow.

For his last few weeks in Glasgow he'd been staying with his sister Jodie and her husband. It was always a joy – if a little exhausting – to spend time with his small niece Becky.

She loved her uncle to distraction and would spend the duration of his visit in a state of high excitement; alternately shrieking with delight at the riotous stories he told her or doing one of her 'impressions' for her new captive audience. Their house was not far from the centre of town, and so he'd decided to walk the short distance to Café Boheme, declining Jodie's offer of a lift.

All around him Tony could see and hear the city stirring itself and coming alive for a Saturday night. It was an uplifting feeling. The streets were busy and full of noise, lights and music. The aroma of various kinds of delectable foods wafted out from the bars and restaurants grouped along the high street. By the time he reached the Café his stomach was growling with hunger.

Glancing through the window, he saw Stella immediately. She sat at their usual table in the middle of the room talking into her mobile. His friend from childhood, Stella Buchanan was under a lot of strain at the moment and he was more than a tad concerned. Newly divorced, a control freak and self-confessed workaholic, she'd been devastated when the PR Company she worked for was liquidated, leaving her without the job that she thrived on.

"Money isn't the problem, angel," she'd explained to him sadly when he'd offered her a loan. "I just don't know what to do with myself now. That job was everything to me, and the thought of starting all over again somewhere new is just too horrendous for me to think about right now."

When he'd suggested that she come down to London for a break, she'd looked thoughtful, shrugged and promised to consider the idea. Tony hadn't been reassured, that kind of indecision was completely out of character. And then unexpectedly she'd phoned sounding a bit more positive and insisted that they meet up for a chat. He could only hope she'd made her mind up the change would do her good after all, and that maybe this was the beginning of the end of the slump she seemed to be in.

By the time he'd walked through the door into the warmth of the restaurant and given his coat to one of the waiters, she was already on her feet. They embraced and she kissed him affectionately on both cheeks.

"So." Stella began, as soon as they'd had their glasses filled from the bottle of Pinot Grigio. She took a deep breath and looked at him, her hazel eyes sparkling with some of her old joie de vivre. "How's the visit going? Becky's not driving you nuts yet, I hope."

"I'm coping," He smiled passing her the basket of warm bread that'd appeared on the checked tablecloth as if by magic. "But you're not going to believe what happened last week."

"Oh?"

He rolled his eyes and took a sip of wine. "Jodie invited Lexy over for tea and brought along my wee nephew Chris to play with Becky." He paused dramatically.

"So far so good." She murmured around a mouthful of heavily buttered bread.

Tony stared at her enviously, wondering how it was physically possible that a woman who ate as much as this one did could be so utterly, stick thin. "It gets better, I promise. Ooh, look – my bruschetta's arrived already. That was quick."

He helped himself to a small portion before manoeuvring his glass and cutlery out of the way to make room for the more virtuous plate of tuna niçoise which the waitress brought.

"Thanks. Anyway, some of the parents from her school have been helping out; you know making costumes and what-have-you for the end of term play they're putting on. Jodie got roped into making a fairy costume; I think they're doing Peter Pan. Well, I say roped into, you know that she secretly likes making kiddy clothes."

"I don't know how she does it, I wouldn't have a clue," Stella declared admiringly heaping some calorie-laden creamed potatoes and swede swirls onto her fork.

Tony caught himself stealing flirtatious glances at her plate of poached salmon and pomme parisienne and hastily took a bite of his own salad. He was determined to look his absolute best next time Si laid eyes on him. If it took self-

10

restraint to get that wash-board stomach back, then so be it. "Well, she bought some of those fairy wings you can get from the fancy dress shop in town and made the most adorable pink dress. She'd even sewn flowers on it and made a garland for Tinkerbell to wear on her head..."

"Aye," Stella stopped chewing and smiled as he chuckled softly to himself.

"Och dear, sorry." He wiped his eyes, "It's not really that funny. It's just that Lexy was saying how sweet it looked and couldn't Becky try it on and wouldn't it be precious. And of course she absolutely refused to go near it and insisted on being a little madam. Then Chris decides *he* wants to wear it, so Lexy put it on him. I swear he looked so pretty with that flower garland on his blond curls, just like a wee girl. And then he was running around the room posing in the mirror, going "I'm a fairy! I'm a fairy!" – Stella, it was hil-arious."

"Oh no!" She cracked up. "You must have been pissing yourself. Did Lexy see the funny side?"

"Of course!" He laughed. "It was so cute! Those kids are adorable."

"Anyway doll," he looked at her across the table as sternly as he could. "I presume we're not here to talk about my domestic life, riveting as it may be. Am I going off to England by myself then?"

She finished off the last morsel of food on her plate and put down her knife and fork with a clatter. "That was heaven. Look I won't keep you in suspense. I did a lot of thinking yesterday and basically I'd like to come with you. If you still want me, that is?"

"That's fabulous news!" He felt immeasurably relieved; at least he'd be around to keep an eye on her. "Think of it as a holiday sweetheart, lord knows I can't remember the last time you had one."

"I know." She seemed to be looking brighter already. "I'm quite excited about the whole idea. Can you believe I've never been to London before? And I'll finally get to meet this gorgeous new boyfriend of yours."

"Let's have a toast to the summer." He finished off the bottle filling them up once again and they chinked glasses before commencing the tremendously important task of studying the dessert menu.

Chapter 3: A face in the crowd

Receiver clamped to her ear, Ida Swann listened as the phone continued to ring. Gypsy was out. Perfect.

On the point of frustrated tears she squeezed her eyes shut. In a couple of hours Steve would be home, and then any plan of action would have to wait. Tomorrow would be too late. By then she might've changed her mind, or even decided to stay and find a way to make life at home bearable. She couldn't risk that. It had to be now, whilst she had the courage. Pushing her hands deep down into her coat pockets, Ida scrabbled for pennies, coming up with nothing but a crumpled business card. Knowing that Steve wouldn't approve, and angry with herself for minding, she smoothed out the card's heavy creases. A name was embossed on it in shiny, black italics. Cecile Benedicte, it read, Boss Model Management.

She dialled the number carefully, crossing her fingers that Cecile would be in and the offices would be open. This was going to be a long shot.

X

Later that afternoon Duncan Cavendish arrived at Boss Model Management's office. Camera slung round his neck, hands full of equipment, bags and car keys he pressed on the buzzer and shouldered his way in. It'd been another hectic day at work. Two of his models were late; the other had gone AWOL requiring a last minute replacement from the agency.

The project de jour had been a shoot for Viva Magazine; it involved taking pictures of a selection of models against a back-drop of wild animals. Subsequently, Duncan, Taylor Cheung – his Assistant – and the rest of the crew had taken the models in a trailer to Regent's Park Zoo. They'd spent an eventful day involuntarily creating chaos wherever they went. It was beyond vexing trying to work around small armies of families with children in tow. Inside the bus, make-up artists tried frantically to apply eye-shadow and lipstick whilst stylists metamorphosed lifeless hair into corkscrew curls. Pandemonium ensued as the genetically blessed darted in and out of the public toilets to change clothes.

Halfway through the shoot, one of the models, Rosa Barr – who's nasal, whining tones had been grating on Duncan's nerves all day – caused a scene when standing against an enclosure a Lemur grabbed a fistful of her hair. Her ear-splitting shriek had probably been heard in Soho. Then to cap it all off, it started pissing it down with rain. However, petty irritations aside it'd been a satisfactory days work and he suspected he was going to be gratified with the results. The pictures were to go with an article on a new brand of make-up. DIVAFACE was set to be huge in the world of cosmetics. Amongst other things, they promised against testing on animals.

It was a relief that Taylor was there to soothe taut nerves and fragile egos as he concentrated on what he did best, flattering, cajoling and inveigling the models into the poses he wanted. His efforts had been rewarded with some mesmerizing, poignant shots of Blaine Feynard with the tigers.

Out, gay and currently gracing the front of Fashion Fatale Magazine, Blaine was the newest queen of the supermodels. Posing for international magazine covers and strutting down runways in his inimitable style, he'd also been known to do specialty slots as drag DJ B. Fey at Club Envy, the hottest night-spot in town.

Looking at him now Duncan found himself fascinated by the boy iconic designer, Alana Dors, had hailed her new muse. He was just not what one expected in a male model. For one thing there was his height, or lack thereof. He was barely five foot ten for crying out loud. On top of that he was androgynous-looking, camp as a Shirley Bassey impersonator, and often snapped cross-dressed. In the same way Kate Moss had shaken up model-kind when she was first discovered amidst the Linda Evangelista and Cindy Crawford glamazons of the time, Blaine was a breath of fresh air... and then some. Thin rather than muscular with amber eyes, tousled auburn curls and almost feline features, he had an air of mystery about him. A curiously wistful smile revealed small teeth that slanted inwards. He also had a larger than life personality, and managed to convey a vital energy to the camera as he posed gazelle-like in front of the lions.

Content he'd got everything he needed from the shoot, Duncan was glad to finish up. At last he was free. A serious looking man and arguably a workaholic; he was undoubtedly a brilliant photographer. He had a quick eye, amazing vision, and a gift for making his subjects relax and perform for the camera. His work was almost always striking and thought provoking. Today, instead of being absorbed by the creation of something beautiful, he'd found himself uncharacteristically distracted. He couldn't stop thinking about a boy named Ash who he'd arranged to meet later at the Black Cock.

X

Ida took a deep breath before quitting the lift. It opened directly into a small waiting area with an intimidating selection of cover shots mounted on the walls. Most of the models seemed to be ones she recognised. A few were really famous, household names even, she realised biting her lip as she noticed a glossy picture of Fleur Ascott on the cover of Vogue. They all looked unspeakably perfect, and she wished fervently that she'd had time to change, or for that slap on

15

some make-up to disguise her black eye. It was the first time Steve had hit her in months, crushing her gossamer thin hopes that he'd changed. It had been one hell of a wake-up call. Self-consciously she put her hand up to feel the damage, convinced that everyone she passed was staring at her face.

Walking through to reception she followed a gaggle of models to a desk by the door and took her place behind them. Silently she watched the poised, polished girls with endless legs and lustrous hair chattering and laughing with the bookers. Glamorous, harassed looking office workers busied themselves around the huge, open-plan chrome and steel workplace, answering phones and sifting through fat portfolios and contact sheets.

To her horror her eyes filled with panicky tears, which she hurriedly blinked away. At this rate Boss were going to turn her down flat without so much as a second glance. Then, with no prospects, no money and no place to live she would be forced to return to Steve, who'd already be livid to find her gone. God only knew what he would do to her this time.

After all, Ida thought numbly, he loves me, provides for me and now I've deserted him. She knew he'd see it as a betrayal.

X

From across the crowded room Nadia Olsen watched the group of young hopefuls clustered around the New Faces desk. Her eyes zoned in on a hauntingly beautiful brunette with a badly-cut fringe and huge frightened bambi eyes.

Nadia scowled, her lovely features darkening. It seemed that no matter how successful you became there was always someone younger, hungrier, *edgier* just waiting to take your place. Of course she was thinking of Trinity Short, an ultra-skinny, sandy-haired teen currently taking the fashion industry by storm with her quirky and strikingly unique looks.

Trinity. The name buzzed around annoyingly like a wasp in her head. The girl had become an irritant ever since

16

Antonio Duvelli whom she'd worked with (amongst other things) several times in the past, had had the audacity to turn timelessly elegant Nadia down for his summer collection in favour of the younger model. It was paranoia inducing to know that there was a line of girls waiting on the side-lines ready to step into your shoes. Everybody wanted their fifteen minutes of fame.

Losing interest she patted her jeans pocket absentmindedly, wondering for the umpteenth time if it would be too desperately unwise to make a quick detour to the toilet for a line of coke before her meeting with Lucian.

Although she didn't make a habit of indulging during the day, this, she told herself, was an exceptional circumstance. She'd danced and drank until the early hours, and her nerves were pretty frayed after only a couple of hours sleep. It wouldn't do to let Lucian the Letch – so called due to his habit of expressing a somewhat more than professional interest in his girls – see her looking like a jittery mess. Especially, as she was relying on her considerable charms to get herself out of trouble and her career back on track. Tedious though being nice to Cecile's right hand man might be, she recognised it as a necessary evil.

Nadia had been modelling since the age of thirteen. Cecile herself had discovered her at Oxford Circus, bunking off school and smoking cigarettes with friends outside Top Shop.

With part Swedish, Spanish and Russian ancestry, Nadia possessed even Cosmo Cover girl features, a lascivious smile and heavy-lidded, cerulean eyes. These contrasted dramatically with mahogany hair hanging half-way down her back, and flawless olive skin. She'd quickly become a favourite with the designers and soon had posing for pictures and making clothes come alive on the catwalk down to an art form. It hadn't taken her long to rise to the elevated status of super, and that's exactly where she was planning on staying.

She deeply resented the fact that she could be summoned into the agency's office like an errant school girl, especially on the strength of one missed shoot, albeit an important one. The people from Verve had sworn never to work with her

17

again. Although she'd pleaded a nasty case of food poisoning, pictures of her clubbing the night away with Damien Black – lead singer of indie band Utopia – surfacing in the tabloids admittedly hadn't improved their temper.

She shook her head furiously. It didn't matter, she was a supermodel and that spoke for itself along with the tens of thousands of pounds she'd made for Boss over the last decade. Surely it wouldn't hurt for people to show her a little more respect?

Although she wouldn't admit it even to herself, her anger was also tinged with fear. She hadn't been working as much as she would've liked lately. There'd been whispers, clients complaining she was too stroppy and difficult. At first, she'd taken these vague warnings in her stride, rationalising that you couldn't please everybody all of the time. It was common knowledge that the more famous you were the more flack you got. It came with the territory.

To fill in the gaps in her normally hefty work load she'd been going out, maybe a teensy bit too much. After all, what was the point in being rich and successful if you couldn't enjoy it? Only now her lavish lifestyle seemed to be catching up with her and the last thing she needed was to get a reputation for being unreliable to boot. To top it all, her Accountant was worried about the state of her finances, hinting she was spending cash faster than it was coming in. Accountants, what did they know? She thought scornfully, didn't he realise that she could earn more in an hour than most normal people did in a month?

Worriedly, Nadia whipped a hand-mirror out of her Gucci bag and checked her perfect pout. Her lips were her signature feature and could get so dry after a night out. A glance in her compact reassured her there was nothing to fret about today. Luckily, make-up concealed a multitude of sins. All she needed to do now was to impress Letchy Lucian and convince him of her professionalism and she'd be working again in no time. It was time to start taking her career more seriously; get back to doing what she did best, working the runways and selling the clothes.

Squaring her shoulders and holding her head up high she marched purposely up to Lucian's office and rapped on the door. Charming men was the only thing she did even better.

X

Ida came back to herself with a start, realising that she'd been in a reverie, lost in thoughts of Steve and their old life together. She looked about her. The room was so noisy; full of people charging around, shouting instructions at each other.

Magazine covers dominated the walls in this room too, the faces appearing to sneer down at her menacingly. Bringing her attention back to the room's other occupants, she noticed that everyone else in the place model or not, was dressed in trendy, high-street gear. They all looked immaculately styled, yet somehow, conversely fresh-faced. Tugging at the bottom of her old, holey jumper picked up from the charity shop she felt horribly scruffy.

What am I doing here? She wondered fighting an almost overpowering urge to just turn and run. Her eyes once again filled with tears that threatened to spill over and make her humiliation complete. What choice did she have anyway? She'd burnt her bridges. There was no turning back. She was so distracted the receptionist had to call out to attract her attention.

"Hello! Is your name Ida Swann?" The bleached blond queried, peering over the top of DKNY glasses.

Ida nodded; managing to give what she hoped was a confident smile whilst surreptitiously brushing her sweaty palms against her thighs.

"Cecile will see you now," the girl gestured towards a glass-walled office to their right. "Please go on through."

Chapter 4: Follow the Yellow Brick Road

Mark listlessly waited for his phone to ring for the best part of the evening before deciding to go out. Of course, there was nothing stopping him making a few calls himself; it was more that he felt someone should phone him, just to see if he was alright. Was he being a drama queen? He wondered. It was a possibility.

The early afternoon had seen him sobbing inconsolably to an ill-timed re-run of 'The Torch Song Trilogy.' Then he'd masochistically chain-smoked on the balcony, tearfully listening to Amy Winehouse's 'Back to Black' before proceeding on a chocolate doughnut bender. He was committing calorific suicide but had lost the will to care. By the time 'Britain's Got Talent' had finished he decided to take his mind off his problems at any cost, even if it meant going out.

In the bathroom he idly perused his selection of shower gels all the while keeping up an unconvincingly cheerful whistling. He finally settled on an aquamarine coloured bottle. Revitalising and energising, the bottle enthused in psychedelic purple and lime green letters. He grunted distrustfully. If only it were that easy. Shower away your anguish and despondency. He scrubbed himself vigorously, using up the last of his Charles Worthington shampoo for good measure. The almost painfully sharp needles of hot water sluiced down his face and between his shoulder blades.

If he and Dario had been having problems he would've found it easier to get his head around the break up. The thing that really killed him was that he'd thought everything was fine; better than fine. They had talked about getting married. Admittedly not for a long while, but it had been discussed and Mark assumed that's where they were headed.

Getting out of the shower he picked up a shirt that Dario had left behind, the fabric still smelled of his aftershave. Holding it against his cheek his misery became an actual physical ache somewhere between his throat and his chest.

Shit. The chocolate doughnut craving was back with a vengeance. Undoubtedly this was some kind of internal defence mechanism, designed to transform grief into an escalating BMI. Not only was he going to be alone, he thought; now he was going to have to contend with being chubby too. Which meant if he wanted to get laid from now on, he'd be forced to join a gym. Mark let out a groan. He hated the gym with a passion. Christ on a bike, life was a cruel bitch sometimes.

Wrapping a thin towel around his waist he returned to the small, but by no leap of the imagination cozy, living room. Across the ceiling splotches of damp spread malignantly, giving rise to a musty smell that no amount of Febreze could dispel. The drawn curtains, dim lighting and fag smoke did little to improve the ambiance. Mark didn't care. It suited his mood. He grabbed his most recent copy of Boyz Magazine and poured himself a very stiff rum and diet coke. He was determined to escape his feelings, and if that meant getting shit-faced, so be it.

Pouring over the pubs, clubs and bars section with a look of single minded concentration he was eventually satisfied he'd found a suitable way to spend his evening. The Black Cock was having a karaoke night. The fact that Dario worked there was irrelevant, Mark told himself, this was about karaoke. *Right.* He knocked back his drink deciding he'd better get a move on if he wanted to catch the free entry before ten. He only had two hours to get ready.

21

X

By the time he left his flat he'd downed several more rum and cokes and was feeling no pain. As he got off the tube it started to drizzle, the streetlights reflecting on the wet pavement giving the surface an orangey glow.

Along the way he passed several restaurants where groups of people gathered outside smoking, laughing and socialising; reminding him of happier times. He felt another glimmer of self-pity and strangled the feeling quickly. He brushed the rain off his jacket and did a little jig as he walked to the sound of a Madonna remix from a bar across the street. This evening he was going to have fun. After all the night was young, so was he and who cared about a man called Dario?

Whilst he'd been getting ready indoors a plan of action had started to form comfortingly in his mind. Mark had always been an enthusiastic planner. He intended to take some time off from work and head off to the coast for a while. The weather was just starting to pick up. Brighton had a decent gay scene, was quite lively and would be enough of a change to do him some good. He needed a break and to clear his head. Apart from anything else the sheer monotony of his life was beginning to get to him.

Reaching the pub and pushing open the double doors music, laughter and eau de alcohol instantly enveloped him. The place was packed. His eyes searched behind the bar, but there was no sign of his ex. His heart sank, although he suspected deep down it was for the best. Also conspicuous in his absence was Si.

Drag queen Morag McDuff was holding court on the stage, and below her a young boy in a half-top was enthusiastically kicking off the karaoke with a truly awful rendition of Will Young's "Leave Right Now." He considered it briefly, but then thought of his empty flat and pushed his way manfully into the larger room. It was already so heaving it was impossible to tell if there actually was any floor beneath the mass of swaying bodies, let alone what it might look like. He waved to

DJ Little John who winked at him, before heading back to the bar for a drink.

The clientele comprised of a random mish-mash of older queens, bear-types and twinks with a few gym bunnies thrown in for good measure. An unfortunately dressed tranny who needed a good shave sat in front of him as he queued to be served. As a space cleared he grabbed the stool next to her and ordered a pint of lager. Surreptitiously he checked out the new barman. He had nice pecs, dark expressive eyes and designer stubble; it didn't hurt to look.

Mark took a large swallow of beer and peered out across the room into the crowd. It was a Friday night and everybody seemed to be in the mood to party. He wished he could join them and get into the spirit of things, but was already starting to feel that coming out had been a mistake. He didn't feel like dancing, cruising, or going on to Vauxhall for some serious clubbing. In fact, it was beginning to feel like he was having a major come down. Plus, the karaoke queen was making him feel old, for godsake, he looked about fifteen.

Dario kept creeping unwelcome into his thoughts. Painfully he wondered where he was and who he was with. And finally, that old chestnut, was he, Mark, going to end up alone? And would he still be alone when he was sixty years old, trying to pick up young boys and hoping they would be impressed with either his wealth or career? Of course, he considered, his mood free-falling like a kamikaze sky diver; that was assuming that at some point in the distant future he might actually end up with either money or something resembling a career. Maybe that was being too optimistic.

He shook his head, realising that this particular chain of thought wasn't doing very much to lift his spirits, quite the opposite in fact. He gulped down the rest of his drink and ordered another one from the barman who'd initially caught his attention.

"Are you alright, love?" The barista asked, a flicker of concern wrinkling his forehead as he carefully placed the pint glass on the beer mat in front of him. "Excuse me for saying so, but you look a bit down."

23

"I'm fine, thanks." Mark smiled wanly in a pathetic attempt to show just how fine he was. He hadn't noticed it until then but he could feel his face was scarred with tears. Mortified, he lifted up one hand to try to furtively brush them away.

The barman looked at him disbelievingly.

"I'm okay, honestly."

For fucks sake, he thought, I'm leaking like a burst pipe today. He felt that if anyone was kind to him, especially a stranger, he really would start bawling out loud. He took a shaky sip of lager, managing a more convincing smile.

"Actually, I've just been dumped and thought a night out might do me some good." He laughed mirthlessly. "Nothing like getting trashed to ease the pain."

"I'm sure it's his loss, honey." He patted him on the shoulder in a motherly way, whilst simultaneously mopping up the beer sodden bar. "Plenty more fish in the sea and all of that... Sorry I'm not very good with advice. I just pour drinks and erm, flirt with the punters."

"That's okay." Mark sighed. He decided the alcohol was making him morose. After all, he had his holiday to think of, that would get his mind off everything for a while. "You're new aren't you? My name's Mark by the way, sorry for being such a mess. I'm not usually like this."

"I'm Andrew. Very nice to meet you, and don't worry, we're all of us a mess sometimes."

"Sooo..." He continued with one eyebrow raised, as Mark watched him rinsing glasses, sipping his drink and tapping his foot against his stool in time to the music, "Are you up for some fun tonight?"

"What kind of fun?" He tried to sound coquettish but it came out in a depressed monotone. Bollocks. He was never going to pull without a major attitude adjustment.

"I meant our karaoke competition, although if you're still here when I get off..." Andrew let the sentence hang in mid-air and eyed him with semi-interest. "Anyway, whatever you do you should at least stay for that. You don't have to be Christina Aguilera." He cast his gaze over to the stage where a

24

plump, blond fag hag covered in glitter had taken over and was wailing out an exuberant and surprisingly comical version of "Something Kinda Oooh" by Girls Aloud. "It's just a bit of a laugh."

"Sounds like fun, but no... I don't think so. Not tonight anyway."

"Go on," Andrew cajoled, "you might even enjoy yourself, I'm doing a turn myself later."

"Seriously, I'd drive out all your customers." He didn't like the direction this conversation was heading. "What are you singing?"

"You're in for a treat. I'm having my drag debut tonight! I'm dressing up in my break and doing a Judy Garland number."

"Sounds great." Mark said noncommittally. "But I'm having an early one, I'm organising a trip Brighton."

"Oooh, I love Brighton, you'll have a ball. I lived there for a while myself a few years back. Got a place to stay?"

He shrugged. "Not really, I figured I'd just check into any decently priced hotel when I get there."

"You'll be lucky. Excuse me a sec, hon." He apologised before hurrying off to serve a particularly drunken and obnoxious group of men who looked like they'd just walked into the wrong pub.

Mark sighed and settled back into his pint. By the time Andrew returned he looked a little flustered, it had got a lot busier.

"Look, I might have a suggestion for you." Andrew leaned across the bar to be heard. "One of my ex's has a two-bedroom flat in Hove, just outside Brighton. If you're interested I know he sometimes likes to let the spare room to bring in some extra cash."

"Look, that's nice of you but..."

"Wait! Let me finish." He protested. "It's a nice place, right by the sea, a bus ride into town – plus, JJ'd only charge you seventy quid a week, and you could very well end up paying that for a night in a hotel. It's up to you of course, but it could certainly save you some dosh, and it'd be doing my friend a favour too, if he's looking for someone."

Mark frowned. He had to admit he was tempted. Of course sharing with someone else hadn't been quite what he'd been expecting, but so what? He didn't plan to sit indoors much anyway and the expense of the whole venture had been worrying him. When he raised his eyes he saw that Andrew was regarding him impatiently, waiting for his answer.

"Come on, what have you got to lose? If you don't like the flat, or if JJ starts to piss you off for that matter," he added dryly, "You can always check into a hotel at the end of the week."

"Well when you put it like that..." He paused for a moment. "I'll think about it, but I can't see any reason why not. Are you sure he wouldn't mind?"

"I'll check with him tomorrow and ask if the rooms free. How long did you want to stay ideally?"

Mark hadn't really thought about it. He quickly weighed up how long he could afford to be off work with how much he really needed a break.

"Um, about a month, starting ASAP?"

"Fine," Andrew extracted a biro from his jeans pocket, grabbed a post-it from behind the bar and jotted down his number.

"Give me a ring. Now I'm off to get changed, wish me luck!" He winked and waved cheerily at him as he shimmied through the bar divider.

"Snap a lash." Mark called out, and then a thought occurred to him. "Hey, wait! What's your friend like?" But the barman had already disappeared upstairs.

Oh well, he thought, feeling a good deal better than he had before. Things finally appeared to be looking up and a nice relaxing sea-side break could be just what the doctor ordered. He could try to get fit while he was down there, do a bit of swimming and even give up smoking, a complete detox!

A few pints later he'd managed to shake off the last of his depression admirably and was considering a) entering the damn karaoke competition and giving Miss Half-top a run for

26

her money b) buying the transvestite a drink and engaging her in conversation about the meaning of life, before finally settling for c) go out and get trashed pre healthy-living trip. Fire was a possibility, then maybe Chariots for afterwards. So much for an early night.

Now, if he could just find out which restaurant Gypsy was working in he could pop in and see her before catching the tube. After all, it was probably a good idea to let someone know about his plans to leave the city for the summer. Purely to stop anyone worrying, he told himself. Nothing to do with wanting to show Dario he was moving on, of course.

Happy with the shape the evening was taking he decided to make a move right away, and got unsteadily to his feet.

Chapter 5: Working 9 to 5

Monday's were the pits. The best way to survive them in Kate's experience was to tackle them head on. This is precisely why she'd dragged herself out of bed at the unearthly hour of six o'clock. A quick life restoring power shower later, she'd blearily dressed herself whilst brushing her teeth and rushed out of the front door all within half an hour of waking.

She removed her coat and hung it up before sitting down at her desk. She'd done little to personalize her niche in the Sales Department. A dying pot plant sat sadly wasting away for lack of sunlight next to several unwashed coffee cups with the company logo emblazoned across them, and what looked suspiciously like mould growing in the middle one. A lurid green wall separated her from the other Sales Team typist, Tamsin Knight (the class-A bitch with whom she had the misfortune to work). This was decorated with a postcard her ex Neil had sent her from his last holiday in Thailand, and a two for one voucher offer for Pizza Express that was way past its validity date. Frowning she ripped them both off and shoved them in the bin.

Nope, definitely not getting too comfy here, but it paid the rent. She groaned thinking of the whole week stretched out ahead of her. Was this really what her life had come too? Working nine to five in a boring dead-end job just to make ends meet? Her shoulders slumped. Where oh where was the

28

excitement in that? Somehow her life had become just like the breakfast bagel she'd picked up en route. Dull, dull, dull.

She switched on her computer and began to efficiently but unenthusiastically sift through the mountain of work that had accumulated in her in-tray. Checking her emails rather depressingly unearthed even more work and a few hours later she was munching forlornly on her food and beginning to wish that she'd never come in. Of course it didn't help that Gypsy was no longer temping and around to keep her company. If only something would come along to bring a little excitement into her life.

"Morning," said Gavin Huntley, Head of Facilities, looking his normal lanky, greasy-haired self as he materialised from behind a small cluster of PA's who were loitering near the kitchen in a huddle. He waved a photocopied piece of paper in her face with a smirk.

"'Ere ya go. How about it?"

"How about what?" Kate peered at it suspiciously. "Hmm, it's an invite to an office party. Gee, thanks!"

"No problemo." He walked away looking pleased with himself.

Brilliant, she thought wryly. That hadn't been exactly the stimulus she was looking for. However, not being in a position to be picky she penciled it in her diary. As she did so she realised that socially she had at last hit rock bottom. She was now officially someone who thought spending a lunch period in the office, getting pissed and making a twat of yourself in front of your colleagues sounded enjoyable. She made a mental note to kill herself.

"How did the move go for your mate?" A familiar voice from behind her asked suddenly, making her jump about a mile in the air.

"James! You scared me, you moron." She exclaimed loudly. Then as her heartbeat slowly returned to normal she gave him a grudging smile.

"Come on; let's go for a fag before everyone arrives." He urged, hurrying her along as she reached for the spare pack of Marlboros she kept in her top drawer.

29

Somehow over the course of her employment they had become smoking buddies, sneaking out for a quick puff as often as they could between work and meetings and during tea breaks. Luckily he was the only person in the building who made her laugh, so it was sort of nice to have a partner in crime.

When they got outside she walked over to the guard rail by the steps and leaned over to him for a light. He obliged and she inhaled deeply letting the smoke fill her lungs.

"Thanks."

"That's alright." He lit his own cigarette and stared out into the street. "It'll be summer soon."

Kate nodded breathing out smoke through her nose.

"I know. I can't wait. It's by far my favourite season; particularly here in the city, there's always so much going on. It'll be way better now I'm single. My ex never really got on with Gypsy or my other friends. Ooh, maybe now we can all go on holiday!"

"Yeah, sounds great." He said vaguely. "Talking about Gypsy, what's she got on at the moment, work-wise?"

She looked at him surprised. "Why do you want to know that?"

"Well we were chatting before she left and she was telling me about her acting and all that. She said she's always looking for extra earners. I might know of something she'd be interested in."

She frowned and took another quick couple of drags of her cigarette before throwing it down on the asphalt and crushing it under her heel.

"Oh. Well I know she just started a waitressing job at the moment, and I think that's about it apart from random extra work." She eyed him speculatively. "What did you have in mind then?"

James gave her an opaque look.

"Wouldn't you like to know?" He teased. "Just give me her number and I'll ask her myself."

"Okay, but first you have to spill."

"There's a job going at this club I'm working for."

30

Kate narrowed her eyes. "Where? I didn't know you had a second job."

"I only started a fortnight ago. It's called the Pink Flamingo. I thought I told you about it?" He trailed off absentmindedly. "Oh no, wait, that wasn't you at all. Whatever. Anyway, I thought it might be her kind of thing."

"Is that what this is really about?" She raised her eyebrows. "Look, if you're interested why don't you just ask her out?"

"Wow! You really couldn't be further off track."

"Right."

"It's the god's honest truth, I swear." He insisted, looking amused.

"Okay well what is the job exactly? If it's working in a cloakroom, then I know for a fact she's not interested. We've both done that before and she hated it."

"No, no, this is more performance orientated."

She waited expectantly for him to elaborate.

"Well." She said crossly when nothing further was forthcoming. "Don't keep me in suspenders."

"It's working with moi, and I am the entertainment of course," James said in a theatrical voice giving a sweeping curtsey to the passers-by on Kreyton Road, "Well, technically my alter ego Miss Geneva Convention is. Didn't you know I'm a drag queen, darling?"

"Oh. And I thought you had a crush on Gypsy!"

He regarded her pityingly. "Yes, I know. The term gaydar really is a foreign concept to you, isn't it?"

Chapter 6. We are Family

Later glancing up at the clock above Tamsin's studiously bent head, and seeing it was five o'clock at long last Kate gave a sigh of relief. Mercifully the day had passed quickly. After James' Pink Flamingo revelation she'd immediately phoned Gypsy, who invited her out with Si and friends for a drink in Soho. She'd been ecstatic to hear of the possibility of a job. It transpired her debut as a waitress had come to an abrupt end after she'd knocked a bowl of gazpacho soup over the restaurant owner's wife. Kate had snorted with laughter. At least gazpacho was served cold.

She whistled to herself, looking over at her colleague who gave her a disapproving look as she switched off her PC and tidied her things away. What a witch.

"'Night!" She called. "Have a great evening."

The other woman grunted and pointedly carried on with her work.

God, martyr much? Kate sighed to herself. She'd thought Tamsin would be pleased. They'd discovered earlier on that she was finally getting her long awaited promotion as PA to the CEO. The news had certainly cheered Kate up no end. However, the prospect of her work load doubling had been daunting to say the least. Her panic had been short-lived however; a replacement had already been hired and this development was what really proved to be the cherry on the icing of the cake. Not only had Danny Jackson been the most gorgeous guy she'd seen for ages he'd also suggested a drink after work tomorrow! She was going on a date!

She swept out of the doors and into the night grinning from ear to ear. Impulsively deciding to treat herself to a cab rather than travelling all the way to Leicester Square with her face wedged in someone's armpit.

Once in the High Street she managed to flag one down almost immediately. Damn but this day really couldn't get any better.

X

At around the same time Kate was leaving work, Si was descending the spiral staircase into the gloom of the Hub's basement.

The Hub was a trendy new Soho cocktail bar they'd all been dying to try for ages. He saw that Dario, Marina and Gypsy had already arrived and were seated comfortably on big squishy leather chairs clutching exotic coloured drinks.

Dario looked up, caught his eye and waved energetically. Si's eyes lit up as he excused his way through the packed and rather narrow floor to where they were waiting for him. "Sorry I'm late guys, the tube was murder. Bloody rush hour."

He sat down and looked around. Despite being so crowded; or maybe because of it, the place seemed cosy and not at all pretentious as he'd half-expected.

Fairy lights twinkled like stars dotted across the navy ceiling and the walls were painted with archaic looking art, lit with more strategically placed lights giving the place a bohemian feel. Different sections of the venue were separated with archways; lending a magical cave like quality and the bar itself was an explosion in psychedelic colours, advertising outlandish cocktails.

Scanning the crowd quickly for celebrities he was a little relieved not to see any. The Hub had quickly become a playground for the rich and famous, but he was not sure how he'd actually react if he came face to face with, say, Ryan Gerrard.

"What do you reckon then?" Dario asked handing over a drink and indicating the strange abstract figurines placed haphazardly round the room. "Pretty weird, huh?"

"I quite like it." He peered suspiciously into the swirling tangerine depths of his drink. "What is this?"

"'Monkey spunk mix." Dario made a face.

"Seriously?!"

"The waitress recommended it. I'll swap it for my sex on the beach though if you like." Gypsy interjected. "In case you don't save up enough for the real thing with Tony."

"Ha ha, very funny. I'll stick with my, erm, monkey cum thanks." He took a cautious sip.

"Not bad at all." He put his glass down. "And I'll have you know I've been working on a money-making scheme, so I think we'll be sunning ourselves in Gran Canaria before you can say 'see you in the sand dunes'!"

"Oh?" Marina demanded. "Can I get in on some of the action? I need cash for more canvases."

"Afraid not sweetie," he shook his head apologetically. "This is a secret."

There was an expectant pause whilst he silently cursed his indiscretion. Luckily just as he was about to get bombarded with a volley of questions a welcome diversion arrived in the form of Kate. Still in her pencil skirt and work-shirt she looked dishevelled; her hair falling around her face and an ink stain on one cheek.

"Oh my god, this place is unreal! Am I seeing things?" She stage-whispered, pointing none too discreetly to a group of people sitting in one of the darkest recesses of the bar. "Or is that really Blaine Feynard over there?!"

"You're kidding! Where?" Gypsy asked, twisting round in her seat, any thoughts about what the hell Si could feel the need to keep from them completely forgotten; to his great relief. "I totally love him, he's amazing." She was just in time to see the model gracefully getting up from his seat and disappear up the stairs with his entourage.

"Oh no, that's so typical, he's leaving!" She cried in frustration, "I can't believe none of us saw him before. This could have been my big chance to meet him and I never even got to say hello."

"Never mind hon." Marina patted her arm. "I don't think you would've been exactly in there anyway."

"Gyps, he's gayer than a drag queen in a rainbow bikini at Soho pride on Old Compton street." Si was matter of fact. "You'd have more chance with Brian Dowling from Big Brother."

"Yeah, but the papers swear he's bi."

"Right." Dario added. "Well, that changes everything. If the tabloids say so, it must be true."

"Oh piss off and let my stay in denial with my celebrity crush." She stuck her tongue out at him.

"Well, I've got some news that you'll wanna hear." Kate said chirpily.

"What? Have they sacked that bitchy thing you work with?" Gypsy asked finishing her drink.

"No. In fact she got promoted."

"So wouldn't that be bad news?" Si was confused.

"Nope. Well, not directly anyway." Kate grinned before lowering her voice dramatically. "It's the new bloke in the office. His name's Danny, he's completely stunning, really nice, and we're going out tomorrow night."

"That's great baby." Si clinked his glass together with hers. "Fast work. You've made mama very proud. I expect a full report the very next day. I want to know everything."

"Yeah, that's fab, Kate." Gypsy concurred. "But we might have to check him out if this gets serious. You know, make sure he's good enough for you."

"In short make sure he's not another Neil." Marina said reading between the lines.

"Neil was fit though." Dario commented. Si nodded eagerly, prompting Gypsy to kick them both under the table.

"Well, he was kind of a shit."

"A good looking shit – Ow! But a total bastard."

"Yeah, definitely better off without him."

And finally, "Danny sounds lovely, when are we going to meet him?"

"Me, introduce him to you lot? Like that's gonna happen!" She said good-naturedly.

Si looked around at his friends happy, alcohol-flushed faces and put his arms around the two girls. "Well, I must say its nice having a family outing."

There was an uncomfortable pause and Dario looked instantly ill at ease.

"God, I'm a tit." He clapped his hand over his mouth realising his gaffe. "I've got foot in mouth disease. I completely forgot about Mark and... I'm just gonna shut up now."

"No. Look, it's okay," Dario insisted. He hadn't really discussed the break up with his friends and didn't much feel like it now. "I don't want to make this awkward for you all. Although things are difficult now, I'm sure we'll be able to hang out together in the future. It just might take a while."

"Do you know how he's doing?" Kate was concerned.

"Well presumably he's coping; he told me he's off on holiday to Brighton." Gypsy said, everyone with the exception of Si (who she'd already spoken to) looking at her in surprise. "He came into my restaurant the other night just before a... erm, soup incident."

"Aha." Said Dario, smiling despite himself, "I reckon that explains an odd phone call I got from him early yesterday morning. Something about a bloke called JJ and jogging and Judy Garland? I think..." He said unnecessarily, "he may have been a bit out of it."

Marina looked unconvinced. "I hope he's okay. I meant to call him I've just been really busy with work, and then Lisa and I had this argument... am I a shitty friend?"

"Of course you're not," Si told her sternly, putting an arm around her. "If it makes you feel better, I only just found out so I haven't spoken to him yet either. How about we both give him a ring tomorrow?"

Gypsy grimaced. "Well I'm afraid I wasn't that sympathetic when he dropped by. But it was my trial night! The last thing I needed was a visit from one of my fuckwit drunken mates."

"Come on guys," Dario said, exasperated. "You can make it up to him when he comes back. Let's change the subject."

"You're right." Si got to his feet. "Now, who fancies another drink before we hit the clubs? Could everyone place their orders, please?"

Kate yawned. "Look, it was great to see you all but I'm knackered. Plus, I've got work and a hot date to look forward to tomorrow." She began pulling on her coat, "I think I need to catch up on some beauty sleep."

Marina got to her feet. "I think I'll join ya babe. Lisa's expecting me home at a reasonable hour."

"What?" Dario looked incredulous, "I can't believe you're all flaking out on us! It's only early." He complained.

Si looked at Gypsy who'd got up to kiss them goodbye. "You're coming out with us aren't you, dear?"

"Is Old Compton Street gay?" She asked. "Is the Pope Catholic? Of course I'm coming."

"'Night you lot of lushes," Kate gave them a tired wave as she and Marina headed for the stairs. She shivered as they pushed open the door and were greeted by the bone-chilling air. Exhausted, at that moment she could think of nothing she wanted more than to drink a pint of water, wash off her make-up and fall into a deep slumber. Thankfully a good night's shut-eye was an achievable desire. If only everything else on her wish list was as attainable.

After biding farewell to Marina and making her way to the Piccadilly line, she fell gratefully into a vacant seat and let herself daydream about winning the lottery, falling in love and finding a cheap flat in zone 1-2 all the way home.

Chapter 7. Falling Angel

Blaine Feynard stepped into the Le Bordeaux's sumptuous penthouse suite, turned to flash his fans in the corridor a radiant, supermodel smile before closing and locking the door behind him. Immediately after completing this simple action his face fell, the mask dropping.

Slumping back against the cool polished wood, he raked his fingers through his hair as he felt a scream start to build up within him. And then just as suddenly as it had started, his body relaxed. All the pent up rage drained out of him and his shoulders shook. Tears trickled furiously down his cheeks quicker than he could wipe them away with the heels of his long fingered, elegant hands.

The crying jag only lasted a few minutes and then it was over, leaving nothing more than a dull ache in his cranium. He took a deep shuddering breath, drew himself up to his full height and composing himself walked slowly across the ankle-deep carpet towards the balcony.

The room was vast, opulent and the hotel probably one of the most exclusive in Paris. Sadly this did little to elevate his mood. Blaine was used to palatial but impersonal accommodation, it made him feel empty. With a stab of homesickness he found himself suddenly longing to be back in the Notting Hill flat he shared with his friends Nadia and Fleur, and his little Pomeranian dog, Dior, who could be such a comfort.

Only two days ago on a shoot for DIVAFACE, he'd considered himself the luckiest man alive. How naive, he thought bitterly, to have believed that if he buried his head in the sand long enough the past would simply go away, or at least have the common courtesy of staying dead.

Suddenly desperate for some fresh air he kicked off his Jimmy Choo's and stepped outside. The view was spectacular. Forgetting his problems for a moment, he propped his elbows on the pebble-dashed ledge and looked down. He imagined he could see the entire city living and breathing spread out below. Car headlights winking and gleaming made serpentine shapes inside orange, yellow and white streetlights. Fluorescent flashes like Christmas tree baubles decorated the exteriors of the bars and clubs causing the city to sparkle in all its night-time splendour. The glow from the prettily illuminated bridges over the Seine reflected on the ripples in the seemingly untroubled black water.

It was just as well to enjoy at least one aspect of the trip, Blaine thought ruefully; after all under normal circumstances he would've been over the moon. It wasn't every day he was flown out to France to attend a premiere in which he had a cameo role.

'Sabine' was the latest Rebekka Redfern film and set to be a blockbuster. It was all he'd wished for, his greatest ambition finally realised to make the leap from modelling to acting and eventually be recognised for his theatrical talent.

Quivering slightly in the wind he wrapped his arms around himself, feeling the nubby material of the strappy sheath of a Versace dress he'd chosen specially for this evening. He adored the dress and it would've cost a fortune if he'd had to pay for it himself. Lately though, everyone seemed desperate for the famous cross-dressing supermodel to be seen wearing their clothes. The world was fascinated with the pulchritudinous gay boy who wore heels and make-up on the runway and worked it better than most of the girls. His modelling career - already successful - was sky-rocketing.

Along with prominent cheekbones and an unconventional sensuality, Blaine had attitude, charisma and an effortless style all of his own. Magazine's world-wide proclaimed him a phenomenon. Now within a few weeks, news of the contract he was verging on signing ensuring his future as the new face of Raoul Fahri's ✿*FX* fragrance would hit the tabloids, undoubtedly making him a household name.

It'd all been coming together so perfectly, until now.

The letter had arrived at his flat yesterday. He'd found it lying innocently on his doormat in an unremarkable, manila envelope. As soon as he'd opened it a cursory once-over of the contents was all he needed. He'd known what it meant immediately. In the back of his mind had actually been expecting it for years. It meant he was about to be blackmailed, or tell the world the truth and risk losing everything.

He slid his chic clutch bag - a present from Raoul himself and encrusted with diamond ✿*FX*'s – off his shoulder. Opening it he fumbled around inside until his grasping fingers found what they were searching for. A piece of paper he'd been carrying around with him ever since it'd come into his ownership. With his free hand he extracted the solid silver lighter Nadia had given him for his birthday last year. Lighting one corner, he tossed it onto the ground and watched it burn, its contents imprinted indelibly onto his mind.

He wondered what kind of miscreant could be doing this to him. And what did they want? That was the real question. There hadn't been a mention of any demands. Was someone just out to torture him? Why?

It was just so spiteful, he thought putting the back of his hand to his mouth in an ineffectual gesture designed to stifle another sob. He'd worked his celebrated butt off to get where he was now and it was unbearable to think it might all be taken away from him. Who had he known during that period which he no longer liked to think of who'd want to hurt him so badly?

Biting his lower lip he wondered if he hadn't bought all this on himself. Had he tempted fate once too often by putting himself in the public eye like this, when of course he knew there would always be the risk of someone from the

40

past putting two and two together... Maybe he should've thought twice before doing something where he'd become so visible. But it had all been such a dream come true for a boy like him. Was he really supposed to have turned down the opportunity to work in the fashion industry? The clothes, parties, travelling, not to mention the glamour... No, he couldn't have done that, was glad he hadn't. Besides, understated and inconspicuous had never really been Blaine's style.

Right on cue, the phone in the adjacent bedroom started to ring and wandering back inside he scooped it up in one hand and tucked it between his shoulder and chin.

"Hello?"

"Room service for Monsieur Angel Saint-Angelo, oui?" The voice of the concierge enquired solicitously, using the low-key name his agent had suggested he choose for checking into the hotel anonymously and discouraging the paparazzi.

"Lovely," he replied sniffing slightly. "Come right on up."

Chapter 8. Who's that Girl?

Thanks to signal failure at Earls Court, Mark missed his train by a matter of minutes. He subsequently found himself succumbing to a Burger King meal and an overpriced pint of lager whilst waiting for the next one. When it finally arrived, crammed full of tourists headed for the coast, the only vacant seat he could find was next to a harassed looking mother and her little boy. The kid spent the best part of the journey trying to stick chewing gum on his favourite jeans. Thankfully in a fit of organization the night before he'd packed his iPod, a copy of QX Magazine and a Gscene gay guide to Brighton to distract himself.

As they pulled away from the platform, his thoughts turned to Dario, Marina, Si and his other London mates. He began to feel hopelessly nostalgic and lonely hurtling towards a strange city where he would doubtless be isolated and friendless (a Brighton virgin if you will). What had started off feeling like a wonderful adventure whilst in the pub was suddenly starting to appear a tad melodramatic and pointless. What exactly had galvanized him into the dubious action of leaving London, his home, for some small, overpriced seaside retreat?

In order to restore his flagging spirits he bought a beer from the hatchet faced attendant wheeling a refreshments trolley. Happily, this coupled with a very optimistic sounding horoscope in the magazine lifted his mood and he almost managed to get back to being excited at the sheer recklessness of it all as he watched the green, sheep-dotted fields roll past.

He eventually nodded off reading a surprise piece about the Black Cock featuring a picture of Lisa posing behind the bar. That, for some reason, made him feel better; it was almost as if she was silently encouraging him from the glossy pages. He didn't wake up until the train shuddered to a halt at Brighton station and everyone started making a rush for the doors.

Disembarking, he felt like death thanks to a deadly combination of alcohol and sleeping in the day. Also it was raining and he was late.

He stuck his head cautiously outside loath to leave the sanctuary of the station and get soaked but at the same time hoping to spot a handy cab. Other passengers with umbrellas rudely jostled and pushed their way past him, as if they relished the chance to rush out headlong into the dreary windswept drizzle.

Mark had noticed mid-journey that the sky had turned a depressing shade of grey and now had to forcibly stop himself from being disheartened again. He mentally bid farewell to his romantic notions of being greeted by welcoming early-summer sunshine and lots of deliciously muscular men sunbathing on the nude beach. Feeling thoroughly cold and wretched, he experienced a surge of adrenaline as a taxi appeared out of the gloom. He attempted a sort of limping half walk, half jog that was the best he could manage whilst carrying almost the entire contents of his wardrobe in a single case. Travelling light was something he'd never got the hang of.

The cabbie, an older man with a grey goatee and multiple piercings, was just rolling down his window when they both heard an ominous click-clack, click-clack, coming up steadily from behind them.

Before Mark quite knew what was happening, the passenger door had been forced open by an elegant, red taloned hand. A mauve bag - with the words 'Miss Bitch' decorating the front in loud gold letters - was thrown inside.

He caught a fleeting glimpse of a striking looking transvestite with an impressive tawny hair-piece, in a sequinned bikini and PVC boots. Then with a flash of royal blue lipstick and a flutter of gigantean eyelashes she'd disappeared with break-neck speed into the back of the car. Grinding his teeth together he simmered with rage. Of all the fucking cheek! She was hijacking his ride.

Infuriatingly the cab driver didn't appear to look put out at all. Quite to the contrary, his craggy face broke into a delighted, welcoming smile as he turned round to address the bored looking apparition. She sat, casual as could be, with her legs crossed swinging her foot in time to the music on the radio.

"Gladys, my dear!" He cried delightedly, as Mark looked around him in irritation. "What a lovely surprise!"

"Ooh, hiya Fred." She tittered merrily, perking up a bit and winking at him cheekily in the mirror. "I almost didn't recognise you with your clothes on." She threw her head back and broke into peals of raucous, throaty laughter making Mark wondered whether she was joking... or not.

"Excuse me for interrupting." He said brusquely appealing directly to the driver. "But I got here first, and I'm in a bit of a hurry." It was, he strongly believed best to assert yourself in a situation like this, after all he was clearly in the right, and if he was firm and yet courteous...

He somehow managed to heave his bag halfway inside the taxi just in time to prevent Gladys slamming the door shut on him. Heavily made-up aquamarine eyes followed him incredulously as he scrambled into the backseat after his things in as dignified a manner as was possible under the circumstances.

"Hi, I'm Mark," he deadpanned after a brief pause.

A moment of silence followed while she digested this piece of information and looked him up and down. Nervously, he wondered if she was considering kicking the shit out of him. After all it certainly looked like those heels (not to

44

mention the nails) could do some serious damage. It took all of his self-restraint to stop himself edging back the way he'd come and making a run for it. But then, thankfully she seemed to undergo a mercurial change of mood.

"You're alright love." She waved her hand carelessly at the door. "I was just about to suggest to Fred that we share." She suddenly gave a surprisingly infectious grin.

"Is that alright with you, Freddie darling?" She yelled.

"Whatever you say Miss Cox-Hardt."

The man was obviously totally ignorant of the bloodbath that could've occurred in the back of his car.

"That'll be fine." Mark agreed quickly.

Miss Cox-Hardt. *Gladys Cox-Hardt?!*

"Good! That's settled then." She reached over his legs and grasping the handle slammed the door shut.

"So, whereabouts you headed, gorgeous?" Meaningfully she fixed him with a lazar beam stare whilst flicking her wig around and touching her tongue to her top lip suggestively.

Mark cringed. If only he'd had the foresight to call a cab from one of the payphones. Was she coming on to him or just trying to make him uncomfortable? Could she really have been on public transport dressed like that? Apart from anything she must've been freezing. And did he honestly want this perfect stranger to know exactly where he was going to be living for the next month? Ho hum, all very good questions. He thought for a moment.

"Er... Hove."

"Oh yeah? Whereabouts?"

"A friend's place. It's near the church I think." He said vaguely. There, that should get him in the area without giving too much away.

"Perfect." She beamed displaying two large rows of square white teeth. "I'll get off there too; it's just round the corner from my flat."

He froze, then nodded pleasantly deciding that if he were to say something along the lines of "How nice" or "That *is* lucky" he'd probably come across as deeply insincere now. This led him to the realisation that he cared way too much

45

what other people (for example random drag queens he was unlikely to ever see again) thought of him.

X

The driver put the car into gear and they lurched off up a steep rain-slicked road full of sharp bends, speeding by rows of unremarkable terraced houses.

Mark stared out of the window, his travelling companion all but forgotten as he drank in the first sights and sounds of the town that was to be his home for the summer.

Sitting across from him, looking over in his direction from time to time and growing increasingly piqued at such an unusual lack of interest being shown towards her, Gladys huffily produced an emery board and started filing her already immaculate nails.

After a few minutes the taxi swung left into a residential street full of patrician looking buildings. He noticed a small green, dotted with statuesque trees shaking their branches in the wind, quaint park benches and beds of unidentifiable red flowers that passed in a blur as they swept by. He felt his mind begin to drift as fatigue took hold of him.

The last holiday he'd taken had been pre-Dario. It'd started off very differently, in the dry burning heat of a scorching Greek summer. He'd hooked up with a French guy called Frédéric the day before he was due to leave. He let his thoughts wander as he recalled them stumbling back to his apartment through maze-like cobbled streets for hours of unforgettable sex.

He sighed and wondered wistfully if he'd be lucky enough to meet anyone on this particular foray into the unknown. Then out of the corner of his eye he caught a glimpse of Gladys. She was extracting a fiver from the top of one of her boots. Classy.

"So, we're nearly there then." She said, noticing his reverie was broken.

"Are we?"

"Oh yes. Just up the road now."

46

He saw, worryingly, that she was looking at him with an ingratiating expression. Not only did it look unnatural on her face but it also filled him inexplicably with alarm. He concentrated hard on looking at the scenery. Ah, he could see they were now on Western Road passing a colourful parade of shops which he was bound to become better acquainted with soon. Oh look! He thought to himself, a Debenhams, a Tesco and Marks & Spencer – that'd come in handy. But it was no use; apparently Gladys was not to be put off by minor trifles like being ignored.

He reluctantly turned round as she cleared her throat for the second time.

"I have a favour to ask." She confessed, putting her hand playfully on his thigh. "I left my wallet at this bloke's house and I'm a bit short. I've only got a few quid to buy some fags tonight, and well... You couldn't pay Fred here for me could you?" She pouted her blue lips appealingly.

Mark looked pointedly at her hand on his leg until she removed it.

"Go on." She urged as the church loomed into view. "What do you say?"

"Oh, alright then," he said with as much grace as he could muster. "On one condition..."

"Fantastic! You're a star!" She slung her bag onto her shoulder as they pulled up on the curb, causing a flock of seagulls to noisily take flight. Pausing, she looked back at him. "Oh. Did you want something?"

"I need directions; that's all." A quick look at his watch had confirmed he was now spectacularly late. And of course not having a clue where you're going seldom proves a great help when it comes to reaching a destination speedily.

"Fine." She muttered ungratefully. "But make it snappy. I haven't got all day."

He tried not to notice the attention that Gladys attracted from passers-by as she exaggeratedly avoided the puddles. The OAP's at the bus shelter turned to gawp at her. Clearly in her element she smiled and waved at them bounteously as she passed. Noticing his mortification she shot him a

47

mischievous look and quick as a hawk swooping in for the kill, surprised him with a kiss full on the lips.

"Uggh...Wha??!" He struggled helplessly in her embrace. "Gerroff!"

"That's for the cab fare." She explained magnanimously.

The bus-stop was abuzz.

"Thanks a *lot.*"

"Pleasure was all mine." She purred unabashed. "Now where did you want to get to?"

"Grace Street." He muttered, giving up and allowing himself to be propelling forwards as she grabbed his arm in hers. They passed Cullens, a tobacconists and greengrocers, before turning left at a set of traffic lights and down a little alley-way. They traipsed down some steps and onto a street that led straight down to the sea.

"You don't have to take me all the way." He protested, "Honestly, if you just point me in the..."

He broke off as she pointed at the street sign above their head. Grace Street, it read.

"Oh, I'm here then. Well, thanks for that." He said. "Maybe I'll see you around."

"You will! I'm all kinds of hard to miss!" Gladys promised as she ran on ahead leaving him to pour over the piece of paper with JJ's address on it.

When he did finally looked up to see which side of the road number thirty-three might be on, she'd already disappeared from view. The only reminder that the encounter had been real (as opposed to some horrible acid flashback) was the unmistakeable but slowly fading sound of spiky heels hitting hard pavement.

X

The road turned out to be a long one, lined with tall, narrow houses. Due to the fast encroaching dusk he was forced to stop and peer short-sightedly at the door numbers, hindering his progress.

Number twenty-nine, number thirty-one....

48

Reaching number thirty-three he saw that a light was on in the top floor – which if the peeling numbers by the doorbells were anything to go by – was definitely Flat C. As he pressed the buzzer twice with no response forthcoming it dawned on him that leaving your light on could be due to anything from forgetfulness to wanting to discourage burglars, he hoped JJ hadn't gone out.

Just as he was starting to give up hope, a window opened somewhere above him and some keys came flying out. They landed with a dull thud on the be-littered patch of earth by the front door and dangerously near his head.

Once inside, he looked around, disappointed to find himself in a rather neglected, ramshackle hallway. It sported individual mail boxes for each of the flats and a few sickly-looking potted plants hanging over the end of the banister.

An unpleasant acrid smell pervaded the air as he mounted the rickety steps covered in worn paisley carpet. What was it? He wondered as he lugged his bag up the steep stairs. Then suddenly he knew, and wished he didn't. Ah yes, cats piss, that was definitely it. Charming.

As he reached the landing at the top of the building, feeling very unfit and panting heavily, there was a soft click and the door to Flat C swung open.

Someone was standing in the shadows waiting for him. Posing seductively in the doorway in a marabou feather dressing gown and struggling (most unsuccessfully) to contain her amusement at the hilarity of the situation was none other than Gladys Cox-Hardt herself.

Mark sighed wearily, so much for his quiet seaside break.

49

Chapter 9. Nice Work If You Can Get It

Cecile Benedict squinted at the Polaroid as Ida sat opposite her looking pensive, hands folded in her lap. Impatiently, she waved it back and forth in the air waiting for the image to appear.

The large high-ceilinged office smelt of a combination of perfume and eau de dog. The latter courtesy of her excitable shiatsu, Baby, who was busily shredding a cushion with the maximum amount of noise and mess.

Cecile, still attractive in her early fifties, wore her raven hair in an asymmetrical bob which showed off her porcelain features to their best advantage. Looking at the photo she felt a surge of adrenaline. This one had something special. She rubbed her temples thoughtfully and watched as 'The Sainsbury's Girl' as she'd already mentally dubbed her, waited patiently for her verdict.

Ida had a nasty shiner, but otherwise she was perfect. Even her ill-fitting clothes and unflattering haircut failed to disguise her potential. She had achingly perfect bone structure, a full mouth, wide-apart eyes and an impossibly slender, elongated frame. Cecile frowned, she hoped the girl wasn't a victim of domestic violence but it looked that way. That could prove problematic.

Meanwhile Ida sat quietly in her chair and tried to convey some sort of outward composure. Inwardly her stomach was in knots. She could almost hear the woman's brain ticking.

What she'd expected to be a quick meeting had already taken three hours as she was interrogated, measured and weighed. Still not satisfied, this intimidating and bossy woman had then persuaded her to change into some clothes her assistant had provided from an earlier shoot. She'd found herself sitting in reception once again, this time waiting to be introduced to some big shot photographer called Duncan Cavendish to have some test shots done.

The pictures were set against a white background in the studio at the back of the office. Someone was summoned to do her hair and styling. This involved much energetic backcombing and copious amounts of cough inducing industrial strength hairspray and make-up. She'd found it uncomfortable having someone else circle her eyes with kohl and cover her lashes with mascara as she tried hard to co-operate by closing, opening and blinking her eyes as required. As soon as that was over Duncan had arrived and after brisk introductions the shoot had begun.

Ida had tried hard to follow his instructions. The bright lights his assistant pointed at her made her feel disorientated to begin with, her eyes started to water and she worried she'd ruin all the painstakingly applied war paint. However, she had to admit once she got into it she found the whole process exhilarating. In her new outfit she actually felt that her embarrassingly long and skinny limbs might even look passable. Also, Duncan was charming and quickly put her at ease. He chatted with her unselfconsciously as if they were old friends, asking all about her life and interests until she'd felt her initial tension start to melt away. He even told her that she was an extraordinary beauty. An extraordinary beauty! She'd never been called that before!

The remainder of her inhibitions gradually began to desert her as the shoot progressed. Experimentally, she tried a few poses that she'd secretly been practicing in the bed-sit whilst balanced precariously on the mattress glimpsing as much of her body as possible in the A4 sized mirror hanging on their wall. He captured her smiling, enigmatic, seductive

51

and serious – from every different angle. The time seemed to pass by in a blur and then suddenly they were finished.

She gradually came back to reality. Heart thumping in her chest she wondered if she'd made a fool of herself or if she'd actually been any good.

Cecile finally looked up with a sigh.

"Your look is terrible." She said by way of breaking the silence. "I mean the hair, the clothes, the styling... None of it will do. You couldn't go and see clients looking like that! We'll have to change everything."

Ida cleared her throat hardly daring to breathe.

"So does that mean you'll represent me?" She asked crossing her fingers behind her back and squeezing them together so tightly they hurt.

"Yes." Cecile nodded her head decisively. "I think if you follow the advice I give you, you could end up becoming very successful indeed. I'm convinced you have what it takes."

It took a few moments for the information she was receiving to register and when it finally did Ida shrieked. Jumping up from her chair she ran round the desk and threw her arms around the startled woman giving her an awkward hug, her smile dazzlingly bright. "Thank you so much! You don't know what this means to me, I'll work so hard I promise."

"Well," Cecile said after her new model had settled herself back down in her seat and she'd managed to regain her composure and un-wrinkle her jacket. "I'm glad that you realise a lot of hard work will be involved, not to mention long hours. You need to be extremely committed."

Eyes wide, Ida nodded, as her thoughts cannoned off in all directions. The possibilities for her future suddenly seemed vast and endless. Only a few hours ago she'd had no hope at all, only the card this wonderful woman had insisted on her taking whilst she was doing her grocery shopping. Now she was going to be given the chance for a real career, for independence! She sat on the edge of her seat hardly able to contain herself; there were so many questions she wanted to ask, so much that she'd need to learn.

It was as if Cecile had read her mind.

"Of course, there's lots that you will have to be taught about... well everything! You haven't got any previous modelling experience, have you?"

"No."

"Hmm. Whereabouts are you living at the moment? With family?"

Ida looked down at her lap. "Well I was living with my boyfriend, but now I've left him... and I'm going to need to find somewhere else to stay." She said a silent prayer that this wouldn't spoil her chances.

The older woman looked thoughtful and paused for a few moments. "Will you excuse me? I won't be a minute, just stay right where you are."

Ida's heart sank as Cecile got up from her desk grabbing her mobile phone and headed out of the office closing the door behind her. Things had been going so well, she stared dispiritedly through the window as she waited for her possible benefactor.

It seemed to take forever for Cecile to return to the office. Ida spent most of the time trying not to get her hopes up too high and preparing herself for the possibility of rejection. When she finally breezed back in though she knew immediately everything was going to be okay though by the huge smile Cecile directed at her.

"This really does seem to be perfect timing, I've just got off the phone with one of our girls and I believe I've found a flat-share for you." She was thumbing through some papers. Her observant grey eyes flicked from the sheets on the desk back up to her newest protégée, missing nothing as she tried to gauge her reaction.

"It's a lovely, fully furnished three-bedroom place in Notting Hill. You'd be sharing with two of our most successful models here at Boss who'll be able to show you the ropes and answer any questions you may have. You're very lucky that this opportunity has opened up, one of our other girls decided to move out yesterday – the room would be ready as early as tomorrow." She added.

Ida could hardly believe her ears, she felt like bursting into happy tears everything was falling into place so unbelievably. A place to live, a career and freedom from Steve and her dreary fear-filled life in Balham!

"Tomorrow would be wonderful." She said, struggling to take in all the good news which was so unexpectedly coming her way. She searched her mind for a catch. Then panic suddenly darkened her eyes as she found one. A biggy.

She dropped her head in embarrassment. "The only thing is... I won't be able to afford it. I haven't been working so I've literally got nothing. That means I can't pay a deposit or even rent up front."

"Don't worry about that." Cecile's tone was brisk and business-like, "I'm treating you as an investment. I wouldn't have agreed to take you on unless I thought you'd get regular work. Believe me; you'll have no trouble in supporting yourself and repaying the small loan that I will arrange for you." She waved away Ida's objections. "It's necessary, so you've got no reason to feel guilty. Now, I'm going to give you the numbers of a hairdresser and stylist that I would like you to contact over the next few days in order to get your image sorted out. Also you'll need a completely new wardrobe – your new flat mates might even help with that and I'll give you some practical advice on the sort of things that are always essential. Usually I encourage my models not to lose their own innate, individual style." She frowned. "Let's just say that yours appears to be a work in progress... so we'll need to focus on that.

I will be in touch about initial photo-shoots with a diverse mix of photographers so we can start building up a basic portfolio for you. They're not always easy to get hold of so be patient, but I will do what I can to pull some strings. I want to get moving quickly with you. Plus you'll need some basic training, your walk is a disaster and your general posture could certainly stand to be improved."

She broke off watching Ida's exquisite little face as emotions played across her perfectly proportioned, elfin features. This girl was going to be big. She'd had the thought

54

before when she'd discovered Nadia and then again when she'd found Trinity Short working as a waitress in a coffee shop in Islington. What a gift for the agency!

"I think we'll cut your hair. Some kind of crop would be good." Cecile continued, cupping her chin in one hand, "Something very modern, very now, but unique to you."

Ida opened her mouth to refuse. After all, Steve hated her hair short. But then she shut it again and nodded mutely, she could do what she liked now.

Suddenly there was a smart rap on the door quickly followed by Duncan's face poking round it.

"Knock, knock!" He said, obviously completely un-intimidated by Cecile as he peered round at them both. "Sorry to disturb. I just wanted to say I'm off now, but it was lovely to meet you Ida and I think you're both going to be very happy with the prints." He winked at her kindly sensing the unease that comes with being the new girl in a strange environment. "You're a natural. Stick with this woman and she'll make you a star."

Cecile sighed loudly to show that the interruption was most unprofessional. "Thank you Duncan. Will that be all, or is there anything I can help you with?"

He shook his head amicably deciding that Cecile had been right, Ida was going to be sensational. In light of how well the photo-session had gone he'd forgiven her for interrupting his date with Ash. Duncan had been planning to surprise him and take him as his guest to a party designer Raoul Fhari was throwing. Perhaps in hindsight though, it would be more fun going solo. Much as he enjoyed Ash, the boy was showing signs of being a bit too interested in his celebrity friends and lifestyle.

"I was just wondering if Ida wants to come to Raoul's do tonight?" He offered on impulse. "It might be a good chance to be seen and meet the right people?"

Cecile looked amused as Ida unsuccessfully tried to restrain her enthusiasm. "Blaine's going to be there tonight and possibly Nadia too, aren't they?" She asked thoughtfully reaching down to stroke her dog as he whined for attention.

55

Duncan nodded. "They'll both be there."

The Director lifted her pet up onto her lap distractedly as he let out a series of short, sharp barks.

"I strongly suggest that you do go along and cancel any other plans that you might have for tonight." She advised. "I'm sure Duncan can sort you out with some clothes to borrow if you need anything. It'll be golden opportunity to meet Blaine and Nadia who you'll be living with as of tomorrow."

"I'd love to come, wow, thanks Duncan." Ida felt her cheek muscles ache; she hadn't smiled so much in years. Then suddenly the full implications of what Cecile had said hit her and she swallowed hard, her throat dry.

"You don't mean... Blaine Feynard and Nadia Olsen the *supermodels* do you?"

"But of course dear." Cecile looked surprised, "How many other Blaine's and Nadia's do you know in the modelling industry?"

"Don't worry angel." Duncan said as he reached over and squeezed her arm reassuringly. "They're both lovely, you'll all get on like a house on fire. And I'll take care of you, you just remember us when you're a superstar, ok?"

Chapter 10. Opportunity Knocks

After work Si grabbed his bag, said goodbye to Marina and made a hasty escape.

For weeks he'd been worrying over Tony's imminent arrival and the state of his finances. He'd hassled Lisa for as many extra shifts as possible and turned himself inside out trying to be the funniest, most charming and flirtatious barman, but the tips still weren't great. And then one night he'd found a simpler solution literally staring him in the face in the form of Phoenix, a stripper who entertained at the Black Cock on Tuesdays.

Thrilled to have found a possible answer to his problems he'd set about quizzing Phoenix and buying him drinks. He discovered that the seriously fit, muscle-man's real name was Leslie (wasn't that a girls name?) and he was disappointingly affected off stage. Nonetheless, he proved to be a goldmine of information, happily giving him tips about performing, how to get gigs and most importantly how to earn as much as possible. Si had been giddy with excitement; he made it sound so easy. This could really work, he might even enjoy himself. He'd decided to give it a whirl then and there. It was such a brilliant idea; he'd had to draw on all his reservoirs of will-power in order to stay schtum.

How did the saying go? He thought to himself, crossing the road into Kershalton Street. That was it, loose mouths sink ships. Or in this case, if anyone inadvertently mentions a word of this to Tony, there's a chance he'll run a million miles.

Putting the key in the lock he noticed blissfully that none of the lights were on inside. The house was his.

X

Within a remarkably productive few hours Si had made himself a cheese and ham omelet, taken a relaxing bubble bath and done the basic choreography to a routine.

Jezebel looked on benignly like a stripy Buddha. He hoped it wasn't indicative of his technique that she'd spent the last ten minutes disdainfully licking her bum.

Experimentally he tried drizzling body oil over his chest as he got down to his underpants, throwing his T-shirt over his shoulder and swaying his hips seductively in the mirror. He was beginning to think he might not actually make a bad stripper.

So engrossed was he in the creative process, he was oblivious to the sound of footfalls on the stairs. As a result when someone rapped loudly on his bedroom door he nearly had a heart attack.

"Si! It's me, Gypsy. Can I come in?"

Flustered, he turned the music down and tried to find his T-shirt which seemed to have disappeared into the ether.

"Er, hang on a sec. What is it?"

The door swung open and she looked around suspiciously.

"What're you up too?" She asked, an eyebrow raised as he sat on the edge of the bed in his underpants, dripping oil and trying and failing to look nonchalant.

"Nothing." He said. "Just listening to some tunes."

"Hmmm."

"Honestly!" His voice was an octave higher than usual. If only he wasn't such a completely rubbish liar.

"Fine." He gave up. "If you must know, I'm becoming a stripper, but I'm keeping it very quiet – this can't get back to Tony."

"You're not serious."

"I'm deadly serious. I need to raise money so we can go on holiday."

"Right, so just now you were…"

"Rehearsing." He said sounding defensive. "Why? What's wrong?"

Gypsy cracked up, before shooting him an apologetic look.

"I'm sorry!" She spluttered, noticing his offended expression. "I've just never imagined you as the stripper… type, I guess."

He continued to look hurt. "Have you quite finished?"

She suppressed a giggle. "Yes."

Then a thought occurred to her. "What if Tony shows up at one of the bars where you're working?"

"Not likely." He sniffed. "Tony only ever goes to those poncy, city bars."

"You met in the Black Cock." She pointed out.

"Yeah, well, that was an exception; he doesn't really do the gay scene."

"Okay, I'll make you a deal."

"What?"

"I'll watch your routine and give you pointers, as long as you keep your pants on." She broke off to allow Jezebel onto her lap. "Oh, and you have to come and give me moral support when I start my new job."

"Oh, where's that?"

"The Pink Flamingo Club."

"Hmm." He said doubtfully, "Is that like Secrets? Are you joining me in the world of exotic dance?"

"No, it's a drag bar. I think one stripper in the household's enough, don't you?"

"Don't judge what you haven't tried. This could be the start of big things for us."

"You mean you taking your clothes off for money, and me working at a tranny club?" She sounded skeptical.

"No babes, I mean it's a fresh start. Who can say where our new career paths will lead? Maybe what we're doing now will determine the course of rest of our lives."

"I'm not sure that would be so great." She said dubiously.

"Look at it this way." He said. "We've just moved into an awesome house, we have new jobs and, most importantly, *I'm* in a relationship now! Things are looking up." He started blotting his chest with some toilet roll. "Oh that reminds me, Tony says that he's bringing a friend down with him. Apparently she's going through a bit of a rough time, so if you know of anyone looking for a lodger that would be mucho appreciated."

"How about your Mum? I mean when Kate moves out."

"Maybe, I'll ask. Pity we already took George, or she could've stayed here." He mused.

"By the way, have you had a chat with him yet? I feel a bit guilty for not making him feel more welcome." His voice lowered to an exaggerated whisper. "To be honest though, he seems a bit unfriendly. He's out most of the time and whenever he is here he stays in his room with the door locked."

"Perhaps he just likes to keep to himself. Anyway, he can't be. I haven't sorted locks on the bedroom doors yet."

"That's the thing; he's put one in himself. Go outside and have a look if you don't believe me, it's a big heavy duty one. Bit rude that, isn't it?"

Gypsy frowned, went to take a look and then sat down again next to him. "Okay, I'm all for privacy, but that's a bit weird. What's he got to hide?"

Chapter 11. Gladys Cox-Hardt

"You knew it was me in the taxi, didn't you?" Mark accused. JJ passed him a cup of tea, his lips curved in a half-smile.

"Perhaps."

"Well, why didn't you say something then?"

"I didn't want to spoil the surprise." The drag queen's eyes glinted mischievously.

Mark suddenly felt overcome by fatigue and depression. "I hate surprises."

"Look, why don't I leave you to get unpacked." JJ suggested. "I've got to go out in a minute to do a punter."

"Punter?"

"Didn't Andrew tell you that I'm a working girl?"

"No. He didn't actually tell me much about you at all." Mark said crossly.

JJ fussed with the flower arrangement in the center of the table. "Well that's easily fixed, why don't you meet me in the pub tonight after I'm done and we can have a couple of bevys?"

"Sorry, I'm actually pretty tired." Mark wanted nothing so badly as a hot bath and some sleep.

He shrugged. "Well, if you change your mind I'll be down in Bardot's after nine. The cab number's on the fridge door, they all know where it is."

61

"We'll see." Mark carried his suitcase into the sparsely furnished bedroom JJ had told him would be his for the duration of his stay.

"Excuse me!" His host cried sprinting past him and throwing open the doors to the wardrobe just before Mark could reach it. "Sorry, I might actually need a couple of things from in here."

He rummaged around for a while, eventually emerging carrying a cardboard box. It contained (amongst other items) a fireman's uniform, a pair of handcuffs and a lethal looking leather whip. He carried it out and disappeared into what Mark presumed was his own room.

"Hey!" Mark called out after him, poking his head into the hallway. "What do I call you? Do you like to be called JJ? Or... Gladys?"

"What do you want to call me?" He asked suggestively, hand on hip.

Mark just looked at him. He wished he'd never decided to leave London. "Whatever."

JJ shrugged and thought for a moment. "I've always liked princess, if you're looking for a term of endearment?" He rolled his eyes at his guest's expression. "JJ will be fine. Honestly."

X

It was dark. The flat was eerily silent apart from the shrill sound of a telephone ringing. Mark groaned and groggily lifted his head up off the pillow.

He'd been in the middle of a dream about trying to climb a huge tangled pile of wire coat hangers. The metal mountain stretched up into the sky as far as his eyes could see. He knew somehow that he'd be happy if he could only reach the top, where he saw blue sky and wisps of cloud drifting by. The harder he tried to reach his destination though, the more entwined his feet got in the hangers. Then he lost his balance and was freefalling towards the ground when someone

62

started blowing a whistle, an awful piercing noise that sounded relentlessly again and again.

Just as he was starting to wonder where in hell he was and why his bedside table had vanished into thin air, he heard the sound of a male voice leaving what sounded like a mildly obscene message. This was followed by the beep of an answering machine and heavy breathing down the line.

Mark stumbled out of bed and into the hallway realising as he did so that he'd fallen asleep fully clothed. He remembered unpacking, then feeling tired and deciding to lie and rest his eyes for a couple of minutes. Except he must've been asleep for hours and now he was overcome with that unpleasantly disorientated sensation you invariably get from being in a strange place, not knowing your way around and being completely unaware of the time.

Searching blindly for a light switch he stumbled along like a mole in the blackness, his hands outstretched, listening as the raspy breathing amplified by the answer machine got louder and louder. Finally it ended abruptly with the sound of the dial tone. The caller, whoever he or she had been, had hung up.

Squinting, he finally located the kitchen light and switching it on, instantly illuminating what could only be JJ's bedroom, mercifully unoccupied.

Mark blinked as he looked around taking in his surroundings. From across the other side of the room a row of mannequin heads stared at him coquettishly from beneath a variety of professionally styled wigs. These ranged from burnished copper, peroxide blond and gothic black to hot pink and pale lilac. Another shelf was completely dedicated to false eye-lashes. Ridiculously long rainbow hued ones, an electric blue feather pair, and sets in vibrant purple, silver and crimson. Beneath the disjointed heads was a selection of shoes that would've made Imelda Marcos green with envy, and incongruously placed on top of the neatly made double bed was the cardboard box with the accessories that JJ had collected earlier. The air was scented with the lingering smell of joss sticks and on a little wooden table sat a sewing

63

machine next to a pile of gaudy coloured curtains that'd been dumped on the floor.

Exploring the flat at leisure, he discovered a spacious bathroom with floor to ceiling mirrors. A tall cabinet above the sink housed a vast collection of skincare products jostling and fighting for space. He was gratified to see a commodious and somewhat grandiose claw-foot marble bath; although the effect was somewhat marred by the hot-pink ashtray balanced on the side, below which he spotted an empty bottle of vodka in the bin.

His bedroom seemed to be the only one blandly decorated in neutral inoffensive shades of beige. The others were all blood red with huge bright Warhol-style prints on the walls. Everywhere he looked there seemed to be clutter and bits of JJ's costumerie covering any surface or sitting space. Even the kitchen, which doubled as a living room, had not escaped unscathed. Lengths of electric blue gauze were draped all over the arms of the black, zebra-print sofa.

Momentarily startled, he happened upon a life-sized cardboard bust of Eartha Kitt dressed as Catwoman standing by the flat screen TV. Next to it, he saw the phone that'd roused him from his nap. It was pillar-box red and shaped like an enormous pair of lips.

Swinging open the door to the fridge, he peered hopefully inside and moments later was sitting down to a snack of cheese and bread with a glass of Papaya juice. The microwave clock told him it was half-past nine and he'd been out cold for nearly two hours.

He washed up after his meal and wandered about indecisively before checking the piece of paper with the taxi company's details which was indeed taped to the front of the fridge. He knew the chances of getting back to sleep were minimal and wondered if maybe a few drinks in Bardot's might not be such a bad idea. After all he was going to be living with the guy for the next month; it couldn't hurt to at least give him a chance.

But why would I willingly seek out the company of someone who clearly rubs me up the wrong way? He

64

wondered frowning and staring at the piece of paper in his hand. For that matter why bother going out at all? He sighed. Did he really want to put himself through it all again, just because he felt alone and there was the possibility of meeting someone? And did he look fat in this top, or should he change into a shirt?

X

By the time the cab pulled up outside Bardot's it was nearly ten o'clock. Mark paid the cab driver and entered the pub, hoping he was in the right place. The interior immediately reassured him that he was. The walls were completely covered in a variety of pictures of the silver screen goddess.

Elbowing his way through the crowd to the bar, he glimpsed a couple of drag queens standing chatting by the jukebox, neither of them looked familiar. He'd been certain that spotting a six-foot, fantastically attired tranny in a gay bar would be the easiest of tasks but suddenly he wasn't so sure. The place was pretty crowded and larger than he'd expected; the music eardrum-abusively loud.

Squeezing to the front he bought himself a pint of cider and settled back on a bar-stool to take in the sights. His eyes were drawn to a wooden staircase leading to a gallery where more customers were seated at tables directly above them. The vibe was buzzing. Everyone was talking and laughing animatedly and he felt his spirits begin to rise as he finished off his drink, suddenly very glad to be out and about rather than sitting at home alone.

"Excuse me."

"Hi." Mark looked over and saw an attractive dark haired man leaning on the bar next to him.

The man smiled showing off even, white teeth, "I was wondering if I could buy you another?"

"Thanks. Don't mind if I do."

The man ordered a drink for Mark and one for himself. He stood up and offered his hand. "I'm Raphael."

"Nice to meet you, I'm Mark."

Raphael handed him his drink and they clinked glasses before enjoying a moment's companionable silence whilst they sipped their pints.

"Are you here on holiday?" Raphael asked in his slightly Spanish sounding accent.

"Is it that obvious I'm not from round here?" Mark asked ruefully.

"No, but if I'd seen you around... I wouldn't have forgotten."

"Oh, right." He blushed like a sixteen year old schoolgirl. "I live in London, but I'm around for a month or so."

"London is very nice city. I visit there last summer and I enjoyed very much."

"Yes, well I like it. So, do you come here often?" Mark cringed at the banality of the line but found himself stuck for conversation that wouldn't involve ex-boyfriends or cross-dressing flat-mates.

"Si. Is good bar. Are you staying close by?" The man moved closer.

"Um, not too far." He hedged, stalling. "Anyway, where are you from?"

Raphael looked into his eyes. "I lived Madrid, but I've been here three year now. Listen what are your plans for..." He stopped mid sentence as something on the other side of the room seemed to catch his attention.

Annoyed, Mark looked over in the general direction his companion was focused on and found himself staring at Gladys Cox-Hardt herself. Resplendent in red hot-pants, dominatrix style boots and a glittery bra-top this time she sported a big blond beehive and the lipstick was an exaggerated prostitute pink, but it was unmistakably JJ.

"Yes. Go on, what were you saying?" He asked distractedly.

"Look at her. What's she doing?" Raphael seemed fascinated and leaned forward to watch Gladys undulate her way over to the box of Freedom condoms on the side of the bar. Without missing a beat, she opened up her sizeable

66

handbag and picking up the box emptied the contents into it – pausing only to give it a shake and make sure she hadn't left any behind. Unbelievably none of the bar staff seemed to notice. Next she walked up to the bar purposely where a chubby older man, clearly a fan, bought her a shot. Rewarding him with a jubilant smile she downed it in one.

The drag queen's eyes lit upon Mark and before he knew it, he'd been descended on, grabbed by the elbow and marched towards the exit. This was staring to become a habit. Frustratingly, Raphael vanished from sight behind him, melting into the crowd.

"What is it?" He asked crossly. "I was trying to have a conversation back there."

"Yes, I could see that." Gladys said, tossing a strand of monofibre over her shoulder. "That's what I've come to warn you about. You're chatting up the weirdo who's been stalking me."

Chapter 12. Big Shoes to Fill

Gypsy was running late for her appointment at the Pink Flamingo club. Mysterious technical difficulties on the tube had resulted in the train crawling along at a pitiful speed only to come to a complete stand-still for what felt like an age at Bond Street. The situation made infinitely more unbearable by the man with bad body odour squashed up against her.

By the time she'd reached her destination her feet were hurting, she'd been rained on and was feeling thoroughly grumpy. Finding a small queue outside the entrance; she took her place and lit up a fag. When she got to the front a tall drag queen wearing a blond curly wig, roller-skates and a superior expression stopped her.

"Ten pounds please."

"My name's Gypsy, I'm working here tonight."

"Well I'm Sasha Bitch and I've never heard of you." She said brusquely.

"James Cadogan sent me. Geneva Convention? He told me I could work a trial evening." Gypsy was starting to get pissed off.

The drag queen raised a painted eyebrow and then disappeared behind a desk inside the entrance, sighing crossly and looking most put upon as he flicked through some paperwork. "Just one moment please."

Gypsy threw her cigarette down onto the street as it started to get speckled with rain. She swore to herself that if she'd come all this way for nothing she would not be responsible for her actions. After a few more minutes she was thankfully summoned inside out of the drizzle.

"There seems to have been some sort of mistake."

"Mistake?"

"We were expecting a drag act, a professional performer to fill our hourly spot." Sasha explained looking down her nose condescendingly. "Our own infamous Ivana Double was in an unfortunate swing mishap last week, most tiresome, she's still in hospital."

"What's the problem? I'm a professional performer."

"Maybe, but despite the amount of slap you've got on you're clearly not a drag act, you are female." She pronounced this last part slowly and deliberately as if speaking to someone with the intelligence of a particularly slow egg mayonnaise sandwich. "We need a drag queen. This..." Sasha gestured around her wobbling slightly on her roller-blades "Is a drag club. Are you getting the picture?"

"But James said..."

"James must have got confused. There was an opening for a waitress recently."

Gypsy opened her mouth to speak.

The drag queen was too quick for her.

"The opening is now closed." She put a long false fingernail up to her chin thoughtfully. "You're not a drag king are you? No, no... that wouldn't work."

"Well I could..."

"Sorry love, drag acts only. Come back when you've got a dick."

The door was shut firmly in her flabbergasted face.

Chapter 13. Too good to be true?

"I'm really glad we're doing this," Danny confessed, taking a gulp of his drink. "I only moved down from Manchester recently so I don't know many people in the area yet."

"It's a pleasure." Kate ginned. "I don't normally socialise with the guys from work. It's nice not to be rushing back to Hounslow for once."

"Oh, so you mean there are no work parties or pub crawls to look forward to?"

She pulled a face. "Well, let's just say that parties at Dennison Advertising are not exactly the stuff of which legends are made."

"Right." He gave her a slightly crooked smile which made her glad they were sitting down such was the effect he had on her. What was it with this guy? She hadn't felt so attracted to anyone in a long time. He was gorgeous.

Kate took a cursory look through the menu. They'd been drinking and chatting for almost an hour in the Covent Garden brasserie and she was still no nearer to knowing whether he'd asked her out because he found her irresistible or simply as a friendly gesture.

Sighing she decided to change tact. "Anyway, they're an okay bunch for the most part. Have you met James Cadogan yet? He's on our floor and we have a drink after work occasionally."

"I don't think so, is he your..."

"Boyfriend?" She shook her head emphatically. "Oh no, definitely not."

"So, are you seeing anyone?"

"Nope." She shrugged. "I've been single for a while. Probably coz the only clubs I've been going to lately are gay. Oh god, I'm turning into a fag hag!"

He raised his eyebrows. "You'll have to come out with me sometime. Maybe tonight after we've eaten if you're up for it?"

"Sounds like a plan." Result! Kate rested her chin in her hands and studied his face, drinking in the turquoise eyes that lit up when he laughed, his dimples and hair that curled around his neck line.

He smiled. "Okay, well let's have a wander around later. I'm sure we'll find somewhere."

She was suddenly glad that she'd made a bit of effort tonight. Okay, maybe a lot of effort. It'd taken ages to straighten her hair and perfect her make-up in the toilets, plus she'd blown a hundred quid on a silver top and some new ultra-stylish ankle boots in her lunch break. But now it all seemed worth it.

"I haven't even asked you about life in Manchester and what bought you down here." She realised suddenly, helping herself to a piece of bread.

He tried to catch the waiter's eye. "Oh, it's a long boring story. Why don't we eat first?" He steered the conversation discretely back to her. "You're not a born and bred Londoner are you?"

"No, I'm a country girl really. I came here to live with my ex, except that all ended in disaster, which is why he's my ex... But here I am anyway, and I love it now."

The waiter jotted their orders down and collected the menus.

"Anyway, I'm looking for a place to live at the moment. I'm staying with a friend. She's great, a real character. She used to be quite a famous actress years ago, and I love her to bits but it takes ages to commute from Hounslow..."

71

Kate trailed off seeing that she'd lost him. His expression was unreadable, he was clearly miles away.

"I'm sorry. I've just remembered a call I have to make; would you excuse me a minute?" He asked. "I'll order us another bottle of wine whilst I'm up, shall I?"

"Yeah, alright, that'd be nice." Was it paranoia, or had she said something wrong? Perhaps she'd just been going on and had completely bored the poor man. Glumly, she conceded that despite a promising start, the date still had plenty of time to turn into a dead loss.

She downed her glass of wine. Fuck it. She wasn't ready to give up yet.

X

Kate woke up the following morning with an excruciating hangover. Slightly discomfited to find herself in an unfamiliar bedroom, she sat up and looked around. Early morning sunlight poured through the slats of a pair of wooden shutters. A breeze wafted in from the open window and she inhaled the fresh air eagerly, stretching her stiff legs out and rubbing the sleep from her eyes.

Now it was coming back to her, she'd just had a *very* enjoyable night with Danny. She had a hazy recollection of them going on to a variety of bars after their meal.

She furrowed her brow in concentration, racking her brain. From this point onwards her picture of the night's events was badly impaired, in direct proportion, she suspected, to her intake of vino.

She could recall only bits and pieces of the club. It'd been hot, noisy and absolutely rammed. At one point dancing amid the throng Danny had stripped off his shirt. She could still see his impressive upper body glistening with sweat as the two of them moved together under the strobe lights. After that, all she could be certain of was that they'd got a taxi at some point, presumably to his place.

A knock on the door startled her.

72

Bleary-eyed, Danny materialised from the floor beneath her. Hair mused up and face indented with marks from the carpet it appeared he'd for some reason been sleeping there.

"Danny boy, do you want a coffee mate?" A male voice shouted through the door.

He looked up at her and she hesitated, then shrugged and nodded.

"Alright, cheers." He yelled back. "Could you make that two?"

"Two, eh? Okay, I'm putting the kettle on in a mo."

They heard someone thumping back down the stairs in a manner which was unsympathetic to raging headaches.

Danny smiled lazily and reached up to where Kate was lying, touching her lightly on the cheek. "That's my flat-mate Seth."

She nodded and offered up a silent prayer that her hair hadn't treacherously turned to frizz overnight and that she'd removed her make-up last night. Otherwise he was probably looking up into a pair of panda eyes.

"What're you doing down there?"

"I think I fell off." He winced in pain and massaged his rib area. "Ouch."

"I hope you're not insinuating that I hog the bed?"

He nodded. "And you snore like a trucker!"

"I do not!"

"Ha! No, I'm winding you up." He grinned. "Although I'm surprised you couldn't hear Seth through the wall. He snores something terrible, the big smelly idiot."

She sat up properly, pushing her tangled hair back from her face. "Talking of neighbourhoods, where exactly are we?"

"About five minutes from Shepherd's Bush tube."

"Shit!" She exclaimed looking at her watch. "It's quarter past nine already."

Danny looked disappointed. "I guess you won't be staying for coffee then."

He pushed his hand under the duvet and ran it slowly up one of her legs whilst leaning over to nibble her earlobe.

73

"I suppose it's nothing I can't postpone until later today." She relented as he covered her body with his own.

The smell of bacon cooking drifted up the stairs and into the room. Outside birds were singing, it was a sunny day and she was about to get shagged senseless by a really hot guy...

I'd have to be stark raving mad to turn all this down just to view another crappy flat; she thought to herself carelessly, house hunting could wait.

X

The morning unfolded slowly. They took their time before emerging from the bedroom. Danny nipped out to shop for the papers and Kate rescheduled her appointment before immersing herself in a hot bath. She lay there for a full fifteen minutes luxuriating in the soapy water before washing the pub smell out of her hair, drying herself and re-dressing in last nights clothes.

Satisfied, she noted that for once her hair was behaving itself and had fallen flatteringly round her face in damp golden-brown waves. Desperate for a caffeine fix she rinsed her face with cold water and headed downstairs, her nose twitched with interest at the lingering smell of fried food.

Entering the kitchen she was greeted by the sight of a scruffy looking man sitting at the table wearing a holey tracksuit and a baseball cap. He was smoking a roll-up and drinking coffee; he smelt strongly of stale curry.

"Morning love, I'm Seth." He glanced up from the magazine he was reading, "Danny's mate."

"Hi. I'm Kate. Danny's erm, work friend." She sat down next to him.

"Can I get you a tea or coffee then?"

"Yes coffee please. That would be brill. I couldn't bum a fag off you too, could I?"

"I'll roll you one."

"Thanks."

He fixed her a coffee, located his pack of rizlas and began to painstakingly shake some tobacco out. Meanwhile a few

74

seconds later Danny wandered in laden with groceries. He dumped two plastic bags on the sideboard and produced a newspaper, a loaf of bread, milk and eggs.

The two men had a brief argument about whose turn it was to do the hovering and Kate smoked her fag and drank from the chipped mug. The radio was playing and she hummed along wondering reluctantly if it were time she made a move. After all, she realised guiltily, Cathy was probably wondering where the hell she'd disappeared to last night. She'd only planned on a quiet evening out, but the best laid plans, and all that...

"Do you fancy going out into town?" Danny asked, interrupting her thoughts. "I need to do some shopping in Oxford Street; we could get lunch if you like."

Her stomach rumbled audibly. She'd already cast a hopeful eye over to the cooker, but the frying pan was disappointingly empty, its contents long gone.

"I'd love to." She said eyes lighting up. "But I definitely have to go see the flat this afternoon."

"You're looking for a place to live?" Seth asked.

"Yeah, I need somewhere nearer the office."

Suddenly Kate's attention was caught by the magazine he was holding. She craned her head to try to get a better look. *Noooo.* She thought, I'm hung-over, confused. It can't be. But the more she squinted at the picture on the front, the more it seemed to look exactly like...

"Seth! Excuse me but could I quickly check something?" She reached over for the mag, which he handed to her with a shrug.

"Ohmigod!" She exclaimed as they both looked quizzically at the model she was pointing to excitedly. "It's Ida Swann. I went to school with her."

Seth looked interested. "She's a friend of yours?"

"What?" Kate asked distractedly. "Oh, well yeah I suppose we're friends, although I haven't seen her for ages."

"You have a friend who's a gorgeous model." He gave a low whistle. "Wey hey."

75

"She looks great. I almost wouldn't have recognised her." Her face flushed with pleasure. "When I knew her she was nice and all, but she always looked so downtrodden and miserable. Her boyfriend was really controlling and awful. God, that's made my day. I'm so glad she's made a success of her life. I have to tell Gypsy and Marina."

"Who?" Danny frowned.

"Gypsy's the one I told you about?" She reminded him. "She, Ida and I went to the same college. I met Marina through Gypsy and we introduced her to Ida years ago and she had a huge crush on her."

Seth looked at her with new respect. "You have a model friend and a lesbian friend too?"

"I apologise for Seth." Danny muttered. "He's a knob."

"I'm a knob?" Seth asked indignantly. "Excuse me. Anyway, we have a spare room that needs renting out. Kate, why not take a look while you're here?"

There was an uncomfortable silence.

"I dunno..." Kate looked embarrassed.

"Why not think about it? You're friends can visit anytime, by the way." He said with a wink. "By the way, did I say I'm available?"

She raised her eyebrows and gave him a Tyra Banks disappointed look.

He chuckled to himself. "Only joking, I'd behave myself. Plus it'd be a laugh living with us. We're not too untidy, rent's reasonable." He looked at Danny. "Come on mate, help me out a bit here, we've got a dish-washer, washer/drier, SKY TV, internet connection."

"Stop it; don't go all hard sell on her, jeez." He laughed before turning back to her. "But seriously, feel free to look around at least; it might not be a bad idea."

She ignored him and turned to Seth.

"Most of my friends are actually gay guys I'm afraid, so if you're just hoping to cop off with a model you'll be disappointed."

"Oh. Well, you can't blame a guy for trying. Your men friends are welcome too... although I'm strictly into the ladies."

"I'm sure they'll be gutted." Danny patted his beer-belly playfully.

X

Later Kate and Danny sat near Trafalgar Square enjoying the weather and finishing off a late lunch of Prèt a Manger sandwiches. Kate licked a strand of mozzarella off her fingers and leaned back contentedly, lifting her freckled face towards the sun. Her eyes flickered open, then closed again as a group of school kids ran by disturbing the pigeons who gathered around them scavenging for crumbs.

They were both tired after braving the crowded streets and trawling countless shops in search of a present for Danny's nephew. They'd finally struck gold in the Gadget Shop. She'd expected him to have had enough by this point, but he'd surprised her by suggesting they browse through some clothes shops while they were there. Amazingly enough he'd been perfectly happy to wait around as she tried on various items; modelling them for him so she could get a second opinion. A man who liked shopping? Was this too good to be true?

She turned around to look at him, shielding her eyes from the sun with her hand.

"I suppose I should make a move." She checked her watch. "Thanks though. I've had a lovely day."

"Oh." He frowned. "Are you still going to look at that flat?"

"I guess I should. It's expensive though."

"Have you thought about what Seth said about the room at ours?" He asked. "I hope he didn't annoy you, he's just you know, Seth."

She shook her head. "He's alright. I was just a bit thrown at the idea of me moving in, to be honest. It's a terrible idea.

77

I mean, don't you reckon? I can't move in with someone I've just had sex with."

"I know what you mean." Danny shrugged. "But it wouldn't be like that. It's not like we'd be "moving in together"." He made exaggerated inverted commas with his hands. "We'd be flatmates; with anything else completely separate. Besides, I like you. It might work. If not, then you're free to leave."

Kate laughed. "That's very sweet. But don't you think it might be a bit much us living and working together?"

"Well, we'd still go out and do our own thing." He stopped and took a swallow of coffee from his polystyrene cup. "Now I totally feel like I'm twisting your arm, which I really don't want to do. Honestly, there's no pressure at all. If you think it's a bad idea, then that's your call. I'm just letting you know, it'd be lovely to have you. We do need to find someone and seeing as you're looking... "

"Go on, convince me! Change my mind; I give you permission to try."

"Really?" He smiled dimples flashing. "We-ll, you'd have your own space; it's pretty much a flat in itself up there. Oh, and it's on the top floor, with a balcony overlooking a stunning garden. There's a kitchen area with a microwave and kettle. It's great value for money, ideally located in the heart of Shepherd's Bush..."

"Hmm. Okay, okay... I'll think about it." She promised, throwing her sandwich wrapper in the bin.

"That's all I ask. Now, are you off to look at the other place? Or shall I give you a quick tour right now and we can maybe grab a DVD before I let you go?" He asked hopefully.

She took his hand and gathered up her bags. "You've got yourself a deal mister."

X

Later Danny left her looking around the studio flat which was on the top floor of their house. She had to admit she

78

could live a pretty self-sufficient life up here. It even had its own tiny en suite bathroom.

The attic ceiling slanted upwards charmingly its old beams visible. The effect was cute and cottagey. Although, Kate mused, lying down on the double bed experimentally, she'd have to watch she didn't bang her head sitting up too quickly in the morning. Still, the main selling point had to be the balcony. Kicking off her flip-flops she opened the door and stepping out wiggled her toes appreciatively as they touched welcoming, sun-warmed tiles. It was just large enough for one person to lie out there; the white iron railing surrounding it almost totally hidden by ivy and creepers. Leaning over and looking down revealed a gorgeous view of the garden below. She stayed out there a few moments, breathing in the fresh air and the scent of honeysuckle. Dusk had fallen, and looking up in the half-light she could see stars in the sky.

Fuck it. It was perfect.

Turning to go back inside, she smiled to herself. Irrespective of what happened with her and Danny, if the price was within her range she was going to take it. How could she not? She was never going to find something else as nice. All she had to do now was break the news to Cathy.

She was just descending the stairs when she heard Danny's voice coming from his room. For some reason, he was talking in an undertone, which piqued her curiosity. Hovering silently on the steps she found herself eavesdropping on the tail end of the conversation.

"I got your number from the ad." She heard him mutter urgently. Then a pause, followed by, "Yes, a man. Six foot, dark hair, fit. Can you do the full works? Well, if it's just a matter of money... it's difficult here; can I come to you, tomorrow?"

There was silence, during which she considered alerting him to her presence, but something stopped her. She wanted to know what was going on.

"Look, I can't really talk. I have someone here. Okay, I'll see you then. Bye."

Heart thudding guilty in her chest, she nipped down to the landing and slipped into the bathroom pulling the door closed behind her. As she heard him run downstairs she realised she'd been holding her breath and exhaled slowly her mind racing.

Chapter 14. Cathy Troubled

Cathy Fraser rested her chin in her hands and stared down at the blank piece of stationery lying on the coffee table as she waited for inspiration. The radio was on low and she could hear the gentle rise and fall of the DJ's chatter.

She realised that if she didn't get a move on she'd still be sitting there when Si arrived, which wouldn't do at all.

Picking up the fountain pen and willing herself into action she took a deep breath and in her large scrawl managed to fill a couple of pages. She sighed, hoping for the hundredth time that she was doing the right thing by ignoring the old saying and refusing to let sleeping dogs lie. She stared down at her barely legible penmanship with a sick feeling in her stomach.

As if he understood Lawrence, one of her three poodles jumped up to rest his curly front paws on her lap. He whined sympathetically and licked her hands as she petted him.

Just then the phone rang making her jump.

Saved by the bell, she thought with relief, pushing Lawrence out of the way and reaching for receiver.

"Cathy? It's me." It was Kate.

"Hello dear." She tried not to sound distracted as she twisted the telephone cord round one finger.

"I just wanted to let you know I'll be home later on tonight."

"I'll look forward to seeing you. Is everything alright?"

"Yes and no." Kate paused. "I've found this bed-sit. I'm considering taking it and I thought I'd talk to you. I'd hate to leave you high and dry."

"Oh, don't worry about that dear. You know I love having you, but if you did want to move on it might be quite good timing." Cathy paused to think. "Si told me Tony's bringing a friend from Scotland, and I'm sure she'd much rather stay here than in some awful hotel. I'll talk to him about it tonight."

"Okay, thanks." Kate said gratefully. "I'll miss staying with you, you've been amazing."

"It's been a pleasure."

"This new place is perfect in some ways." She trailed off. "It's in the same building as the new guy at work I was telling you about."

"Aha! The one you went out to meet yesterday night?" Cathy asked, smelling gossip.

"Well yes, and it was a brilliant night but despite that and how fabulous this room is... I don't think things are going to work out with Danny. In fact, I don't even know whether I should move in there or not now, I'm so confused!"

"Sweetheart, you're not making any sense at all. Whatever's the matter?" Cathy's voice filled with concern.

"It's just..."

"Yes?"

"Well we've spent some time together and I thought he was a really lovely guy." Kate broke off.

"I don't understand."

"I heard him on the phone this morning. He couldn't even wait until I'd gone. Oh fuck it Mrs F, what's wrong with me? I mean first Neil, and now this... I'm seriously thinking of taking a vow of celibacy."

"But what exactly did you hear? I'm sure it can't be that bad."

"Well it's not great." Kate said. "I think he was hiring a rent boy."

X

Night had fallen by the time Cathy had finished her conversation with Kate, tidied away all evidence of her communication and carefully folded the letter in its envelope. She addressed it with haste and slid it covertly under a place mat before springing into action in preparation for Si's visit.

Dogs under foot, she ran the vacuum around the room, took out the rubbish, and fetched glasses and a bottle of brandy from the kitchen. Finally she rushed upstairs to make sure she'd hidden the ancient album of wedding photos she'd unearthed from storage before lunch.

The doorbell rang just as she was examining her flushed face in the mirror and self-consciously she tucked a wisp of grey hair back into place.

"Darling!" She cried as Si opened the door gave her a big hug.

"Hello mum." He was wearing jeans and a tight black top, his two tone hair spiky with gel and she noticed he had a new silver bar through one eyebrow.

"Come in, come in." She led him into the living room where he collapsed into the sofa, swinging the large canvas bag he was carrying down to rest between his legs.

"You're looking well." He eyed her pink cheeks with suspicion as she sat down next to him and poured them both a small glass of brandy. "In fact, I reckon you're up to no good. You've got that look in your eyes."

"I don't know what you're talking about dear." She said guiltily.

"Hmm." He took a sip of the amber liquid, the corners of his lips twitching with amusement. "I suppose I'll give you the benefit of the doubt."

Cathy avoided his eyes and removed a dog hair from the sleeve of the man's velvet smoking jacket she liked to wear around the house.

"I like your new piercing." She said changing the subject. "Very fetching."

"Thanks." He fiddled with it, "It's still a bit sore."

83

She lifted her glass to her lips. "You look like you've been away."

"Sunbed." He admitted sheepishly.

"Cheat!" Her mouth twisted in a wistful smile. "You look so much like your father did when he was your age." She paused, her heart heavy as she wondered how much her son had minded the absence of a father figure in his life. Of course she'd always tried to be both mother and father to him, but she felt a sudden need to know what effect it had had on her boy, growing up without a Dad. It seemed to have a heavy bearing on the painful direction her own nostalgic wonderings had been leading her of late.

"Do you ever..." She broke off, choosing her words carefully, "think about him?"

Si paused for a moment. "No, not really. I did when I was a kid sometimes. But not now, I've got you and you're the best."

"I'm glad, I do try to do the best I can for you my dear."

"I know." He patted her hand reassuringly.

"I'm afraid I'm going to smoke." She warned, reaching for the packet of Marlboros in her pocket. "Don't make a fuss."

He gave her a reproachful look.

"It's my house and I'll do as I like." She sighed. "I'm trying to stop, but I've been a little stressed lately." She inhaled deeply as he lit the tip with his Zippo. "Silly really."

"Oh, by the way, I spoke to Kate and she's found somewhere else to live." She looked up at him, "So I'd be happy of the rent money if Tony's friend would like to stay."

"That's great news." He said brightening up, "Her name's Stella, Tony's told me all about her and I'm sure you'll get on. But I'll speak to him first anyway and get her to come over for tea and a visit so you can both make up your minds."

"Lovely."

He avoided her eyes, "I'm afraid I can't stay long tonight. I'm er, busy."

"Oh?"

"Just meeting a friend, no one you know." He said quickly, subconsciously fingering the straps of his bag.

Immediately she felt uneasy and made a heroic effort to fight down a wave of panic.

I'm being paranoid; she thought to herself. This is what keeping secrets does to people. All the same she was suddenly very glad that she'd written that letter. She sensed her mind wouldn't quieten down until she had some answers.

Chapter 15. Marvellous

Weaving around wind-blown afternoon shoppers, Gypsy navigated her way through the crowded Covent Garden Plaza, mobile phone clamped to her ear.

"What street did you say it was on?" She asked, reaching the other side and looking around for landmarks.

"Coulter Road, for the third time." James snapped crossly down the line.

"And you said the shop's called 'Fabulous'?" She hiked her bag more firmly around her shoulder and headed off in what she thought was the right direction.

"No, no, no. It's called 'Marvellous'."

"I hope you realise this is all your fault." She reminded him, piqued at the irritated tone in his voice.

"Whatever Gypsy, I was trying to do you a favour."

"Some favour! That door whore, whore being the operative word, was rude to me."

He sighed. "That's just Sasha Bitch." He explained. "Don't take it personally. Clue's in the name? She's vile to everyone."

"I don't care." Gypsy huffed. "No one gets away with talking to me like that; this is war."

"Yes, about that. I don't know if this is such a good idea."

"It's a *marvellous* idea." She grinned.

"I honestly don't think you'll get away with it."

"James honey," she replied confidently, "You underestimate me."

"You're too short for one thing!"

"I'll wear higher heels."

"But your facial features can't be changed.... and what about those curves?" He protested.

She paused outside Lloyds Bank to light a cigarette, sheltering the flame from the wind with one hand. "Ever heard of stage make-up and clever dressing? It was you who told me I can find everything I need at this shop." She reminded him.

"I still don't think you can pull it off." He said crushingly.

She inhaled deeply. "Look, I'm buying wigs, headdresses, a costume, false eye-lashes, cosmetics, nails and the biggest pair of fuck-me platform stilettos I can find." She reeled off her shopping list impatiently, "Plus I'm a performer. It's what I do. I'll be a natural."

"What about all the money you're going to have to spend?"

"You have to spend money to make money. It's an investment darling. I'll make it back and more if this works out. Honestly, you're starting to sound like a real worry-wart."

"I don't want to piss on your parade; I'm just trying to be a friend." He said snippily. "Why not just ask for a job as a female drag queen? Lots of girls do that whatsit... faux queen thing. Plus, look at Pam Ann – she's a woman, she's very successful."

"Where's the fun in that? Besides that bitch made it quite clear that nothing but a conventional queen would do. Trust me this is going to work." Gypsy said firmly, "Oh, and not a word to anyone okay? I don't want to tell the guys until I've been hired. I don't even want you to tell Kate, I mean it James."

"Fine, my lips are sealed."

Her eyes lit up as she spotted the attention grabbing window display on the other side of the road; it boasted wigs and feather headdresses galore.

"I've gotta go now hon, I think I've found it."

"Whatever. Knock yourself out." He said condescendingly, "But the day you pass as a drag queen will be the day I get mistaken for David Beckham."

X

The second resident of number sixty-nine Kershalton Street to pay a visit to the Covent Garden costumerie that day was a stressed-out Si. Unbeknownst to either of them he arrived barely an hour after Gypsy had left, jogging over in a tearing hurry to get back to work before his break was over.

A Sales Assistant had pointed him in the right direction and distractedly he perused the aisles, swooping with glee on a pair of imitation leather chaps and searching for a price tag.

Phoenix was proving an invaluable contact on the stripping circuit. As well as getting him on the books of an agency, he'd already set him up with a couple of small gigs to start out with. These, he decided, would be perfect practice for the hen party he'd been booked for in three weeks' time. Initially he'd only considered gay venues, advertising exclusively in the gay press. However, when a posh sounding lady had phoned him the other day he'd decided to take her up on her proposal. Considering the amount of money on offer it would've been rude not to. Besides, he thought browsing through the shops selection of cowboy hats, it might be fun. It'd undoubtedly all be worth it when Tony arrived and they started planning their vacation together. He picked up a lasso and examined it critically before adding it to the 'maybe' pile he'd mentally accumulated.

X

"Has he gone yet?" Ash hissed, peering round the stock room door.

Michelle, his supervisor, rolled her eyes and continued pricing cans of glitter spray.

"Yes, he's gone. You can come out now."

88

"I can't believe it." Ash said joining her behind the till. "That's the second customer today that I know from my local gay bar, and they're both friends of Duncan's, what are the odds of that?"

"Is that why you were hiding? Don't you want your snobby boyfriend knowing you work in a shop?" Michelle asked sarcastically.

"Ha!" He snorted putting his hands on his skinny hips. "Duncan doesn't know the first thing about what I do for a living, if you know what I mean honey, and that's the way I'd like it to stay."

"Yep, there's nothing like honesty to kill a relationship." She said crisply.

"It's none of his business." Ash protested busying himself with the other price gun. "So I sleep with guys for cash. So what? I never lied; I'm simply withholding the truth. Besides, he's never shown the slightest bit of interest in how I spend my time when he's not around. We're not married."

Michelle shook her crimped, purple hair. "No need to get defensive."

"You're making me defensive."

"Okay, so are you telling me that you'd still be interested if he wasn't some hot-shot photographer?" She asked teasingly.

"Maybe." He looked thoughtful. "He's got an enormous cock."

"How romantic."

"Well I'm not in the best of moods with him right now, so it's not the optimum time to be asking me these questions.

"Are you still sore about missing that party?"

"Of course I am!" He said pouting. "I would've killed to be there. I mean, Raoul Fahri... can you stand it? It was all over the papers the next day." His eyes took on a faraway expression. "There were pictures of Blaine Feynard chatting to Vincent Santelli, you know, that gorgeous hairdresser off the telly I've got a thing for? There were celebs galore... Nadia Olsen, Ryan Gerrard and Rebekka Redfern. And what does

89

Duncan go and do? Invites some new model instead of his own boyfriend."

"Wow, so he's really in the dog-house then?" She ripped open a bag of skittles with her teeth and handed it to him.

Ash sucked in his breath. "I might be persuaded to forgive him, if he's very, *very* good." He delved into the bag.

Chapter 16. Straight Talking

After telling Danny and Seth she was going to move in, Kate went and sat in the garden, ostensibly for a smoke, but really wanting a few minutes alone to take stock. What had she just agreed to? Had she lost her mind? Christ.

She frowned, lighting up a fag, inhaling sharply and tossing the match into a flowerpot. How should she handle this? Burying her head in the sand and pretending she'd never overheard Danny's conversation was a tempting prospect. Groaning, she lowered herself on to the grass and splayed her legs out in front of her. It wasn't as if they were even dating. Why did it all have to be so complicated?

She didn't mind admitting that she was confused. After all he struck her as being an upfront kind of a guy who was making no bones about the fact he was completely into her. If he was into guys, surely he'd just go and date one.

She couldn't quieten a little voice in her head which insisted that moving in with a bloke you've just started seeing is guaranteed to end in disaster; even if he didn't have a penchant for anonymous sex with male prostitutes. But on the other hand she *really* liked him.

Sighing, she carefully buried her fag butt in the flowerbed under some stones. The last of the afternoon sunshine was warming her back and shoulders. A bed of fragrant peonies fluttered their petals in the breeze. In the shrubbery by the fence a magpie suddenly burst through the leaves causing a ruckus as it crashed through the undergrowth and wheeled up above her into the sky. She watched it for a while until it was just a tiny speck finally fading from view into cotton candy like clouds drifting along the sky now tinged with pink. It was so pretty and tranquil; she was in no hurry to go back indoors.

She sat sprawled on the lawn for several more minutes staring meditatively at her surroundings until the sun disappeared from view leaving her shivering in her thin cotton top.

X

Later on Kate found herself agreeing to stay for the evening. She still hadn't broached the subject of the phone call and bringing it up was very much on her mind. They sat on the sofa eating popcorn and watching rubbish TV.

"I'm so glad you're moving in." Danny murmured. He moved behind her and started massaging her shoulders. "How lucky am I to have met someone like you on my first day at work."

Someone gullible? She wondered, swallowing and trying to compose herself. "What do you mean?"

"You know, just that you're hot, funny and the answer to our prayers in terms of finding a lodger." He replied, and she could hear the smile in his voice as he trailed his fingers up and down her back making her shiver.

Nuts. She thought to herself. She hadn't felt this way about anyone in a long time.

"That's sweet. I'm having fun with you too." She said finally.

"Why do you sound all weird?" To her disappointment he stopped what he was doing to her back. "What's wrong?"

"I just think it's all going a bit fast. Perhaps it'd be easier if we just kept things plutonic." Kate took a deep breath and moved to the other side of the couch. "I mean we work together, and soon we're going to be living together..."

"We went over this already; I don't think those things need to affect us... not if we don't let them."

She avoided eye contact. "We're hardly an 'us' are we? Come on! We barely know each other."

"I don't understand what your problem is." He was unhappy. "Look, if you're not interested, just tell me so I can stop making a twat out of myself."

"Danny, it's not that. It's *so* not that." She took his hands. "Shit, this is ridiculous. I'm just going to be upfront, I need to ask you something okay?"

"Fine, go head. I'm all ears." He looked at her expectantly.

She fidgeted with remote, turning down the TV and pulled her legs up underneath her. Silently she prayed he wouldn't think she was some kind of spying, neurotic pain in the ass.

"Well. What is it?"

"Have you ever, erm, been with a man?"

He looked completely thrown. "No. Have you ever been with a woman?"

"What? Erm, no." She thought for a bit. "I mean, yes... I have actually. It was only once though, I was in secondary school and very drunk. But that's not really the point." She shook her head. "You're not going to make this easy for me are you?"

"I don't get it?" He frowned. "Hang on, are you asking me if I'm gay?"

"Well... yes actually."

He stared at her. "Kate, only a few hours ago we were having sex." Then he stopped as understanding seemed to dawn. "Wait. Are you asking me to like take part in some kind of threesome?"

"No, no! This is so coming out all wrong. I heard you on the phone yesterday..."

He was confused. "What are you talking about?"

She sighed. "It was after we got back from town. I wasn't listening in, but I couldn't help overhearing. You were calling one of those numbers to you know... *hire* a man."

"What?" A look of disbelief crossed his face. "You think that I was phoning up guys for sex?" He sounded incredulous.

93

"Well, what was I supposed to think?" Kate was defensive. "That's what it sounded like. It's just my luck..." she trailed off when she saw his shoulders start to shake and he lifted his head up. He was nearly wetting himself with laughter.

"It's not funny!" She spluttered crossly, though inwardly her stomach lifted with relief. "Look I'm sorry; I obviously got my wires completely crossed, will you tell me what's so hysterical?"

"I can't believe you! What are you like?"

"Gimme a break, okay? I've clearly made a mistake. It's none of my business who you were calling anyway, let's just drop it." She begged, mortified.

"I don't think we can." He said slowly.

She picked up the remote control again, "We can. You don't have to explain anything to me."

He took it from her hand and threw it back onto the floor.

"Yes, I do." He regarded her solemnly. "Because, Kate, I really like you."

She looked away. "You do?"

"Yes, you idiot."

He tilted her face up towards his and kissed her.

"Oh, and if it makes you feel any better, you're not the only one who's jumped to the wrong conclusion about my sexuality." He added.

She stared at him quizzically.

"Your friend at work, James? It was bizarre; he was pretending he knew me from some club."

"What?"

"It was really strange. When I said he'd mistaken me for someone else, he gave me this look, like he thought I was lying!"

"Weird!" She ran her hand up his back. "I've no idea what that's all about."

"Anyway," Danny carried on. "I want to explain what you heard on the phone."

Oh god, she thought. Here it comes, whatever *it* is. Mentally she prepared herself for the worst.

"I am looking for a man, in fact that's the reason I'm here in London." He took a deep breath. "You heard me calling a private detective; I was trying to see if he can help me find my identical twin, Julian."

"You have a twin brother?" She was gobsmacked. "So, why don't you know where he is? Did you fall out?"

"No, that's the whole point. Five years ago he disappeared off the face of the earth, literally just vanished." He stood up, agitated. "I've got to find him Kate, and I'm pretty sure he's living here, in this very city."

Chapter 17. Dodgy Dealings

Jumping up and down on her queen-sized bed, Ida punched the air and let out a yell of pure joy. Gleefully she bounced back onto the carpet and grabbed the copy of 'Fashion Fatale Magazine' she'd purchased only moments ago. She held it out at arms length staring at her picture splashed across the cover. A slow smile spread across her face and she hugged it tightly to her chest before resuming leaping inelegantly round the room grinning like an idiot.

Perturbed by all the excitement Dior, Blaine's dog, edged his snout suspiciously into the bedroom. She ran over and scooped him up in her arms covering his doggy head with kisses.

Her life was now divided into two parts. Pre and post Boss. It'd only been six months since she'd joined. Already it seemed a life time ago. She hardly recognised herself or the world as she'd previously known it. During that time she'd been taught to walk, dress, pose and conduct herself like a professional model. She'd had make-up tips, bought a whole new wardrobe and met countless new people. She was working incredibly hard but loving every minute of it. As promised, Cecile had helped her comprise a basic portfolio which was growing with every shoot she did. Now tonight, she was going to be taking part in a fashion show at Earls Court Stadium.

Releasing Dior, she sat down at her dressing table and stared into the mirror. Such a short time ago she'd been nobody. A big nothing, and now she was a working model on the front of a magazine. She devoutly repeated the words to her reflection as she did every morning.

"I, Ida Swann, am going to be a supermodel."

Positive affirmations couldn't hurt. Fingering her fringe she stuck her tongue out at herself. She still wasn't crazy about the haircut, although she conceded that it was certainly 'a look'... it just wasn't very her.

When she thought of strutting down her first catwalk in only a few hours time, her nerves tingled deliciously with a mixture of fear and exhilaration. Of course then there would be the after-party! Duncan should be coming; he'd turned out to be an amazing friend. Although she frankly detested the boy he was seeing. She found Ash sarky and rude.

Turning on the radio she danced into the kitchen singing tunelessly to herself as she filled up the kettle and put two slices of bread in the toaster.

This morning she felt like the happiest girl in the world. She loved modelling, the way her confidence was growing and the new life it was giving her. Of all the gifts she'd received though, the most precious had to be her freedom and her new home with her two famous housemates.

Of course on the day Cecile had signed her, and suggested she attend Raoul Fahri's party, the prospect of meeting them both had terrified her. Duncan had been an absolute angel that night. He'd got her a bit pissed and made sure she met lots of other friendly people who'd put her at ease before leading her over and making the introductions.

Ida pulled a face as she recalled Nadia's initial frostiness. Blaine though had been an absolute darling right from the start, really down to earth and wickedly funny. Although Nadia could have been friendlier, Blaine had pointed out that Nads – as he affectionately called her – was easily threatened by new blood in the business.

Imagine internationally renowned goddess Nadia Olsen being threatened by little old me! She laughed to herself.

97

From what Ida gathered the two models had been the best of friends for years. For the sake of peace in the house she tried her best to get along with them both, although Blaine was unequivocally her favourite. After all, he was the one who'd taken her under his wing, given her words of advice when she'd felt like a clueless outsider and generally been a hundred percent supportive. Plus he cracked her up! Nobody had ever made her laugh until her stomach ached before. He had a mind like a sewer, an infectious cackle and a razor sharp tongue you wouldn't want to be on the wrong side of, but he was fun. Besides, Nadia was almost always out somewhere working or partying, so it didn't really matter that they hadn't exactly hit it off.

Life was fantastic. If only she could forget about Steve. In the dead of night she still occasionally woke up fresh from a nightmare, soaked in sweat and full of paranoid fears that he'd track her down. She shuddered as if someone had walked over her grave.

Steve's in my past, he can't hurt me now. She told herself firmly as she buttered her toast and poured herself a cup of strong black coffee. As for Nadia, she'll just have to get the used to the idea that I'm here to stay.

X

Much later that evening, all thoughts of her ex temporarily obliterated, Ida was elatedly sipping champagne. She listened to the murmur of polite conversation, clink of glasses and bursts of muted laughter with a thrill of excitement. The show had been a great success. Even better than that, *she* had been a great success.

It felt like she'd never come down off the high she'd got from working that runway. The whirr and flash of clicking cameras, the strobe lights, awesome clothes and throbbing music had made her forget herself. It was as if she'd come alive, suddenly loving the scrutiny that would've once paralysed her.

She kept spotting celebrities, including designers, actors, and even politicians. Then of course there were the usual society girls, pop singers and bright young things on the fashion scene. They'd all been clamouring to meet her. Ida was set to be the next big thing in fashion, and she couldn't get enough of the attention. She was shocked to realise she felt hungry for more, as if this was what she'd been starved of her whole life. If this was a drug, she was an addict.

Duncan whispered something in her ear and she giggled. As she did so she realised the champagne and line of coke Ash had produced had gone straight to her head. It felt wonderful. She floated inches above the floor, luminous, accepted and comfortable in her own skin.

Circulating around the room her gaze was drawn to Nadia, who was laughing hysterically at something a member of Guyz'n'Sync said to her. Unsurprisingly her flatmate hadn't bothered to throw a single word of congratulations her way. However, she'd already decided she wasn't going to let the other model's animosity ruin her evening. Tonight was her night and she was having the time of her life. She made her way towards the bar in search of another drink.

"There you are." Blaine materialised from the crowd looking stunning, if agitated, in a Tia Wong dress.

Ida was pleased to see him. "Did you watch me? It felt pretty amazing. What a buzz!" She was animated in her joy.

"You were wonderful darling." He assured her, "A real pro, you looked like you'd been doing it for years. I felt very proud." He squeezed her arm affectionately.

"Really?" She smiled blissfully.

"Truly."

She noticed that he underneath his bonhomie Blaine was looking decidedly ill at ease and fidgety, his face strained.

"B is everything alright?" She watched him knock back a triple, his hand shook almost imperceptibly.

"Actually, no it's not. I'm going to call a cab." He replied in an odd tone of voice. "You stay and enjoy your night though lovely, you've worked hard for it, we'll catch up tomorrow."

Her heart sank briefly at the thought of her night being cut short, but some things were more important.

"Forget it." She put her arm around his bony shoulders. "I'm coming with you. It's a circus here anyway and I'm tired." She lied.

The supermodel nodded gratefully and allowed himself to be gently led through the crowded room to the foyer.

X

Ida waited impatiently until the cab pulled away from the exclusive Soho nightclub before turning to check on her friend and mentor. She noted with concern that he was sitting with his head slightly bowed, shoulders turned downwards as if the punch had been knocked right out of him. There was a snuffling noise as he groped in the pockets of his faux fur coat, dabbed under his eyes with a tissue and blew his nose loudly.

"Okay, what gives?"

"Here." He waved a piece of paper at her. "Read this and tell me what you think."

She took it from him wordlessly whilst he stared out of the window into the night traffic.

The message was spelled out in letters someone had painstakingly cut out of newspapers and magazines. Ida's first thought was that it was a joke, some kind of sick prank.

It was typed on plain white paper. She read it out under her breath and then scanned the letter once more searching for clues.

It read...

A little note from your no 1. fan
(and particular admirer of your early work)
I urge you to enjoy the view from the top, while
you still can.
Forever, Grace.

"I don't understand… Are you being blackmailed?" Ida puzzled as the cab swerved down Judd Street.

He shook his head helplessly. "That's just it. I don't even *know*. Whoever it is hasn't made any demands, not a single one. I haven't a fucking clue what I'm supposed to do."

"Is this it? Or have you had other letters?" She asked, folding it back up.

He bit his lip. "This is the third."

"God, what does Cecile have to say about this?"

He paused and then sighed.

"Oh B." She sighed. "You haven't told her have you?"

He shook his head.

"But she's your agent; this is exactly the kind of thing she should deal with."

He flinched. "No! You have to promise to keep this to yourself. I can't tell anyone at Boss."

"Alright. But I don't get it. Why?"

Silence.

"You haven't shown this to anybody but me?" Ida asked gently as he began to cry.

"No, not even Nadia…" He broke off overcome by emotion. "She's been out the whole time. It's been so hard dealing with this on my own. I've been so scared."

"It could be nothing." She tried to console him. "You must get letters from obsessed fans the whole time. I understand this must be upsetting, but surely you know this Grace person can't hurt you. Unless there's something you're not telling me?"

He turned away. Getting information out of Blaine suddenly seemed about as challenging as getting Nadia to accept her. The words blood, out of and stone came to mind.

"Do you know who Grace is?" She pressed.

Reluctantly he nodded, his face hidden in the darkness.

"And she has something on you?" She hazarded a guess.

"Sort of." He put his head in his hands wretchedly.

"Listen to me," She urged. "Whatever's going on, you don't have to deal with it alone. I wouldn't have got through the last few weeks without you, you're a real friend and I can't

101

thank you enough for all you've done. Besides, you're not the only one to have a less than picture-perfect past, believe me girl." She added darkly. "If you want my help, you've got it. But you have to tell me what's really going on."

He found her hand with his own and squeezed it before wiping away the last of his tears.

"I don't know who's writing the letters, I wish I did."

"But you said..."

"I know who Grace is... or was, but she can't have written them."

She was puzzled. "How do you know? The letter *is* signed by her."

"Oh *bugger* it Ida, someone's trying to freak me out!" He gestured in frustration. "Grace doesn't exist any more. It's what my name used to be... before I had my sex change."

Chapter 18. The Start of Something

Tony parked the car in a vacant spot on the pretty, suburban street, turned off the engine and shook Stella awake.

"We're here already?" She asked groggily letting her head drop back and moving it around from side to side gingerly.

"Yep, this is the address that Si gave me." He replied taking another look at the map spread out on his lap before folding it and shoving it in the glove compartment. He sighed, drumming his fingers on the steering wheel.

"Are you nervous?" Stella asked, sitting up and stretching.

"A bit." He admitted checking his reflection in the mirror.

"Well I suppose you are about to meet your bloke's mother."

"I hope she likes me."

"I'm sure she'll love you." She muttered sleepily, smothering a yawn.

"If we're lucky she'll love us both." He unfastened his seat-belt. "This'd be a great place for you to stay babes. Look how pretty it is around here, and we passed a tube station a couple of minutes ago."

She looked uncertain. "We'll see, I want to meet her first."

"You're the boss."

"So what's the plan? Did you say you're dropping me off and going on to meet Si in Chelsea?"

"Sure am. I can't wait." He beamed, clearly excited. "Do I look like I've lost weight to you?"

She examined him and prodded his tummy critically.

"Oh my goodness, abs of steel!" She proclaimed.

He looked at her suspiciously. "Are you being sarcastic?"

She ignored him. "Come on handsome, let's go." She hastily slipped on her jacket. "Will you guys come and pick me up in a couple of hours?"

"I told you we will."

She took a deep breath and slid a polo mint into her mouth before handing the pack to him.

"Okay. I'm ready when you are."

X

Cathy was busily planting bulbs in the front garden when her two visitors arrived. Her face broke into a welcoming smile. Straightening up she brushed the loose soil off her palms before wiping them on her skirt.

"Hello!" She cried, running over to greet them. Tony offered her his hand and she clasped it with both of hers, taking a long appraising look at him.

"So, you're my son's young man." She gave Stella a wink. "Unless you're Jehovah's Witnesses, that is. You're not are you?"

"No! I'm Tony and this is..."

Cathy interrupted. "Ah yes, the newest addition to the family – that's me and the dogs by the way – it's lovely to meet you dear." On cue, three large and excitable poodles rushed out and milled around their legs. "I used to be Cathy Fraser, although most people these days seem to refer to me as 'Si's mum.'" She added wryly.

"Hello there, nice to meet you." Tony said looking flustered.

Stella leant over to kiss her on both cheeks. "I'm Stella Buchanan. It's so kind of you to offer to have me stay."

"Nonsense. I'll be glad of the money and the company. Anyway, let me show you round, you might hate the place!"

104

Cathy said, looking over their shoulders into the street. "But where's that boy of mine?"

"Oh, I'm meeting Si in a bit." Tony explained. "We'll get a bite to eat and then come over later. Give you two a chance to chat."

"That's very thoughtful of you." She fussed with a peacock feather earring. "You know I've heard so much about you from Si; it's nice to finally see what all the excitement is about."

He turned pink at the compliment. "I've heard lots about you too, all good of course."

"I expect to have a proper talk with you when you return this afternoon for cake and tea." She admonished.

"I'm looking forward to it."

"Come on then Stella dear," She ushered her inside, "Let's not keep him waiting; we don't want to stand in the way of a glorious reunion now do we? I've made a new batch of chocolate fudge in honour of the occasion. I do hope you'll try a piece."

"Of course." Stella replied.

"It's got a little hash in it, and lots of good dark chocolate." She said. "I find it gives it that something extra."

X

Tony spotted Si instantly on entering the gloom of the Queen's Arms. He was sitting near the jukebox wearing a navy shirt unbuttoned to the waist, his streaky hair slicked back and a faraway look on his face. For his own amusement he walked round the back of the room and crept up on his lover from behind.

"Hey gorgeous, can I buy you a drink?" He drawled huskily over his shoulder.

"Oi!" Si exclaimed his eyes lighting up, "You scared the life out of me."

"Sorry." He leant over to give him a big hug. "I couldn't resist."

"I bet you say that to all the boys."

105

"Only you." He smiled self-consciously and changed the subject. "Now, about that drink. I've travelled all the way from Scotland to get to this poxy gay bar, my mouth feels like my throat's been cut."

"Sit down." Si ordered patting the seat next to him. "Two pints of Grolsh coming up and then I want to hear all your news."

"Do they serve food here?" Tony asked hopefully, "I'm starved."

"You bet. I'll grab us a couple of menus."

An hour and several pints later, they had lapsed into companionable silence as Tony finished off the remains of his penne pasta and Si used a chip to soak up the last of the gravy on his plate.

"I wonder how Stella's getting on with your mum." Tony speculated draining his glass and taking a quick look at his wristwatch.

"I'm sure they're fine." Si said, and belched discreetly. "Let's give them another half an hour."

"Don't forget I've still got to drive to your place and unpack."

"How could I forget that?" Si asked. "It's all I've been talking about for the past two weeks; I've driven Lisa and Marina mad. You're actually quite famous in the Black Cock now you know. Oh crap!" He suddenly stiffened in his seat and tried to hide behind his menu.

"What is it?"

"Don't look now, but that's our mysterious lodger George with that tall, dark guy in the corner." He muttered talking out of the corner of his mouth.

Tony was perplexed. "So?"

"So," Si hissed, "this is the most I've ever seen of him since he moved in. He's either fanatical about privacy or just plain rude."

"Och, so what?"

"Shhh! I want to see what he's up to."

They both watched as the two men muttered to each other in the darkest corner of the bar, an exchange took place and George slipped something into the other man's pocket.

"Someone's out shopping." Si speculated.

"Hmm, he's probably just given him his number. The other guy's hot; doncha just love Latino guys? Besides why do you care what he's up too?"

"Well, we'll never know, they're leaving."

The barman turned up the music and Si tried valiantly to control the sudden urge he felt to chair-dance, knowing that'd make him look instantly butch as a ballet shoe. He tapped his foot on the floor in time to the music instead, smiling sheepishly as his boyfriend clocked him.

Tony leant over to kiss him, his stubble grazing Si's chin.

"What was that for?" Si asked as Tony pulled back and stared at him, a slow smile spreading over his face.

"Since when do I need a reason to snog my boyfriend?"

X

Back at the Fraser residence on the porch overlooking the back yard, the two women reclined lazily in Cathy's battered old swing-sofa, sipping camomile tea. As they chatted and caught the last rays of the late afternoon sun, a gentle breeze played across Stella's face. She felt herself relax for the first time in ages.

The garden was tiny, with a little flagstone path leading to a rundown looking tool-shed. The flowerbeds, she noticed, had just begun to bloom and all around the lawn plants were bursting into vivid colour. Next to the shed, there was a bird feeder suspended over a rhododendron bush.

As she watched, quick as a flash a squirrel jumped up onto it and started stealing seeds, eating them daintily with its front paws. Over by the back-fence the dogs scampered around, ruining the heap of dead leaves and twigs that someone – Cathy presumably – had carefully swept into a neat pile. Ignoring them and basking in the sun a fat black

107

and white cat lay sprawled out on his back in the dirt, clawing the earth contentedly.

She took in the scene inhaling deeply; the smell of newly cut grass taking her instantly back to her childhood.

"It's a lovely house." She commented.

"Thank you." Cathy poured some more tea into their cups, "And what did you think of Si's old room – the one you'd be staying in?"

"It's nice."

The inside of the house was homey and cluttered with worn out furniture and a wide array of ornaments. Memorabilia and mementos from around the world were displayed on dressers and mounted on the walls. The living room was painted cream with shelves set in one side holding numerous photos of Cathy in her acting years, Si growing up, and what Stella presumed were snaps of other family members and friends.

She'd been shown all three bedrooms and the moderately sized bathroom on the second floor. Si's old room was the most spacious, with a king-sized bed, huge wardrobe, quaint wooden dressing table and mirror.

Cathy nodded. "I must say, I'm very happy here. You'll have to excuse the mess of course; I have a young friend of Si's staying until the weekend."

"Well, I think I've made my mind up. I'd like to stay." Stella decided. "That is if you're sure you want another lodger so soon after you get the house back to yourself."

"Nonsense, like I said the money's handy and I'd be bored out of my mind without someone else around to keep me company." Cathy beamed. "That's the best news I've heard all day." She reached for her packet of cigarettes and offered Stella one.

"I hardly ever smoke... but actually I wouldn't mind one, what the hell." She accepted a Marlboro and lit it, drawing the smoke deep into her lungs.

Stella found herself wondering what the hell had got into her. She felt positively rebellious. She didn't know if it was the building and its setting, the mellowing effect of the chocolate fudge or the compelling presence of Cathy herself, but somehow this rather ordinary looking little house in the outskirts of Hounslow seemed to be casting some sort of spell over her. Even the smells of baking from the kitchen and the sounds of the neighbour's kids playing next door were beguiling and seemed designed to bewitch.

"So," her new landlady asked casually, stirring a lump of sugar into her tea. "Do you have any plans now you're free from that dreadful sounding company you worked for?"

"Oh, I'm not sure." Stella sighed, "I'm staying in London for an extended holiday really while I get my head together. I'm afraid I may need to re-evaluate a lot of things. Perhaps I'm having a mid-life crisis." She gave a nervous laugh.

"Of course you're not." Cathy said crisply. "You're much too young for a mid-life anything. As for the other bit though, do you think your life needs an overhaul?"

"Maybe." She replied staring into the distance suddenly lost in thought. "I don't know. I suppose so."

"Are you attached?" Cathy asked curiously.

"You mean married, with kids and all that?"

The older woman nodded questioningly.

Stella laughed, "No, I haven't had much luck in that area I'm afraid." She leaned closer, taking another sip of tea, "Also, my romantic history's followed a less than conventional path. Believe it or not I even had a five year relationship with a woman in my early twenties. Anyway, it didn't work out." She broke off. "Then I fell in love with a married man. We were seeing each other secretly for years. Then finally he left his wife for me, there were no children thank god, and we got married. It was all I'd wanted for so long; the answer to my prayers." She broke off, her eyes filling with tears. "Then it fell apart. The divorce came through six months ago. What a mess. He was having an affaire with a work colleague; I suppose I got what I deserved." She added bitterly.

"I'm sure that's not true."

Stella shrugged suddenly wanting to change the subject. As she looked around the porch a large photograph in a silver

109

frame caught her attention. It showed a classically beautiful blond enjoying a chat with Princess Diana.

"Is that you?" She asked, reaching out to hold the picture and get a closer look.

"Yes, of course I was a lot younger then and a little bit famous."

"You look beautiful." Stella exclaimed touching the glass. "And you haven't changed much." She added truthfully. Cathy wore her blond hair much shorter now; her expressive eyes were framed by mascara-heavy lashes but apart from that she wore no make up. Her cheekbones were still impressive, her skin only slightly lined with age. They looked at each other for a moment, totally comfortable in the silence that had fallen.

"Well, thank you." Cathy's cheeks flushed, as she got up and busied herself collecting up their empty plates and tea-things. "You know, I think I'm going to like having you around."

Chapter 19. The Man from Bardot's

"Why didn't you tell me you had a stalker?" Mark asked later on as JJ removed his make-up and expertly brushed out his wig.

He shrugged, looking surprisingly vulnerable in a too-big navy dressing gown, all traces of bravado having disappeared along with his three-inch lashes. "I haven't had much chance."

"Don't you think it would've been pertinent to my coming to stay?" Mark demanded.

"Well I didn't want to put you off! I needed the money." JJ put down his comb. "Besides it's my business, I didn't think it'd affect you."

Mark let out his breath noisily; this pissy little queen was really starting to get on his tits.

"Didn't think it would affect me?" He pronounced each word slowly and deliberately. "It never crossed your mind I might not particularly fancy getting involved with nutters or living with a hooker for that matter?" He could hear his voice becoming distinctly shrill. "I came here for some downtime by the sea, for a nice, hard-earned break so that I could try to sort out my life after being dumped. The last thing on earth I want is to get dragged into someone else's problems."

"You don't have to get involved." JJ's bottom lip quivered alarmingly, his sea-coloured eyes filling with tears. "But it'd be nice if you could show some compassion and stop yelling at me. I've got a monster headache." He pressed his fingers to his temples with a pained expression. "Having a stalker is no picnic let me assure you." He gave him a contemptuous look. "But I'll shut up now; I wouldn't want to ruin your holiday."

"Don't you dare try and turn this around on me." Mark warned, but his anger had lost its edge and he suddenly felt very old, ancient... at least a hundred.

They sat in silence for a while listening as the church bell chimed out the hour. It was midnight.

"You don't have to stay here, there are plenty of hotels." JJ finally sniffed, dabbing his eyes with a tissue.

After a few moments Mark let out a long sigh. "Well I'm here now aren't I? Just tell me how long this has been going on?"

"About a month." JJ took a digestive biscuit from the open pack on the table and offered him one. "The first time I saw him I was out walking a friend's dog. Her name's Sasha Bitch – my friend, not the dog – she's fabulous." He broke off as Mark shot him a baleful look and carried on hastily. "Anyway, I was walking her Dalmatian and I noticed this man was following me... your Raphael from the pub, if that's his real name."

"Well, that's what he told me."

JJ looked dubious. "He also pretended not to know me which simply tells us he's a big, stalky liar."

"Why would he lie to me, a random stranger?" Mark pointed out, grudgingly accepting another digestive.

"Ah, but what if you weren't so random?" JJ continued. "I reckon he'd been following me all day, saw us together on Grace Street earlier and that's why he was hitting on you, to get to me."

"Oh my god, could you be any more paranoid and self-obsessed?"

"Can you please stop with the insults and let me finish my story?" JJ looked pained. "So there I was, walking the dog and I thought the guy was cruising me only whenever I looked over my shoulder he'd turn and pretend to be staring in the other direction."

"Is that all you've got?"

"Of course not! Since then, I'm certain I've been followed loads of times... when I'm out shopping, on my way to a punter's or a gig.."

"You being certain doesn't amount to actual proof." Mark said.

JJ ignored him. "Then someone tried to break into my flat. I was shit scared!"

"Did you call the police?"

An expression of horror crossed his face. "No way, I wasn't gonna get the pigs involved, they hate me."

"That's what they're there for." He felt another burst of frustration.

JJ shook his curly head stubbornly his eyes shifty. "We don't have a good relationship. Besides, I took care of it; no harm came to me... I locked myself in the bathroom."

"That's not taking care of it."

"It was time well spent. I gave myself a facial, a pedicure and I exfoliated my entire body."

Mark sighed, "Still not really the point is it?"

"I don't know." He paused frowning. "I'm actually a bit confused about the whole thing. Until I recognised Raphael as the man following me I'd assumed it was Elliott trying to break in..."

"Who the fuck's Elliott?" Mark boggled.

"Just a client who was a bit, you know..." JJ made a psycho noise and stabbing motions in the air. "He told me that he was in love with me, and if he couldn't have me, neither could anyone else..." He trailed off as he saw Mark's face.

"I think he's harmless really. Unless he gets drunk of course," his eyes widened dramatically, "Then he turns into a stark raving lunatic."

X

The next day they put their differences aside and wandered down to the gay beach to soak up some rays.

"You must be well pissed off with me. Andrew should've told you the score about me being I'm an escort." JJ conceded.

113

"And this whole stalker business..." He gave a low whistle and shook back his curly hair.

They stopped and Mark arranged his beach towel over the pebbles, pulling his sweatshirt over his head and folding it up to use as a makeshift pillow.

"It isn't quite what I expected." He admitted.

JJ squinted at him through his shades.

"It bothers you, doesn't it? Me being on the game."

"It's really none of my business."

"But you don't approve..." JJ persisted.

Mark sighed and finished off covering his chest and arms in tanning oil. "I couldn't care less."

This is the life, he thought. Present company excluded, this was exactly what he'd had in mind when the idea of a holiday in Brighton had first occurred to him. Seagulls crowed overhead and he could feel his skin tingling in the delicious heat as his entire body started to relax.

Letting his mind wander he listened to the sound of the waves breaking on the shore, droplets of water moistening his toes. The sea-air filled his nostrils, tangy and salty; miraculously the sky was unblemished by clouds, post-card perfect.

He'd got up that morning feeling tired and out of sorts after the late night drama he'd unwillingly become party to the following evening. However, in the interest of peace he'd reluctantly agreed to a conciliatory brunch in a sea-side café before being shown the sights.

Surveying the area through sleepy half-closed eyes, he noticed there was now no shortage of these. A group of fit looking lads had arrived and dumped their belongings not far away.

For the next half an hour, JJ was blissfully silent as he listened to music on his iPod. They lay there, cooking gently, sitting up for the odd fag break or to indulge in sips of warm, flat coke from the bottle propped up between them. Nearby waves broke sending frothy white spray crashing over the stones whilst further out to sea sunlight danced and sparkled off the crests of turquoise waves. Adding to the area's natural

114

beauty, their neighbours stripped down to their swimming trunks revealing youthful, carelessly muscular physiques as they lazed about chatting and drinking cans of lager.

"Tut tut." JJ said slapping Mark's thigh and breaking his reverie. "You shouldn't be using oil babe, not with that pale skin."

Looking up crossly Mark saw his companion was examining his bottle of tropical tanning oil.

"Oi, give that here." He said, grabbing it. "I've got olive skin actually and please don't call me babe."

"Sorry hon." JJ shot back mischievously and then eyed the guys further up the beach. "You don't like me very much do you?"

"It's not that I don't like you just that I'm trying to relax." Mark said turning over onto this back.

"Do you fancy me?" He asked.

Mark sighed. "I'm not looking for anything right now; it's too soon after my ex."

JJ pulled a face. "Jeez, you need to relax. I wasn't asking you to marry me; I was thinking more along the lines of some no-strings sex."

"Well, thanks, but you're not my type."

"Suit yourself." He pulled a cigarette out of the packet offering Mark one. They smoked silently for a while, each looking out across the ocean.

"I'm sorry about your boyfriend." JJ broke the silence. He picked up a pebble and threw it into the water. "And that you're having a crappy holiday."

"Well, today's been alright." Mark conceded.

"Let's go to the pier later." JJ suggested, "Then we could go out for dinner if you like, and make a night of it."

"Okay." Mark paused. "Tell me, is the drag for the punters or do you actually perform at clubs and stuff?"

"Well sure, some punters like me dressed up, but others prefer me au natural." JJ replied airily. "I've got a residency at the Pink Flamingo Club in London, and I get loads of bookings on the scene around here."

"But what do you do?" Mark persisted, eyebrows raised. "What does your act involve?"

"Oh I'm so glad you're showing a little interest." JJ looked pleased. "Well I probably veer more toward the avant-garde than your typical sea-side drag queen. Oh I sing, dance and do all the usual patter, but I like to throw in something a bit experimental. Come watch me next week at Bardot's if you like. I'm doing a lip-synching fan-dance to a Beyoncé track."

"Huh, I might just do that." Mark stood up. "Come on, I'll race you into the sea."

JJ looked around worriedly, "What about our stuff? I wasn't going to say but I think I see our friend Raphael hanging round by the steps. Don't look now!" He said, as Mark swung his head round.

"Shit." Mark swore under his breath. "You're right; I reckon that's him." He thought for a minute. "If you're really worried why don't we head out to the pier first and go for a swim afterwards."

"Sounds like a plan babe." JJ said. "Oh! Your back's gone all red – I told you not to use that tanning oil."

Chapter 20. Amateur Dramatics

After finishing up at work Kate made her way through the after-hours throng to join Danny in the nearby pub. It was barely a month since she'd moved into the house in Shepherd's Bush but despite an admittedly rocky start, things couldn't be going better for them. She was determined to help out in his endeavors to find his estranged twin; even if it did seem to be taking up most of their spare time.

She found him sitting at a secluded table, kissed him hello and waited while he went to get the drinks in.

"So, do you think the gossips have sussed us out yet?" He asked on his return, handing her a glass.

"Ta. Probably." Kate took a sip of her vodka and orange. "But who cares? Our sex life is none of their business."

"True." He raised his eyebrows. "Are you okay? You seem stressed."

She sighed. "Sorry. I'm not in the best of moods. James is acting all off with me, which is a huge bummer considering he's the only one at work I like, present company excluded."

"Right. He's the guy who thinks he knows me?"

"Yeah. I'm worried I've done something to piss him off. We used to chat the whole time but now he's avoiding being alone with me. It's bizarre."

"Maybe he's jealous." Danny suggested.

She snorted with laughter. "Love yourself much?"

117

"I don't mean that." He insisted. "Maybe he's annoyed I've been monopolising you."

"I doubt it." She eyed the clock on the wall. "Never mind I'll just have to have it out with him. Look, if we're still going to crash that drama group we'd better get a move on."

Danny pulled some folded sheets of paper out of his jacket pocket. "I've got the address and I printed a map off before we left. It's somewhere in Hounslow." He thought for a minute. "Hey, that's near where you lived isn't it?"

"Perfect! Do you mind if we pop in and see Cathy on the way?"

"No problem." He was studying the map.

"So." She rested her chin on her knuckles. "What do you want to do when we get there? We don't actually need to join? Like spies?"

He laughed. "Of course not! I'm just going to be honest and tell them I'm looking for my brother, found out they've got a member called Julian Jackson, and I've come on the off-chance it's him. It's unlikely to come to anything, but I've got to check it out."

She was visibly relieved. "Phew! I mean I would've given it a go... but acting really isn't my forté. I get really self-conscious... it's like a phobia."

"Aw, and you'd be willing to do it anyway for me?" He leant over and kissed her. "Bless you."

"No big deal. Anyways, how did you find out he's in a theatre group?"

"Google." He took a swallow of his pint. "Don't know why I didn't think of it before. Acting's always been his biggest passion so it's a good place to start." He held out the page for her to see. "This website was last updated a year ago though, so there's a chance the group's moved or dissolved. We could have a wasted trip."

"How do you even know he's in London?"

"I got that out of his closest friend but she swears that's all she knows." He shook his head. "We're both due an inheritance from out late Aunt. I guess that's what's finally given me the motivation to come looking for him."

She was sympathetic. "Were you very close?"

"Yeah." He muttered, staring down at the table. "We've always had this bond, even though – looks aside – we're so different. That is up until about a month before he took off. It was weird, he started acting really out of character and there were some huge family rows."

"Out of character how?"

He took another gulp of his drink. "Well, for a start he quit his job completely out of the blue. He distanced himself from me and the family, his friends... He shut me out totally."

"Look, tell me if you don't want to talk about this." Kate said gruffly.

"That's okay. Thanks for supporting me; it means a lot you know." He squeezed her hand.

"It's fine." She drained her glass. "We'll do this together"

X

Mrs Fraser was pleasantly surprised to find Kate and a male guest shivering on her doorstep. She invited them inside, put the kettle on and soon all three were seated around the kitchen table enjoying hot drinks and slices of homemade chocolate cake.

"So you're the one Kate's been telling me about." Cathy smiled mischievously after Kate finished explaining the story of his brother and their plans to find him. "I'm so glad you two sorted out your differences."

"Thanks for reminding me." Kate rolled her eyes. "Actually Mrs F, you never heard the end of the story. It turns out what I actually overheard was Danny trying to hire a private detective to find Julian, not a... erm... male escort."

Danny started chuckling to himself and the older woman caught his eye, threw her head back and roared with helpless laughter until eventually Kate joined in.

"Oh dear." Cathy sighed wiping a tear from the corner of her eye, "You're too much Kate."

"Anyway," he continued, "I didn't have enough information for this investigator to be very hopeful of success.

119

Plus the amount he was going to charge was extortionate. I don't have that kind of money."

"I see." Cathy narrowed her eyes and clasped her palms together. "So you two are going to track him down yourselves."

Danny nodded. "Exactly. The theatre group meets at the Town Hall every Friday at seven, so we're just going along."

"Have you thought what you'll say if you do find him?"

He paused. "He's my brother; I'll know what to say."

Cathy cut herself another sliver of cake and swept the stray crumbs off the table. "I don't mean to pour cold water on your plans, but have you considered the possibility that he doesn't want to be found."

"Regardless of that, I have to make sure he's alright." He frowned. "Julian's always had a knack of getting in over his head. As a kid he'd always wind up having some kind of hassle and I'd have to look out for him; or he'd piss someone off. He can be a right gobby bastard. I suppose I'm afraid he might be in trouble now."

"Yes." Cathy stared off into space. "I suppose that's one reason people run away."

"God! I can't believe I forgot to ask." Kate said suddenly, "How's it working out with Stella living here." She lowered her voice to a whisper. "She's not upstairs now is she?"

"No, she went out." Cathy looked cagey and busied herself pouring more tea. "Actually we get on splendidly, so in that respect it's going very well. However, the poor love has been going through a lot lately." She put the teapot down and fell silent for a moment. "It's good she's come here for a break, but that said, it hasn't all been plain sailing."

Kate and Danny exchanged glances and waited for her to elaborate.

She frowned. "Well, you know she lost her job and then there's the divorce; it's all exacerbating this condition she struggles with."

"Condition?" Danny asked, confused.

120

She raised her eyebrows and pushed her chair back from the table. "It's easier if I show you. Why don't you both follow me into the living room?"

They trailed in her wake as she pushed the door open and motioned them inside.

Spinning around, Kate turned to look at Cathy.

"Oh my god!" She gasped. "I can't believe it's the same place."

"It looks alright to me." Danny said. "Am I missing something?"

The entire space had been totally de-cluttered, varnished and scrubbed. Surfaces gleamed and glistened in the overhead lights. The carpet was freshly shampooed, and the ornaments positioned symmetrically. Even the various remote controls lay at right angles to the paper on the coffee table's pristine surface.

"It's spotless!" Kate exclaimed, flabbergasted.

"I know." Cathy shook her head grimly, before adding in an undertone. "And you should see upstairs."

They stared at her waiting for an explanation.

"Obsessive Compulsive Disorder." She explained with a sigh. "It's a terrible affliction."

X

An hour later, after they'd made their excuses and left, Kate and Danny found themselves walking down a poorly lit alleyway leading to the back entrance of Hillbrook Town Hall.

"This was a stupid idea." Danny muttered steadying her as she nearly tripped over the curb in the darkness. "I bet they don't even meet here anymore."

"There's no harm in trying." Kate protested. "And if I'm not mistaken... I can hear music."

They both stood and listened as sure enough the faint sounds of someone playing the piano accompanied by male voices singing floated through an open window further down on their left.

121

"Come on, it must be in here." Danny led her over to a little blue door and twisted the handle. He could see a light shining through the cracks of the wood in the room inside. "Fuck, it's locked. So what now, do we wait for them to finish?"

He stood back and looked about in frustration. Kate shivered; her teeth were chattering like castanets in the night air.

Just as Danny was about to suggest they give up and come back another time he noticed a small buzzer set into the wall half-hidden by shadows. He pushed it, and they waited expectantly as they heard a bell go off inside the building.

A few seconds later the door was opened by a wizened looking man wearing John Lennon style glasses and a harassed expression.

"Yes, can I help you?" He asked clearly not pleased at the interruption and shooting distracted glances over his shoulder where the sounds of a rehearsal were clearly audible now.

"We're sorry to bother you, but perhaps you could help us..." Kate began with a polite smile. But the elderly gentleman cut her off mid-sentence as he squinted through his glasses at Danny his eyes widening in recognition and his frown quickly collapsing into a huge, toothy grin.

"Julian, is that really you?" He asked pushing his spectacles further up his nose and throwing his arms around him in an enthusiastic embrace.

"My dear boy!" He exclaimed. "I can't tell you how happy I am that you've come back to me in my hour of need." Then, to their horror he burst into tears.

Awkwardly Danny let him sob into his jacket and patted the old man's back shooting Kate a helpless look. What the hell were they supposed to do now?

Chapter 21. Unexpected Allies

By midmorning sunlight dazzled the rain-slicked pavements transforming London's uniform greyness and lifting Stella's spirits. So when Cathy suggested a walk she found herself acquiescing despite her recent despondency. It was the first time she'd left the house in days, having fallen into something of a funk.

She took her time getting dressed, finally teaming a pair of denim shorts with espadrilles and a halter-neck top.

Cathy was waiting for her at the front door, dog leads in hand and a pair of sunglasses perched on her head.

Together they set off down the road, Stella grabbing an over-excited Olivier whilst Cathy took Lawrence and Liz. Together they all tumbled off passed the shops and down a little lane leading to the park, breathing in the sights and smells, the sun warming their skin as they walked.

On reaching the park, Cathy signalled for them to release the dogs and they both sat down on a bench. Stella stretched her legs out in front of her as they watched the poodles run around exuberantly, reveling in their freedom.

"I'm sorry for being such a state these passed couple of days." Stella said after a moment. She reached into her carry-all for a bottle of mineral water and offered it to the other woman.

"Please don't apologise." Cathy shook her head; eyes warm with humor as she took a large swig from the bottle and set it back carefully on the grass. "The house hasn't been so clean in... well... ever."

"God." She groaned closing her eyes and grimacing. "You must think I'm mad. I'm not usually like this."

"Tell me to mind my own business, but would it help to talk?"

Stella sighed, letting her hands fall into her lap. "That's kind of you. I'm just not very good at sharing. It's embarrassing, I feel like such a failure."

"Just because you're going through a difficult time?" Cathy smiled at her kindly. "That doesn't make you a failure dear, it makes you a warrior."

"I find it hard to handle not working." She admitted. "And I guess the divorce really knocked the stuffing out of me. Finding out he was cheating was the nail in the coffin, but if I'm really honest our relationship began to disintegrate as soon as we came out into the open. The reality didn't live up to my expectations, or his." She paused sorrowfully. "He left his wife for me, and then I wished he hadn't. I'm a home-wrecker, that doesn't exactly fill me with pride."

"We all make mistakes." Cathy said looking at her. "Besides he's the one who abandoned his first marriage, not you. I think you have to let him take at least some of the responsibility for that."

"I suppose." Stella reached in her pocket for a tissue and blew her nose.

They sat in silence for a while. Cathy wordlessly reached for her Marlboro packet, pausing to light up and take a deep drag of her cigarette.

"I don't speak about my marriage to Si's father very often." She said breathing out the smoke, her eyes unreadable as she gave a mirthless chuckle. "But it wasn't a very happy union... a marriage of convenience you might say. I was pregnant and Karl did what he thought was the right thing."

"You didn't plan on starting a family?"

"Good lord, *no*! I've loved Si to pieces since the day he was born, but having a baby was certainly not on my agenda at that time." She stared into the distance. "Si was conceived during a particularly drunken party after one of the plays I'd been in. Karl, the father, was an actor with our company. If I hadn't got pregnant we both would've put it down to one of those things that happen under the influence of too much vodka."

"But instead you decided to get married!?"

"I know." Cathy gave her a wry smile. "It sounds ridiculous, but things were different then, and when Karl offered to marry me I thought maybe it could work. He was so charming and good-looking; I'd had a secret crush on him for ages. I was terribly naïve and self-centered... I would've made a hopeless single mother." She sighed. "Besides he convinced me it was what he wanted, his family was very keen for him to find a wife." She shrugged. "Of course, the marriage turned out to be a disaster. Not surprisingly we resented each other terribly and things turned acrimonious."

"I'm sorry. Tony told me that Si's father had died just before he was born, but I had no idea that things were hard for you even before then." Stella covered Cathy's hand with her own and squeezed it gently. "I suppose we all have our share of shit to deal with."

"True. Have you not seen anyone since your marriage ended?" Cathy asked. "No young man on the horizon to take your mind off the divorce?" She thought for a moment. "Or woman for that matter."

"I don't think I'm in any fit state." Stella shook her head. "I think I need some time out. What about you?"

"God no, I'm much too set in my ways now. Whilst we're talking about our past though, I actually had a thing with a girl when I was a teenager." Cathy revealed. "She was beautiful, a bit like a young Angelina Jolie."

"Oh? What happened?" Stella asked, surprised.

"We spent the night together after a party and I thought about it for ages afterwards." She said wistfully. "Things were different then, there was a lot more homophobia. She was very precocious and something of a pariah in school; didn't keep her sexual preferences secret." She flicked the ash off her cigarette and snorted. "You can just imagine what the

125

other school girls made of that... Well, let's just say she didn't have the easiest time. I got scared, I didn't want to be ostracized too so I ignored her and acted like nothing ever happened. I've regretted it ever since. It's the one thing in my life I'm truly ashamed of."

"Well you were only a kid." Stella screwed her eyes up in the glare of the sun. "How do you feel about Si being gay?"

"I love Si exactly the way he is." Cathy was emphatic. "My son is the most precious thing in my life, and my best achievement to date." She turned to her, mock-threateningly. "Your friend had better treat him well, or he'll have me to deal with."

"Tony's the best." Stella assured her hastily. "We've been friends for ever and he's a great guy."

"I'm only messing with you, dear." Cathy winked at her. "I'd never presume to interfere in my son's relationships; I'm hardly in a position to be giving him advice. I mean look at me..." She turned her palms up in despair shaking her head dramatically. "I'm hopelessly middle-aged and my years of romance are long gone."

"I doubt it. You're wonderful; a really special person and I think you're going to meet someone who'll appreciate that in you." Stella said honestly. "This has been lovely, just what I needed. Thank you."

"You're more than welcome. Now I, for one, am absolutely gasping for a cup of tea." Cathy called the dogs who obediently raced back from where they'd been playing in the shrubs. "Anyway, I've enjoyed our chat. I believe that people come into each other's lives for a reason. Maybe we'll benefit from each other's company." She leaned down to pet a panting Liz, who licked her hand. "I know I already have. I've had a lot on my mind lately, and you've been a marvellous distraction."

Stella helped her put the other two dogs back on their leads.

"Anything I can help with?" She asked as they set off back to the house. The dogs gamboled around their legs, tongues lolling out of their mouths in the heat.

"I'm not quite ready to talk about it yet." Cathy said taking her arm in hers, "But when I am, you'll be the first to know, I promise."

Chapter 22. Faye Kinnett at the Flamingo

As she lowered her microphone Gypsy beamed at the audience giving them all what Si liked to call her 'actressy smile.' The last few beats of the music faded into silence as the crowd erupted into a frenzy of applause and whistles. The noise of drunken punters stomping their feet and calling out her name resonated ecstatically in her ears. It was safe to say the performance had been a success.

"Thank you all darlings." She growled affectionately into the microphone in the deepest baritone she could manage, before she blew them all a kiss and did an over-the-top curtsey – no easy task in her new ten-inch heels. As the applause died down Norma Lee Swallows, queen of femme realness and compere for the evening came to take the mike from her.

"I'd like you all to give it up for Faye Kinnett!" She yelled. "This is Faye's debut performance here at the Pink Flamingo Club, and I'm sure you'll all be looking forward to seeing her again very soon." She looked at Gypsy questioningly.

Gypsy nodded and gave another slightly obscene smile thanks to a massively exaggerated lip-line.

The audience roared their approval.

Making her way back-stage Gypsy floated on a cloud of their noisy appreciation, she felt so ALIVE... Pretending to be a drag queen had been a blast, the best experience she'd had for years. Also, she'd noted with some satisfaction that even her adversary (as she'd come to think of her), Sasha Bitch, had seemed to enjoy the number. Thank god she had a naturally deep singing voice.

On arriving at the club, confronting Sasha had caused her a few anxious moments. However, although every bit as bolshy and unwelcoming as before it'd soon become clear the drag queen didn't have a clue Faye Kinnett was the very same act she'd sent packing not long ago.

The painstakingly constructed drag disguise had worked at treat. James, she thought triumphantly, would have to eat his words. She finally had a job. She was going to be one of the Pink Flamingo Girls. The most beautiful words she'd ever heard came as Norma Lee hissed into her ear. "You're soo hired" in between smiles.

She was a bit disappointed not to have spotted James' face in the crowd or Miss Geneva Convention as he was otherwise known, but it couldn't be helped. Knowing him, she thought crossly, he was probably cruising in the toilets and had missed the whole thing! She couldn't wait to tell him they were going to be working together. Now all she had to do was make her escape without cocking up the whole project. Thank fuck, she had the changing room to herself.

Taking a moment to stand in front of the mirror she struck a pose and admired her reflection. The transformation had taken a lot of thought and hard work, but she absolutely looked the part. Her own mother wouldn't be able to pick her out of a line up. Plus all the effort she'd put into choreographing a routine had paid off. Luckily she was a damn fine singer if she did say so herself. Through the walls she could hear the crowd enthusiastically responding to Sasha Bitch, she'd watched her do a number earlier and had to admit the cow had talent.

Humming to herself she gathered up her stuff and headed for the exit. She'd decided that getting undressed at the club was way too risky; after all if anyone were to spot her sans costume things could get very problematic indeed.

Chapter 23. Current Affaires

Stella wandered around the corner shop absentmindedly picking up cans of vegetable soup and macaroni cheese before putting them back on the shelves. In truth there wasn't really anything she needed to buy, she'd already done her weekly grocery run. Swinging her empty basket on her arm she sighed loudly, the trip to the store had been nothing but a poorly disguised ruse to get out of the house. The tension was becoming unbearable, and she had a feeling that getting things out into the open was going to be left to her.

Finally grabbing a giant sized bar of Galaxy chocolate and a copy of Fashion Fatale Magazine she trudged up to the counter to pay. Handing over a crumpled fiver she wondered if it was worth giving Tony a ring. But no, she thought, dismissing the idea as unwise. It'd put him in an impossible situation, Cathy was his boyfriend's mum. If only she had someone to confide in.

Walking out into the street the weather seemed to reflect her mood. The skies were overcast and grey, atmosphere muggy making her feel suffocated.

Sniffing the air and sitting down at the bus stop she predicted a thunder storm. Tearing open the wrapper, she broke off a piece of chocolate and let it melt on her tongue, as she tried to decide what to do for the best.

On the surface everything in the Fraser home seemed to be going swimmingly. Cathy had helped her through what'd proved to be a difficult time and she'd had the space to consider her future career prospects. They'd even considered the idea of going into business together.

Thanks to some therapy her OCD was settling down. She was grateful for the patience and support the other woman had shown her. Cathy had taught her to laugh again and got her more than a bit stoned from time to time. Their business venture gave her hope for the future. Before she knew it she was looking forward to getting up in the morning rather than dreading it.

Yes, the break in Hounslow seemed to be helping her relax and recharge. Things were looking up. And yet, if all was really as peachy as it seemed why had Cathy been acting strangely for the past week now?

Why, Stella asked herself nibbling on the Galaxy bar, had the easygoing camaraderie between them that she'd so enjoyed almost totally disappeared?

As her bus came round the corner she threw the empty wrapper in the bin before climbing on board.

She thought she knew exactly what was the matter with Cathy, but the real question was did she have the guts to do anything about it?

X

Cathy was watching 'Runway Wars – Battle of the Supermodels' when she heard the key rattle in the front door. Hastily, she tucked the letter she was holding deep inside a pocket of her Japanese style dressing gown and busied herself by filling the kettle with water.

"Hello darling. I'm just making a camomile tea, would you like one?" She asked brightly, reaching for a couple of mugs off the dresser.

Stella pulled up a chair and put her magazine on the table quietly. Looking over her shoulder Cathy noticed that her lodger's expression was unusually solemn.

"What I'd really like, is to talk." Stella said quietly.

131

"This sounds serious." She abandoned the kettle and sat down so they were facing each other. "I hope nothing's wrong?"

"Well that's what I want to find out." Stella said carefully. "I mean have I done something to upset you? You've been jumpy and stressed... things have just seemed strained lately."

"Really?" Cathy avoided her eyes. "I'm sorry; I've just got a lot on my mind."

"Look, I think I know what's going on." She stopped and thought for a moment. "I just wish we could talk about it. I'm sure we could resolve the whole... situation."

"Oh dear! Have you been talking to Si?"

"No." Stella was bewildered. "Have you told him?"

Cathy looked shocked. "He hasn't heard anything from me, that's the point. I'm worried he's found out some other way. Has he mentioned anything to you?"

Stella shook her head feeling like somehow she'd lost control of the conversation. "I don't understand. If you haven't told him, how would he know? Anyway, does it really matter what he thinks? After all he's a grown man and it's really none of his business."

"Hold on dear, if you didn't find out from Si, how do you know what's going on?" Cathy's voice rose in panic. "Did someone phone the house while I was out? For god's sake you would tell me if someone left a message wouldn't you Stella?"

"I think we may have our wires crossed." Stella said slowly. "What on earth are you talking about?"

The actress looked flustered. "Oh dear, how foolish of me... I shouldn't have bought all this up. Please, go on and finish what you were trying to say before I rudely interrupted."

"Okay." She took a deep breath. "I've noticed a difference in you these last few days... a difference in the way you are with me, specifically."

"Like I said I apologise if..."

Stella put a hand up to stop her. "Please just hear me out."

"Okay, go on, I'm listening."

"I don't want to freak you out," she paused meaningfully. "But the bottom line is I have feelings for you."

"Oh!" Cathy's mouth dropped open. "Well *that* is not what I was expecting." She looked uneasy.

"I'm sorry." Stella groaned. "Shit. I've got this all wrong, haven't I? You didn't have a clue..."

"No, that's not entirely true. It's just your timing is off I'm afraid." Cathy reached for her hand to take the sting out of her words.

"Should I have kept quiet? Have I just made things really awkward?"

Cathy sighed. "No, that's alright. Better that it's out in the open and you haven't been imagining things. I can't deny there's something between us. It's just that to be frank I've got so much else on my plate... That sounds awful, what I mean is I've got a problem and it's taking up all of my head space."

"Oh?"

"Do you remember, I said I'd talk to you when I was ready?"

Stella thought for a bit and then nodded recalling their conversation in the park.

"You said that I'd be the first person to know."

"Right, well I think the time has come for me to unburden myself, so to speak."

"Go ahead," Stella urged. "Whatever it is, I'll do anything I can to help."

Cathy reached into her pocket and brought out the letter, clasping it in one hand. "You know that Si's father died shortly before his birth?"

Stella frowned. "Yes... of course, you told me. I'm so sorry."

"Don't be." She said crisply. "I lied... to you, to Si and to everybody else... Karl Fraser is alive and well. In fact I saw him the other day enjoying a latté in Old Compton Street."

133

Chapter 24. The Twenty-Seventh Hen

"You'll have to forgive me." The man who'd introduced himself as Donald Willis said as he led Kate and Danny into a kitchen area adjoining the main hall.

"I'm not myself today as you can see." He removed his glasses giving them a wipe on his jacket sleeve, perched them back on his nose and stared at Danny shaking his head to himself. "You really are the spitting image of Julian. I'm so sorry for earlier."

"Not at all." Danny said kindly. "It's me who should be apologising, the last thing I wanted to do was upset anyone."

"Well you caught me at a bad time I'm afraid." Donald said wringing his handkerchief in his hands. "It looks like our little group will be closing down due to lack of support." He inclined his head in a birdlike manner in the direction of the hall. "We only have five members left now, and we used to be quite a successful bunch."

"Do you think we might be able to talk to them?" Kate asked, hastily adding. "After they've finished rehearsing I mean."

He shook his head doubtfully. "They wouldn't be much help I'm afraid. Julian left the Hillbrook Group nearly three years ago and all the actors who would've known him have left us sadly. But maybe I can be of some assistance."

Danny nodded. "Anything you could tell us would be great; you see I haven't heard from my brother since he

134

disappeared from Manchester years ago. It was pure fluke that I found a listing for your theatre group members on the internet." He shot him a hopeful look. "I suppose you don't have any contact details or an address?"

"Not current ones I'm afraid." The man held up a hand, disappearing into the hall before returning with a battered looking duffel bag. "I had his home number but I last rang ages ago and a girl answered, she'd never heard of Julian so he'd obviously moved on."

Rifling around inside the bag he produced a large, black Filofax, ripped out a piece of paper and handed it to them triumphantly. "I only have this to hand because someone else was here recently asking after your brother. A bit odd that. Nothing for years and then suddenly everyone seems to want to know about our boy."

Danny examined the scrap of paper and frowned, handing it to Kate.

It read simply:

Grace Gillespie/Julian Jackson: 0207 734 0221

"I don't know who this Grace is..." The old man added, reaching for a packet of Hobnobs from the cupboard and offering them round. "But I think Julian mentioned living somewhere in Soho, if that helps?"

"Who else was asking about him?" Kate asked curiously, taking two biscuits. "And when was this? That *is* a huge coincidence."

He looked at them unhappily.

"It was a young man about the same age as you two. He turned up last week and told me that Julian owed him money, I'm sorry to say." His gaze flickered apologetically towards Danny and he swallowed nervously. "He wasn't very pleasant. In fact he demanded that I tell him if I knew of any... misdemeanors on Julian's part whilst he was with the Hillbrook Group."

"What did you tell him?" Danny asked quickly.

135

"Nothing! There was nothing to tell." He protested indignantly. "Julian was a dear soul and such a talented actor. We became friends and he helped me through some difficulties... That's why I was so delighted when I thought that you were him... before."

"Tell us more about this man who was asking after him." Kate encouraged. "It sounds as if he upset you."

"He did rather." The elderly thespian admitted. "He seemed to want me to dish the dirt, asking if I knew what he did for a living and all sorts. Of course even if I'd wanted to - which I did not - I couldn't have told him much. Julian didn't discuss his personal life with us. It was all about the acting you see."

"And what did the man look like?" Kate asked.

"He was tall and Mediterranean looking... maybe a bit on the skinny side." He broke off, eyes closed in concentration. "Nice legs. I can't remember what he was wearing."

"So you don't know what Julian's day job was?" She asked.

"He never said, dear." Donald glanced at his watch. "He did tell me he was leaving because he'd found work and had no free time." He stood up. "I could be wrong, but now you come to mention it I think I recall him saying that a friend had got him a job at someplace called Cordelia's... so maybe that's a bar or restaurant. Anyway, that's really all I know."

"Okay." Danny scraped his chair back. "Well I think we've kept you long enough. Thank you very much for your time."

Kate smiled and stood up extending her hand to be shaken, as the actor leaned forward to give her a whiskery kiss on both cheeks.

"No trouble at all, I hope you find him." He said anxiously squeezing her arm. "If you do, *do* tell him to pay us a visit won't you? Hang on a tick..." He reached into his pocket and handed her his card. "Just in case I can be of any further assistance, or if you know anyone who might like to join a super little theatre group..."

136

The old man stared at Danny wistfully. "The resemblance is truly remarkable." He muttered, adding hopefully. "I don't suppose you're at all interested? Perhaps acting runs in the family?"

X

Later on the two of them opted to discuss their findings at a burger bar near the tube.

Kate picked half-heartedly at her plate of vinegary chips, took a slurp of diet coke and wiped her hand inelegantly over her mouth.

"Well, I suppose we could try that number Donald gave us." She suggested finally. "I know he said Julian's moved, but we could find out the address and investigate. Maybe we'll find someone else he knew while he was living there... like this Grace Gillespie person."

Danny nodded slowly. "I guess it's worth a shot... and I can phone directory enquiries and try to find out where Cordelia's is. I mean if he worked there they may have a forwarding address."

"It's weird that someone else has been there before us." She mused as Danny stared into space, mouth set in a grim line. "You're worried, aren't you?"

"Of course I fucking am!" His anger surprised her. "It just confirms my worst fears! Julian's got himself into some sort of trouble and I can't do a thing to help." He paused and lowered his voice as a couple with kids at the table next to them turned to look. "This isn't just some jaunt where we get to mess around and play detective you know. This is my family."

Kate's mouth fell open. "I can't believe you just said that. It's not like I've nothing better to do."

"I know... I just meant..."

"Save it." She snapped getting to her feet. "I'm knackered and I've got an early start tomorrow so I'll see you later."

"Wait." He caught her hand. "I'm sorry; I don't know why I said that." He sighed and rubbed his eyes tiredly. "It's been a long day; why don't I just get the bill and we can go home together."

He tried for an apologetic smile but she avoided eye contact, looking out of the window into the street. It had started to rain.

"Please babe, forgive me. I'm an idiot. I really do appreciate your help. Let me take you out for dinner tomorrow and make it up to you. I promise it'll just be us, no talk about twin brothers whatsoever."

She knew she was being petty but still felt annoyed. The fact she had a headache coming on didn't help.

"I can't. Si asked me to entertain Tony as a favour while he's working." She pulled on her coat rummaging around in her wallet for some money to leave as a tip. "I'm taking him to some god-awful hen party."

"If it's going to be awful, don't go." He said sensibly, which irrationally irked her. "Tony's a big boy, he can look after himself, come out with me instead."

"Sorry, I promised Vienna. She's an old school friend. Well, I say friend – she was actually a bit of a cow." She muttered as they made their way out into the damp night air. "I'm bringing Tony as an honorary hen. It might be fun. There's going to be twenty-five drunken women going crazy, free food and champagne, and a stripper if we're lucky. It sounds more entertaining than a trip to the pub."

"Ha! How do you think Tony's going to feel being the only bloke amidst twenty-odd pissed females?" He laughed.

"Well, I haven't met him before." Kate said defensively. "I thought it might be a laugh, you know like an ice breaker... Oh fuck it; I did say there's going to be a stripper."

Once on the train, they lapsed into silence, each thinking their own thoughts. Kate leaned back into her seat wearily; upset that tonight they'd had their first row, however small. Also, she couldn't help thinking Danny was right. Tony mightn't be too pleased at the prospect of being the twenty-seventh hen even if they did get free booze. One thing was for sure, if memory served her correctly the only way to survive an evening of undiluted Vienna was with alcohol and lots of it.

138

Chapter 25. God in Nirvana

Standing in the foyer of the Sandersby Hotel, Vienna Valentine gleefully waited to greet her guests. Even Fleur Ascott the model, who was strictly speaking more of an acquaintance than a friend, had agreed to make an appearance. Consequently, not wanting to be outshone she'd made an extra effort tonight. A glance in the floor length mirrors assured her it had paid off. The sleek, strapless dress cost a bomb but clung in all the right places without being tarty. She rustled around in her ruffled silk clutch bag and smoothed cherry gloss onto her lips. The news that her old school nemesis Gypsy Wright wouldn't be coming was the only fly in the ointment as far as she was concerned. Was it wrong to feel the teensiest bit smug she was marrying a man who was not only good-looking but also wealthy?

Vienna gave a small sigh of satisfaction. The news had doubtless got back to her through Kate anyway. She'd heard Gypsy's career had never really picked up and she was still single. Très pathetic, who was the popular one now? She grabbed a celery stick from the h'ors d'oeuvres a passing waiter offered.

Piqued, she recalled her earlier conversation with Kate. Really! It was too much of her to insist on bringing a man to her hen night. She'd only agreed on hearing he was gay. After all, she thought cheering up slightly, gay men loved her. It'd be nice to look as if she were the center of attention when

139

Fleur arrived. Irritatingly though, Kate and aforementioned honorary hen seemed to be verging on the tardy.

"Vienna darling!" She was distracted by a horsy looking woman dressed in Gucci waving at her from the steps.

"I haven't seen you in forever, how are you?!" Vienna gushed, flicking her fair hair over one fake-baked shoulder and giving her a double air kiss.

X

"It looks like we're going to be late." Kate groaned as the cab crawled forward another few feet in the rush hour traffic before coming to an abrupt halt.

"Nay problem." Tony replied good-naturedly. "I'm not sure about all this hen business anyway to tell you the truth, but we'll make the best of it."

"Thank you for agreeing to come with me." She said, hoping that the night wouldn't prove to be a total disaster. "I didn't want to go alone because, quite frankly, it's likely to be full of pretty horrendous people. But I thought it might be okay having someone to laugh at it all with. Anyway, I've been looking forward to meeting you."

She hoped that she'd pulled off the small deception. Tony didn't need to know that Si had begged her to entertain his boyfriend out of guilt for all the extra hours he was putting in at work.

He smiled at her. "I'm enjoying myself. It's great meeting all of Si's mates, and a free dinner at the Sandersby sounds like an opportunity not to be missed."

"Mmm." She murmured, thinking he seemed like a nice guy and that maybe she should've spared him an evening of Vienna induced hell. Adjusting the straps of her top she did a quick lipstick check in her compact mirror. These days it was kind of a novelty to dress up and go somewhere nice. Hrmph, she snorted, thinking it made a change to trekking around after the illusive family members of an ungrateful boyfriend.

"I think we're nearly there." Said Tony as the cab veered off Charing Cross Road.

"Do I look okay?" She asked worriedly, gesturing to her hair which she'd piled on top of her head with a butterfly clasp.

"Relax, you look lovely hen." He said before laughing at his choice of words. "I can't wait to tell Si that I spent the night as an honorary girl, and he thinks I'm so butch."

The cab pulled up outside the hotel and they both gathered up their coats and the chocolates Kate had bought earlier. They split the money for the fare and she pulled open the door for him.

"Ladies first." She teased. "Come on; let's get into the spirit of things.... We'll have a good time, right?"

"Aye doll, it'll be grand. Stop worrying so much!" He called over his shoulder.

X

Knocking back another glass of champagne, Kate looked around for Tony in the crowd of semi-sozzled hens. What'd started off as a rather stilted affair was quickly descending into alcohol induced debauchery.

Propping up the bar and watching twenty-odd Sloane Rangers go mad under the effects of too much Bolly and dodgy disco music, she thanked her lucky stars that she hadn't had to endure the night solo.

Unhappily, she'd spent dinner seated between an anorexic looking girl who said little and spent the evening staring enviously at Kate's delicious but mean portion of swordfish steak, and a tubby brunette with a voice like a fog-horn. She was harbouring a bitter resentment against the latter for finishing the last of the caramel flambé just before it reached her.

Predictably, after makings such a fuss about how she 'simply must come, darling. It wouldn't be the same without you,' Vienna was seated so far the other end of the table that Kate had barely been able to make her out. Even more annoyingly she'd pounced upon poor Tony and insisted that he sit next to her while he made 'help me' gestures behind her

141

back. Ah well, she thought as she spotted him coming back from the gents. He seemed to have been holding his own. However now it was definitely time for Plan B, get good and pissed.

"Isn't this horrible?" She groaned as Tony sidled up to join her at the bar.

"What do you mean?" He asked chuckling. "I'm having a ball, this is hilarious."

"The karaoke was certainly interesting." Kate giggled ordering a double Bacardi and coke for them both. "I can't believe you sang. You're a braver hen than me."

"Well, you don't mention that to anyone else on pain of death, right girlie." He threatened accepting the drink and taking a large gulp. "But you did say we should get into the spirit of things."

"Look at Vienna over there with her tongue up Fleur Ascott's ass." Kate pointed to the other side of the room where the beautiful black model had been cornered by la Valentine... her eyes had taken on a glazed, trapped expression. "If you look closely you can almost see her losing the will to live."

Suddenly the music quieted down, the guests on the dance floor stumbling to an undignified halt as someone dimmed the main lights. A tall, beaky looking woman climbed up to the makeshift stage area near the bar.

"Dear God." moaned Kate, dramatically clutching Tony's arm. "What more can we possibly be subjected to in one evening?"

"Oooh, I think it's time for..." He started.

"Ladies, may I have your attention please." Tall and beaky boomed into the mike. "I'm delighted to inform you that our stripper for the night is about to make his entrance!"

The hen's yelled out their approval and someone shouted an unladylike 'get your knob out!' as the catcalls began and everyone clustered nearer the bar.

"Ouch." Kate shrieked. "Someone just elbowed me in the tit! Shall we move to the front? These lot are dangerous."

142

"You betcha." Tony leered steering her through the crowd of girls - suddenly rowdy as football hooligans.

Michael Jackson's 'Don't Stop 'til You Get Enough' started thumping out of the sound system as a semi-naked man in chaps and a thong, his face almost entirely hidden under the huge brim of his cowboy hat stepped out onto the dance floor.

"Please welcome, our stripper girls. His name's Ivan, *Ivan Ewjun*...ooh!" Beaky squawked excitedly. "And he wants to entertain you."

The audience went wild as the stripper threw himself energetically into his routine, posing and dancing in time to the music as he started to remove his costume.

As the light reflecting from the giant, rotating disco ball fell on him Kate stiffened in shock. Her jaw dropped cartoon-character style as she recognized the all too familiar features. It was none other than their Si. She whipped her head round to register Tony's reaction but his face was unreadable, mouth set in a thin line as Si/Ivan poured oil seductively down his chest, twirled his hips and bent down to show the crowd his bum, to cries of delight from the hens.

Kate covered her eyes with her hands and tried desperately to pretend she wasn't there. This was definitely not a good turn of events. She took a peek through her fingers and hastily closed them again. Shit and double shit, she thought, on the verge of hysterical laughter as he disposed of his G-string and stood butt naked except for that ludicrous hat.

Si meanwhile was surprised at how confident he felt, stripping in front of this mob of girls. It was certainly a change from the usual gay venues which were actually much more intimidating. He'd been dreading the party, but to his relief it was turning out to be a piece of piss. Everyone was drunk and in fine spirits, and with any luck he could have a quick shower and be home by midnight.

Coming to the grand finale, he stood starkers before the circle of screaming women as the track finished. He whipped off his hat with a flourish, and searched the faces in the crowd before sending it spinning off in the bride-to-be's general direction.

He saw Tony a second before the cowboy hat hit him square in the midriff...

Their eyes locked... Tony's expression glacial and Si's registering total horror.

And then the music started up again, and it was his cue to take a bow and leave the dance floor. He pasted on a smile for his public, forced to watch helplessly as his boyfriend started to push his way towards the exit followed by Kate. Blindsided he was promptly tackled by a violently pissed hen. Manfully several taller girls tried to disentangle him and they all ended up in a heap on the slippery floor.

After he'd showered, changed and collected his wage, Si found himself wandering disconsolately along the Strand. There was no sign of Kate or Tony waiting for him outside. Shocker.

Feeling traumatized, he considered his options carefully before calling Dario on his mobile. He clearly wasn't going to be getting a very warm reception back at Kershalton Street.

The phone was answered almost immediately.

"Dario, it's Si. Whatcha doing?"

X

Three hours, two ecstasy tablet and countless pints later Si and Dario were taking part in a mass drug induced work-out - otherwise known as dancing - on Nirvana's main stage.

Dario was naked to the waist and clutching a can of Red-Stripe as a man who looked exactly like Vincent Santelli the hairdresser (or at least he did in Si's drug addled mind) slid his hands down Dario's jeans and pulled his head back by his hair as they begun to kiss hungrily.

In search of further refreshments Si stumbled away from them and off the main floor, jostling his way through the crowd, the music ringing in his ears. His shirt was drenched with sweat.

144

He checked his watch and bought another beer from the barman. It was nearly closing time, but he didn't feel remotely inclined to go home. Dario also clearly had other plans. Just as he was considering getting a cab to Vauxhall to blow some more of his hard earned money, he caught the eye of the stunningly attractive older man he'd been ogling earlier.

His admirer was sitting further up the bar and beckoned him over. Si downed some more of his drink and wandered towards him. He decided that he was definitely too drunk to care about the consequences of his actions tonight. After all, he was on the verge of getting dumped. Plus this was the man he'd pointed out to Dario earlier; he was so gorgeous they'd nicknamed him God.

"Hi there, I'm Si." Si introduced himself giving his best flirty smile as he approached. The man regarded him appreciatively, he had striking blue eyes and silver hair.

"Very nice to meet you." God said finally. He took a sip of his drink and crinkled his eyes at him irresistibly. "Although it's a shame we didn't meet before, I was just about to head home." He gave him a slow smile. "I don't suppose you'd like to come with me?"

Chapter 26. Drageratti

Gypsy downed her pint and waved a ten-pound note at Freddie the bartender, holding one finger unsteadily in the air to indicate that she'd like another one.

If he was surprised to see drag queen Faye Kinnett dangerously pissed and wearing a dress made entirely of wilting peacock feathers at three in the morning he didn't show it. Freddie was used to the diverse crowd of punters that frequented the illegal after-hours watering hole. The place bustled with club kids, drag acts fresh from the Flamingo, tranny chasers and other passing flotsam and jetsam of the night, including tourists, addicts, insomniacs, and prostitutes. Cordelia's had real character... if you weren't put off by drug busts, occasional stabbings and the fact that it cost a tenner for a warm pint of lager.

Gypsy had not been in the mood to get picky. She'd been desperate for a drink. In fact several drinks, swallowed down with a few more. Ignoring the smoking ban she lit the wrong end of a cigarette before stubbing it out in disgust.

"Is everything okay?" Madeline, the beefy blond tranny asked commandeering the barstool beside her. "You look wasted."

"Wow, nothing gets past you does it Mads?" She cradled her be-wigged head in her hands dramatically. "Leave me alone. Can't you see my life's over?"

146

Shrugging Madeline made her way over to the pool table, patting her on the shoulder gingerly as she passed. In Faye Kinnett's current mood it looked like she might bite, literally.

Taking a swig of her fresh pint Gypsy/Faye swung her head around to give the other customers a belligerent once-over, muttering incoherently under her breath to no one in particular. Freddie busied himself at the other end of the bar.

How dare Sasha Bitch and Tyra G'eye-Out have her demoted to door-whore? Oh the humiliation, after it had all been going so well! Bitter tears welled dangerously behind her false lashes. But, she vowed to herself savagely, she would not give up. Faye Kinnett would be returned to her rightful place on the Pink Flamingo's stage. It was just a matter of time.

"I think you've had quite enough of that madam." An arm stretched out to remove the glass from her hand.

"I'm pefec-ly shober." She retorted crossly, making a bid to grab it back and nearly sliding off her stool. Her head lolled backward and she found herself looking up into the heavily kohled eyes of James Cadogan. "Gimme that back Jamesh." She demanded.

"Hrmph. Geneva if you please." He retorted patting his asymmetrical purple wig and pursing his lips.

"Pleeeeshe Geneva babesh." She begged, not noticing as a strategically placed feather dislodged itself and fall to the floor.

He sighed and arranged his fake fur stole over her shoulders to stop her from flashing the bar.

"Freddie darling!" He yelled, sitting down next to her. "One glass of vodka and coke for me and a large black coffee for Missy here, if it's not too much trouble." He took in her dishevelled state with a raised eyebrow as he waited for their drinks to arrive.

"Soo." He said finally as she took a reluctant sip of coffee. "Are you going to tell me what you're doing in this godforsaken dive looking like someone's just run over your cat, or do I have to beat it out of you with a stick?"

147

She laughed drunkenly. "I can't take you sheriously with that hair, not after seeing you in a shuit and tie all those days at..." She broke off looking confused. "Where did we work 'gain?"

"You're avoiding the issue. I take it you haven't looked in a mirror yet? I wouldn't advise it honey pie..."

Gypsy sighed and slumped over the bar supporting her chin with the palms of her hands.

"I'm not in a very good place."

"So I gather. What appears to be the problem?"

A deeper sigh. "I've just been shacked."

"Shacked?" James asked uncomprehendingly.

"SHACKED." She yelled into his ear.

"Oh, sacked. I see... well, that *is* bad news." He agreed flapping his hands in an effort to get her to keep her voice down. "What did you do?"

"Nothing." She said sullenly.

He looked at her reprovingly. "Nothing? Really?"

"Nothing much." She admitted taking another gulp of coffee. "As you're aware, I haven't been a hundred percent truthful about every tiny, insignificant detail of my life. Well... Tyra found out I'm a genetically correct man and went apeshit."

"Woman." James corrected.

"Swat I'm saying." She wailed plaintively. "I mean I can't help being gerretically correct, it's rashism... you know wat I mean? Oh buggery bollocks. This is your fault anyway. I never would've gone there and been insulted if it wasn't for you."

"Oh no! Don't you dare try and pin this on me. I *told* you to be honest. You could've just been a faux queen from the start, there's no shame in it. But OH NO! That would've been just too easy! Your problem is you have to make everything more complicated than it needs to be, you big drama queen."

He sighed. "Why not just be grateful for what you've got?"

She stared at him as if he had suddenly grown an extra head and started speaking in Japanese.

148

"Come on darling. You've been performing at the Pink Flamingo for months now despite the fact they don't allow female acts, and you've gone down very well." He cajoled, sipping his watered down vodka with a little moue of distaste.

"You've been all over the gay press and performed at loads of venues. Honestly, I'm sure you'll have no problem getting another job in one of the clubs. People know the name Faye Kinnett now, money can't buy that sweetheart. I don't mind saying you proved me wrong. I admit it. I thought you should've just stuck to straight acting; but you've got a real gift for cabaret." He gripped her by the shoulders. "Now, is a teeny little set-back like being outed at the Pink Flamingo really the end of the world? Or is it possible you're over reacting?"

"But ish my spiritual home, innit?" Her voice wavered and sooty tears streaked their way down her pan-sticked cheeks. "They really love me, and I really reaaally love them."

"It's not like you can't go back." He said wearily, concluding to himself that talking to drunks was beyond frustrating. Gypsy would almost certainly remember none of this in the morning. Well, he'd done his bit thank you very much. He was damned if he was going to talk her out of suicidal despair all over again once she sobered up.

"Huh! They're making me door whore." She spat angrily.

"There you go then!" He cried enthusiastically. "That's not being sacked... they've just changed your role somewhat. I think you'll make an exquisite whore de la door."

"Not for long, I'm coming up with a whole new act." She said emphatically tossing back her tangled synthetic curles. "I'm going to start rehearsing just as soon as I've finished getting drunk."

With that her eyes snapped shut and James found he was supporting her entire body weight as she leaned into him, an arm slung around his hip.

Scowling, he checked for signs of life and just as he was becoming concerned a loud, guttural snore emanated from her lip-stick smeared mouth.

"Oh perfect. Freddie! Call us a cab will you, love?"

149

Chapter 27. Trouble in Paradise

Jolted awake by a sharp rapping on her bedroom door, Kate groaned and pulled the duvet over her head. A moment later she discerned the sound of someone entering the room along with the clatter of cutlery. Reluctantly she emerged from the warm cocoon of bedclothes. Danny was making his way gingerly over, a fully laden breakfast tray balanced in his hands; his hair was all mused up and he wore an endearingly sheepish expression. She rubbed her eyes and smiled at him, smothering a yawn.

"I thought you might be hungry." He put the tray down on her nightstand taking care not to spill the orange juice or coffee. "I hope you like croissants. They're the chocolate ones; I won't be offended if you'd prefer some cereal."

She heaved herself up into a sitting position, and blinked at the sun streaming in through the windows. I must have forgotten to draw the curtains last night, she thought feeling her hangover kick in. Weakly she reached for the orange juice and drained the glass.

"My hero." She gasped when she'd finished. "What did I do to deserve breakfast in bed?"

"I wanted to make it up to you for being a moody sod." He admitted sitting down on the floor. "Also, to be honest, it was a ruse to wake you."

"So basically, you were bored."

"Well, yeah. I've been up for hours." He said helping himself to a bit of croissant. "I was doing some investigative work on Julian but came to a dead-end about two hours ago. And Seth's no use... he's on the Internet pretending to be a lesbian." He shook his head at her disbelievingly. "When I last checked he was in a chat room introducing himself as sexy Cindy from Chiswick."

"*What?*"

"You know, so he can talk dirty to lesbians on the net... Sometimes I'm embarrassed to be his mate." He sighed in mock despair.

Kate manoeuvred the tray onto her lap and began tucking into her breakfast. "You do realise that the lesbians he's chatting to are probably straight men too." She said trying to keep a straight face. "In fact, the whole chat room is probably exclusively male; I'll bet there's not a single bona fida lesbian there."

Danny guffawed. "I have to say, the thought did cross my mind. I mean 'big-bosomed Brigitte from Bromley'? *C'mon.* He's got to be talking to some other wanker with the exact same idea."

"Yep." She nodded her head solemnly. "Let's not tell him."

"Definitely not."

"So, what time is it anyway?" She stretched her arms above her head.

Danny looked at his watch and tutted loudly. "It's passed twelve. How was the hen night, by the way?"

"Oh shagging hell!" She exclaimed as the events of the previous evening came flooding back. "You're not going to believe this!"

X

By the time she'd relayed the details of the previous nights debacle to Danny, his earlier good mood seemed to have disintegrated.

151

"Are you listening to me?" She asked waving a hand in front of his eyes. "It was awful. Si was standing there stark bollock naked surrounded by all these drunken girls. Tony just stormed off home. He was furious; I didn't know what to do."

He gave a half-hearted chuckle. "That is too much! Your friends are mad."

"It's not funny." She said. "Si looked like he wanted to die. Tony's only just moved in with him."

Kate searched her boyfriend's face with her eyes, not liking what she found there. His expression was distant and troubled, mouth downturned at the corners.

"Okay what's wrong? What happened with your investigating?"

He sighed. "Sorry. I just feel like I'm getting nowhere and it's pissing me off. I phoned Directory Enquiries and found out there is no Cordelia's listed." He ran a hand through this hair. "I also tried that number that the theatre group bloke gave us."

"And?"

"Well I spoke to a woman named Tracy Lucas. I managed to talk her into giving me the address of the flat. Apparently it's a bed-sit in Berwick Street." He paused. "I guess we could go and check it out but I don't hold out much hope of finding anything there."

"So she definitely hadn't heard of Julian?"

"No. She said she'd only moved in a couple of months ago. I did ask for the landlord's details, but this Tracy says he's only recently back from living in Australia, so he probably won't be much use. Oh and she'd never heard of Grace Gillespie either."

Kate cast her mind about desperately, trying to think of something that would help take the defeated tone out of his voice. If Danny gave up hope of finding his brother who was to say he'd even want to stay in London?

"Look, I think we need a fresh perspective on this." Purposefully she got up and began searching for the portable phone they were constantly misplacing. "Why don't I give Si a ring and see if we can go over to his place?"

Danny eyed her doubtfully. "I don't know."

"Come on!" She encouraged injecting a note of optimism into her voice. "I'll just check he's recovered from last night, and then we can get him to help us. If he can't think of anything we'll still have time to go round and look at the Berwick Street place." She put her hands on her hips. "What harm can it do? I really think an outsider's perspective might help. C'mon, three heads are better than two."

X

A few hours later a rough-looking Si led Kate and Danny into the living room where he'd spent the best part of the day convalescing.

"Sorry about the mess." He said, indicating the empty crisp and take-out wrappers. "I wasn't expecting company."

"Wow. You look like shit." Kate said taking in his disheveled appearance and the dark circles under his eyes. "Do you want us to go? I tried calling, but you must've been asleep."

He shook his head. "No, it's nice to have company. It'll help take my mind off the fact my life's falling apart."

"Right, yeah." She shuffled her feet uncomfortably. "Anyway, I wanted to introduce you to Danny here. Long overdue, I know."

Si pasted on a smile. "Sorry, I'm feeling a bit under the weather. It's good to finally meet my favourite copy-typist's man though." He grasped the other man's extended hand weakly.

"Pleasure." Danny grinned. "Mate, are you sure you're up to company?"

Si nodded. "Some friendly faces to cheer me up are exactly what the doctor ordered." He shot a look at Kate. "I suppose this one's filled you in..."

153

"Ehm, yeah. So you're a stripper." Danny took a seat whilst Si took their coats and hung them up in the hall. "Good on you. That must take a lot of balls."

"Yes, I think Kate got an eyeful she wasn't bargaining for." Si chuckled, then winced and clutched his head. "Ow, fucking ouch... I've got the worst headache... son of a bitch."

"Do I detect a slight hangover?" Kate asked sympathetically.

"That's the understatement of the decade. I wouldn't get too close, I probably smell." He sniffed his armpits experimentally and grimaced.

"So, what did Tony say when you got home?" She asked taking a swallow from a half-full bottle of Pepsi on the table.

Si coughed. "I didn't make it back until a couple of hours ago."

Danny let out a low whistle. "I don't know if that means the same with blokes; but if it does, you're in big trouble."

"You're not wrong." He looked at them both with a pained expression. "When I staggered in this morning I bumped into him having a cup of tea in the kitchen. Let's just say we had words. In fact, he had words, I just stood there feeling fragile while he shouted at me and stormed off to spend the day with Stella."

"So where did you go after the Sandersby?" Kate asked gulping down more coke and passing the bottle to Danny. "And more importantly why didn't I know about your stripping sideline?"

"I didn't want anyone to know." Si said quietly. "I thought the less people knew, the less chance of Tony finding out. Ha! You can imagine my surprise when he rocked up to my first hen party... the one place I was absolutely certain of anonymity. Oh the irony. Anyway, I couldn't face going home afterwards so Dario and I went clubbing at Nirvana."

"Oh I bet that went down well." Kate pulled a face.

He hung his head. "That's not all. I got absolutely trollied and ended up at some bloke's house."

"Oh dear." Kate frowned. "Was it good at least?"

"No idea." Si raised his palms heavenward. "The last thing I remember is having a drink at his place... next thing I'm waking up on his couch. Maybe I just passed out..."

All three of them jumped as the door opened and a head poked cautiously around.

"George!" Si was surprised. "I thought you were out. Come and meet my friends Kate and Danny. Guys, this is our lodger."

The man gave the three of them a deer-caught-in-the headlights look. "I didn't know you had company. I've, er, gotta run." He finally mumbled retracting his head and vanishing as quickly as he'd appeared.

"Charming." Si said.

They heard the front door open and close followed by a door slamming upstairs.

"And that'll be Gypsy. Welcome to our lovely home. Honestly! I don't know what's going on with that girl. She's spent the morning in her room with a 'Do No Disturb On Pain Of Death' note stuck to her door."

Kate and Danny exchanged glances.

"I'll introduce you to her another time." Kate muttered before turning her full attention to Si.

"Anyway, we were wondering if you could help us out with something."

Si raised an eyebrow. "What sort of a something?"

"We need your sleuthing skills."

"Oh?" He leaned forward and lit a fag. "Go on."

Kate smiled at him. "I'll let Danny explain; after all it's about his brother."

"I'm listening." He said giving them his full attention. "Tell me everything."

Chapter 28. Bad Hair Day

After Danny and Kate had left, Si set about cleaning up the house. Painstakingly he scrubbed, dusted and hoovered, opening up the windows to let in some fresh air. Once the place was spotless he felt somewhat better and forced himself to eat some leftover stir-fry. The house was eerily silent. He felt agitated and desperate to talk to someone.

Climbing the stairs he hesitated at the top, eyes drawn to the padlock on George's door. Their anti-social lodger was clearly still out. Walking over, he examined it and then, feeling slightly foolish, got down on his stomach and pressed his cheek against the carpet as he tried to get a glimpse underneath. He could see nothing but dust balls and darkness. Guiltily he stood up and brushed himself off before warily approached Gypsy's room.

He re-read the note on her door dubiously.

At least he had a genuine excuse to wake her now. George's behaviour was increasingly bizarre. Only the other day Tony had complained that he was rude, verging on monosyllabic and acting strung out. He was also simply the most unfriendly person Si had ever met. It was getting to the point where he actually felt uncomfortable sharing a home with him. If Gypsy agreed, maybe they could arrange to rid of him. Plus, he admitted to himself, he needed a shoulder to cry on. Fuck it. He was going in.

He knocked twice and listened with his ear pressed to the door for sounds of life. From inside there was the faint sound of moaning. Slowly he turned the handle and stepped inside.

X

"What the fuck? Who's there!" He heard Gypsy croak.

"It's me... Si." He whispered, feeling his way towards the bed. The room was pitch black but as his eyes became accustomed to the dark he could make out a Gypsy shaped lump under the bedclothes.

"Hold on." There was a fumbling noise as she knocked various objects off her bedside-table. Suddenly the room was flooded with low light.

"Good lord! What the bloody hell happened to you?" Si spluttered, shocked. He involuntarily took a step back towards the door one hand inching its way up to his mouth in horror.

To say Gypsy did not look her personal best would be putting it very kindly. Her hair was a tangled bouffant mess, spewing hair grips at angles, her face hidden behind a blotchy smear of what appeared to be stage make up partially removed with a hose. Panda eyes and lipstick smeared across her chin completed the look with a large pink false eyelash clinging to one cheekbone. To a startled Si it looked like some kind of poisonous caterpillar.

"Can't you read?" She asked pointing at the door. "Bugger off!"

When he didn't move she started lobbing pillows at his head. This assault stopped abruptly as she happened to glimpse her reflection in the mirror. Her mouth opened in a perfect 'o' and she dropped the pillow in hand onto the floor at his feet.

"Jesus... I'm *hideous*."

"It's not one of your best looks." Si agreed, edging nearer.

"My head hurts!" She pulled the duvet around her like a shawl and allowed him to sit down beside her.

157

"That seems to be a common problem today." He looked at her matted hair grimacing slightly. "Heavy night then, pet?"

"Bleugh! It was awful, they're making me go on door duty at work, and then I went to the shittiest bar in the world and got hammered. I don't even remember getting home."

"You've been so busy I've hardly seen you since you got that job. I don't even know what you're doing?"

"Faux drag." She muttered. "Singing in clubs wearing wigs and too much slap."

"Come again?"

"Have you heard of Faye Kinnett?"

He looked at her. "Hmm, I think so. Isn't she a drag act? I saw something in QX the other week."

Frowning she peeled off the fake eyelash. "*She* would be me."

"What?" Si shook his head. "You're telling me you're a drag queen?"

She sighed loudly. "Faux drag means a woman dressing up as a man dressing up as a woman, with me so far?"

He nodded hesitantly. "Just about."

"I've been doing faux drag as Faye Kinnett at the club and some other places, which in itself would've been fine. Anyway the problem was Sasha Bitch pissed me off something chronic, which resulted in me passing myself off as a real drag queen to sort of er, prove a point. They found out and demoted me to door whore."

He scrunched his face up as if in pain. "This is too much for me to take in today. How come you didn't tell me any of this? I mean how exciting! Obviously not the last bit about you being demoted."

"I don't know. I didn't want it to get out. I just thought it'd be best if I told no one."

Si shrugged. "Well it could be worse, believe me. I haven't told you about *my* Saturday night yet."

"What do you mean?" She asked finally noticing that Si wasn't looking his usual perky self either.

"Well, I had a stripping gig last night at a hen party."

"Go on."

He paused for a moment. "And you'll never guess who showed up…"

Gypsy thought for a moment. "Not Tony!"

"Give the lady a gold star."

"What was *he* doing at a hen party?"

"Never mind that, the good bit is yet to come." He continued. "I threw my cowboy hat into the crowd during the finale and it practically landed on my boyfriend, who up until this point I hadn't noticed, so I'd cheerfully continued doing my routine and getting naked." He said. "Anyway, he gives me this look… and storms off. So like an idiot I go out, get trashed and wake up at some bloke's house with absolutely no memory of what we did, or didn't, get up to."

"Shit Si…"

He held up a hand to silence her. "Hang on, I haven't finished yet. When I finally get home he's waiting and we have a blazing row. Oh and now he's gone. The end."

She rested her head on his shoulder.

"Okay darling, you win."

He managed a watery smile. "I do, don't I."

"Does he know about the other guy?"

Si looked alarmed. "No! So don't for godsake say anything."

"Of course I won't."

"Hmm." He frowned at her. "I can't believe you didn't tell me about all this drag stuff you've been up to, I'm a little hurt you didn't trust me."

Gypsy got up and paced the room. "It's hard to explain, but I liked the fact that no one knew. It was just something that was… I dunno… all *mine*." She sighed. "I didn't want you guys to make fun of it, I suppose. I've trained for years to be an actor, but this feels like something I could really do. It's not just a laugh, you know."

He got up and gave her a hug.

"You're a funny little thing." He said fondly. "Now go and sort your hair out."

She sniffed. "Thanks, I will. And you and Tony are going to be okay. Why don't you buy him flowers, or take him out to dinner to say you're sorry?"

Si shrugged. "I don't know if I am sorry, I mean what's wrong with stripping anyway? I think I just embarrass him in general."

"Bullshit."

"We'll see." He said. An idea was starting to take shape in his mind but he needed to talk to Tony before it could go any further. "Let's go downstairs and get you a mug of caffeine. We need to talk about some other stuff too."

"Oh god, if I *must*. I suppose I'm not going back to sleep now anyway." She followed him into the corridor.

X

"So let me get this straight." Gypsy said later, Jezebel purring on her lap. "Kate came to see you with her new bloke, and they're trying to track down his evil twin brother?"

"Identical twin brother." Si corrected. "Not necessarily evil."

"And you're going to help them?" She stroked the cat's tummy. "God Si, this sounds like something out of a bad soap opera."

"I know. Anyway, what I really wanted to talk to you about is our lodger."

"George? What's he got to do with it?" She swallowed down the last of some soluble aspirin and water and stuck her tongue out. "Yech."

Si looked at her. "Don't take this personally honey, but I think you'd feel a lot better if you washed your face."

She waved away his suggestion with a careless gesture. "I'll jump in the shower in a minute. Now, tell me what you were going to say about George."

"I think he should move out. For a start, he's been off with Tony." Si began slightly defensively.

"Well that's not exactly the crime of the century and you're the one who chose him in the first place."

"I know, but he's always off his face. Plus he's rude, standoffish and secretive, he makes me nervous."

"Okay." She chewed the skin around one of her nails. "He does seem a bit weird. He's away for weeks and then he suddenly reappears when you least expect him."

Si nodded. "And personally I think it's a bloody cheek to fix a lock onto his door without asking anyone. Makes you wonder what he's up to in there."

Gypsy got up and rinsed her glass with water. "I don't know babes. He's antisocial... but apart from that he hasn't really done anything." She shrugged. "Some people would consider him the perfect housemate. I mean we hardly notice him, it's not like he plays loud music, or makes a mess or doesn't pay his rent. I suppose he does bring some pretty dodgy looking mates home."

"Right, so you agree. Wouldn't it be better to get someone... more normal?"

"You mean normal like us? A stripper and a woman who impersonates drag queens for a living?" She laughed.

He remained silent, she had a point.

"Let's just give him a chance." She sat back down next to him. "Maybe he's shy or something. I don't know!" She threw her hands up in the air as he snorted derisively. "If it's still not working out in a couple of weeks then we can have a house meeting."

"Alright." He said reluctantly. "Now, can you see my mobile anywhere? I need to check that Dario's still alive."

Gypsy located it on the dresser and leaned over to grab it for him.

"What's up with him?"

Si frowned as he tapped in the number. "He was clubbing with me, and it could be the drugs but I think he was all over Vincent Santelli."

"Vincent Santelli the hairdresser?!"

"We'll soon find out..."

X

Dario was soaking in a hot bath over at the flat he, Marina and Lisa shared above the Black Cock when the phone rang. This was followed by someone banging on the door.

"Dario! Phone!" It was Marina.

"I'm in the tub, take a message okay?!" He yelled back.

He heard the sounds of her running down the hall and relaxed back into the soapy water. Having only got home an hour earlier he was absolutely shattered.

Smiling lazily he thought back to the night just passed... non-stop sex in a luxury penthouse apartment with none other than Vincent Santelli. He submerged his aching shoulders with a contented sigh. Could Vincent *be* any more gorgeous? Quite apart from the fact that he was a minor celebrity thanks to his own reality TV show. Not that he cared about that, not really. He silently blessed Si for dragging him out to Nirvana. For the first time since the break-up he could say to himself categorically that he was over Mark, over feeling guilty about Mark, over even thinking about him.

He turned on the hot water tap, wanting to prolong this sacred time spent alone and uninterrupted with his thoughts before his shift downstairs began. Sponging shower gel over his torso, he wondered when they would next hook up. Already he knew it was more than a weekend fling. For fuck's sake, Vincent had cancelled an appointment with Nadia Olsen so they could spend the morning together. He felt a huge grin spread across his face at the thought of the supermodel having to suffer a bad hair day simply because Vincent couldn't get enough of him.

The sound of Lisa and Marina bickering outside the door momentarily distracted him. He frowned as a thought he'd been trying to suppress danced unwelcome into his mind intruding on his happiness. This particular problem was one he'd been aware of for some time now. It was just so stressful and overwhelming he'd been ignoring it. The good old head in the sand approach. Time was fast running out now though, dammit. As the women's voices rose he sucked in his breath and lowered his head underwater to block them out.

162

He told himself firmly that it was nothing he couldn't sort out. But there was no getting away from the fact he urgently needed a visa if he wanted to stay in the country. He was going to have to be proactive. Under no circumstances did Dario plan on allowing himself to be deported. He simply couldn't leave London, especially not now.

Chapter 29. Grace Gillespie' Story

Ida and Blaine only stopped at the house long enough to change and put Dior on a leash. They set off at a brisk pace up the road, Dior trotting at their heels.

"Let's just walk around." Blaine was matter-of-fact. "I don't want to go to a café in case we're overheard."

Ida put a restraining hand on his arm. "Why don't we go back home? Getting mobbed is the last thing we need right now."

He shook his head and wiped his sleeve across his face as fresh tears sprung to his eyes.

"I can't be there right now!" His voice cracked alarmingly. "Whoever's been writing the letters knows where I live. They were hand-delivered."

"Fine, but let's go left here, otherwise we're going to end up on the main road and we'll be all over the tabloids next week." She led him round the corner and they sat down on a bench. Patiently she held his hand as he took in great hiccupy gulps of air.

"Look, try to calm down babe. Then tell me what's going on." She handed over a tissue from her handbag.

Blaine stared at her, his face drawn and blotchy.

"I already told you." His voice was strangled. "Someone's found out about my past, you saw the letter."

Ida took a deep breath. "So you're... trans?"

He laughed cheerlessly. "I know it's not what you were expecting to hear. But believe me honey, it's true."

"You're telling me you were honest to god born female?" She struggled to understand. "But you're famous for being a cross-dressing man!"

"Yes." He said patiently. "And that's exactly what I am. Just think of it as an admin error in the womb."

"And you're name was Grace, like in the letter?" Ida grappled for the right words to say. "How the hell have you been able to keep this a secret?"

"I lied about my past, obviously." He admitted. "It was no one else's business. Then when I started becoming famous I couldn't tell anyone, the press would've had a field day. Like you said, I'm known for being the outrageous gender-bending male model. There are a lot of ignorant people who just wouldn't get it."

"I suppose."

"What's freaking me out is I don't know what this person wants from me. You read the letter." He looked at her desperately. "What do you think it means?"

"This is the third one?"

He nodded.

"I don't know." Ida squeezed his hand. "Why don't you take a deep breath and start from the beginning? Tell me everything."

"Yeah, okay." Blaine picked up Dior and cuddled him to his chest. "Well, I was christened Grace Gillespie and lived in Sidcup with my Mum; Dad had disappeared long ago. I always knew I was really a boy trapped in the wrong body and by the time I was eighteen I couldn't stand living a lie anymore. It was confusing though, coz I fancied other men and as for being butch... Look at me, Ida! I was camp as tits, just like I am now. There's no way my mother would've understood, she was very old-fashioned, I had a strict religious upbringing... So, I left home as soon as I could."

"Go on..."

He reached feverishly in his pocket for his cigarettes and handed her one. They both lit up in silence before he took a lungful of smoke and continued.

"Anyway, I hung round in the gay bars so I could be with other gay guys, but it was horrible constantly being mistaken for a woman. I had big boobs, a high voice and really feminine features. Testosterone's changed my face completely! You wouldn't recognise me if you saw what I looked like back then. Seriously, there was nothing male looking about me." He sighed. "So anyway, I knew if I cut my hair short and wore men's clothes I'd just look like a more masculine woman – which is the exact opposite of what I am.

It was a tough time. I worked in a shitty bar called Cordelia's and shared a tiny bed-sit with another mate. I knew that if I couldn't get a sex change I didn't want to live anymore." Blaine sighed. "I worked in a strip joint and started saving everything I earned. Those weren't good years. I don't like to think about it now, any of it." He shuddered.

"Anyway, eventually I had various operations, and started taking testosterone. By the time I'd had my last round of surgery I passed completely. I was reborn as Blaine Feynard.

I didn't want anyone to know about my past. There was no one to miss Grace, not really. I hadn't had any close friends, apart from this one guy, JJ. But I was scared he wouldn't understand so when I got the go ahead to start on hormones I just disappeared. Then a year later I got discovered by Boss and the rest is history."

Ida gave a low whistle. "So everything written in the magazines about your life pre-modelling is..."

"Total bullshit." He confirmed. "I gave myself a whole new background and family history. I didn't want to tell Cecile the truth. I didn't want to give her any reason to rethink signing me."

"Well I can understand that."

"I refused, and still refuse, to play down the fact that I'm effeminate though. I'd come so far to be true to myself, I wasn't about to start living another lie. That's why I sometimes do drag at the Pink Flamingo as B Fey. Anyway the designers like me as I am. So, now you know." He stared at the ground, shoulders hunched. "What do you make of it all?"

There was a long pause.

"I think you're brave." Ida said finally. "I think you've had an amazing life and I honestly find it hard to believe you were ever a woman... I mean you're such a gay man."

"Yeah, well it was just my body that was female."

"Babe, I'm honored you've trusted me with all this."

"Thank you. For listening to me and being there, we've not been mates for long, but I won't forget this."

"Any time." She put an arm round his shoulder. "I'm glad to repay the favour. I dunno how I would've coped these last few months without you"

He gave her a watery smile.

Ida thought for a moment. "You really don't have any idea who could be behind the letters?" She asked finally.

"I don't think it could be anyone who met me post transition." He sounded pained. "Someone from the old days must've recognised me somehow. That part really pisses me off."

"What about boyfriends or family?"

"No." He frowned and chewed on his lower lip anxiously. "My mother died soon after I left home." He waved her concern away. "It's alright. I've had a long time to grieve for her. As for my Dad, I never met him."

"What about that JJ guy?" Ida prompted.

"He'd never do something like that! He had secrets too. We had a lot in common, both running away from things. We had such a strong bond. I wish I knew where he was now."

"You never know, maybe he'll turn up one day." Ida hugged him. "I'm glad you told me. You don't have to deal with this on your own anymore."

"Thanks darling." He squeezed her back gratefully. "And you won't breathe a word to anyone?"

"Course not." She was offended. "But I want you to tell me if you get any more letters, phone calls or anything."

He nodded. "Okay."

"I think someone's trying to scare you. You know so you'll cave when they finally come to you with whatever demands they have, probably money. You're not to give them anything." She told him sternly.

"But..."

"Trust me, okay?" She stood up and they began to walk slowly home.

"Oh bloody hell Ida. I bet you weren't expecting all this drama after your big night. The tangled webs we weave, eh?!

"Indeed."

She found herself thinking of Steve. Blaine's disclosure had changed their friendship somehow, and she felt she might be able to talk to him about her own past one day. Tonight wasn't the right time, but sometime soon.

Chapter 30. Vienna and the Black Cock

Vienna arrived at the Black Cock in a foul mood. She'd just had a meeting with Leonard Fitz-Patrick, Director of 'Queen of the Night' the West End Musical. Being her new husband's close friend and associate she'd assumed herself practically guaranteed a small part at the very least. Unfortunately Leonard had other ideas; he'd wanted her to audition for fuck's sake.

She gulped down a white wine spritzer. On reflection, it mightn't have been a bad idea to have something prepared for that eventuality, but hindsight was of little use to her now. Leonard had not been impressed. Well, neither would her hubbie when she told him how she'd been treated. It'd been so humiliating. He'd actually suggested singing lessons... SINGING LESSONS! Indeed!

Vienna knew that she had a beautiful voice, obviously this was a man who wouldn't know talent if it painted itself purple and did one-handed cartwheels naked in front of him.

Huffily she ordered another drink and peered round the pub for signs of Gypsy. The last thing she felt like doing was sitting in a bar waiting for her deeply unreliable school 'frenemey' to appear. The catch up she'd suggested seemed more than a bit redundant with no exciting news to gloat about. Now she came to think about it, Gypsy was always at least half an hour late for everything. Damn her.

"Rina?" Lisa elbowed her girlfriend in the ribs. "Who's that girl doing the Macarena with Jeremy?" She narrowed her eyes and sighed. "She looks familiar, but I can't place her."

Marina looked up from her magazine and raised her eyebrows at the sight of an extremely drunken woman stumbling around with an even drunker Jeremy amidst much clapping. She recognised her instantly as a friend of Gypsy's. Her lips seemed to have inflated considerably since she'd last seen her, and judging by her gravity defying boobs they weren't the only thing to have been augmented. Right now her pale blond hair was backcombed to the hilt and she was poured into a tiny mini-dress. "It's one of Gypsy's mates. God, she's been here ages, I saw her knocking back the vino before seven."

"Well it shows." Lisa said pointedly. "And it looks like we're going to have to throw Jeremy out again. He promised me he'd behave himself after the last time."

"So what's new?"

Lisa put her hands on her hips. "At this rate we're going to have to get rid of them before they do themselves or someone else an injury. If you deal with the girl I'll ask Dario to help with Jezzer."

"What, now?" Marina was unhappy. "It's my night off."

"Tough." Lisa retorted sounding stressed. "If you don't I'm just going to have to kick her out myself and I'm only going to lose my rag. Do you know how many other things I should be getting on with right now?"

"Okay, okay... I'll see what I can do."

"Thanks, love you." Lisa blew her a kiss as she hurried off behind the bar to find Dario.

Folding away her copy of QX resignedly Marina made her way through the bar to where the inebriated society girl was crawling around on the floor trying to recover a shoe and helped her up.

"Come on, why don't you sit up here?" She led her over to one of the chairs giving Jeremy a warning glare as he tried to grab his dancing partner back.

Vienna looked up, eyes unfocused.

"I know you!" She cried triumphantly, nearly poking Marina's eye out as she jabbed a finger at her. "You're Gypsy's friend... Maureen?" Her voice was surprisingly husky. It sounded as if it belonged to someone else; someone who'd spent the last decade chain smoking. I'm just here to see Gypsy except she's a little late."

"Looks like you've been stood up." Marina handed over the escapee perspex heel.

Vienna grabbed it treating her to a dazzling, game-show hostess smile, revealing toilet-bowl white veneers. "Yes, I've been waiting, and waiting and WAITING... and now ay'm a bit pished."

"Well she's not here and it's nearly closing time. Will you be okay to travel home? Maybe I should call you a cab?" Marina looked doubtfully at her; she didn't seem in a fit state to travel anywhere.

"Ay've just moved house... Oh dear, can't remember zackly where we live." Vienna thought hard, her eyes nearly crossing with the effort. "Somewhere in Knightsbridge?"

Marina sighed.

"No! Silly me! I mean Battersea."

"Okay look... you can stay in the flat tonight, but only coz you're a friend of Gypsy's. I'd feel guilty if you got attacked and cut into small pieces on your way home." She added darkly.

"Ooooh, I think I've pulled." Vienna slurred still laughing. "Did you know this is a gay bar? I've had such a good time!"

"Mmm." Marina ignored her, caught Lisa's eye across the room and gave her a murderous look. "Now come on, try not to fall over... one foot in front of the other."

Taking her completely by surprise Vienna attempted a drunken snog. The smell of alcohol was overpowering.

Swearing under her breath, Marina extracted herself and manhandled her charge up the stairs towards the flat. Angrily

171

she resolved that next time she had a night off it'd be spent as far away from the pub as possible.

X

"Oh shag!" Gypsy exploded checking her watch.

James jumped, splashing vodka and coke on to his top. He brushed himself off and gave her a hard stare.

"Well? What is it, then?" He asked impatiently. They'd bumped into each other by chance in Compton's and had been drinking and gossiping for the last hour.

She thumped her hands on the table in frustration. "I completely forgot, *bugger* it. I said I'd meet Vienna at the Black Cock tonight about two hours ago. Oh fecking hell."

"Uh oh." He tutted.

She tapped a number into her mobile phone and then listened for a few moments. "She's not picking up."

"Don't you worry your pretty little head; she'll be long gone by now. No offense darling, but everyone knows what you're like." He leant forward. "Now there's this fab new club I've been dying to check out. Are you're up for it?"

"Maybe." She was distracted. "Isn't that Duncan over there by the pool-table?"

James craned his neck in the general direction she was looking at.

"So?"

Gypsy was already on her feet. "I need to ask him to pass my number on to Ida Swann, you know... the model?" She explained her eyes fixed on Duncan's back. "We used to know each other and I wanted to get back in touch."

"Just don't direct his attention this way." James pointed to the stairs. "That's his boyfriend Ash snogging the face off some random guy."

"No problem. Didn't you know tact is my middle name, James?" She smirked before heading off in Duncan's direction.

X

The next morning, flummoxed to find herself in a strange room, Vienna blearily tried to think through her bone-crushing headache. Where in the hell was she?

Far more worryingly there appeared to be a lump under the duvet beside her, a lump which looked suspiciously like a sleeping body. She frantically tried to get her brain into gear. But it was no use; the evening remained an ominous blank in her memory. Lifting the covers cautiously and peering underneath only confirmed her worst fears. She was naked.

Cautiously she began edging her way to the end of the mattress, taking special care not to wake... whoever. Just as she'd swung her legs onto the floor a loud yawn emanated from under the bedclothes. Without warning an arm flung itself over the empty space where she'd been lying. An unmistakably female arm.

Vienna's heart began to thump in panic as she got a flash back of being in some kind of an embrace with someone, a girl. Could she have... got drunk and slept with her??? She began scrabbling around on the messy bedroom floor for her clothes. Fuck. She'd only been married two minutes.

"Hello there."

The voice made her jump as a mussy-haired Marina, that lesbian friend of Gypsy's, emerged from below the quilt.

"You okay?" Marina sounded half-asleep; she put her head back down on the pillow before muttering. "If you're looking for your shirt someone spilt beer on it, just grab something of mine and give it to Gypsy after, alright?"

Spying a black T-shirt slung over the door that didn't look too crumpled Vienna slipped it over her head, collected up her shoes, a speedy exit had never seemed more in order.

X

Later on, alighting from a Circle Line tube at Sloane Square Vienna was feeling fragile.

In a state of paranoia she fumbled around in her bag for her tube pass before joining the throng of passengers heading towards the exit. She felt as if everyone knew exactly what she'd been up to the night before. She was convinced a group of teenaged boys had been whispering about her... Then a girl on the train had broken public transport etiquette to give her a friendly smile. Something was clearly very wrong.

Feeling in urgent need of ten gallons of espresso and a new head she tried to quiet her nerves whilst power-walking homewards. After all, she'd just woken up in bed with a woman. She was in shock. Perhaps her anxiety was a natural side effect. Or, she thought hopefully, maybe she'd been drugged. She jabbed her keys into the front door hearing the locks click open comfortingly. Yes that must be it; maybe some kind of hallucinogenic. Of course, it was the obvious explanation. How awful!

Once inside she kicked off her shoes and leaned her back against the front door. At last she felt herself start to unwind. Now for that coffee and then the world would start to make sense again.

Catching a glimpse of herself in the hallway mirror she stiffened. She pulled the T-shirt off, tearing it over her head and laying it right side up on the floor. 'NOBODY KNOWS I'M A LESBIAN' it read.

Chapter 31. Paranoid Proposals

Several hours later, a sleepy eyed Marina stumbled out of bed. Orlando the cat greeted her enthusiastically, rubbing his face against her bare ankles in a wanton display of cupboard-love; she clearly wasn't the only hungry one.

She sniffed the air, from the kitchen came the unmistakable smell of...

"Pancakes!" Dario confirmed cheerfully as he poured more batter into the frying pan and adjusted the strings of Lisa's apron around his waist. "I thought I'd make us a nice breakfast, and voila!" He indicated the kitchen table, where a steaming plateful of the sugared crêpes sat waiting for her beside a pot of tea. "I got golden syrup."

She blinked, wondering if she'd somehow entered a parallel universe. The table was laid for two. In the middle a vase of flowers jostled for space with a bowl of lemon-halves and containers of jam, syrup and sugar.

"It's not Shrove Tuesday is it?" She sat herself down squeezing some lemon on top of her mouthwatering plateful.

"Nope." Dario tossed the pancake he was cooking into the air, barely catching it in the pan. "Oops!" He turned the gas off and eased it onto his plate before pulling up a chair opposite her. "It doesn't have to be a special occasion for me to do something nice for you, does it darling?"

"Well no, I suppose not." She broke off and chewed on a mouthful. "These are really nice. Thanks."

175

He just smiled. "Tea?"

She nodded and he poured them both a cup, passing her the milk and sugar.

"All I can say is that seeing this Vincent bloke must be agreeing with you." She helped herself to two lumps and lots of milk. "You certainly seem happy."

"Oh Marina! I am. I'm sooo happy, I think it's really love this time."

"Woah, take it easy! You've only just met him."

Dario looked misty-eyed. "I've never felt like this way before though. Honestly, we had the best evening last night."

She sighed. "I'm glad for you. I had to share my bed with a drunken punter."

He waggled his eyebrows at her comically. "And that's not good?"

"No! It was a friend of Gypsy's who came in and got absolutely paralytic. She was in such a state I had to let her stay upstairs. God, she snored like a lawn-mower, it's a wonder I got any sleep at all."

She finished her breakfast and dumped her plate in the sink.

"Oh, would you like me to fetch you a coffee while you get dressed." Dario asked.

Marina looked at him suspiciously, wondering if the real Dario had been kidnapped by aliens and this was a convincing impostor. A few minutes later he knocked on the door, a steaming cup in one hand and a newspaper in the other.

"For you Madam." He said cordially handing them both over.

She eyed him warily. "Okay, that's it! Tell me what you want."

He took a deep breath and sat down on her bed his eyes big and hopeful.

"Now you come to mention it, there is one tiny little favour I need to ask you Marina sweetheart." He said in a wheedling tone.

She folded her arms across her chest. "Oh yes?"

176

"It's actually quite a big ask. But you're my most trusted friend, and I'll understand completely if you're uncomfortable with the idea."

"Uncomfortable with what idea exactly?"

"It's just that, well... God, this is harder than it looks in the movies."

"Dario? What the..."

"I hate to put you on the spot sweetie-pie, but without your help I'm going to have to go back to South Africa." His forehead wrinkled in angst. "I'm going to be deported."

"Bummer. Wait a minute, what do you mean without my help?"

He dropped to one knee grimacing slightly and looked up at her sheepishly.

"I was rather hoping you'd agree to marry me?"

Her jaw dropped open and he grabbed her slack hand.

"Please Rina, best friend in the whole world?"

There was a moment of stunned silence whilst Marina tried to gather her thoughts enough to respond.

"Hang on a second. You actually thought that I'd agree to this just because you made me pancakes?!" She spluttered finally.

"With syrup." He reminded her and then shut up quickly as he caught her warning look.

Chapter 32. Intruder

"Hi honey, I'm home!" JJ sang out from the bath as he skillfully finished shaving his legs whilst smoking a fag.

"I thought you were out." Mark caught sight of him through the door and hastily averted his gaze.

"My regular Tuesday man cancelled." JJ washed the shaving foam off his calves and stubbed his cigarette out in the ashtray, inadvertently dripping water all over the carpet. "You don't have to act all coy; we're all boys here." He pulled out the plug and stood up shivering. "Be an angel and pass me my towel will you?"

Mark grabbed it from the radiator and held it out for him. "I was going to get a DVD and some take-out this evening. If you're not doing anything, do you fancy it?"

"Yippee! Can I choose?" JJ wrapped his hair in the towel, turban-style.

"That depends, what did you have in mind?"

"Hmm, not sure. I'm easy, really."

Mark raised an eyebrow. "Well, I know that."

"Ho, ho; very funny. You're just jealous." He opened the bathroom cabinet and reached for a jar of anti-wrinkle cream which he began massaging into his face in smooth circular motions. "It's obvious you want me."

"Absolutely, you're right. I've always pictured myself walking in on a prospective boyfriend doing the hovering in a hot-pink bikini."

"I already explained... I was expecting Fred. Honestly, the way you go on at me, baby." JJ turned to face him, lower lip trembling mock tearful. "Sometimes I think you don't love me at all."

"Whatever." Mark smiled despite himself.

X

In the end they settled on 'The Girl with the Dragon Tattoo' and some Chinese. Mark busily transferred the various cardboard containers onto plates whilst JJ bought a blanket for them to sprawl on in front of the TV, throwing down some cushions for good measure. He switched off the big overhead light substituting it for two lamps that cast a cosy glow over the room.

"Here you go." Mark carried the steaming food in on a tray. "I have to say I'm a huge fan of take out... but I think it's all I've ever seen you eat. Do you never cook?"

"Not if I can help it." JJ pressed play on the remote control and arranged himself on the floor. "Sit!" He patted the space next to him.

"Well, how about if I cook for us tomorrow? Do you like Indian food?"

JJ took a mouthful of crispy seaweed. "Mmm. Yeah, I never say no to an Indian... or anyone else for that matter!"

Mark ignored him. "I'll cook lamb rogan josh and teach you at the same time, it's not hard. What do you say?"

"Alright, ta."

"You know what?"

"Que?" JJ looked at him, pushing back a strand of curly hair from his forehead.

"I know it's none of my business, but if acting and performing is your passion why don't you pack in the escorting and really make a go of it?"

"Darling." JJ grinned showing off his dimples. "I didn't know you cared. Don't you like the idea of sharing me with all those other men?"

179

"I'm just concerned. I mean you've already got a stalker... maybe two! You said one of them might be an obsessive client, I believe you used the adjective psychotic?"

"Thanks, but I know how to take care of myself."

They were interrupted by someone rapping loudly on the front door.

JJ jumped, spilling soy sauce all down his dressing-gown. "Bugger!"

"Are you expecting someone?" Mark asked frowning.

"No." JJ looked at him uneasily, and then they both heard the unmistakable sounds of someone trying to jivvy the lock.

"Stay here, I'm going to have a look." Mark got up stealthily and crept over to the front door where the handle was being twisted and turned from the other side.

"I can hear someone talking." He whispered. "I think there are two of them."

"Jeez Louise!" JJ yelped. "What do we do?"

"Shhh! Stay there." Mark got down on his knees and leaned toward the door. Bracing himself he lifted the flap of the letterbox as slowly and quietly as he could.

What he saw made him drop the flap so quickly he nearly jammed his fingers. Peering back at him was a pair of brown eyes staring beadily into his.

Chapter 33. Mixed Messages

Kate was typing away, finishing a spreadsheet for a two o'clock deadline when she felt a tap on her shoulder.

"Hey." It was James looking shifty. Sorry to disturb, but I have a message from Danny for you."

She frowned, setting aside her notes and glancing at the clock.

"Oh? And here was I thinking that you might've come round for a chat like you used to." She said pointedly. "Why are you his messenger boy all of a sudden? Where is he?"

"I know I've been a bit off lately. Please Kate, I think you should go talk to him. He's erm, waiting for you in the stationery cupboard."

"The stationery cupboard?!"

"Yeah." He gave her a look that instantly made her think he knew more than he was letting on.

"James, what the..."

"Just go okay." He patted her on the shoulder. "There's a lot you don't know about that boy, I've seen him... oh anyway, he'll want to tell you himself. I'll catch you later."

X

The stationery cupboard was huge, its aisles crammed full of supplies. It was also one of the few places in the building you could get a moment of privacy.

"Over here!" Danny emerged from behind several crates of printer ink. "Sorry for all the subterfuge, but this couldn't keep."

"What's all this about? I do have work to do you know." She said archly, and then her eyes widened dramatically. "Is this some kind of sexual fantasy thing? Like the mile high club only more corporate?"

He moved closer bringing his face nearer to hers. "Well that wasn't the plan," he murmured huskily, "but if you're up for it I won't say no."

"Danny! Stop it, someone could walk in." She pushed him away. "Look seriously, I'm busy. Tell me what's going on; James' obviously clued in, it'd be nice if I was too."

"He's not, I only told him to come get you." Danny looked puzzled and then shook his head. "Anyway, you're not going to believe this but I had a phone call from someone about Julian." He breathed. "I couldn't wait until five to tell you. Plus, I've arranged to meet him."

She was suitably shocked. "You've arranged to meet your brother?! Blimey, that was easier than we thought."

"No, not Julian. Someone who knows him." He said impatiently. "Let me explain."

"I think you'd better. Hang on a sec." She shuffled around uncomfortably finding them both boxes to sit on. "That's more like it, right, go ahead."

"Okay, well I got a call put through to me from reception." He began. "This guy demanding to know if he's speaking to Mr Jackson." He took a deep breath. "He says he wants to talk about Cordelia's and Grace Gillespie."

"Grace Gillespie! From the piece of paper that theatre group guy, Donald, gave us!"

"Exactly! That's when it hits me; this guy reckons he's talking to my brother."

"Go on." She urged staring at him expectantly.

"Well I had to think on my feet; so I said we should meet up to talk face to face. He suggested next Monday in a place called the Ku Bar." He paused. "Fuck knows why he thinks Julian works here though. That's a mystery."

"Hmm." She shook her head puzzled. "But why didn't you tell him the truth?"

"No way! If he found out I'm just the brother he probably would've hung up."

"So you're going to go along and what? Pretend to be your twin and see what you can find out?" She was worried.

"Uh huh, pretty much."

Kate looked at him unhappily. "But if this *is* the person who went to the theatre group then it sounds like Julian's in deep shit. God, this bloke could be in some kind of gang or anything."

He stood up. "Come on, this is great news! I'll sort something out so it's safe, like maybe bring someone with me, don't stress."

"Right, it sounds dodgy as hell to me. Did you get his name?" She joined him at the door.

"Bollocks! No. He assumed I knew him, I think." Danny shook his head. "I'd know his voice again though; he had a Spanish accent."

183

Chapter 34. No Business like Show Business

Stella drizzled bleach into the sink, scrubbing around the base of the faucet until her elbow ached. Feeling lightheaded from the fumes she rinsed off the area with hot water and finished up.

Wandering downstairs she came across Cathy chatting animatedly on the phone. It sounded like it could be work related. Her eyes gleamed as she thought of the plans they'd already made for creating Fraser Buchanon Actors and Entertainment Agency. The excitement and hope she felt around the project was undeniable. This was truly the start of a new career she could really put her all into. She sighed. The only downside was plunging headlong into a new business left precious little space for them to just *be* together.

"So?" She asked as the other woman finally hung up.

"It was Donald Willis from the Hillbrook Theatre Group; you know the one that Kate put me in touch with?"

"Do you think he'll be able to spread the word?"

"Oh, I think we can come to some sort of arrangement." Cathy said happily. "He needs help publicising his group. I dare say a certain well known actor's support will make the whole difference."

"Brilliant! Now we need to look into getting ourselves an office, I know it's expensive but preferably in the West End." Stella grimaced slightly. "We're staking our entire savings on this, doll. You do think it'll be a success, don't you?"

"Of course it will!" Cathy said passionately, clasping her hands together. "Don't forget I've spent my whole life in the business; I have contacts coming out of my ears. Put that together with all your public relations know how... and well, with a lot of dedication and hard graft, I know we'll succeed. This just feels right, don't you agree?"

"Yeah, it does." Stella nodded. "I just needed to hear you tell me again, I guess. It's wonderful, but scary too." She took a deep breath and smiled. "I'm so grateful to Tony for dragging me down to London with him. I mean not that long ago I had no job, no prospects and no one in my life. This is amazing Cathy. I can hardly believe it's all really happening."

"Well you better believe it." Cathy grinned and then looked thoughtful. "We'll have to think about hiring a couple of people to help us. Maybe Kate could be tempted away from her job? She'd make a splendid PA."

"What about clients?" Stella asked.

"I've got some ideas... which reminds me, family and friends! I want to tell everyone our news." Her face lit up. "What do you think about a dinner party?"

"Absolutely," Stella acquiesced. "And didn't you say you were thinking of representing Gypsy? You could run it by her then." She sneaked a glance at her partner. "Also, it might be.... you know, a good opportunity to let Simon and Tony know about us? If you don't think it's too soon..."

"Oh! You mean like a *coming out* party?" Cathy raised her eyebrows.

"Kind of." Stella eyes slide away bashfully. "I was thinking a celebration of the coming together of Fraser and Buchanan, in both senses of the word."

"Mmm." She looked slightly worried and splashed some brandy into a glass. "I suppose we should start drawing up a guest list."

"Are you sure?" Stella sensed her reluctance. "Because if you're having second thoughts, about me *or* the agency..."

Cathy shook her head mutely.

"Come on, talk to me." Stella cajoled.

185

"I'm sorry. It's nothing like that." Cathy's shoulders slumped. "It's Karl, damn him! I know I said I'd try and put this out of my mind but I won't feel right until he fucks off back to Sydney."

"Listen, you told Si his father was dead because you thought it was the right thing to do." The relief in Stella's voice was plain; this clearly had nothing to do with their relationship. "What were you supposed to say? Daddy ran off and left us because he didn't want to know and was too much of a coward to say so?"

"Yes! No..." With a trembling hand Cathy took a swig of her drink. "I don't know, maybe that would have been better, at least it would've been honest."

"I hate to see you beating yourself up like this; you've always done your best for Si. You adore him."

Cathy stared at her despairingly. "Well I don't think the feeling will be mutual when he finds out I've been lying to him his entire life. Oh, it was all very well when Karl was in Australia. I mean it's quite literally the other side of the world. But now he's back, what if they find out about each other? Si would never forgive me."

"You don't even know Karl's back here for certain." Stella pointed out. "It's been years; how sure are you that it was even him you saw in the café?"

"I married the man; I know what he looks like." She said grimly.

"You've got to let it go, or you'll drive yourself mad. Even if he is back, so what? It's a big city."

"It's a smaller world than we think, darling." Cathy said softly. "Si's been so secretive lately. I can't help thinking he already knows somehow."

"That's irrational. From what you've told me there's no way Karl could find him even if he wanted too. Besides if Si knew he'd confront you right away."

"I don't know. I *do* know that I can tell when my son's hiding something."

Stella picked up the phone and pressed it into her hand.

"Let's pick a date for the dinner right now and then you can call and invite him and Tony. I'm sure whatever's going on with him is completely unrelated to you or any of this Karl business, okay? Talk to him, you'll see I'm right."

"Yes, okay." Cathy sighed and nodded, but she couldn't shake the nagging feeling that her past was about to catch up with her.

Chapter 35. An Unwelcome Reminder

"This is great." Tony said kissing his boyfriend as they snuggled up together on the sofa watching TV. "Have I ever told you how much I love you?"

Si chuckled. "If I'd known this was the response I'd get I'd have rented this movie weeks ago."

"No idiot." Tony smiled tracing his jaw line with his index finger. "I mean us, you surprising me with dinner like that. I hate being mad at you."

"Agreed. I hate you being mad at me too."

"And thank you for the gorgeous meal; you'll make someone a lovely husband one day." He joked. "Apart from the whole being a stripper thing..."

Si snorted. "Isn't that what we're meant to want?" He quipped. "A whore in the bedroom and a chef in the kitchen? Or something like that. Anyway, my stripping days are so over, I couldn't keep it up long-term."

Tony grinned at him sliding a hand down his jeans. "Really. I've never noticed that being a problem."

"Ha, ha." He closed his eyes briefly and covered Tony's hand with his. "Did I mention Gypsy's working at the club tonight and George's gone to Brighton? For once we can do whatever we want, *wherever* we want."

"Is that so?" Tony rolled on top of him, tugging at the zipper on his flies.

"Wait." Si pushed him back and leapt off the couch. "I have something for you first!" He called over his shoulder. "I bought it after we fought, I can't wait any more! I'm dying to see your face when you open it."

After a few minutes he returned carrying a large, rectangular object covered in Miss Piggy gift wrap.

"Ta da!" He struggled over to the couch and set it down in front of his lover.

"What's this? You didn't have to get me anything." Tony gave a token protestation, completely failing to hide his delight.

"Open it! For godsake the suspense is killing me." Si danced around impatiently as his boyfriend got up and began peeling off the paper.

There was a moment of silence as Tony stared at the beautiful abstract painting he'd admired a month ago at a friends art exhibition they'd attended.

"You went back and bought it for me?" He was deeply touched. "It's too much Si; it must've cost you a fortune."

Si gave a small smile. "Well, I blew all my stripping money on it, so it may be a while before I can come on holiday with you. But I thought it was worth it. You raved about it all the way home."

Tony sat quietly looking at the exquisite paint strokes. "I love it... I love *you*, thank you."

"Come on then." Si said taking his hand. "Why don't we find a home for this in our room and then finish what we started?"

The phone rang, interrupting them.

"Hold that thought, why don't you go on up? I'll join you in a sec." Si kissed him forcefully on the mouth and grinning watched him walk upstairs. He grabbed the receiver on the third ring. "Yeah, this isn't a good time, can I call you back?"

"Hi." A familiar voice drawled. He recognized the slightly amused tone immediately and his breath caught in his throat. It was unmistakably the voice of God, from Nirvana.

189

"Sorry to disturb you, but I found your wallet down the side of the sofa when I was cleaning." God said casually. "Your number was inside."

Immediately awash with guilt and anxiety Si furtively glanced at the top of the landing to check for signs of Tony reappearing. "Er, thanks. But not to worry, I already cancelled my bank cards, so I'm only a couple of pounds and a library card down."

"That's a relief." God said sounding slightly sardonic. "Well it'd be nice to see you again anyway, if you're up for it?"

"I'm sorry, but I have a boyfriend and it's a bit complicated." He lowered his voice putting his hand over his mouth.

God didn't sound in the least bit put out. "Understood. Look, why not give me your address and I'll just send the wallet back to you."

Si clutched the phone, relieved and anxious to escape. "That's kind, thanks."

"No worries." God replied cheerfully. "Now, I'll just grab a pen... right, got one. Shoot."

X

Later Si and Tony were propped up in bed sharing a tub of Ben & Jerry's cookie-dough ice-cream when the phone trilled again. Si stiffened as he picked up the receiver, unconsciously leaning away from his lover's chest as he held it to his ear, but it was only his mum calling for a chat.

As they talked, Tony watched him, idly spooning up the rest of the melted dessert. Eastenders blared out of the television and Jezebel lay curled about his feet, snoring softly and flexing her claws. He felt his eyelids growing heavy; it'd been a long day. A few minutes later Si hung up and snuggled back under the covers.

Tony handed him back his spoon. "How's mother dearest?"

"You're not going to believe this." Si licked it clean and pitched the empty carton into the bin. "But I think something's going on between Mum and your friend." He waggled his eyebrows suggestively.

"What?! No way." Tony snorted. "The whole world isn't gay, you know. I think I'd have heard about it by now if Stella was a lesbian."

"I could be wrong." He admitted. "But she was going on about how *close* they are now and how *happy* she is."

"Huh! They're just getting along is all."

"Time will tell. We've been invited to a dinner party next Saturday at their place." Si said. "Oh and I suggested we invite Duncan, he's been in a bitch of a mood lately. I think Ash is giving him the runaround, maybe this'll be a chance for them to spend some quality time together."

Tony raised an eyebrow. "It is frustrating that you keep talking about people I've never met; and no offence but your friends seem a little odd. I mean, I like Kate and Gypsy's alright... apart from being a female drag queen and all. Don't you have any normal friends?"

"Normal? Not so much, no. But what's normal anyway?" Si pondered for a moment. "Ooh, that reminds me. Danny, Kate's boyfriend, is supposed to be meeting this dodgy sounding bloke in a few days who thinks he's his twin brother. Did I tell you about that whole saga yet?"

Tony moaned. "Stop it! No more tonight, please."

"Anyway, what do you mean about my friends?" Si was indignant. "Your own best friend is probably seducing my mother as we speak?"

"Enough already!" Tony protested. "What do I have to do to shut you up?"

Si smirked at him. "Well, I have a few ideas seeing as you're asking..."

Chapter 36. Live to Tell

When Blaine finally arrived home from the airport Ida was waiting for him, waving a copy of the Daily Herald frenziedly. "Oh my God! Are you okay?"

"Give me a break gurl! For heaven's sake, let me get in first." He snapped, looking frazzled and clearly in a foul mood. "Bloody traffic! It took hours for us to get back from Heathrow and the flight was a total nightmare. *God*, I need a drink."

The taxi driver helped stow his bags in the hallway and chastened, Ida grabbed a chilled bottle of Chardonnay from the fridge and set about opening it.

"So." She said finally, her back to Blaine as she poured the wine into glasses. "What the hell happened in Milan, and why do I have to wait until now to find out about it? Don't the phone's work over there?"

He massaged his temples and lunged for the glass which she proffered.

"I'm sorry darling." He drained it in a single satisfying gulp, holding it out for more. "I just couldn't face talking to anyone. I wasn't thinking straight. I *should've* called afterwards to let you know everything was okay, but there were back-to-back shows, it was hectic! What can I say? I'm sorry."

Ida stared at him, thinking that although his make-up was immaculate as usual, he looked gaunt and brittle; as if she hugged him he might snap in two.

"I can't believe you collapsed in the middle of the runway! You made all the front pages, what happened?" She took a sip of wine and tried to calm down; there was no point in upsetting him even more, after all.

He fluttered his hands about in a gesture of despair.

"I honestly don't know sweetie. I haven't been eating well; my sleeping pills stopped working... I'm all over the place." He ran his fingers through his short red-brown hair. "That's why I'm thinking if I'm offered the ✿*FX* contract I should just turn it down. I mean there'd be a lot more work and pressure and I'm clearly not up to it right now." He avoided his friend's eyes and looked at the kitchen clock.

"You can't do that. That'd be professional suicide and you know it!" Ida looked at him sternly. "And I'm worried about you. For godsake eat, heroin chic is so over."

"I want out Ida; it's all getting too much."

"Seriously? Modelling is your life, I understand that you're going through a lot at the moment, but giving up?" She frowned, and then her eyes grew round with understanding. "Oh shit. You've had another letter haven't you?"

Blaine let out a long defeated sigh, looked like he was going to say something and then nodded, hanging his head.

"Well?"

"It wasn't as cordial as the first three." He attempted a smile. "I won't go into all the gory details but whoever it is threatened to kill me and poor defenseless little Dior if I sign with Raoul Fahri. They also reminded me that if I talk to the police the press gets to know all about Grace Gillespie."

"Fuck, that's bad." She acknowledged. "I suppose its common knowledge that you've got a dog thanks to all the gossip mags."

He nodded, brightening slightly and reaching down to ruffle his pet's ears affectionately. "Ooh yes, he's *always* getting papped. He was in OK last week. He just loves the attention, don't you baby?"

193

"Right, well this just confirms what I've already been thinking. You can't go on like this. I mean it's affecting your health."

"I'll live."

"Let's hope so. But quite frankly you look like a skeleton." It was no time to spare his feelings. "I think it's time for you to call a press conference."

"What are you saying?"

"I'm saying that if you're ready to throw the towel in anyway you've got nothing to lose by telling the world the truth." She finished her wine off. "Look at it this way, the media attention will be great for raising your profile. Who knows, it may even work in your favour."

"Are you out of your mind?"

Ida shook her head. "Think about it. Once this is out in the open, you won't have to worry about it coming out any more. You'll have nothing to hide B, and this sick psycho-fuck will have nothing on you. You can go straight to Cecile who'll sort it all out with the police. FYI this is serious as hell you realise; okay it could be an empty threat, but what if it's not? Your life could be in danger."

"Gee thanks, you sure know how to make a boy feel better."

"So will you consider it?"

"I don't know. I'm so stressed right now I can't think. Sometimes I wish I was just a nobody!" He declared picking Dior up.

She raised her eyes and let out a sigh. "Well, I think it's your only way out, but it's up to you."

"The media will go crazy. Good grief, they'll find out I was a stripper and everything." He stroked the dog's ears as if to soothe himself. "I may never work again."

"It's a gamble you'll have to take." She said decisively. "Besides, I think you *should* tell them the whole story. It'll save you from worrying about assholes crawling out of the woodwork and selling stories."

Blaine looked unconvinced. "Maybe I should tell Nads. See what she thinks before I make a decision?"

194

"I don't think Nadia's in the best place to be offering advice right now."

"What do you mean?"

"I didn't want to bring it up but she's really gone overboard with the drugs lately." Ida sighed. "Everyone's talking about it."

"Nads is okay." He said defensively. "She's just got a new boyfriend, that indie rock guy. He's the reason she's partying so much."

Ida shrugged. "She hasn't been home all week and Cecile says she's losing work big time."

"I'll talk to her." He promised. "Damien Black! That's his name..." He chewed on his lower lip. "It sounds like he's a bad influence, huh?"

"Nadia can take care of herself; don't you think you should be focusing on your situation? What do you reckon? Tell the world the truth and set yourself free."

"Hardly! We'll be prisoners in our own home if I do that." Blaine looked at his nails and shuddered. "The paparazzi would literally camp outside in droves. It'd be a nightmare. I think there's a very real chance I'd have a breakdown if I had to cope with that in this state, and I'm not being melodramatic."

"Okay, I can't deny it'd be full on." Ida admitted, sloshing the last of the wine into both glasses. "They're nothing if not persistent."

"Like mosquitoes." He added. "I hate them."

They drank up in silence listening to the ticking of the clock and the gentle patter of rain falling. Outside it had grown dark and the wind railed against the window-panes.

"I don't want to be alone tonight." Blaine admitted in small voice. "You aren't going out are you?"

"No. I've got an early casting tomorrow; I need to be up at five." She grimaced. "Look, I had a sort of idea when I was talking to Duncan the other night, it may help with our press problem."

"Oh?"

195

She lit a Marlboro. "Theoretically speaking, let's say you go with the whole coming out scenario. What if I knew somewhere anonymous you could stay after you break the news? Somewhere *no one* would think to look for you?"

Blaine lobbed the empty wine bottle into the bin. "Is there such a place? You mean like a deserted tropical island?"

"Actually no, I was thinking you could stay with an old friend of mine right here in Blighty, just until the dust settles."

"Hrmph." He snorted. "Not very glamorous, darling. I liked my plan better. How do you know they won't sell me out?"

Ida was affronted. "I'm not an idiot! This person was the closest thing I had to a best friend back in the days."

He raised his eyebrows. "Maybe. A break would be amazing."

"Well, I have to ask first, but the beauty of it is no one can link the two of you, and this is no celeb. Who'd think to look there? As long as you stay indoors and lie low, that is." She eyed him meaningfully; Blaine had never really taken to lying low in her experience.

"I don't know if I fancy it after all to be honest sweets." He fingered his diamond teardrop earrings. "Staying with some dodgy geezer I don't know from a bar of soap and just hoping he doesn't tell the paps coz you *used* to be friends."

"Actually I think you two may like each other, besides, she's a girl not a dodgy geezer."

"Huh! Dodgy bird then. You know what I mean, a total bloody stranger." He retorted crossly.

"Fine, it's up to you. I just think it's a better plan than your other options – A) wait around to be murdered or B) drop out of modelling altogether and get a job in Kentucky Fried Chicken."

"Point taken." He put a finger to his lips. "I'll consult my horoscope and get back to you."

"Okay, in the meantime shall I phone her and see if she's even willing to have you, theoretically speaking?" Ida persisted.

"Yes, go on then, girl."

196

Walking over to the hallway mirror and peering into it anxiously he traced the hollows in his cheeks with his fingertips.

"I think I'd better order in some food. You're right, the waif look just isn't very me, is it darling? I'm positively haggard!"

Chapter 37. Introductions

"I'm starving!" Si announced as he and Tony walked up Old Compton Street towards Balans restaurant. They'd stopped at Costa for a coffee on the way and browsed in several book stores enjoying a lazy afternoon stroll in town.

"I love summer, everyone seems so much happier." He sighed contentedly. "Plus they wear less clothes."

"Aye, it's nice here now." Tony slipped an arm through his. "But you don't have to keep taking me out to eat you know. I'm just as happy cooking something, or even having a picnic in the park."

Si faked alarm. "You can't possibly mean that. Balans' food is divine and they have very cute waiters." He smiled. "Besides, tonight you finally get to meet the rest of the gang."

"I know. I'm just saying." He shrugged as they made their way inside and Si indicated to a generic, model type that they were joining friends. Following him to the back of the packed restaurant they quickly spotted the others and hurried over.

"Hello there guys!" Marina was wearing a maxi-dress, her hair piled haphazardly on top of her head and skewered with what appeared to be paint-brushes. "Take a seat, we haven't ordered yet."

"Hi Rina, hey there Dario." Si leant over the table to kiss them both. "This is my gorgeous boyfriend, Tony."

Dario reached out a hand. "It's so lovely to finally meet you. I'm the hot one – I expect Si's told you all about me."

Tony looked embarrassed as he took a seat. "Hey, it's nice to meet you both."

"And I'm Marina." Marina said with a friendly smile. "Would you like some wine? We got a bottle already."

"Thanks, I'll wait and get a Grolsh." He demurred.

"Well I won't say no." Si reached for the bottle and splashed some into his glass. "So, what is this big news you have to tell us.... or do you want to wait for Duncan?"

Marina and Dario exchanged glances.

"Well, let's run this by you two first and then we'll catch Duncan up when he arrives, he called to say he'd be a little late." Dario said finally, looking over at Marina who nodded slightly.

"The thing is..." She said looking up at them expectantly. "You'll have to keep this strictly confidential because it's, erm, not altogether within the confines of the law."

"Sounds interesting." Tony munched on a bread-stick and Si made an inquisitive face.

Dario took a sip of wine before blurting out. "I've fallen in love with Vincent Santelli."

"Dario! The important news first, alright?" Marina scolded.

"Huh! Well it's pretty major to me." He said indignantly.

Tony looked surprised. "Wow, that bloke off the TV... I didn't know he was gay."

"Vincent Santelli!" Si was aghast. "Seriously? You thought he was heterosexual. He makes Mark from Ugly Betty look butch."

Dario looked put out. "*Excuse* me."

Marina motioned they should all be silent.

"Let's start again." She suggested. "Now, the reason we're meeting here tonight, apart from the fact that we wanted your fabulous company." She added quickly. "Is to tell you I've agreed to marry Dario so he can stay in the country."

An astonished silence followed.

199

Si was the first to speak. "Sweets can't you get into trouble for that? Don't you think it's a little, well... extreme?"

"I'll get deported otherwise." Dario muttered. "That's extreme."

Tony shook his head, thinking that this evening was doing nothing to prove him wrong regarding Si's friends.

"Well, congratulations, I guess." He murmured.

"Thanks!" Marina beamed at him. "Lisa was the one who talked me into it, I mean it sounds mad but actually if Dario has to get hitched then I'm the obvious choice."

"Of course, it's perfect." Si said. "You're a lesbian with a girlfriend; Dario's gay, in love with a celebrity hairdresser and soon to become an illegal immigrant... I'm sure you'll be very happy together living above the Black Cock complete with downstairs darkroom. Why not at least get married to someone who's the right gender for you?"

"Like who? I don't think Vincent and I are exactly there yet. Think about it Si." Dario admonished. "The very fact we do already live together is what will make it work. Otherwise if people checked out our living arrangements things could get awkward. Besides we're friends, we know each other already and Marina's not going to want to marry anyone else."

"I just hope you've thought this through." Si said sounding worried.

"We have, trust me." Marina handed round the menus. "We're even going to have a big wedding to make it look more realistic."

"A church wedding?" Tony asked looking dubious.

"Oh no!" Dario shook his head. "Registry office deffo, but we want a big crowd and an after party of course! We thought we'd ask Duncan if he'd do the pictures."

"Wow." Said Si, "You've got it all planned out. Well, I hope we're invited is all I can say. Have you thought about what kind of dress to wear yet, Dario?"

"Ha ha, that's so amusing." Dario sniffed. "You won't be laughing when Marina makes you chief bridesmaid."

"Really? You were thinking of me?" Si looked chuffed.

"Actually babe," She admitted apologetically. "I already asked Gypsy, or should I say Faye Kinnett. She's also going to entertain at the after-party with some other acts we're booking."

"She told you about her alter ego? And she already knows about the wedding?" He looked hurt.

"Yes, I called to invite her tonight, but she's out trying to secure equal rights for femme drag artistes at the Pink Flamingo Club." Marina said, eyebrows disappearing under her fringe. "Or at least I think that's what she said."

"It means she's working as door whore again."

"Oh." She looked at Dario, who shrugged. "So, can we count on your discretion?"

"Of course." Si nodded.

Tony made a motion as if he was turning a key to his lips and throwing it over his shoulder. "Right, let's get some service around here." He suggested. "I'm starving. I think we've had enough drama... time for some food."

"Now you're talking, I'm positively wasting away over here." Dario agreed.

At that moment Duncan wandered over pushing his way through the crowded room and scowling furiously.

"Did any of you know that Ash is a rent boy?" He demanded looking round the table crossly without bothering to say hello.

Tony sighed; a steak and chips had never seemed so far away.

Chapter 38. A Blast from the past

Gypsy had just put the phone down after a lengthy conversation with James when the damn thing started ringing again. She paused from struggling into a tight monochrome mini-dress. After a final triumphant tug, she zipped herself up and grabbed the receiver in one hand whilst brandishing a mascara wand in the other.

"Hello, switchboard." She chirruped, sweeping liquid liner over her lashes with a practiced hand and peering at herself in the mirror. Hmmm, she thought, maybe nude lipstick would work with this look. Unfortunately after an earlier hair modelling assignment her normally dark, shiny locks were backcombed into a giant beehive and secured with so much hairspray, deconstructing it would take hours.

"Gypsy speaking?" She prompted.

"Oh good, I thought I had the wrong number." It was a woman's voice, unfamiliar.

"Who is this?" She asked impatiently.

"It's Ida, Ida Swann."

Gypsy sat up straight and abandoned her make-up.

"You're shitting me! Ida, is that really you?"

"Yes, it's me. I hear that Duncan is a friend of yours? He said you'd like to get in touch, so I thought I'd give you a ring."

"Fantastic! Wow, we've got so much to catch up on I don't know where to begin. Are you still with that bloke, was it Steve?"

"Actually I left him not that long ago. Turns out he was a total bastard. He used to beat me up, it was pretty much hell the whole time we were together."

"I'm so sorry, I had no idea. Why didn't you call? You could've *talked* to me."

"Oh god Gyps, we haven't spoken in so long. Besides, it's all ancient history. I'm alright now, I promise."

Gypsy sighed, picking up her lipstick and smoothing it over her mouth. "Well I'm glad about that, and congratulations honey.... you're fucking famous! It's unreal!"

Ida laughed. "Yeah, thanks! It's taking some getting used to. How goes it on the career front with you? Are you still acting?"

"Yep." She blotted her lips with tissue. "I've done quite a few commercials and I get odd bits in films now and then."

"Well, I believe in you. You were always brilliant at school."

Gypsy smiled down the phone fiddling with her black hoop earrings. "It's so good to hear from you sweetie, we'll have to meet up soon and talk properly. But I'm going to be more than fashionably late for a dinner party if I don't get off the phone right now."

"Damn. Sorry, I called at a bad time, huh?"

"Well yeah, but I'll be about later."

There was a brief silence.

"Actually, I have a favour to ask you."

"What?" Gypsy was intrigued, what an earth could she offer her fabulously successful erstwhile friend.

"It's a biggy." Ida warned. "You can say no."

"Go on. Spit it out!"

"Here goes." She heard Ida take a deep breath. "I have a friend who's in a bit of trouble. Nothing illegal, not that kind of trouble... anyway he's also a celebrity which complicates things somewhat."

"Yeah?" She'd forgotten all about being late. "Who is it?"

"I'll tell you that later. The point is, he's about to go public about... something. The press are gonna go nuts and he's been under a lot of pressure lately." She broke off. "You must think I'm only calling because I want your help.... I won't mind if..."

"Ida, just tell me!"

"He needs somewhere to hide out, away from the paps where no one can find him."

"You don't mean..."

"It'd only be for a little while, until things calmed down." Ida added quickly.

"You want me to hide a celeb for you?"

"Well... yes. He'd be no trouble really. Although you'd have to agree not to tell anyone and I mean *anyone*. Gypsy... *Gyps*?"

Gypsy remained silent, her mind working overtime. "Could I tell two trusted friends? You see I don't live alone, they'd have to know." She asked thinking fast.

"As long as you can count on them to keep their mouths shut, I guess." Ida sounded reluctant. "Look, maybe I shouldn't have asked. Why don't we just arrange to meet up soon, and I'll find somewhere else for my friend to stay."

"I'll do it." She tried not to sound too excited. She never had been able to resist a bit of scandal or a drama for that matter, and this promised both.

"Are you sure? I can't give you very much notice I'm afraid."

"When does he want to come?"

Ida sucked in her breath nervously. "Tonight?"

"Tonight?! Well, as I said I'm out until late."

"Late's good. I wouldn't be able to drop him off until about midnight."

"Okay. I'll expect... both of you then?"

"I can't believe what an angel you are! Thank you soo much." Ida gushed.

"Hey, what are friends for?" She replied glibly, fastening her handbag shut and blowing her reflection a kiss into the mirror. "Looks like I'll see you later then babe. Ciao ciao"

204

Chapter 39. An Unexpected Guest

His mother had dressed to impress, Si noted as he and Tony were led into the dining room. Cathy was resplendent in a black low-cut gown, ruby earrings and blood red lipstick. In stark contrast, Stella sported a loose pony tail and wore a flowing skirt and top. Her arms were decorated with silver bangles that moved and jangled as she prepared the drinks.

The table had been laid with care, cutlery and glasses gleamed and a beautiful arrangement of flowers sat in the center. Candles created a soft, romantic mood. Cathy fussed with the napkins before joining them by the porch.

"I'm so glad you could come tonight, both of you." She said warmly as they stood around sipping brandies. "It should be a lovely night, I thought I'd leave the garden door open so we can get some air it's so mild."

"What time will the other guest's be arriving?" Si asked helping himself to some Bombay mix.

"Soon." Her face was passive and inscrutable. "Stella and I wanted a chance to talk to you both before the party starts, so to speak."

Si looked at Tony but his boyfriend was studiously ignoring him. "Well. What is it then? Don't keep us in suspense."

Cathy took Stella's hand. "Stella and I are starting up an Actors Agency."

205

Si and Tony exchanged startled glances.

"That's fantastic news! " Tony exclaimed breaking into a broad grin. "I thought for a moment…"

Cathy put a hand up to stop him. "Actually that's not quite all." She was unable to keep the smile out of her voice as she put her arm round the other woman's waist. "The other thing we wanted to tell you is… we're together. I mean, as a couple."

Tony gaped at them before turning to Si who was looking infuriatingly smug.

"Do tell me what you think." Cathy reached over to take her son's hand. "I know this may come as a shock, but really this is the best thing that could've happened to me, I'm so happy."

Si smiled. "I knew it. I *knew* something was going on… and honestly I couldn't be happier for you guys."

Cathy reached over to stroke his cheek.

"Fuck me; I can't say I'm not surprised." Tony exhaled loudly pausing before catching Stella unawares with a huge bear hug. "Good for you though. I haven't seen you looking so well for years. I'm so pleased for you, my love, for you both."

"Stop it! You'll make my cry and ruin my makeup." Stella laughed throwing her arms around his shoulders.

"Well, I am glad you both approve. This is going to be a wonderful evening." Cathy adjusted the neckline of her dress self-consciously. "It was a bit of a gamble, you know. If you'd hated the idea this dinner would've been really awkward."

X

An hour later the dining room was full of laughter and the clatter of knives and forks against china. Cathy had finished serving everyone, and was now looking every bit the exuberant hostess. Stella watched her throw back her head, laughing infectiously at something Orlando Koffer - one of her actor friends - had just whispered to her. Kate and Danny were regaling the table with the story of their progress on the Julian front whilst Gypsy and Si bickered like siblings.

206

"Would you like some more mint sauce, Simone." Gypsy asked solicitously as she spooned some next to her delicious looking lamb and crispy roast potatoes.

"Don't call me that!" Si muttered contemptuously taking the jar and staring at her with mock horror. "And *why* do you have a pineapple on your head, this isn't fancy dress, you know?"

She rolled her eyes. "I had a hair modelling job as you very well know and I was too busy to re-style it."

Just then Duncan burst into the room followed by a tall, distinguished looking man with grey hair and the most beautiful cerulean eyes Gypsy had ever seen.

"I'm so sorry we're late!" Duncan cried swooping down to kiss Cathy on both cheeks. "The bus broke down, would you believe it. This is my date, Karl. Ash will not be joining us."

The man stepped out from behind him, his lips curved in a smile at the expectant faces looking up at him from around the table. Si suffered an immediate coughing fit, almost choking on his mouthful of wine as he found himself looking straight into the memorable eyes of God Himself.

Meanwhile Stella couldn't help noticing something was wrong with her partner. Cathy's face had gone a deathly white, making her rouge stand out unnaturally. She frowned, bewildered and increasingly concerned. Finally the penny dropped... Karl. Somehow the unthinkable had happened. Karl Fraser had engineered an invite to the party; Lord knows how he'd even known about it. She watched, transfixed with horror, as muttering something under her breath, Cathy excused herself and raced off to the kitchen.

Not seeming to see anything amiss, Duncan sat down and pulled out the empty chair next to him for Karl.

"Hi there." Gypsy said oblivious to the potential time bomb that had landed and thrown her hosts into disarray. She gave Duncan a smile before turning to his date and stretching out a hand to be shaken.

"Lovely to meet you, I'm Gypsy, and this is Si, his boyfriend Tony. Oh and Kate, Danny and erm, I'm not sure of everyone else's name." She waved an arm to indicate the remainder of the guests.

Karl took her hand in a firm shake. "Hello, good to meet you."

They made small talk for a while but Gypsy fought to give him her full attention. Ever since Kate had introduced her to her boyfriend earlier on that evening, she'd found it impossible to stop surreptitiously checking him out. Again and again she found her eyes drawn to Danny. Although she'd warmed to him immediately, one thing was bugging the hell out of her. He looked so familiar somehow. Despite wracking her brains she couldn't place him.

Meanwhile Duncan carved himself a slice of lamb off the joint and chatted to Tony explaining how he'd finished things with Ash, for good this time, whilst Si hastily tried to recover his composure.

As Danny turned round unexpectedly and caught Gypsy staring leaving her red-faced, there was a loud crash and shattering noise from kitchen.

Gypsy looked away startled. "Oh dear, was that the sound of a glass breaking?"

People stopped talking mid-sentence, a pregnant silence ensued until Stella got up to investigate and muted conversation tentatively resumed.

Karl looked across the table at Si, poker faced as he ate his meal and engaged in small-talk with Donald Willis. Mentally he prepared himself for his wife's return to the table. As he'd suspected, it looked as if Cathy had been keeping more than a lesbian lover under her hat.

X

Later when Si snuck out to the kitchen Karl followed on the pretext of getting a glass of water.

"Hello." He said walking up behind him. "I thought I might as well return this seeing as you're here." He extended the battered leather wallet in one hand.

208

Si turned around and froze in the action of scrapping his broccoli into the bin.

"What the hell are you doing here?" He asked angrily.

"Having dinner." Karl was composed. "Duncan and I hooked up the other night and he mentioned he was going to this little shindig. I did guess we had a mutual friend in common when he talked about his mate Si who worked at the Black Cock."

Si felt a burst of rage. "Why did come? My boyfriend's right next door."

"Relax. I'm not here to see you." Karl remarked mildly. "I used to know your mother actually, here take this will you." He pressed the wallet into Si's hand.

"What? I don't believe you... Mum acted like she'd never set eyes on you." But his anger ebbed away leaving him feeling uncertain and foolish.

"It's a bit embarrassing, she's obviously forgotten all about me. We used to work together." Karl helped himself to a fresh glass from the cabinet and began filling it with tap water.

"So you really didn't come here to find me?"

Karl chuckled. "Don't flatter yourself. I'll admit I did wangle an invite to dinner – but that had nothing to do with you. Like I said I wanted to see your mother."

"Look, please could you keep quiet about me spending the night at yours." Si looked away from him. "Tony and I have only just got through a rough patch we don't need more trouble."

"Let me put you out of your misery." Karl said kindly. Nothing happened that evening."

"Really?" Si relaxed visibly. "I mean... I wasn't sure. Thank fuck for that. No offence."

Karl shrugged good-naturedly. "You passed out about five seconds after you arrived."

"Right. Well, thanks for telling me." Si gave him a sheepish smile. "Sorry if I was a bit paranoid. Let's go back in shall we or all the lemon meringue pie will be gone."

209

"Now *that* would be a tragedy." Karl followed him out of the room.

X

Cathy waited until she'd waved goodbye to the last of her guests and Stella had taken the dogs out before turning to face her husband.

"Hello Karl." She said in an icy tone. "I was wondering when you'd come back. Twenty two years is rather a longer time than I anticipated, but better late than never." She sat down like a queen in her armchair and gestured that he should take the couch.

"I'll give you five minutes to explain what the fuck you're doing here before I throw you out, you bastard." She said smiling pleasantly and checking her elegant silver watch.

"Starting right now."

Chapter 40. Letting Go

Si and Tony arrived back at Kershalton Street an hour or so after Gypsy herself, having enjoyed a couple of pints in town en route. She watched them from the bay windows, peering around the heavy damask curtains and had the front door open before they'd even located their keys. Ushering them both into the sitting room she glanced furtively up and down the damp street before pushing the door shut and joining them on the sofa.

"I've got something to tell you both." She said sounding serious. "And it's very important that you don't mention a word of this to anyone outside of the house."

Tony frowned and continued his tussle to detach Jezebel's claws from his denim-clad leg where she'd velcroed herself. Si took a gulp from his can of redbull hoping the caffeine would sober him up for whatever Gypsy had in store for them. He decided that last pint had probably not been prudent.

"Okay, I'm going to have to explain this in a hurry, and we should tidy up a bit while I'm talking." She said, propelling herself into action and throwing cushions on armchairs whilst simultaneously gathering up rubbish for the bin.

"Well, come on then! We have a guest arriving in...." She looked at her watch and bit her lip. "About twenty minutes."

"Guest?" Si queried, puzzled.

It took her a good fifteen minutes to explain the favour that she'd agreed to do for Ida as they helped her clear food debris and lager cans away. When she'd finished, Tony was shaking his head ruefully and muttering to himself.

"A mad house, that's what this is.... What have I got myself into?"

Si meanwhile was trying hard to contain his excitement, a celebrity living with them! This was the BEST news ever! He mentally ran through a list of prospective supermodel flatmates. He tried to decide whether he'd prefer their mystery guest to be Rosa Barr, Nadia Olsen or Kat Romanoff. He'd always thought Mina Foxe sounded like she'd be a right laugh, but how fab to be sharing a bowl of cornflakes with someone like Fleur Ascott or Trinity Short in the morning? – Then a thought occurred to him.

"Gyps darling, I know it's easily done taking into account the measure of which he enriches our lives... but aren't you forgetting our fourth housemate?"

He sprayed air freshener around the room and arranged the magazines into a fan shape on the coffee table. "You know... the one with social phobia and a problem with manners."

"Aye, it's no bother far as I'm concerned, but shouldn't George get a say?" Tony raised an eyebrow. "Besides, he seems like a shifty lookin lad to me, can you trust him to keep this a secret?"

Gypsy knocked back the glass of wine she'd poured to steady her nerves.

"That's taken care of." She said checking her hairdo in the mirror for loose strands. "I told him that we'd be having a model who needs a bit of privacy after giving the press some pretty major details of his life, and he was very sympathetic."

"He was? Ooh and it's a *male* model?" Si voice rose in glee. "Why didn't you say? I just assumed it'd be a girl. This puts an entirely different slant on things!"

"Yeah, I don't know who, but it's a bloke." Gypsy said. "Oh and I may be glossing over a few details. George actually wasn't thrilled."

"Did he kick up a fuss?" Tony wanted to know.

212

"He gave his notice, he's moving out in a month." She emptied the ashtray and light up a Marlboro. "But Si didn't want him here anyway." She added defensively. "Let's face it; he won't be a huge loss."

Si shrugged and rested his head on his boyfriend's shoulder. "This model will be paying rent?"

"Yes, I'm sure we'll be financially compensated for our trouble." She replied breezily.

"Hang on a sec. Where are we going to put him?" Si asked doubtfully. "You can't just park a celebrity on the sofa with Jezza and throw an old coat over him you know... What will he think? This is just too embarrassing for words."

"Relax guys." She said looking stressed. "I've got a queen-sized bed; he'll just have to share with me. It won't be for long."

"Huh! I distrust your motives Mz Wright." He said narrowing his eyes suspiciously.

"Oh, shut up Simone." She retorted. "I need time to think, time to prepare and to..." She broke off having lost her chain of thought.

Seconds later, the doorbell rang.

X

The tall, thin figure shivering on their doorstep behind Ida was swamped in a huge mohair coat and Jackie-O style sunglasses. Nevertheless it was immediately obvious to the occupants of number sixty-nine that their guest was none other than Blaine Feynard.

Gypsy found herself wondering if God had a sense of humour and wishing she'd drunk more wine. She felt almost paralyzed by the sheer randomness of having her biggest celebrity crush show up literally at her front door.

Ida smiled at her gratefully as she and the boys ushered their guests inside. Her fear dissipated somewhat as she noticed how wan and pinched the supermodel's face looked, and how alarmingly his legs resembled twin toothpicks.

213

Si tried not to look disappointed and rushed off to the kitchen to put the kettle on. Meanwhile, rising admirably to the occasion, Tony greeted them warmly, taking Blaine and Ida's coats as they followed Gypsy into the - still not exactly tidy - living room.

After a polite half hour of small talk over coffee during which Ida and Gypsy caught up on old times and Blaine remained fairly subdued, Si and Tony retired to bed.

A hush descended on the household as the three of them were left to discuss the living arrangements, the silence only broken by their muted conversation and the ticking of the kitchen clock.

From outside the house retained its air of normality.

A police car's siren and the sound of late night traffic through rain-slicked streets barely disturbed the blanket of night-time quiet that fell over the residential area.

X

Unnoticed by anyone, a dark blue Volvo reversed into Collingdale Terrace and then made a sharp left turn before quitting Kershalton Street. A pink pair of furry dice dangled from the rear-view mirror and its battered trunk sported a sticker which read *"Can go from zero to bitch in 2.2 seconds."* The side doors were liberally decorated with rust.

George Duboit put his foot down on the accelerator and eased the car into second gear as he swung into the Fulham Palace Road. It couldn't be a coincidence that Blaine of all people was here, right now at his place. First the very bloke he'd been gathering information on in Brighton shows up as a guest and now this! Somehow things had gone badly awry and he was ready to tell Raphael they could forget the whole plan.

However that said, he thought, coke fuelled mind feverishly ruminating on possibilities, maybe he could at least still make some money before cutting his losses. He reached for his mobile phone and tapped in a number, keeping one hand loosely on the steering wheel.

214

The phone rang once, twice, three times before its owner picked up.

"Finally." A female voice snapped down the line. "I've been ringing you all evening. I need you to come by my place, tonight George."

The line went dead in his hand. He grinned to himself and started humming the theme tune to 'Dynasty'; a detour seemed to be in order.

Chapter 41. Espionage at the Ku Bar

The next evening brought threats of gale force winds although the temperature was surprisingly mild. Kate and Danny had arranged to meet Si at Piccadilly Circus after work. They had little trouble spotting him amongst the crowds. He had on huge platform buffalo's making him a good head taller than most of the other afternoon shoppers, plus he was wearing a Superman T-shirt.

"Are you sure you don't mind doing this?" Kate shouted to make herself heard. She put her free arm round his waist as the three of them set off down Argyll Street. "We can go by ourselves if you want."

"No way! I'm not about to miss out on the action." Si protested indignantly.

"Well, I really appreciate you coming." Danny pushed the hair out of his eyes as the wind whipped at his clothes. "Although you could've dressed down at bit mate. Talk about inconspicuous." He looked pointedly at Si's feet and sighed.

Si was abashed. "Sorry. I didn't think."

"Anyway, we're nearly there so we should separate now."

They came to a halt at the end of Carnaby Street. Si swaying dangerously thanks to his high-rise footwear and the blustery weather.

"Right, what's the name of the pub?" He asked, steadying himself and bending down to tighten the velcro on his boots.

"The Ku Bar." Kate supplied. "It's on Frith Street."

"The *Ku Bar?* I go there the whole time; you didn't tell me it was a gay bar."

Danny's face registered mild surprise, and Kate shrugged. Obviously it was news to them too.

"Curiouser and curiouser." Si mused. "Well, hopefully by the end of tonight we'll know a bit more than we do now. Although that's not really saying much. Why don't you go on ahead, Danny? You've plenty of time. Kate and I'll come ten minutes later. Sit somewhere obvious and we'll act like we don't know you, okay?"

"Okay, here goes." Danny grinned at them both nervously, giving Kate a quick kiss before he set off down the road. He turned his coat collar up against the wind feeling for all the world like a character in a James Bond film. Looking over his shoulder he gave them a little wave before disappearing into a crowd of Japanese tourists.

X

Half an hour later Kate sat up straight to get a better view of her boyfriend as Si returned with a second round of drinks. They'd chosen seats on a little sofa by the window which gave them a birds eye view of Danny propped up against the bar with a beer, alone as of yet. Hopefully Si would have no trouble slipping out and tailing whoever showed up after they were done.

She smiled nervously as he handed her a Bacardi and coke and slid into the space next to her.

"I can't stand the suspense." He confessed taking a gulp of his drink. "It's positively painful, are you sure Danny got the right Ku Bar? There are two you know?"

"Absolutely." Kate sipped at her own drink through a straw, and then used it to stir up the ice cubes. "It's only ten past. He'll be here, we just have to chill out and act natural."

"Okay, you're right. Let's talk about something else then, like we're just out for a drink." He thought for a moment. "I know what I've wanted to ask you! What do you think about Cathy and Stella getting together?"

217

She shook her head. "I can't believe it! I'm pretty stunned."

"I had an inkling I must confess."

"How do you feel about it? I mean, it's your mum."

He paused reflectively. "I'm glad she's happy. After all, she's been single since my Dad died. I'd kind of expected her to stay on her own forever which would've been pretty sad."

"The agency sounds like an excellent plan too." Kate said brightly. "That'll give her something to get her teeth into."

"Yeah, they're both really into it, exciting times!" He looked at her. "You know they've got their eyes on you, missy, for a receptionist."

"Well, I'm in, if the pay's right. It's not like working for Dennison Advertising fills me with joy. Also, it's a bit much Danny and I working together as well as living together, you know?"

They fell into a companionable silence as they drank and stole glimpses through the throng of punters.

"What on earth was up with Gypsy at dinner?" Kate asked finally, dragging her eyes back to Si.

He arranged his features into a neutral expression. "What do you mean?"

She looked at him. "Didn't you notice? She was all hyped about something and she said she wanted to talk to you and Tony. What was all that about?"

"Things are looking up at the Pink Flamingo Club." Si lied glibly. He was still very aware of the fact that Blaine Feynard's presence in the house mustn't be divulged. Even if it *was* all he could do not to shout it out to complete strangers on the bus.

She wore a doubtful expression. "Oh I'd figured it was something to do with Fraser Buchanan wanting to sign her up."

"Erm, yeah, she told us about that too."

"I think she liked Danny." She chewed on a nail. "Although she didn't really say, just that he reminded her of someone but she couldn't think who. I really wish she'd remember." She eyed him meaningfully.

218

He got her drift at once. "Ooh! You think she could've met Julian?"

"I know it's such a long shot. But we've both been so preoccupied with this search and getting nowhere."

"Hmmm. I think you're clutching at straws darling, sorry."

She sighed. "It's okay, you're right. It's all getting to me a bit, to be honest."

By the time they'd drained their glasses and Kate had gone to buy more, the pub was packed. She handed Si his pint and nodded over to where Danny sat amongst the other punters. "Fuck Si, it's nearly half past. Is anyone here yet? Some fat bloke's blocking my view."

He craned his neck. "Mmm... Well, he's not alone."

"Omigod!"

"Don't get too excited. From the looks of things it's a group of kids on their way out clubbing. Uh oh. I think he may need rescuing."

"Oh." Her shoulders drooped. "Bollocks!"

Si was already on his feet. "You stay there, I'll be right back."

He made his way over to where an awkward looking Danny was surrounded by boys in their late teens. They were persistently trying to engage him in conversation.

"There you are, darling." Si said throwing his arms round him and giving him a big smacker on the lips. "I was just beginning to think you'd left me and copped off with one of these lads. You know how jealous I get."

The boys backed off reluctantly as the two of them walked back over to where Kate was waiting anxiously.

"Well, that's that then." Danny said grimly. "He's not turned up."

"I'm really sorry." She got up to give him a hug. "But we'll think of something else, we'll find Julian soon I know it."

He looked away, his expression brooding. "Fuck it. It's no good. Trying to find my brother in this city is like looking for a needle in a bloody haystack. I give up."

Si tried to intervene. "I'm sure there are other avenues you can explore."

219

"No." Danny shook his head. "Thanks guys, for all your help. But I'm just going to let this one go. Your mum was right Si; he obviously doesn't want to be found. If he does, he knows where the family are. I should never have come here... It was stupid."

"Danny..." Kate put a hand on his arm.

He sighed. "Just leave it, Kate."

"But what will you do?" She asked, racking her brain for some brilliant words of encouragement and finding they eluded her.

"I don't know, go back to Manchester, I guess. What else is there to do?" He said gruffly. "Look, I'll see you both later. I need to be by myself for a bit to think."

Silently they watched him walk out into the night, disappearing round the corner down Old Compton Street.

"I guess I'm not worth sticking around for then?" Kate said in a hollow voice, as Si put his arm around her.

"He doesn't mean it. He's just upset, chicken."

She sniffed. "Come on, let's go. I think I'll stay with Cathy and Stella tonight, if they'll have me."

"I'm sure they'd like that." He kissed the top of her head and they both made their way back to the tube, their progress only slightly hindered by Si's footwear.

Chapter 42. Queen of the World

Gypsy schlepped through the supermarket lost in thought as she steered her trolley through aisles of canned fruits and vegetables. She'd gone shopping partly because they were fast running out of groceries at number sixty-nine but predominantly because she needed to get away from their resident supermodel.

She picked up a couple of cans of tuna for Jezebel before heading to the magazine section, like a moth to a flame. (She simply couldn't stop thinking in eighties song lyrics and if that wasn't a sign of infatuation she didn't know what was). Si had been right, she admitted to herself; in retrospect it had perhaps not been the wisest of moves for their guest to share her room and most definitely not her bed.

A week had passed since the socialite had landed in their lives. No one could have forecast the meteoric rise in Blaine's fame since his story broke. Waves of controversy and speculation swept the nation; the model's name seemed to be on everyone's lips. Consequently there was nowhere Gypsy could go where she wasn't bombarded with his image. Even the television was no longer safe, the last time she'd flicked over to channel five Blaine's revelations were being discussed on the Jeremy Kyle show.

As she passed by the row of glossies she saw his flawless face in place of the ubiquitous Katie Price or Kerry Katona. There was no doubt about it, she thought picking up a copy of the Sun with a shot of him looking stunning and enigmatic. Yet again she'd fallen for someone entirely unsuitable. What an idiot. The headlines leapt out at her.

BLAINE FEYNARD! QUEEN OF THE WORLD WAS ONCE A GIRL! See page 2 for the full story.

Perturbed, she thought to herself that there was nothing worse than being madly in love with someone whom ninety percent of the population were currently fascinated with; especially when you were also the wrong gender. In fact getting Blaine to reciprocate her feelings would be on a par with trying to climb Mount Everest in ballet shoes... wrong er... footwear. She took a couple of the magazines she thought he might be interested in.

Already they'd spent days holed up in her room together reading through the tabloids, Blaine shrieking with laughter at the more amusing blatant lies and Gypsy trying to distract him from the pieces that were upsetting. It seemed that the world couldn't get enough news of the über camp male model who'd been born female. It gave her no relief whatsoever that she was far from the only one to be struck down by a bad case of Blaine-it is. Actually it made her feel slightly sick. None of the others actually knew the real person like she did. Work also provided little relief as she struggled with the depressing reality of being stuck on the door at the Pink Flamingo Club.

Half-heartedly she filled up the trolley with ready-meals before heading over to the wine and spirit aisle. Kylie's 'I Can't Get You Out of My Head' was now playing over the tannoy. Unbelievable. The worst part of the situation was that in Blaine's seclusion she'd become his willing companion and enabler. Now it seemed she was headed in the direction of new best friend as well. The fact that he trusted her so implicitly made her feel guilty. Although she'd tried, her feelings could not be described as remotely plutonic.

If only they didn't get on so well. Their talks took them through the long summer days spent inside and the sleepless nights when the bored model would become restless and full

222

of energy. It was clearly making him miserable being coped up like a hostage, although for the time being it seemed his best option.

Si and Tony's presence eased the tension somewhat and after the initial strangeness of the situation Blaine and the other occupants of the house had relaxed around each other. Their guest was undeniably entertaining, keeping them all amused with stories of his old days in Soho and tales of fellow celebs. Gypsy had already skived nights off work, unable to say no when he pleaded with her to stay and keep him company. She seemed to be powerless to stop her crush from developing. Letting out a long sigh she vowed to adjust her attitude. A friend was clearly what he needed right now.

Mindlessly she bagged her purchases and set off home. If only he wasn't so comfortable walking around naked; although she wasn't sure how to put a stop to that without sounding like a prude. Maybe she'd just try harder not to look; unless it was absolutely unavoidable of course...

X

By the time she'd got home it was late afternoon. Si wasn't due back until after the pub closed, and Tony had already set off to meet his city friends for drinks. She methodically loaded the groceries into the fridge and wondered when Ida would next be in touch.

Pottering around making coffee she absentmindedly opened a packet of ham for Jezebel, arranging the last two slices on a piece of white bread with ketchup for her lunch. If only there was someone she could talk to...

The phone lay on the table, stubbornly silent. She willed it to ring. Nothing happened. Besides, who could she tell without giving away Blaine's presence in the house? She was just agonising over whether she could break her promise in order to chat in confidence with Kate when the man himself sashayed into the room wearing nothing but a bath-towel slung around his hips.

223

"How were the shops?" He asked, seeing the newspaper and swooping on it. "For Christ's sake! I would've thought they'd be bored of me by now!"

"Nope." She took a bit of sandwich. "You're still hot news, but don't worry someone from TOWIE will have implants, or gain a pound and then all this'll be forgotten."

"Hmmm. I wouldn't bet on that." He bent over her to scan through the story, skin radiating warmth. "I just hope I haven't blown my chances with the ♻FX contract."

"Have you spoken to your agent yet?" She moved her chair away a bit and picked up a purring Jezebel.

"No." He wrinkled his forehead. "I'm not ready to find out how this will affect my career yet. I don't even want to speak to any of my friends for fear of what they'll tell me. I left Nadia a letter before I left, but apart from her and Ida nobody else had a clue this was coming."

"Don't worry about that now."

"Easier said than done. And I can't stand being stuck inside like this; I was so damn envious of you for being able to go to Tescos without being hounded, it's ridiculous. I mean I never go to Tescos anyway."

"It won't be for long, just think of this as a rest." She advised. "If it helps I'll stay and keep you company for as long as you want."

He sighed. "You don't know how grateful I am for all you're doing for me baby. I don't think I could've got through this without you." He laughed his inimitable laugh. "Si even says I've put on weight, that cheeky minx, but I had been forgetting to eat, what with the stress. I know I complain but it's such a relief not to have this hanging over me anymore. I feel free in an odd way, even though I've not left the house. I'm in hiding, but I've got nothing to hide. Does that make sense?"

"Yeah." She avoided his eyes and got up to wash her plate. "I'm glad we've been able to help."

"You've done more than that, you're an angel. I love you darling." He gave her a hug that she returned reluctantly although it made her heart hurt.

224

"I feel so cooped up though. If only I could have a night off from my life... you know what I mean?"

Gypsy stood in front of the sink, about to wash up her plate when inspiration struck.

"Maybe you can." She blurted, mind racing.

"How's that gurl? What do you mean?" He studied her curiously through long lashes.

Silently she cursed herself. She knew she was on the verge of suggesting something reckless, irresponsible even. However, she was also unable to resist trying to make him feel better.

"Go and have your bath, and then I'll tell you what I have in mind, okay?"

"You're the greatest!" He squealed. "Come with me though and we can chat at the same time."

She followed him upstairs wondering why the hell she was doing this.

I am weak, she chided herself uselessly. I have all the inner strength of wet tissue paper.

X

Blaine massaged conditioner into his hair; droplets of water ran down his perfect chest making Gypsy want to lick it.

"Do you really think I'd get away with it?" He asked as she perched uncomfortably on the toilet seat.

"I don't see why not. I've got wigs, headdresses and heaps of make-up."

"A disguise..." He mulled over the idea before sinking under the bubbles until he was entirely submerged. He resurfaced, hair slicked back against his head, causing water to slosh out onto the floor. "I suppose it could work. I mean I'm in drag a lot anyway. If I used really heavy make-up, and say wore glasses and a wig with a fringe I could look completely different. Also no one's going to expect me at the Pink Flamingo now. That's interesting that you work there as a faux queen. What made you decide to do that?

225

"It was to prove a point mainly, it's not important." Gypsy said vaguely. "Anyway, are you sure you're up for it?"

"Are you kidding?" His eyes lit up. "It'll be fantastic to go there incognito. I'll need your help sorting out something to wear though." He looked at her expectantly. "Oh please, please let's go tonight! I need to go crazy for one night. Someplace no one cares who the hell I am. I'm so tired of people kissing my ass just coz I'm famous."

Gypsy squeezed her eyes closed and hoped to god that Ida wouldn't find out about this.

"Okay." She decided, caving completely in the face of a nude Blaine in her bath. "Let's do it! And maybe afterwards we can go on to Cordelia's or some other shitty dive where you won't be spotted."

"Oh yeah baby, the crappier the better!" He laughed and then squealed with excitement. "Do you know how much I hate all those poncy parties where the most exciting thing that happens is people bitching about each other's outfits and latest surgery results? I want to go to a proper club, with real people, like you!"

"You haven't seen me dressed up as a drag queen yet, have you?" Gypsy smiled, his enthusiasm was irresistible. "I look quite... different."

"I can't wait!" He declared. "I'm so excited! You're a genius sweetie."

"We need a look for you." She regarded him thoughtfully, eyes narrowed. "I reckon my long, ash-blond wig would look fabulous. And I've got the perfect rubber dress. If you're still recognisable after we're done I've got a mask that could work."

"What will you wear?"

"Well, I've got this head-dress I made out of playing cards glued into fan shapes. That would go with my long magenta wig, black corset and hot pants." She was starting to get into the idea despite her misgivings. This could be a great evening after all. "If anyone asks who you are I'll just introduce you as my friend... erm... What do you want to be called? Ooh I know, how about Ann O'Nimmity!?!"

"I LOVE it". He declared pulling the plug out with his toes.

"So have you performed at the Flamingo, or just done door work?" He asked.

"I've done a few shows." She grinned modestly. "Faye Kinnett's gone down quite well on the cabaret scene actually; apart from the recent set-backs I told you about."

"Faye Kinnett!" He cackled. "I have to come see you do your thing after all this is over."

Blaine stepped out of the bath in front of her dripping water on her jeans and grabbing a towel.

"Can I ask you something?" He looked at her curiously.

"What?" Her throat had gone dry.

"Aren't you into me at all?"

Gypsy felt the blood rush to her face. "I erm, thought you liked men?"

He was tickled. "I do, of course. It's weird. I have a girl crush on you… and I'm all for trying new things. Does that freak you out?"

"No." She felt wrong-footed and completely unprepared for this revelation. Shagging Blaine would not be a wise move, she thought as his towel dropped to the floor. But then again, who cared?

Chapter 43. Crazy for You

"What is it?" JJ gasped, arms clutching his dressing gown protectively to his chest as Mark jumped away from the letter-box like a scalded cat.

"Someone's there! Bloody hell!" He expelled his breath slowly and straightened up. "That scared the crap out of me." He was flustered and more than a little annoyed with himself. "What was that you were saying about being able to look after yourself?"

JJ shrugged helplessly.

"Wait!" He cried as Mark began fiddling with the lock. "What are you doing?"

"I'm sorting this out once and for all." Mark said determinedly sliding the catch back and turning the handle.

The door swung open to reveal a cute-looking guy with sandy hair, wearing a T-shirt and a bemused expression.

"Hi." He said, peering in at their startled faces. "Don't panic, but someone was just trying to break into your flat. It's okay though, I think I scared him off." He looked over in the direction of the fire escape worriedly. "He disappeared that way."

Mark simply stared wondering what the hell was going. JJ however had no such qualms. "Elliot! What the hell are you doing here?! I'll call the police if you don't stop harassing me."

"Gladys, please! Let me explain."

228

"I've got nothing more to say to you. For the love of god. I'm never going to want to go out with you. EVER. I'm sorry, but you were just a client to me... you are not now nor will you ever be my boyfriend, okay?"

"I know." The man said simply. "That's why I'm here."

Mark frowned. "So you're not here to make trouble?"

"Absolutely not!" Elliot looked upset. "I'm sorry if I've come at a bad time, but I just wanted a quick word with JJ here. I don't want to cause any problems for the two of you, please believe me, quite the opposite in fact."

"Oh, we're not... together, I'm just the lodger." Mark said defensively, as JJ pulled a face and mouthed the word 'DEN-IAL' at Elliott behind his back.

"If I could just come in?"

"What more could you possibly have to say?" JJ wanted to know. "We've been through this time after time. I'm not in the mood for a scene. We were just about to watch a movie."

Elliot shuffled from foot to foot nervously. "Sure. I can come back when it's more convenient if you like? I just need a few moments to apologise for the way I've behaved in the past. You see I'm an alcoholic... and that doesn't excuse my actions, but I go to AA and I'm working a twelve-step program that's keeping me sober. Making my amends to the people I've harmed is a part of my recovery. That's why I'm here."

Mark gave JJ a look and he sighed and nodded his ascent. "Oh alright then. You might as well come in."

X

Half an hour later Mark and JJ sat at the kitchen table, all thoughts of the movie forgotten as they listened to Elliott's story. He told them how he'd used alcohol to drown out his fears along with his inability to accept his own sexuality. They listened as he explained how drinking had insidiously taken over every area of his life, wreaking complete havoc and bringing him to a hideously dark rock-bottom before he had finally sought help and gone to Alcoholics Anonymous.

229

"Hmm. You do sound different." JJ commented, propping his chin up with one hand and cradling his coffee cup in the other. "And you look a hell of a lot better. You're actually quite hot now."

Elliott smiled. "Well I suppose you've never seen me sober before. It's a bloody miracle. I can't apologise enough for causing you so much grief." He shrugged. "But if it's any consolation you'll never hear from me again after today. I know this won't mean much to you guys but I'm finally at peace with myself. It's ridiculous; all this time I've been a gay homophobe. How messed up is that? I've started reading this book called the Velvet Rage, which I totally recommend by the way. Oh and I came out to my family last week."

JJ let out a cheer, and Mark clapped politely causing Elliott to redden with pleasure.

"Well if you don't mind. I would like to ask you something." JJ said innocently. "What was it about little 'ole me that made you so... nuts?"

Mark shot him a look and kicked him under the table. "Enough alcohol can really fuck you up, clearly."

JJ rolled his eyes. "Seriously, I'd like to know."

"This isn't all about you." Mark chided.

"No, no. I don't mind." Elliott intervened. "Obviously I was in denial about liking men." He took a nervous puff of his cigarette. "You look like a beautiful woman in drag... I guess it felt like it didn't really count as gay sex, because you were such a stunning girl."

He broke off as JJ preened fluttering his lashes.

"Yes, I see." The escort smiled prettily, and flicked back a curly lock of hair. "I suppose I really can't blame you."

"Well that's why I thought to avail myself of your services in the first place, and then I got a bit obsessed. I thought you were going to be the one to save me from myself. The amount I was drinking, not to mention all the drugs, made me completely loose touch with reality." He eyed them apologetically. "Obviously I have some issues that need resolving, but I'm completely over that one now. In fact I'm going to avoid relationships for at least a year. Casual sex is

230

something I'm looking forward to exploring though. With other men of course.... erm not either of you." He added hastily. "I'm sorry; this is very difficult for me."

JJ clasped his hands together. "Well, I'm so proud of you honey... I don't know what to say."

Elliott looked at Mark, who smiled wryly mouthing the words 'DRAMA QUEEN' at him.

"Why don't we have a group hug?" JJ suggested.

"I really didn't expect you to be so generous about this." Elliott's eyes grew watery, as all three of them clasped each other awkwardly around the shoulders. "Things are going so well for me now... it's such a turnaround. I'm even going to Brighton Pride tomorrow with a group of gay guys from the meetings." He sniffed and wiped under one eye. "If there's anything I can do to make it up to you for all the trouble I caused just name it."

Mark patted him on the shoulder. "Well you already scared away a potential burglar, or worse a guy named Raphael who's been following Gladys here."

Elliott managed a wobbly smile. "I suppose I did do that." He turned to JJ with a look of disbelief. "Bloody hell; don't tell me you've had more than one stalker?"

JJ shrugged modestly with a 'what can I tell you smile' before a thought occurred to him. "Hang on a sec. Did you say I could ask you *anything*?"

"Of course, whatever you like."

JJ slipped an arm through Mark's. "Well, how about we join you and your friends for Pride tomorrow and then we can hit the clubs? I've been monopolising this one dreadfully... and he is supposed to be on holiday."

Mark realised it was the closest he'd get to an apology.

"That would be grand." Elliott beamed looking at Mark, who gave him the thumbs up. "Now, I'll let you get back to your evening. Shall I drop by tomorrow morning then? Around ten?"

"Fabulous!" JJ said as they saw him out into the corridor and waved goodbye. Once Elliott had disappeared he spun round to face Mark with a look of horror on his face.

231

"Oh my GOD! You realise what this means? I've got less than ten hours to plan my outfit for Pride!" The drag artist threw his hands up in horror.

"What about the film?" Mark asked hopefully. "And the rest of our Chinese?"

JJ tossed his hair back in exasperation. "Oh, never mind that. We've got work to do."

Chapter 44. Parenthood

"Is he my son?" Karl demanded angrily, all traces of good humour disappearing from the cornflower-coloured eyes that Cathy remembered so well. The onslaught of the years suited him, she noted impassively. Even the grey hair and crow's feet didn't detract from his undeniable looks. Somewhere inside her she felt a stirring of long buried emotions... anger, bitterness, affection. Gripping the arms of the chair she turned away. The clock ticked in the oppressive silence.

"Yes." She finally sighed, the admission taking all the breath out of her body.

He did a double-take. "But you wrote to my sister and told her that you'd had an abortion."

"You're my husband Karl; you left me without so much as a note when I was carrying your baby. Don't you dare try to take the moral high ground with me!" She trembled with emotion.

"I know I behaved badly." Karl suddenly looked every bit his age. "It's no excuse but I was just a kid. I felt trapped... we'd only slept together that one drunken night and then suddenly all that responsibility. It wasn't meant to be forever, I just had to get away. But then when I thought you'd had a termination... Why did you lie? I could've been a good father even if we were never going to work."

"How dare you!" Cathy's eyes widened, her voice turning shrill with fury. "I don't know how the hell you even knew

233

about Si, let alone how you managed to gate-crash my dinner party. But I won't have you waltzing into my home and lecturing me. I did the best I could! It's all very well for you to talk about the father you could've been, it was a different story back then though, you just disappeared. You coward."

Karl flinched as if she'd slapped him. "I suppose I deserved that. So, where does Si think his father is?"

"Dead." A sob caught in her throat. "And that's the way it's going to stay."

"Cathy, I can understand why you're not thrilled to see me, I wouldn't blame you if you hated me. But you can't deprive Si of the right to get to know his Dad, surely you can see that. I'm sorry if I hurt you..."

"That's an understatement." She said in a choked voice her shaking hand fumbling with her cigarette packet. "I know we were never exactly a love match but you were my best friend. How could you just leave me in the shit and swan off to Australia to find yourself on Bondi Beach or whatever the fuck you were doing? Without a word, Karl, not one word."

He bowed his head in a gesture of defeat. "I'm sorry. What I did was very wrong, no doubt about it. You couldn't really have expected our marriage to work. Surely you guessed that I'm... gay."

"Yes, and obviously marriage wasn't the answer. It was your friendship and support I really needed." She shook her head. "I can't believe you're here. And the last person I'd expect you to show up with is Duncan. You're not serious about him are you? I mean he's the same age as our son."

"That's none of your business."

"Alright. Well can I ask how you even knew Si existed?"

Karl smiled wryly. "We met by chance. I recognised the surname of course and when Duncan told me about Si's fabulous mother the actress I wondered if he could be mine. Then hearing about your dinner party I couldn't resist the opportunity to find out. But I had an inkling. Don't you think he looks a lot like I used to at his age?"

Cathy ignored the question and was silent for a moment.

234

"I saw you recently, you know." She said finally, taking a drag of her cigarette and getting up to pour them both a glass of wine. "Or would you prefer coffee?"

He held out his glass. "I think we could both do with the alcohol, don't you?"

She nodded and poured them each a large measure before settling back into her seat and crossing one leg over the other. "It was in Soho, I recognised you at once. You gave me the fright of my life! I've been in such a state worrying that something like this would happen."

"Oh dear. Is it as dreadful as you expected?" He asked with a little smile which she returned.

"*Hideous.*"

He took a sip and looked at her appreciatively. "You haven't changed a bit you know. You're still as beautiful as you were in your teens."

"Thank you." She replied demurely. "And you're still the same charming bastard that I remember."

He threw his head back and laughed. "You made quite a name for yourself, even though you must've been struggling as a single mother at the time. I saw you in 'The Orangery.' Marvellous acting, you should've got an Oscar."

"Thank you." She twisted a lock of hair between her fingers. "It all seems like such a long time ago now; I threw myself into my work and my son of course."

"Our son." He corrected.

"Yes... our son."

"You went and did it, you became hugely successful!" He continued. "I was so proud of you, you know. I followed all of your work; I saw every film you appeared in."

"What about you?" She asked curiously. "Are you still in the profession?"

"God lord, no!" He chuckled. "It's years since I acted. I've spent my time running a Spa in Sydney. Lately though, I started to get homesick, so here I am. I don't know what life holds in store for me now I'm back in England."

"Do you have a partner?"

"No one since Josh." He said quietly. "We were together for a long time and he died back in the nineties."

Cathy frowned and reached over to as if to touch him, before retracting her hand unsure how to be with him now. "I'm so sorry, Karl, truly I am."

"It's okay. I've had a lot of time to deal with it." He paused. "So, I hear from your friend, is it Gypsy? That you're seeing Stella now, the lady who gave me daggers."

"Yes... yes, I am." Her eyes lit up. "She'll be back soon with the dogs."

He gave her a crooked smile. "I'm glad you've finally found someone who can make you happy. About Si though, tell me, how is he? Doing well in life?"

"Oh yes. I'm so proud of him. He's a wonderful young man. At the moment he's working in a bar, and he's got a lovely boyfriend who you met, Tony?"

"Yes." He looked at her steadily. "You know I'm going to want to get to know him, don't you?"

Cathy closed her eyes briefly as if in pain. "Give me some time, Karl. Don't you think you owe me that much?"

He nodded and stood up. "Well, I'll leave you in peace for now. But I'll be in touch in a few days, okay?"

She handed him his coat and opened the front door. "I don't suppose I've got much choice, do I?"

Chapter 45. ✡FX

At eleven o'clock Gypsy silenced her alarm clock and shivering pulled the sheet back over her naked body. Blaine lay beside her fast asleep, traces of make-up still visible on his skin. Out of the corner of her eye she could see Jezebel curled up snoozing in the dress he'd left crumpled on the floor. Beside it lay a tangled wig.

Even this small awakening was too much effort; she closed her eyes again and leaned more deeply into the warmness of his body, sighing contentedly. The evening had been an alcohol fuelled rollercoaster of activity.

By the time they'd finished getting ready they'd both looked utterly fabulous if she did say so herself, and the evening at the Pink Flamingo had unfolded in a kaleidoscope of feathers, diamante and champagne. Introducing Blaine to her friends and colleagues as Ann O'Nimmity had gone without a hitch and soon they were all having a blast. She'd had a few anxious moments in the beginning, sure that someone would recognise *that* famous smile, but as the evening progressed it'd become obvious everyone was clueless as to whom they were chatting and dancing with. She wanted to hold onto every glorious detail of the night in case she never had such a good one again. Exactly the right mix of people, the perfect atmosphere and some great drag acts.

Gladys Cox-Hardt was up from Brighton for the night - slick, polished and hilarious as ever she'd performed a special

237

burlesque number. Sadly Blaine had missed her show as they'd been watching Lola Lypsinka doing a performance in the Pink Room involving a pole. It was one of those magical nights out that hardly ever happen, the ones you're always chasing and seldom ever find.

Afterwards, she remembered bumping into Tyra G'eye-Out and James aka Geneva Convention and they'd carried on drinking and partying at Cordelia's, a big crowd of the Pink Flamingo regulars joining them. Here too, Ann had gone down a storm. No one had seemed to want the night to end. Then when they finally stumbled home she hadn't been at all sure there'd be a repeat of the following afternoon. Especially as Ann had attracted the attentions of Nathan, a regular at the club, who was ridiculously muscular and gorgeous. By some miracle though (which she was still trying to fathom) it was herself and Blaine who'd somehow ended up in the toilets pissed and snogging. She had a hazy recollection of the taxi home and of the two of them having very drunken sex.

She sighed. It would undoubtedly be a huge mistake to let herself get used to the current state of affairs. Much as she was into Blaine, much as he seemed intrigued with her right now, she wasn't stupid. He might be open to experimenting, but she saw the way he'd eyeballed Nathan. If she was brutally honest with herself it was almost certainly thanks to copious amounts of alcohol and the fact that bringing a shag back to hers would've been awkward that she was the one in bed with him now.

Rubbing her eyes she yawned and willed herself to feel the pain of that particular reality. Yet somehow already having had an idea of the score she felt considerably less upset than she'd have thought. After all, she'd known he was gay from the off. Strangely she was finding herself pretty happy to accept the fact that they'd probably go on to be friends. As far as his usual type went he'd been typically upfront during the many conversations they'd had prior to getting together. Blaine was a sucker for masculine guys. Preferably black. If they had a gigantic cock so much the better. Enough said really.

238

X

As the day was drawing to a close there was cause for celebration at number sixty-nine. Si, Tony and Gypsy sat around the kitchen table clasping glasses of bubbly as an almost hysterical Blaine relayed the conversation he'd just had with Cecile Benedict.

"Congratulations!" Si cried clinking his glass against Blaine's. "Aren't you glad you finally worked up the nerve to call her now? Thanks for the champers too by the way."

Tony grinned. "Yeah. That's amazing news. We're so chuffed for you."

Laughing, Blaine put his glass back on the table after taking a long swallow. "You don't know what this means to me. I want to jump up and down and do cartwheels! I'm relieved and excited all at the same time. But bless you all, I couldn't have gone through with this if I hadn't been able to stay here. You've all saved my career, thank you my darlings."

Gypsy finished her drink and lit a cigarette. "I know how much you wanted the ✿FX contract. You totally deserve it babe."

"That's not even all!" He said, exhilarated at the thought of returning to work. "Cecile says almost every magazine in the country wants me for an exclusive. I can take my pick! Plus the work has been flooding in. I'm wanted for more promotional stuff than I can handle. And, get this! Several casting agents want me to test for some film roles. I'm going to get a chance to pursue my acting! Gurlz, this is my dream come true!"

"And do you really mean it about getting Vincent Santelli back in the country?" Si interjected. "Can you honestly do that? I mean Dario will be thrilled he's been moping like you wouldn't believe, but isn't it kind of a big ask?"

"Already sorted, love." Blaine grinned round at them all. "I told Cecile that I'll do the front cover of 'L'amour' and an interview on the condition I get Vincent flown in to do my hair." His eyes gleamed. "I don't think you realise how much

239

of a big deal being the new Mr ♕*FX* really is. I can pretty much ask for whatever I want now, and it's the least I can do to say thank you."

"And now you're free." Gypsy said. "You'll be able to go back to your flat, start living your life again."

"I *know*. I should get back tomorrow." He hugged himself excitedly. "My little Dior will be missing me. Although Ida promised she'd be looking after him, I know he pines when I'm not around."

Their eyes met and he winked at her, flashing a conspiratorial grin. Wryly, Gypsy smiled back. Although she was disappointed this most likely spelt the end of their fling, she couldn't help but be happy for him. No regrets. After all, they'd had an amazing time together.

"A toast!" Si chimed in. "A toast to Blaine Feynard, the most talked about model in England!"

They all raised their glasses once again.

Chapter 46. Stay

Kate decided to stop in at the Black Cock for a drink on the way home. After a tense day at the office with Danny all she wanted was a pint and to see a friendly face. Unfortunately when she arrived she discovered Si wasn't working that evening. It looked like she'd just have to make do with the alcohol.

Sitting down at a table she took a large gulp of beer and picked up her phone. She tried Gypsy first but the line went straight to voicemail. Mark's number no longer seemed to exist which was slightly worrying, but she wasn't in the right head space to wonder about that now. Dario was engaged (in both senses of the word) and even Vienna, who she tried out of sheer desperation proved unavailable. Ho hum.

Flicking through an abandoned copy of the Pink Paper she considered calling Si to see what he was up to on his night off. Perhaps he and Tony would fancy having a drink with her, or maybe that would be a bit of bus man's holiday. She thought about it and discarded the idea. Being a third wheel was never ideal. Just when she was about to give up her mobile started vibrating, nearly falling off the table and she grabbed it eagerly. It was Gypsy.

"Hey Kate, sorry I missed your call I was having a little nap." Her friend's voice sounded bleary

"That's okay! I'm just relieved you're in. I need to talk to someone."

241

"Man problems?" Gypsy hazarded a guess.

"Yep." Kate sighed. "Danny's given up on finding Julian and says he's going back to Manchester. What do I do now? How do I convince him to stay?"

"Well if he wants to go there's not much you can do hon."

"Don't say that. What about me? Us?" Kate wailed. "He hasn't even taken that into consideration. I mean I'm his girlfriend, you'd think that'd count for something."

"Yeah, but if the only reason he's in London is to find his brother and that's not happening..." Gypsy's voice trailed off. "It's a cliché but sometimes if you love someone you really do have to let them go. Trust me; I'm doing that myself right now. It's a bitch. But if it's not meant to be what else can you do."

"I didn't know you were seeing anyone in the first place?"

"That's because I can't talk about it for a couple more days. I've been sworn to secrecy."

"I'm your oldest and most trusted friend." Kate reminded her.

"I know, but this is... complicated" Gypsy said carefully.

"Oh dear. You're having man problems too?"

"It was only casual and I'm pretty sure it's over already. Which is fine, I'd like us to be friends." She sighed. "But it'll take a while."

"Shall I come over and we can have a misery fest?"

Gypsy groaned. "Sorry babe, no can do. I'll explain another time, but I can't see anyone tonight. Plus I've got the most outrageous headache, I feel rough as a robber's dog."

"Oh." Kate was disappointed.

"It's self-inflicted so I deserve no sympathy." Her friend continued. "I went to the Pink Flamingo last night, not working... drinking. That's why my head now feels like a boiled egg that someone's trying to crack open with a hammer. Then, like a complete masochist I went on to Cordelia's. I tell you, that place is always lethal. Ending up there is a sure sign you should've gone home hours ago."

Kate's head snapped up. In her excitement she nearly knocked her drink to the floor.

242

"Gypsy Wright! Did you just say you went to a place called... Cordelia's?"

A brief pause followed. "Yeah... so?"

Kate clutched her handset to her ear and raised her other fist triumphantly in the air.

"Yes!" She yelled out loud before lowering her voice. "Right, I need you to tell me everything you know about this place." She continued urgently. "For example... is it a bar? A club?"

"Hold your horses." Gypsy sounded bemused. "What an earth is so fascinating about that shit-hole? I only go there because the Pink Flamingo crowd does, that and the fact you can drink all night."

"Please hon, this could be important..."

"Well I don't see how. But okay, I'll just grab my fags and then I'll tell you all about it in great, boring detail. I want to know what this is all about though..."

X

Lying wide awake in her bed, Kate heard a church bell chime the hour. It was three o'clock. Apart from the sound of Danny snoring gently beside her, all was quiet in the house. Even Seth and his new girlfriend next door seemed to have (thank god) called it a night, yet still sleep eluded her. Groaning, she turned her head on the pillow and willed her brain to stop racing.

On returning home earlier that evening she and Danny had reached an uneasy truce. Nothing had really been resolved and yet they'd gone to bed and made up the best way they knew how, finally falling asleep in each other's arms. The facts, however, remained the same. The threat of his impending return to Manchester hung silently in the air between them.

She sat up and switched on the bedside light. She just had to tell him what she'd learned on the phone to Gypsy, even if it did cause an argument.

243

"Wasssamatter?" Danny grunted trying to pull the duvet cover over his head as she shook him awake.

"We need to talk." She whispered urgently, pulling on his arm. "Please? I can't sleep. There's something I need to tell you."

He let out a giant yawn, and struggled into a sitting position. "What do you want? It's the middle of the night."

"I think I've found out what Cordelia's is."

He opened his eyes more fully, and focused on his girlfriend. She sat beside him in one of his over-sized T-shirts shivering and looking pale in the moonlight. Reluctantly he abandoned the idea of slipping back into unconsciousness.

"Okay." He sighed. "I'm awake... just about, and listening."

She took a deep breath. "I know that you want to forget all about Julian and go back home, alright? And if that's how you feel I accept it. But I think you should stay until after Marina and Dario's wedding, at least."

He frowned at her, confused. "What's that got to do with Cordelia's? And why would I want to go to your friend's wedding?"

"Gypsy *knows* the place Danny. It's some illegal bar in Soho where the crowd at her club ends up after hours."

He stared at her, a slow smile spreading across his face. "No way!"

"Way." She looked pleased with herself.

"Why didn't you tell me earlier? Why wait until the middle of the night?"

She looked down at her hands. "I wasn't going to tell you at all. I didn't want you to be mad at me or think I'm that desperate for you to stay. I've got some pride you know."

"I'm sorry; I've been a right moody twat, haven't I?" He reached over and smoothed back a loose strand of her hair affectionately. "I want to be with you Kate. When I go back home we'll find a way to make it work."

She raised an eyebrow. "You mean a long distance relationship?"

"We'd have weekends... and holidays, we can make it work." He said hugging her to him. "By the way, I don't think

244

I've ever really said thanks. You've been so great helping me with all this family shite."

"You're welcome. Anyway, getting back to Cordelia's, I asked Gypsy for the address but apparently she's always got a lift with people after the club, she said she wouldn't know how to find it sober. I've tried the internet too, but nothing."

"Ah. Very helpful your piss-head mates are." His eyes glittered solemnly.

"However," She added. "And this is the good bit. Some staff from the Pink Flamingo will be at the wedding. In fact, Gypsy said they'll probably end up there later that night, so if you were to put off leaving for a week or so..."

"We could go in person." He finished for her.

"Exactly."

Chapter 47. Say Goodbye

Mark was in the middle of washing the dishes when the phone rang. It interrupted the companionable silence that had settled over the room as he scrubbed away the remains of the lamb rogan josh and Gladys Cox-Hardt fixed her wig in the mirror, painstakingly applying a frosting of lip-gloss to her mouth.

"That'll be the phone!" Mark called out over his shoulder. "And by the way I must congratulate you, that was a delicious meal... cooked in part, by you."

"Aww, shucks. It was nothing." Gladys grinned, looking pleased as she reached for the portable phone with one glittery blue-taloned hand.

"Hello, Hove whorehouse. How can I help you?" She sang gaily into the receiver.

Mark shook his head with a little smile as he finished the last plate and set to work on the drying. He heard the excited rise and fall of the drag queen's voice as she carried the phone with her out into the hallway.

His stay certainly hadn't been the idyllic break he'd envisaged, he thought to himself wryly. However, it surprised him to realise he'd been so busy keeping up to date with JJ's dramas that he'd hardly had time to think about Dario. Of course, he still missed his friends and London, but they'd actually had quite a lot of fun in the past week.

Carefully he dried off JJ's favourite tea-cup and positioned it in its proper place next to the vase of flowers by the window. Brighton Pride, for instance had been wonderful, and they'd been lucky enough to get glorious weather. He stole a quick glimpse at his forearms. Yes, there was more than a hint of a tan. Also, who would've thought that Elliott's friends would be so entertaining and not to mention hot? He'd had an unbelievable night with one of the more delicious ones called Jeff, who as it happened was a fireman by trade... a fireman! He'd also been to see Gladys in action at several of the clubs and bars. It seemed unbelievable that almost two months had passed since his arrival.

Mark sighed to himself. He wasn't sure he wanted to go back to reality. Maybe he could stay on here, get a job in a bar. He smiled at the idea. Although he'd grown oddly fond of said cross-dressing rent boy, a lifetime of Gladys would undoubtedly prove too much. Besides, he couldn't run away from his life for ever, could he?

"Fabulous news!" She cried bounding back into the kitchen waving the phone in the air.

"Oh yes?" He wiped his hands dry and flopped down on the sofa.

"I've just been booked to perform at the after-party of a wedding in London." She proclaimed triumphantly. "The Pink Flamingo last weekend, now this. I've got gigs coming out of me ears!"

"Wow, you are in demand! So when is this joyous event?"

"A week today!"

"Well, if you don't mind maybe I could come along and get a lift back to the City? I should be going home... you know earn some money myself." He tried to keep his tone light.

"Oh, right." She looked deflated. "You're off then."

"Well, yes. I've already stayed longer than I intended." He pointed out.

"Funny. We didn't have the best of starts. But we got along alright in the end, didn't we?" The drag queen sniffed loudly.

He smiled at her. "Yeah, it's been a laugh."

"Apart from being stalked..."

"Right."

"And that time when Elliott scared away a burglar."

"Mmmm."

"Sorry about that time you walked in on me and Fred." Gladys continued regretfully. "I should've locked the door, but it was difficult, what with being tied up. You shouldn't have had to see that."

He sighed. "It's okay, with therapy I'm sure I'll get over it."

She gave him a puppy-dog look. "You taught me how to cook."

"Aah. It was nothing. At least you'll be able to vary your diet of Super Noodles with a good Indian curry once in a while, huh?"

Her fake eyelashes fluttered with emotion. "Pride was fab, wasn't it?"

"The best." He agreed.

"But I never got to do you up in drag. Not even once, like you promised!" Her face clouded over again. "I could make you look stunning."

"Let's swap numbers; keep in touch. Give me a ring when you're up my way." He said slinging an arm around her bare shoulders. "I'll come back and visit too."

"Do you promise?" She asked aquamarine eyes teary.

"Yeah, someone's got to make sure you're not getting yourself in strife again." He said sternly. "I do wish you'd get yourself off the game though, it's dangerous. Besides, you're not going to be young and beautiful forever. Why don't you go to Uni or something? Or even really make a go of it with the performing. As you pointed out, you're in demand. Why not give it your all – make it a full time career?"

"Maybe." JJ removed his wig and set it carefully on the table. "I'll think about it. Do I get a proper hug?"

"Yeah, you do."

They held each other tightly for a while.

"Don't you get all mushy on me!" JJ warned.

Mark ruffled his short black curls. "So, what about this lift then?"

A mischievous expression danced across his companion's features. "Well. I'll drop you off... on one condition."

"Oh no! What's that?"

JJ dimpled at him evilly. "You have to let me dress you up in drag, as a one off." He thought for a moment. "*And* you have to come to the wedding as my guest and watch me perform."

"No way! No, no, no..." Mark held his hands up in protest.

"But I'm going to do a whole new number!" He pleaded.

"It's the drag part I'm objecting too."

"Come on! Don't be such a killjoy. It's only for a wedding party, no one'll know."

He sighed, why did JJ always manage to get round him? Was he really such a pathetic pushover?

"Oh and FYI, I really mean it about reconsidering my line of work." He broke off peering in the mirror again. "Although I don't love you for bringing it up, maybe I *am* getting too old for this lark."

"Well I don't think that's an imminent concern. You're younger than me."

"Yes well. I didn't want to say anything, but in gay years you might as well be dead. Now what do you say about the wedding?"

"I'll do whatever you want. Just shut up.... please." Mark gave in.

JJ beamed his brilliant smile. "You won't regret it, sugar. I'm gonna dress you up as an early Madonna for the occasion. I have just the thing; you're going to look sensational. Although not quite 'like a virgin;' I'm no magician."

Chapter 48. Monstrous

The day of Dario and Marina's wedding dawned bright and breezy. The latter being especially true for Gypsy, who found herself strapped to a giant crucifix and suspended above the entrance to new bar 'Monstrous' on Greek Street. Sasha Bitch had grudgingly scored her a gig as one of five 'screaming virgins' for the promotional opening gala. Photographers and members of the gay press congregated below having been lured by promises of free food and alcohol.

On first hearing about the job, she'd been torn. On the one hand she could hardly afford to turn down work; but then again she'd given Marina her solemn promise she'd spend the afternoon helping with final wedding preparations. Being naturally indecisive she'd finally agreed on taking part with the proviso that she be virgin no 1. The plan was to oscillate the five of them in order to prevent everyone screaming themselves hoarse. By going first she hoped to finish early, get home to scrub herself clean of stage make-up, fake gore and the like before changing into her wedding best.

Worryingly, the crucifix itself didn't seem to be very sturdy. She couldn't help thinking that Health & Safety would have something to say about the terrifyingly flimsy fixtures pinning it to the wall. Her falling off and being rushed to A & E would hardly be the kind of publicity the bar was looking for. Besides which, she did not have a high pain threshold. Already the rope securing her wrists and waist were digging into her skin uncomfortably and Sasha hadn't even given her the signal to start screaming yet, more's the pity.

After getting dressed, a quick check in the mirror had satisfied her that the transformation into blood-smeared siren was complete. Her face was a ghostly white, hair and neck dripping with sickly sweet corn syrup. She'd put in special effect cat-eye contact lenses for added shock value, and then finished the look with vampy red lipstick. The pièce de résistance though was definitely her dress. This was a gloriously gothic vintage ball-gown Geneva Convention had found for a tenner in a charity shop.

There were three female and two male "virgins", all of whom were currently hanging around somewhere below her bare feet, smoking cigarettes and waiting for the big double doors to open up.

Of course, if she'd paid attention to her horoscope that morning she would've sensibly at stayed home. Jasmina Jakes who was in her opinion, always dead on the money in her predictions, had warned that today was a time for quiet reflection and that pushing your way into the limelight could result in public humiliation. Unfortunately by the time she'd read it she'd already been en route. Besides, she thought darkly, the newspapers had given her a lot more to worry about lately.

On thumbing through a battered copy of the Daily Herald earlier that week she'd gawked in disbelief at the shock headline on page four. It seemed that her and Blaine's anonymous night at the Pink Flamingo hadn't been as anonymous as she'd hoped. She'd read and re-read the article in something approaching panic. It contained two slightly blurry pictures, one of Blaine as Ann O'Nimmity and herself as Faye Kinnett dirty dancing on the stage - their faces almost but sadly not quite unrecognisable underneath their drag paraphernalia. The second and worst showed them in clinch in a back alley in Soho, taxi visibly waiting for them in the background. The main spin of the story had been on the gender bending antics of the infamous supermodel. However, the fact that he seemed to be getting it on with a woman had also unsurprisingly caught their attention.

She groaned at the headline. "Blaine Faye Kinnett!" The reporter had gone on to describe her as drag queen impersonator 'Faye,' the creation of little-known (rude!) actress Gypsy Wright, latest in the long line of Blaine Feynard's lovers. This had sent her into a tailspin of anxiety as she'd not been at all sure how he'd react to this very public revelation. Since he'd left Kershalton Street they'd had several long chats over the phone. During one of these he'd made it clear that much as he adored her, a repeat performance of that night was not on the cards. She'd accepted this with good grace. But now here their fling was for everyone to read about in the papers. She just hoped that their friendship would survive intact. The only small comfort had been that there no longer seemed much point in keeping it a secret. It'd be immensely reassuring to run up a huge phone bill spilling her guts to Kate. Also now she was a client of Fraser Buchanan, from a professional point of view Stella had been quick to point out that although personally damaging, it was certainly not going to hurt her burgeoning career.

Looking down uncomfortably from her trappings, she came back to the present with a start. There was an excited hubbub amongst the small group gathered below. As the bouncers and doorman bustled out into the street, it looked as though the doors were finally opening.

Thank Christ, she thought, just as the circulation was about to be completely cut off from her arms. Sasha gave her the nod amidst a flurry of movement as the guests began to be ushered inside. She swallowed hard in an attempt to lubricate her vocal chords.

It was time to start screaming...

252

Chapter 49. Revelations

Meanwhile, the other side of town Mrs Fraser paced nervously up and down the garden too overwrought to notice the beauty of the flowers or that her little patch of lawn needed watering. Stella had retired upstairs to select an outfit for the wedding and give her some space, and the dogs were busy wolfing down their breakfast in the kitchen.

Cathy walked over to the ramshackle tool-shed and sat down on a piece of rockery. In less than twenty minutes her son was due to pay a visit, and she felt sick to her stomach every time she thought about the news she was going to give him. How could she possibly find the right words to tell him about his father?

She fingered the petals of a gladiola thoughtfully, her brow furrowed. Over the past weeks she'd reluctantly met up with Karl another couple of times, and had countless heart-to-hearts with Stella. It'd been enough to convince her that she was doing the right thing. Si did deserve the truth; of that she was quite sure. What he did with the information of course was entirely up to him.

By the time he arrived at the front door she felt stronger within herself, and as ready for the moment of reckoning as she was ever going to be. Forcing herself to make bright small talk she led her only child into the conservatory. Then before joining him in the swing sofa, she fetched a plate of chocolate fudge, a half bottle of brandy and two glasses. If she was going to do this she might as well be good and stoned.

Looking into Si's face the resemblance to her former husband was undeniable.

"Mum, what's up?" He asked as she continued staring at him. It was obvious something was on her mind.

"I've got something I need to speak with you about dear."

"God, you're not ill are you?" Si was alarmed. "You're scaring me."

"It's nothing like that. But you'll have to bear with me... this is hard."

He frowned. "Okay, I'm listening. You can tell me anything."

"Very well, here goes." She gave a shaky little laugh before taking a slug of brandy. Avoiding eye contact she began to tell him the story of her friendship with another promising actor in her theatre company and the events that led up to her pregnancy and his birth. She managed to tell him the truth without faltering, although her voice shook when it came to explaining how she'd deceived Karl's sister and how hard it had been raising a small boy, whilst pursuing her acting career and scratching a living.

Cathy carried on talking, seemingly lost in the past for a good ten minutes. When she finally came to the end, her voice trailed off and she looked him in the eye for the first time, desperate to see what his reaction would be.

Si just stared at her, his eyes wide with shock. It was as if he'd turned to stone.

X

Seconds passed like hours as mother and son sat in silence. Cathy tried to speak, but her words seemed to die in her throat turning into a muffled sob. She wrung her hands and frantically puffed at a cigarette before pitching the butt out into the bushes.

Si shifted over in his seat as the full impact of what she'd revealed hit him like a number ninety-four bus... He had a

254

father, somewhere... All these years he'd believed him to be dead. His eyes filled with unexpected tears, he didn't want to be upset, didn't want to cry for this man who'd abandoned his wife giving no thought to her welfare or that of his unborn son. Looking over at his dear old mum, who'd spent her whole life showering him with love; his heart ached to see the anxiety etched into her face. How fearful she was that he'd hate her, or blame her for hiding the truth. Wordlessly he turned and wrapped his arms around her, filled with compassion for all she'd gone through and sacrificed. More than anything he wanted to reassure her that she was forgiven.

Cathy closed her eyes tightly as she rubbed him on the back feeling weak with emotion. "I thought you'd be angry or even worse, disappointed in me." She gave him a watery smile as he gently pulled back, his hand patting hers.

He shook his head. "I'm not mad, not with you anyway. I'm just so sorry to hear how hard things must have been for you. And I suppose I'm in shock. My father's alive."

"I'm sorry I lied to you."

"It doesn't matter, you did what you thought was best." He squeezed her hand. "I'm glad you told me, but it won't make any difference. He's dead to me."

She averted her eyes. "I'll respect whatever decision you make, of course. But for what it's worth I've spent quite a lot of time talking to your father since he came back." She took another fortifying mouthful of brandy and passed Si his glass before continuing. "He's a very different person from the young man I once knew. I think you'd like him a lot. You must've guessed that he wants to see you, very much."

Si's features darkened with anger. "Well I don't want to see him. Do you know how many years I spent wishing that I had a Dad like all the other kids? I needed him then, not now. He's about twenty years too late!"

"Don't you even want to know more about him?" She asked carefully.

"I know all I need to know."

255

She sighed; sometimes her son could be as stubborn as a mule. He certainly didn't get it from her side of the family.

"Well, this is a lot to take in, why don't you give it some thought? Besides, there is actually one more thing I should tell you." She released his hand and passed him a piece of chocolate fudge, helping herself to a square at the same time.

Si took his and leaned back into his seat. "Go on, hit me."

"You've actually already met him... He came to my dinner party." She eyed him warily to see how he'd react to this bombshell. "Oh, *I* didn't invite him. Oh no, he engineered an invite through Duncan to see me and *you* no doubt. I don't know if you remember him or even spoke to him much? His name's Karl?"

Realisation shattered Si's fragile shell of composure like a sledgehammer. Karl, the hottie from Nirvana, was his *father*? His head fell back against the sofa uselessly as his mind struggled to keep up with all the layers of truth that were being revealed to him. The chocolate fudge was doing little to help matters.

Chapter 50. Dario disappears

The Black Cock was closed for business the afternoon of the wedding. The staff however had been up since six, as joined by a few of their faithful regulars they scrabbled about frantically preparing for the grand event. Whilst the rest of the country was obsessing over Big Brother and football respectively, Lisa and the other baristas had been busy organising an after-party to remember. Not to mention preparing themselves for awkward questions. The two newlyweds-to-be had spent hours patiently testing their knowledge of each other and getting their stories straight for members of the outside world. Consequently, paranoia was running high. To make matters worse the day had hardly begun before an obvious glitch threatened to spoil their plans.

"Li-sa!" A pajama clad Marina ran into the bar and found her girlfriend balancing precariously on a ladder whilst trying to secure some netting to the ceiling.

Sitting at a booth Jeremy, Sally and her girlfriend Freya had formed a production line, blowing up and sealing balloons before passing them to Steve – another customer who'd been roped into helping out – who was suspending them into the net. It looked as if they had a long way to go before there'd be enough to make an impact, and Jeremy already seemed worryingly out of puff and more than a little pissed.

"What is it, Rina?" Lisa mumbled through a nail clamped in her mouth.

She dashed over to the bottom of the ladder, knocking over a box of party decorations in her haste.

"It's Dario! He didn't come back to the flat last night. I've just checked his room and it's empty - plus his mobile's going straight to voicemail. I don't know what the fuck to do!"

"Bollocks." Lisa hammered the nail into place and climbed down to ground level. "I thought you were going to talk him out of going to G.A.Y last night?"

"I tried but he kept going on and on about Kathy T performing and how he'd leave straight afterwards. Ash was no help either, he practically kidnapped him!"

Lisa looked stressed. "Well, it's *his* wedding for godsake. Ooh, that boy does make me angry sometimes. We'll just have to carry on getting ready and hope he shows up in time. I don't think he's really going to risk being deported, do you?"

"I hope not." Marina said doubtfully. "But it's totally panicking me, and Gypsy and Kate promised to help me sort out my hair and clothes and neither of them have turned up!"

"Calm down." Lisa took her by the shoulders. "I'm two men down as well, Si promised me he'd be here an hour ago and Ash was going to help too." She sighed and ran her fingers through her short brown hair crossly. "Well at least I know what happened to him.... He'll be in the same place as Dario I imagine, and Lord only knows where that is. If we're very unlucky, in a K-hole."

She frowned surveying the pub to see what more needed to be done. Suffice to say, it was a lot. A hysterical girlfriend was definitely going to slow down progress. "What are you still doing in your pajamas?"

"Oh yeah." Marina looked down at her slippered feet. "I've been running around trying to call everyone and get them here and totally forgotten to get dressed."

"Well go upstairs and get showered and changed *now*." Lisa ordered bossily propelling her stairwards. "I'll come up in a bit and help you with your hair and stuff myself if

258

necessary, although I'm sure the girls and our missing groom will be here by then, alright?"

"Okay." Marina agreed looking only slightly reassured. "Damn, I'll be glad when this whole shebang's over. I've got a bad case of nerves."

"Everything will work out fine, you'll see." Lisa said patiently. "But go on, upstairs, now!"

X

The first thing that Dario was aware of on waking was the unfamiliar sound of a Boeing-747 taking off, and then a short while later another one landing. Cursing, he felt a sharp pain in his temple. Muzzily he shifted his aching head off the empty vodka bottle he'd been using as a makeshift pillow and let it thud onto the carpet. His eyelids flickered in the midmorning sun seeping in through slats in the rustic wooden shutters. A thought occurred to him. It struggled up through layers of grogginess and hangover like a bubble before breaking on the surface of his mind and causing him to sit up, stomach contracting in dread. He didn't have window shutters in his bedroom.

Now that the thought bubbles had started, they could not be stopped. Groaning and wiping some saliva from his chin he realised that A, it was late and B, he had an awful feeling there was something crucially important he'd forgotten to do. He looked around the room dazedly, trying to piece together the events of the following evening.

He remembered Ash dragging him along to a club where they'd bumped into a group of friends and got progressively more and more slaughtered. He had a vague recollection of buying drugs off a girl with purple hair, and then horror of horrors Kathy T had been in the middle belting out her latest number one and (oh please God no!) had he tried to climb up on stage with her!?

As the full force of his mortification hit him, he clapped his hands over his face. No wonder his subconscious was trying to suppress his memory, he cringed. The bouncer had

259

been forced to manhandle him back into the crowd. Oh the shame! Then after that, he recalled a car journey in which he'd been chatting away to a good-looking blond called Matt? Mattie? Something along those lines anyway. Ash had been in the back with two more men, then... nothing.

He frowned, scrunching up his face in an effort to concentrate. What had happened next? He tried his hardest to focus. Ah yes, a drinking game. Five of them sitting round in a circle and downing shorts. His very last recollection involved telling the group how it was VERY IMPORTANT that nobody let him fall asleep; although maybe he could shut his eyes quickly, but only for five minutes max.

Jesus! He jumped to his feet feeling a wave of nausea as he realised what day it was. At that moment a disheveled looking Ash burst into the room naked except for a hand-towel tied around his waist.

"Fuck me! I thought you were going to come and get me when the trains started running!" Ash cried wild-eyed, hair sticking up at right angles. "We're never going to get home in time for the wedding!"

Dario moaned softly. "Oh crapping hell. Where in god's name are we?"

Ash grimaced. "Um, I'm not sure how to tell you this."

"Ash." He said in a warning tone, taking a step towards his friend.

"Okay, okay. We're very close to Gatwick Airport." He spluttered backing away. "And don't go mad, but I should remind you that we left our stuff in the cloakroom. Mattie had to buy all the booze and fags last night and he says we owe him fifty quid... plus we're miles from a cash point with no money to get home."

"Shit." Dario slumped into the nearby armchair, suddenly feeling strangely calm. Everything had gone so utterly wrong, that having hysterics would clearly change nothing. "Give us your phone then. I'll have to call Marina and tell her we're stranded."

"Erm, I've no credit." Ash said sheepishly. "We'll have to wake up our host and see if we can use his."

260

Dario exhaled noisily, features darkening with rage. Sometimes he didn't know why he bothered hanging out with Ash; it always seemed to be one crisis after the other when he was with him.

Chapter 51. Fleeing the Scene

Mark stared out of the window silently saying goodbye to the last glimpses of the seaside town as they whizzed by. Nostalgically he realised he'd miss Brighton life, it'd come to feel like home. Meanwhile, Gladys Cox-Hardt struggled with the clutch, bracelets jangling, and steered them with some difficulty around a sharp bend before kicking off her vertiginous stilettos in exasperation.

"Bloody things! I can't accelerate in heels to save my life." The drag queen muttered flicking a strand of crimson hairpiece out of her eyes impatiently. She slammed her foot down on the break causing them to lunge forward before lurching to a halt as they hit the beginning of what looked like a long traffic jam.

"Bugger!"

The car stalled and she revved the engine furiously before the little Skoda came to life. Mark squeezed his eyes shut and offered up a quick 'thank-you' to the Heavens. Breaking down in the middle of the main road whilst dressed as Madonna would in his book, most certainly fall under the dictionary definition nightmare. Already his wig was itching, the clasps of his strappy sandals were giving him jip and his corset was too tight. Worst of all, he aptly felt like a complete tit in the pointy bra JJ had insisted made the outfit; as for the shade of lipstick he'd been coerced into the less said the better.

262

He was already having serious regrets about allowing JJ to have his wicked way with him... although the peroxide curls did have a certain je ne sais quoi. The tiresome part was that they were already running horrendously late for the gig. This was, he conceded to himself, in part his fault for fussing over his foundation and taking too long to pack. Although JJ had forgotten to set the alarm clock after their drunken night out in Bardot's – Mark's final farewell to the Brighton gay scene.

He craned his neck out of the window for a last look at the train station. What had started out as a perfectly sober and respectable evening had deteriorated rapidly when Gladys got in an argument with a couple of lesbians. She was still blistering with rage over the whole incident.

"Can you believe the nerve of that dyke?" She demanded, just as Mark had begun to hope the subject had finally been worn out. "I've never been so insulted in all my life!"

"Well, you did say she had a face like a smacked arse." Mark ventured as the car crawled forward another few feet. "I'd say you gave as good as you got."

Gladys snorted. "Ha! That's only because she said I had a masculine looking face. I don't, do I?" She peered anxiously in the review mirror pouting her lips at her reflection.

"No." He replied wisely. "And I suppose she didn't have to call you the Brighton bike. That was an inflammatory remark if ever there was one."

"I *know!*" The drag queen bristled. "And that's exactly why I was forced to point out that she was merely jealous because she couldn't give it away."

"Yes. Do you also remember telling her a group of blind, drink and drug addled sex addicts on the pull would probably rather drink their own vomit than touch her with a barge pole."

"Mmm." Gladys looked thoughtful. "Do you think I went a teensy bit too far?"

"Maybe a tad."

"Still! That's no reason for her to set that ferocious looking dog on me!" She rallied, blaring her horn at the unmoving traffic.

Mark smiled despite himself. "Come on now, you know that was her girlfriend."

"Whatever." She snorted. "It wouldn't have got physical if she hadn't pulled my wig off. She's lucky I only threw my pint over her, waste of good alcohol that."

"Yes, well it wasn't a night out that I'll forget in a hurry, that's for sure." He concurred. "I wish we hadn't slept in though."

"Huh! I don't know why you care. It's me that's working today, and I'm not stressing." Gladys reminded him taking her hands off the wheel to examine her flawless gold nails with satisfaction. "So what if we're a tiny bit off schedule? As long as these cars shift in the next five minutes we'll be fine."

A few seconds later the cars started moving forward again and the traffic dissipated. Mark settled back into his seat as they sped onwards, at last gaining a respectable distance from the town. Green fields of lush countryside started to undulate before them. Gladys gave him an I-told-you-so smirk before stepping down on the gas. They hurtled forward, Mark pinned back by the sudden acceleration. Her fake boobs jiggled up and down as they shot over bumps in the road at approximately a hundred miles per hour. Humming to herself she reached over and turned on the radio filling the car with the vocals of Cher Lloyd.

It took a while for Mark to realise the siren in the background was not part of the music and they were actually being followed by a police car. Turning his head, carefully so as not to disturb his painstakingly gelled and hair-sprayed faux waves, he noticed with alarm that it's blue lights were flashing furiously as it wee-wahed along behind them.

"Jeez-us! What do I do?" Gladys cried as she spotted the vehicle in the mirror, steering going haywire with indecision.

"Pull over goddammit! What's *wrong* with you?" Mark yelled and they swung into a lay-by as she braked savagely bringing them to a shuddering standstill.

Silently they stared at each other, the engine ticking as it cooled.

Mark made a face. "This is not looking good... Oh Christ! And it just got worse!" He clutched her shoulder.

"What is it?" She swiveled her head around to try to see, before undoing her seat belt and turning to get a better view. "Oh you've got to be kidding me...."

The police officer walked towards them with a purposeful expression. Her mouth was set in grim line, hands clenched into fists. It was the woman from the night before. Except today, Mark thought defeatedly, her face really did look like a smacked arse, which did not bode well at all.

Chapter 52. Nadia

Blaine scribbled a quick autograph for the cabbie and sashayed over towards his flat, key-ring twirling around his fingers.

Home sweet home. Finally. He felt a flush of happiness; everything was turning out so well, the future looked bright. Cecile Benedict had welcomed him back to the fold with open arms, full of good news about fantastic proposals not to mention congratulations over clinching the ✡FX deal.

There was going to be a lot of work ahead and it filled him with excitement. The best bit was the worst had already happened. The public knew all about his past and loved him more than ever. Nothing could touch him now. He felt like a huge weight had been lifted from his shoulders. His agent had even used the term 'publicity masterstroke', although all he felt was enormous relief that he no longer had anything to hide. No more skeletons in his closet... Well, maybe *one* more. A cloud flitted over the sunny horizon of his mood as he thought about the article he'd spotted in one of trashier rags about himself and Gypsy. God knows what people would make of that! He hardly knew what to make of it himself. He'd never been attracted to girls before, and part of him wished he'd kept everything on a more plutonic level. Admittedly he felt a bit guilty. Gypsy might know the score as far as his sexuality went. But to have her picture all over the papers... well she hadn't asked for any of that. He had no idea how she was taking the news or even if she'd seen the story. Chances were if she had she was probably cursing him and Ida and wishing she'd never agreed to help out in the first place; although really, it was anyone's guess. Close as they'd got, he felt in some respects she was still a girl who played her cards close to her chest. Gypsy and her friends had charmed him, giving so much of their time, laughter and hope when he'd had none and expecting nothing in return. None of them seemed to give a damn what he did for a living either - once they'd got over the initial awkwardness of meeting such a familiar face.

A tiny frown creased his perfect forehead as he wondered if a real friendship with the quirky faux queen would be possible. Especially now that his career was taking off in a way he hadn't even dared dream. The very fact that she hadn't treated him like some untouchable goddamn princess was worth a lot. Plus her obvious insecurities which she tried so hard to hide touched him. He found himself reminded a little of himself when he was younger... once upon a time.

He shook himself out of his reverie and opened the front door. He'd spent the whole cab ride mentally gearing himself up to talk to Nadia, and not just about his coming out either... now he felt his stomach knot in apprehension. Cecile had had a word in his ear about how bad things had gotten lately with Nadia's drinking and drugging and pointed out that if anyone could get through to the model it was him. If the rumours he'd heard were to be believed (and let's face it, now their agent was confiding in him they must be) it looked as if she was spiraling down into a deep abyss of addiction, effectively flushing her brilliant career down the toilet.

Unhappily a quick phone call to Ida had confirmed the news that Nadia's latest lover and partner in crime, Damien Black had indeed eloped for a quickie wedding with their old housemate Fleur. Blaine was fuming. Fleur and Nadia had been really close at one point as well. What a bitch. Talk about kicking someone when they were down.

Sighing, he thought how glad he was to be coming home, everything would be okay. He'd be there for his friend, together they could get through anything.

Blaine knelt down to go through the pile of unopened post and was nearly knocked over by a boisterous Dior who attempted to lick his face clean of make-up. Picking up the excitable canine he trotted upstairs aware that he'd better get a move on, Vincent Santelli had invited him to attend Dario and Marina's wedding that afternoon.

It wasn't until he reached the landing and saw that his bedroom door was ajar that he felt the first stirrings of unease. He was positive he'd left his room locked. Pushing his way inside, his hands flew to his mouth as he surveyed the wreckage in horror. It had to be burglars... Oh God!

Inching further into the room he switched on the light. The floor was covered with papers and his desk had been completely ransacked; photos and private letters spilling out onto the carpet. Flabbergasted, he saw that the box he kept hidden in the back of his closet was now sitting on top of the bed. It'd contained all his old photographs of his family and himself before his transition. Now its contents were emptied carelessly all over the place.

Trembling violently he staggered back into the hallway and checked the lock on his door; it didn't appear to have been tampered with. How the hell did they get in? He wondered, creeping down the stairs to inspect the windows. Then a thought struck him making his blood run cold. What if the intruder was still inside?

Armed with a stiletto, a careful investigation of the ground floor revealed nothing. No broken windowpanes or anything else to suggest a burglary. Feeling lightheaded and panicked he wandered back upstairs, should he call the police? There didn't seem to be any signs of a break in...

Nadia!

Blaine let out a whimper as he realised she should been in. Cecile had said that she'd just had a telephone call from her at the house. He nearly lost it completely. What if his friend had been attacked by the same psycho who'd been blackmailing him and was lying in a pool of blood somewhere this very second?

Irrationally and feeling a bit like an B-movie actress, he snapped on the light in the bathroom and drew back the shower curtain, taking a deep breath and preparing himself for the worst. He let out a sigh of relief when it revealed an empty bath. He checked Ida's room finding nothing so sinister as a neatly made bed and a pile of washing on the clothes bin. Biting his lip he turned the door handle to Nadia's room and pushed it open.

Again all looked normal, except what was that strange buzzing noise? Walking around the king sized bed, he let out a shriek at the sight that confronted him.

Nadia, his best friend in the world, was lying on the floor, limbs arranged in a horribly unnatural angle. Her face was waxy white and there was a dribble of blood running down one nostril and past her open mouth. Lying beside her head was a cracked mirror, some rolled up fifty pound notes and a whole lot of cocaine and other drug debris.

"Oh Nads, you silly cow, what have you done?" He asked, the tears welling up in his eyes as he grabbed her and shook her violently by her shoulders.

"WAKE UP dammnit! Don't you dare die on me or I'll never fucking forgive you!"

Nadia's head lolled lifelessly back on her neck. She looked like a broken doll. Blaine sank to the floor next to her and started to sob, a huge torrent of anger and sorrow overwhelming him. The unsettling buzzing noise, he realised, was the phone. The receiver was off the hook and clasped in one of her bluish tinged hands.

Gently, he pried it out of her grasp, pressing the hang-up button until he had a dialling tone. His fingers shook so much he could hardly tap in the number for the emergency services.

Please god; don't let me be too late, he prayed as it rang.

Chapter 53. A Shocking Discovery

By the time Kate had extricated herself from a crowd of Hare Krishna's and got her bearings she realised she'd somehow lost Danny in the melee. Irritated, she brushed her windswept hair out of her face and walked down Lisle Street feeling hot and bothered.

Already it was eleven o'clock and they were going to be late to help Marina out at the Black Cock. To make matters worse after a hectic hour's shopping in the ridiculously seething West End; their search for both a present and a decent pair of shoes for her to wear to the wedding had proved fruitless. Now to top it all off they'd only gone and got separated. Scrabbling in her handbag for her mobile, she felt well and truly exasperated. This was ridiculous.

Just as she was dialling the number of her carelessly misplaced boyfriend a gaudy neon sign over the entrance of a bar caught her eye. She stopped what she was doing, her eyes widening. She could hardly believe what she was seeing. For right in front of her, in a nondescript side street in all its tacky, window-blackened glory was a club proclaiming itself as Cordelia's.

Catching her breath, her heart started racing with the excitement of her discovery. Could this be *the* Cordelia's? She stood in the middle of the pavement regarding it speculatively. Well, it certainly looked the part, she decided, divey as hell.

She clamped her phone to her ear once again. She could hardly wait to tell Danny. Thank god for the Hare Krishna's after all, she thought as it rang. What were the odds of her just running into the place by accident like this? She decided it was even more random than spotting Gypsy and Si's odd housemate George in Balans a couple of days ago. And he'd been sharing a bottle of wine with Nadia Olsen, the supermodel, of all people. She couldn't wait to share that bit of gossip with the housemates.

"Kate? Where are you?" Danny's voice sounded crackly, like he was out of signal.

"I'm in Lisle Street baby. Do you know it?" She asked unable to keep the note of triumph out of her voice. "I think there's something you're going to want to see."

X

Twenty minutes later she had revised her opinion and began to have grave doubts concerning the wisdom of barging headlong into a potentially dangerous situation.

Danny gave her a reassuring smile as he returned from the tiny bar bearing two weak looking and eye-wateringly over-priced pints of lager. He set them both down on the table where she was seated nervously. She tried hard to look nonchalant as a couple of crack-addict types in the corner eyeballed her suspiciously.

"Ten quid for that round." He said giving a low whistle. "And I asked that surly bloke behind the bar if he knew anyone called Julian and he hadn't got a clue. Although he did say he's only been working here a couple of weeks." He added. "Your friend wasn't kidding; this really is a dump."

Kate shrugged. "How do we know this is it though? There must be more than one Cordelia's in the whole of London. I mean what would your brother be doing in a place like this anyway?"

"I don't know, but I'd like to find out." He said, taking a sip of his beer and grimacing.

271

"Maybe this wasn't such a great idea, Danny." She frowned speaking in a low voice. "Is it just me, or are the people around here looking at us like we're aliens... or worse, tourists? I think we should finish our drinks and leave. I mean, we came and looked and learned nothing. We're running late as it is. We'll doubtless be back tonight if this really is where Gypsy's friends hang out..." She trailed off miserably. "The people here frighten me."

He gave her arm a squeeze. "Okay, you're right. Let's drink up and get out."

Her face suddenly drained of colour.

"Kate?" Danny turned his head round sharply to follow her line of view. An overweight woman wearing red lipstick, a headscarf and a great deal of loud blue eye shadow was bearing down on them, her features contorted with fury. Instinctively he shrank back in his seat.

"You got some bleedin nerve darkening my doors again, yer flaming no good thief!" The woman yelled, pointing a chubby finger in Danny's face, several of her chins quivering with indignation. "How dare you walk back in here bold as brass! Didja think I'd just forgive yer? After you stole from me, when I treated yer like me own flesh an' blood?"

Danny found himself momentarily shocked into silence, and it was Kate who leapt to his defense.

"You've made a mistake, this is Danny." She said trying to sound reasonable. "We've never been here before. We've come here to find his twin Julian... is that who you think stole from you?"

The woman shot Kate a look before launching into another diatribe, bosom heaving alarmingly with emotion. She placed her hands on the table in front of them and leveled her face with their own menacingly. "Don't insult my intelligence. I want my cash NOW!"

Danny rose to his feet taking Kate firmly by the arm.

"Look lady, we don't want any trouble. If my brother owes you money then we'll only have some chance of reimbursing you if you tell us where we can find him. This is all a misunderstanding!"

"You lost yer mind?" The woman asked with a disbelieving snort. "I don't know what you're talking about... an' I don't much care. Pay up or get out, right this minute."

He shook his head helplessly and they pushed past her and fled up the rickety stairs.

"Christ!" Kate yelped as they escaped into the sunlit street now full of Sunday afternoon shoppers. She clutched him around the waist, before doubling up in hysterical laughter as they legged it down the road. "I thought we were going to get beaten up by her heavies!"

"Shagging hell." He let out a snort of disbelieving laughter. "But you know what this means don't you?"

She stared at him. "She definitely knows your brother. In fact it sounds like he's made quite an impression! We're on the right track. Wouldn't you say that's progress?"

He grinned. "I most certainly would. Now come on, or we're not even going to make it to the registry office on time."

"What about my shoes?" She cried, looking down at her trainers in dismay.

"Fuck the shoes. Come on!"

Chapter 54. Policemen and Paparazzi

Out of breath Gypsy sprinted through Hammersmith Broadway scattering shoppers in her wake. She pelted down the steps to the subway, nearly slipping as she barged her way through a group of tourists. She checked her watch and, mid-jog, felt around in her bra to make sure her money and receipt were still there. Satisfied all was in order, she bunched the hem of her ball gown up in her hands and pelted out into the Fulham Palace Road.

Marina would doubtless be furious with her; she thought ruefully, legs nearly buckling from exertion as she was forced to slow down a notch. But for once this was not a case of the infamous Gypsy tardiness. The assistant supervising proceedings had mistakenly thought the screaming virgins were rotating after an hourly shift. After shrieking her lungs out dutifully for a full twenty-five minutes (because after all she was a professional) she had practically no voice left and her croaky demands to be released had failed to attract anyone's attention.

Annoyingly once she'd eventually been freed, late and furious, all concerned had been highly unsympathetic. She wasn't even paid more, which had not improved her mood. The fact that Sasha had commented on what a fantastic actress she was to carry off the part of a virgin so well had failed to appease. To top it off she'd never seen the Piccadilly line so crowded on a Sunday. Growing increasingly annoyed she'd been forced to endure the whole journey standing in front of a group of sniggering passengers who seemed to find her costume hilarious; the funniest thing *ever.* By this time she felt as if her sense of humour had been surgically removed. *Bloody* Sasha.

When at last she reached Kershalton Street she'd slowed to a pitiful, blister-induced hobble. The sun blazed down on her back, burning the skin on top of her shoulders and she was dripping with sweat. Clutching her side in an attempt to ward off a persistent stitch she was relieved to see a very familiar figure sitting on a bench near the house.

Giving a feeble wave she screwed up her eyes in the heat, squinting at what appeared to be Si slumped down with his head in his hands. He showed no sign of having seen her, and drawing nearer it became apparent that all was not well. As she panted the last few feet and came to a standstill in front of him, he looked dazed and confused, staring at her as if she was the last person on earth he was expecting to see.

"Si! Thank god." She gasped bending down and resting her hands on her thighs as she got her breath back. "I thought I was going to be late."

He looked at her blankly.

She frowned. "Come on. Don't you know what time it is? Why aren't you ready? You haven't even styled your hair." A note of concern entered her voice. "Oh my God, you haven't styled your hair! Something's wrong, what is it?"

He shook his head slightly and lifted a hand to his scruffy barnet as if the thought had only just occurred to him.

"Didn't I? Oh, alright, I'll come now." He sounded strange.

"Well let's get going babes. I don't think Marina and Dario'll want me to show up wearing this old thing, do you?" She grinned at him and lifted her paint-smeared skirt elegantly giving a curtsey.

When no response was forthcoming she started to get a little worried.

"Darling, what's the matter?"

Si just looked at her beseechingly.

275

"Come on, you can tell me." She soothed crouching down in front of him and taking his hand in hers. "What's up?"

"It's my father..." He began falteringly, causing her eyes to fill with sympathy; in all their years of friendship she had never known him to express grief over his father's untimely passing.

"I know hon. It must be hard."

"No you don't." Si snatched his hand back, his expression wild. "My father's not dead... he's God, you know, from Nirvana."

She regarded him sternly. "Si Fraser! I can't believe you took drugs before your best friend's wedding. Come on, I'm taking you home for a cold shower and lots of coffee and.... fuck knows what'll help, you're clearly off your tits." She started pulling at his arm purposefully but he shrugged her off.

"I'm not on anything." He said more calmly. "Well, actually I'm a bit stoned. But that's beside the point. I mean *God*... not God, God. You know, *my* God. The guy I told you I met at Nirvana after Tony saw me stripping."

"You what?" Uncertainty clouded her features. "You're delirious... I think you may have sunstroke." She tried to feel his forehead but he ducked away.

"I just came back from Mum's. I think I'd better tell you exactly what she told me." He sighed patting the empty space of bench beside him and giving a mirthless little laugh. "You're gonna love this."

It took him ten minutes to explain by which time Gypsy looked just as baffled as he had previously.

"So let me get this straight." She said slowly. "Your father is.... Oh! Did you have sex with your Dad?"

He shook his head. "No, thank fuck. I just slept on his couch."

She put an arm round his shoulder. "What are you going to do? Do you even want to see him?"

"I don't know. It's all such a mess." He began laughing wildly, before he stopped catching her frightened look. "Sorry love, just a hysterical reaction."

"Right, fun-ny. Well, I suppose we'd better get changed."

"Yup." He stood up and linked her arm in his. "Don't worry, I'll be fine. It's a bit of a head fuck."

"Of course. I can't believe it." She rested her head on his shoulder. "You've got a Dad."

They rounded the corner preoccupied and completely unprepared for the sight which greeted them.

Number sixty-nine was surrounded by paparazzi. Photographers swarmed all over the tiny strip of garden out front and hung around the porch area, cameras at the ready, making the place look like some kind of surreal film set. More alarmingly a couple of police vans were parked on the kerb near the front of the house.

They both stood stock still, mouths hanging open as they surveyed the media circus which had appeared with startling incongruity at their front door. Then just as Gypsy was thinking things couldn't get any more bizarre, Si grasped hold of her arm and pointed as the front door burst open and two uniformed officers began manhandling their very own lodger George outside towards the back of one of the vans.

The paps leapt into action, bursting into an orgy of clicking and flashing as reporters called out to him. Microphones were shoved under his nose as he was pushed roughly inside the vehicle. His eyes flicked up towards where they stood staring in shock and then slid away again, a strange tick going in his face as he maintained a stony silence.

"Jesus." Si muttered putting an arm against the wall for support. "Gyps, I think the world's gone mad."

"Mad as a fish." She replied hoarsely. "No, make that ten clinically insane fish and a boxful of frogs."

Peering into the fray she spotted Tony arguing furiously with one of the reporters, gesticulating wildly. Suddenly he noticed the two of them looking on from the sidelines and called them over.

"Come on sweetie." Si told her firmly. "I think it's about time we found out what in the name of God... strike that... what in *hell's* name is going on around here."

277

As the two of them jostled their way into the crowd she was alarmed to feel Si's grip loosen on her hand. Then she lost him completely as he surged ahead, elbowing his way over to where they'd seen Tony before her vision was obscured by a beefy looking bloke in a tracksuit.

The blood thudded in her ears as the mass of strangers swallowed up the space in front of her.

Oh shit, I'm going to freak out, she thought to herself clapping her hands over her ears to block out the noise of everyone shouting. This is it; I'm going to have a panic attack. Then just as she felt she was about to collapse, a skinny blond woman with badly applied fake tan was peering into her face down her hook nose.

"It's Gypsy Wright!" The patchy-faced woman shrieked excitedly scrabbling around her neck for her Dictaphone. "Gypsy. Can you tell me how it feels to be linked with one of the most talked about models of the century?"

She blinked as a flashbulb exploded in her face, temporarily blinding her. "Er... I..."

"Gypsy! Over here!" Someone else yelled.

There was a murmur of excitement amongst the photographers as word spread and they began to flock around her, completely blocking any possible escape route. Disorientated she turned around straining to look for her two other housemates.

"Gypsy! What's with the costume? Are you doing a show?" A pasty looking teen with bad acne enquired holding a tape recorder up to her mouth.

"Please... Leave me alone." She whispered trying to push through the bodies. Disturbingly she felt she now knew what it would be like to be trapped in the midst of a rugby scrum.

"Give us a smile." Click, flash, click, click...

She managed a sickly grin and tried to duck under an obese woman's arm towards the nearest policeman.

"Help!" She croaked, cursing Sasha again for her lack of voice.

A greasy looking man with slicked back hair and dazzlingly white teeth stepped out in front of her and tried to ward the other reporters off with his hands.

"Okay, enough already guys... Leave the young lady alone."

"Thank you." Gypsy gasped weak with gratitude.

"My pleasure." He blinded her with another smile. "Let me introduce myself, my name's Ronny Fielding and I'm a representative of Insider Magazine." He led her out into the road to groans of disappointment from the others.

"Right." She blinked up at him. "Can you tell me what's happening here?"

"First off can I just check with you that George Dubois has been living here at this address?" Ronny asked.

"Well, yes..."

"I'm sorry to be the one to break it to you, but he's in the process of being taken into police custody." He looked at her brightly. "Were you aware he's a major drug dealer?"

"No!" Her eyes nearly popped out of her head.

Ronny raised his eyebrows and pursued his lips. "Yep, it appears the cops have been trying to track him down for some time now." He leaned closer. "Word is that he supplies a lot of local celebrities, including Nadia Olsen. Incidentally she's lying critically ill in hospital even as we speak from an overdose. My sources tell me that your George's also suspected of extortion and blackmail regarding another certain well known model."

"Blaine?" She breathed.

"Do you have any comment?" He asked scribbling eagerly in a notebook.

"No... No comment."

He smiled at her ingratiatingly and produced a business card from inside his jacket pocket which he pressed into her hand. "Well, why don't you give me a call sometime if you're interested in giving Insider the opportunity to hear the truth about your affair with *Mr* Feynard."

She glared at him. "No way, get lost."

279

"I wouldn't be so hasty if I were you." He urged with a condescending grin she found repellent. "The tabloids are just going to make it all up if you don't give them anything to go on. Why don't you get in there first, the public wants to hear the truth, Gypsy."

"I don't think so." She said frostily.

"Not even for ten grand." Ronny asked playfully. "Keep my card. You may change your mind."

"Get out of my way you CUNT!" She snapped pushing him in the chest and making a run for the front door. Hands tore at her dress as she lunged forward into the house. All she could think about was phoning Blaine and warning him about the press and the awful things she'd just been told.

Briefly the thought flashed through her mind that once again her picture was probably going to appear in the papers... and once again she was almost unrecognisable beneath stage make-up. Despite herself, a bubble of laughter welled up in her throat. All these years she had dreamed of making the headlines, she certainly hadn't planned on being dressed like a corpse for the occasion.

She slammed the door shut behind her, locking it as she did so, and collapsed in a heap in the hallway. Waiting until her breathing returned to normal, she reached out to grab the phone off the table and pulled it into her lap. As she did so a ten-pound note fluttered out from her bodice and landed at her feet.

Glamour, this was not.

Chapter 55. Gatwick Reunited

"It just had to be her, didn't it?" Gladys snapped testily at Mark, drumming her finger nails on the steering wheel. "Out of all the police officers on the south coast this weekend, I would have to get fined by her, the only lesbian I've ever insulted."

"Temper, temper." He remarked irritatingly. "After all, you were speeding and what goes around comes around, it's karma."

"Karma, my ass." The drag queen retorted.

"And I'm sure out of all the lesbians in all the bars you frequent, she can't be the only one you've insulted." He continued. "There's her girlfriend for a start, remember? The one you called a ferocious dog?"

Gladys flashed her sea-coloured eyes at him dangerously, causing the car to swerve across the road. "I hope you're not trying to imply that my manner is usually anything but congenial?"

He chose not to reply and shrugged instead, humming along to the radio and looking out of his window at the passing countryside.

"Mark? Your silence is speaking volumes and I'm finding it insulting."

He sighed. "Look, don't get me wrong, you're a great guy. It's just that sometimes that gets lost underneath layers and

281

layers of... well... bitch. I mean I wasn't all that keen on you when we first met."

She looked hurt. "I thought you found me exotic and irresistible."

He laughed gaily.

"I'm serious."

"Oh." He stopped laughing and looked uncomfortable. "That's not exactly how I would've described you to be brutally honest. It's just that you seem to have this kind of defensive thing going on. It's like you expect to get a hard time off people, so you get in there first. I'm only telling you this because I want you to know how lovely the real you is. Maybe if you weren't so off putting, well... you might have more friends."

"I have plenty friends." Gladys huffed before beeping her horn at a slow moving Ford Fiesta in front of them. "Move it you cunts, you're making me late!" She yelled out of the window.

He shot her a look, one eyebrow raised. "Name three."

"Stop distracting me." She complained frowning at the road ahead. "Is this have-a-go-at-JJ day or something? First of all that evil troll gives me a speeding ticket out of spite... I could tell she was enjoying it, and now you're picking on me too."

"Three names."

She sighed. "Okay then, fine. You, Elliott and Fred. Happy now?"

"Punters and stalkers don't really count." He pointed out.

"Whatever. So you and Sasha Bitch then, even if she can be a two-faced back-stabbing ho-bag." Gladys smiled with admiration. "I've got a lot of time for her, such a talent."

He gave up. "Shall we play a game?"

"What like?"

"Eye spy?" He suggested.

Her mobile started to vibrate off the dashboard, landing on Mark's lap.

"Hold that thought sugar. This could be one of my friends calling now." She reached out and flipped open the tiny silver phone.

"He-llo, Gladys Cox-Hardt speaking."

He tuned out and began thumbing through a magazine.

"Change of plan." She told him when she'd finished her call. "I've just had the bride-to-be on the blower."

"Ooh, is the wedding off?" He asked hopefully, he couldn't wait to get out of his corset, it really was ridiculously tight. No wonder medieval women were always fainting all over the shop and having to be revived with smelling salts, he thought. He felt much sorrier for them now he could personally emphasize with their plight.

"Nope. It seems the bridegroom had one too many on his stag do and got himself stranded in Gatwick. She wants me to pick him up on the way."

Mark was horrified. "Absolutely not! Look at me?! That wasn't part of our deal."

"Too late, I've already said yes. Besides, I'm the only one travelling up this way. Look babe, if the groom doesn't show up there will be no wedding." She paused for impact. "And if there's no wedding there's no point in me going up to London in the first place."

"But I'm dressed like a hooker." He wailed, holding his pointy breasts to illustrate the fact. "I don't want to be seen like this until we get there, where I can blend in and hide."

Gladys grinned, her dimples flashing. "You're beautiful. The hooker look is *sooo* you. Seriously, you're the spit of Madge in her early years. I've done a good job if I do say so myself."

Agitated, he fussed with his platinum hair. "I don't know how you talked me into this in the first place."

"Don't get your Calvin's in a knot; it won't be far out of our way." She said breezily.

"Bloody heteros and their stag nights." He sulked. "How the hell did he end up in Gatwick anyway? An aborted escape attempt?"

"Mark?"

283

He looked over at her moodily. "What?"

She gave him an exasperated look. "Shut up will you, I'm trying to remember the way."

"Fine." He rolled his eyes and picked up the magazine. "I won't say another word."

"Good."

"Fine then."

"Ma-rk, shuddup!"

X

Another trying forty minutes later and they'd parked in a grey looking suburban street near Gatwick Airport. Undoing her seatbelt Gladys thumbed through her mobile trying to decipher the directions from a text.

"Come on." Mark urged desperately wanting to get the ordeal over with. "This must be the right road. Look, it says Sedgwick Avenue."

She frowned. "I know, but I can't see number seventy-two. Damn it, I think Marina might have sent me the wrong address."

"I've got a friend called Marina." He sighed, feeling a wave of homesickness for his London friends. The ones who didn't make him wear wigs, or make it their life's work to embarrass him.

"Hang on a sec." Gladys pointed directly ahead of them. "Look over there! At the top of the street; I think that could be them."

Mark squinted in the sunlight; he could vaguely make out two figures running towards them. Hurriedly he rifled through his handbag and jammed on an outsized pair of sunglasses. This was going to be humiliating. He covered as much of his face as possible with his wig before glancing up again through the monofibre strands. He did a double take. It couldn't possibly be...

The two men were much closer, and extremely disheveled looking. He broke out into a sweat, eyes widening in panic as their faces came into view. His brain scrambled

284

around wildly for an explanation, but nothing came to mind. The figures were unmistakably his ex-boyfriend Dario and Ash from the Black Cock. His mouth opened and closed like a goldfish, but no sound came out. A strange ringing noise started in his ears and he squeezed his eyes shut tight in horror.

"Oi!" He heard Gladys call as she slid down the window and poked her head outside. "Is one of you gorgeous boys getting hitched today?"

"Yes! Thank you, thank you for coming!" Dario sounded out of breath and not at all surprised to see a flamboyantly attired tranny riding to his rescue. "I'm the groom, Dario."

"And *I'm* a bridesmaid!" Ash trilled jumping in front of his friend and leaning down to give her a kiss on the cheek.

"Lovely to meet you both, I'm Gladys Cox-Hardt." She purred smiling suggestively at Ash. Hiding behind his shades, Mark could hear that she'd effortlessly moved into full on flirt mode. If only she had an off switch.

"Hot, hot, *hot*! If he wasn't getting married though, I'd swear he was a sister." She whispered to him out of the corner of her mouth. Then she gestured for the other two to get in the back. "Come on! Don't be shy. We wouldn't want to be late for your big day now."

Mark took a deep breath. "Wait!"

He opened the car door and shakily got out onto the pavement, wobbling like a newborn calf in his heels. He staggered towards Dario and Ash, who were staring at him in expectant silence. He felt a twinge as he looked into his ex-partner's familiar eyes... he was still a good-looking sonofabitch even when he'd obviously had very little sleep.

"It's me." He said impatiently, as Dario frowned and Ash looked puzzled. With a frustrated sigh he removed the glasses. "It's me, Mark."

"Mark?" Dario took a step closer, his face falling in stupid surprise. "Oh my god.... is it really you under there?"

Ash pointed at him and let out a surprised shriek of laughter.

285

"Fuck! It *is* Mark! Look at that, he's actually got quite good legs."

Gladys leaned out of the window. "What on earth's going on? Mark, you know these two?"

"Yeah." He took off his wig and threw it to her. "This is my ex, Dario... and his friend Ash."

"Okay, whatevers, leave me out of it. I'll be ready to set off when you guys are." She stuck her head back inside and lit up a cigarette whilst pretending to ignore the scene that was unfolding itself in front of her very eyes.

Dario looked at him. "What the hell are you doing here? How did you know about the wedding?"

Mark was bewildered. "I don't know about the wedding, or at least I didn't know. You're getting married?! Did I miss something?"

"Er... You guys? I think I'm going to keep Gladys Knobsbig or whatever company in the car." Ash said shuffling from foot to foot as the two of them stared at each other, not even glancing over in his direction.

"See you in a minute then." He added as they neglected to respond.

"It's Marina." Dario explained. "She agreed to marry me so I can stay in the country. I wanted to tell you but no one knew how to get hold of you." He broke off confused. "I thought you were in Brighton? What are you doing in drag, and with the entertainment?"

Mark cracked a smile. "This is unbelievable! I don't know whether to laugh or cry, this isn't how I wanted it to be... seeing you again."

"You mean you didn't imagine yourself in a bustier and lipstick?"

"No, not exactly." He wiped his eyes, his face growing serious again. "Look, this doesn't mean... You really hurt me you know. I can't just go straight into being friends, as if nothing's happened."

"I know that." Dario looked at his feet. "So... how was Brighton?"

"I did alright. I was staying with her." He tilted his head over towards Gladys who was chatting away with Ash who'd joined her in the passenger seat. "I should have known those two would get on like a house on fire." He muttered.

"Look, why don't we talk on the way up to London." Dario said avoiding his ex-lover's eyes. "I've got a lot to tell you, and I want to hear all your news too... but Marina's gonna kill me if I miss the wedding, and I'll get deported...."

Mark nodded. "You make a good point. After you."

They both climbed into the back of the car awkwardly.

In the front Ash was trying on Mark's wig and helping himself to Gladys' makeup, the two of them seemed to be bonding nicely.

As Gladys switched on the ignition the engine roared into life and the houses began to blur together into one greyish mass as they picked up speed and zipped along the little roads.

Furtively Mark tried to sneak little glimpses of his ex out of the corner of his eye. He had prepared himself for a traumatic day, but really, this was taking the piss.

Chapter 56. Rescue Me

As they left Gatwick behind them and drew closer to London the atmosphere in Gladys' old, red Skoda lightened. This was partially due to the music. It would've been hard for a tense mood to prevail as they listened to the camp tracks she'd put on in preparation for her gig. Ash had given Mark back his wig after pouncing with satisfaction on a longer and more glamorous one with realistic caramel highlights. He'd also found a sparkly dress and stilettos which he proceeded to wriggle into from the seat.

Dario and Mark's conversation had gradually disintegrated into recriminations and sniping over the demise of their relationship. Gladys, who refused to be subjected to pre-show animosity on the grounds that it could affect her performance, (and who refused to be out-diva-ed on the grounds that *she* was the star) made it very clear they could either shut the fuck up or find another ride. To ensure harmony was restored to the drag-mobile she passed around some refreshments consisting of pre-rolled joints and a bottle of Malibu. This resulted in a drastic change of ambiance and much singing along to Rhianna.

After screaming their way through a few numbers Dario and Mark began filling each other in on recent events. Meanwhile Ash and Gladys loudly regaled each other with stories of clients from hell and swapped tips on how to give the world's best blowjob.

Dario hesitantly told Mark about Vincent and how the famous stylist had come to be his newest boyfriend. He then went on to elaborate on the details of his marrying Marina. As if that wasn't enough news for one sitting, he found he couldn't wait to tell all about Blaine Feynard and Gypsy being all over the papers. He realised he'd missed having his best friend to talk too.

Not to be outdone Mark reeled off stories of his action-packed summer with the unpredictable Miss Cox-Hardt, he entertained him with tales of how he'd helped fend of stalkers and ex-punters, how Elliott had ended up introducing them to some of his fit friends (including the fireman he'd hit it off with), and what a fabulous time he'd had at Brighton Pride.

All things considered, Mark reflected, the journey seemed to be going a lot better than had seemed likely under the circumstances. Thanks to Gladys' speeding it even started to look amazingly as if they might be on time after all.

No sooner had Mark had the thought than the drag-mobile made a serious of alarming noises. The car began jerking around wildly causing it's passengers to bump up and down violently in their seats to the screech of tires. They swerved, veering around into the next lane of traffic and narrowly avoid collision with a van. Struggling to maintain control of the wheel, Gladys finally managed to force the vehicle onto the hard shoulder of the motorway where it screeched to a bone-jolting halt.

The four occupants sat in stunned silence exchanging appalled looks as traffic zoomed passed them London-wards.

It took nanoseconds for the initial shock to wear off and then everyone began shouting at once.

X

Gladys put two fingers between her lips and gave a shrill whistle, then when that had no effect, raised her hands above her hairpiece and clapped loudly.

"Right!" She yelled, twisting around in her seat to face all three of them. Ash's eyebrows shot up, he hadn't yet witnessed the drag queen in assertive mode.

"Now that I have your undivided attention, I want everybody out of the car NOW!"

Mark refused to be ordered around. "I'm not setting foot outside dressed like this."

"Out!" Gladys insisted. "Out! Out! OUT!"

Ash was the first to comply, quickly followed by Dario who shrugging his shoulders scooted over to the middle seat and reached over his ex-lover to unlock the door. "Come on. I think she means business."

Gingerly Mark lowered a high-heeled foot onto the gravel. He muttered under his breath as he joined Ash and Gladys by the side of the road. He'd never felt more ridiculous. The only saving grace being that the traffic was moving so quickly he had no way of gauging people's reactions. Dario got out last, smirking slightly at the sight of the three of them.

"This is so not funny." Mark tossed his blond curls and swiped at Dario's leg with his handbag. "You won't be laughing if we miss your wedding and you have to leave the country, dickhead."

Dario blew him a kiss. "It'd almost be worth it to see you looking like this!"

Ash was adjusting the straps of his sequined dress. "Can I bum a fag off someone?"

"Here." Mark threw him his pack. "Now for fuck's sake what are we going to do? Do you think it's fixable?" He asked Gladys who'd been peering under the car's bonnet.

"Erm." The drag queen avoided his eyes. "I would say so... yes."

"Great! Well let's hurry up and get it sorted then." Dario urged. "I can't miss this wedding. Marina will never forgive me, and as for Lisa..." He closed his eyes in horror at the thought of what Marina's girlfriend and his boss would have to say.

"What is it?" Mark asked eyeing her suspiciously. He put his hands on his hips as realisation dawned. "You forgot to fill her up, didn't you?"

"Don't attack moi! I can't be expected to remember every little thing." Gladys snapped defensively. "Besides, I'm the one doing all of you lot a favour. Without me you'd be stuck with public transport." She reminded them.

Mark ground his teeth together. "Without you, I wouldn't be wearing fake tits and standing by the side of a motorway."

"Fine! I suppose none of you ungrateful bitches wants to hear my solution then." She turned her back on them and sashaying to the other side of the car.

Ash finished his cigarette and stamped it out with one heel. "I do!"

Mark sighed. "Okay. Tell us your brilliant plan then. This had better be good."

She swiveled around with a radiant smile, fluttering her fake lashes at her attentive audience. "Well, alrighty. If you're all ready to listen now?"

"We are!" Ash promised.

"Right then ladies." She announced ignoring a snort of disapproval from Mark. "We have a wedding to get to. I'm a professional, and that means I never let my fans down."

They looked at her expectantly.

"The most sensible, no the only solution is for us to hitch-hike into town."

Mark opened his mouth to protest and then closed it again, it didn't seem that they had much choice; options were limited to say the least.

X

It wasn't long before all four of them were waving and shouting at the road-side, inhibitions tossed to the wind as they watched the cars whiz past again with increasing frustration. Each tried their best to capture the attention of the speeding traffic whilst passing around the remains of the Malibu.

291

Clearly in her element, Gladys who'd started the car's engine and put on the music, treated the Sunday afternoon travellers to a dance and lip-sync routine. Dario went for the more conventional approach of jumping up and down and waving his arms in the air, occasionally sticking his thumb out at the oncoming vehicles, to little avail. Ash was surprising everyone with some pretty impressive dance moves to the music belting out of the drag-mobile's window, whilst Mark who'd commandeered the majority of the alcohol began voguing sullenly. Eventually the group caught the attention of a passing fire-engine.

"Oh my! I think I've died and gone to heaven!" Gladys stage whispered to Dario as the big red truck pulled over beside them. A couple of highly amused looking firemen poked their heads out from inside.

"This is like my favourite fantasy." She went on dreamily. "Except of course you lot aren't here, and there are more of them."

The firefighters clapped respectfully as they all clambered aboard accompanied by whistles and yells of approval. Gladys gave a modest curtsey and nearly fell back onto the road in her high heels to uproarious laughter.

Feeling self-conscious and hoping that their saviours wouldn't turn out to be violent tranny-hating homophobes; Mark allowed himself be introduced to Steve, Jerry, Owen and Connor who were all sitting in the back drinking coffee from a thermos and chatting amongst themselves. It transpired that they were heading back to their base in Soho after a training day. When they heard the story about the wedding there were snorts of helpless laughter and raised eyebrows but they cheerfully agreed to drop them off. Dario, Gladys and Ash were enchanted and beside themselves with gratitude. Mark wished longingly for a pair of jeans and a nice bland T-shirt.

As the engine roared into life and they sped up the motorway, a fifth fireman emerged from the front. His nicely muscled arms were laden with packets of sandwiches which he passed around his colleagues. He was tall and well-built

292

with dark close-cropped hair and melting brown eyes which flickered briefly over Mark and his embarrassingly enormous cone shaped breasts... The man frowned, shook his head and looked again. Mark's own appraising look froze as they stared at each other.

Jeff, unmistakably *his* fireman from Pride was the first to regain his composure.

"Mark? God! Sorry, it took me a moment, but in my defense you do look a bit... different." The corner of his mouth twitched slightly. "Have you erm... done something to your hair?"

Damn. Mark thought. He'd forgotten how sexy Jeff was. Oh shite. He wondered how many ex shags with were going to see him in this ridiculous get up. He fluttered his hands in an abortive effort to hide his chest.

"You know, I'm flattered but if you wanted to get my attention you could've just called." The fireman said with a grin. "I left my number with your friend, the drag queen." He looked around at Ash and Gladys who were trying to flirt with Steve and Owen simultaneously and Dario who gave him a coy wave. "*One* of the drag queens... What in hell's going on? It looks like the Pink Flamingo back here."

Chapter 57. A Wedding to Remember

Marina hovered anxiously outside the Town Hall, taking sanctuary on the sunbaked steps outside. She'd begun feeling claustrophobic and panicky waiting inside with all the guests.

Lisa had been a superstar thank god, she thought affectionately, or she wouldn't have been coping nearly as well as she was. Her girlfriend had taken charge of all the after-party arrangements, as well as ferrying over several guests who'd helped with the preparations. Jeremy who'd somehow managed to get drunk even under her eagle eye had been settled in a seat with a Styrofoam cup of black coffee.

She noticed that Sally and a few other regulars had formed a little huddle inside, chatting amongst themselves and pretending not to be impressed by celebrity guests Vincent and a strained looking Blaine who were standing together and exchanging pleasantries. Seeing Lisa swoop down on the couple and begin introducing them to the Black Cock punters she smiled. As the bride, looking after the guests was probably her responsibility by rights but she simply couldn't face everyone asking where the groom was for the hundredth time.

Crossing her fingers behind her back, she sighed. It was out of her hands now, all she could do was hope that the party host, Gladys Cox-Hardt, would make good on her promise to get him there on time. Otherwise all their efforts would be for nothing.

"Hey! Looking good, Rina." Duncan Cavendish surprised her by taking her photograph. "Love the dress and the hair." He bounded up the stairs to give her a hug.

"Thanks." She said smiling a little self-consciously as the wind blew her blonde curls around her face. "Why don't you go inside and get a drink?"

He blew her a kiss. "I'm on my way."

She waved him inside and threw her cigarette away. Seconds later she spotted Stella and Cathy getting out of a taxi on the other side of the road.

"Oh dear! I hope we're not late." Cathy cried, looking very elegant and completely OTT in a black cocktail dress and diamond earrings. "Marina you look simply divine."

"Ta." She allowed herself to be kissed on both cheeks by each woman in turn. Stella, she noted, was dressed in a bizarre muumuu arrangement worn with lots of chunky bracelets. They made the most incongruous couple, she thought with some amusement, adding. "You're not late. We're still missing five guests and the main man."

Cathy looked concerned. "Is Si here yet?"

"No." Marina bit her lip. "Why don't you go inside? I'm sure everyone'll arrive soon."

They wandered over to where Lisa was waiting to welcome them.

Oh God, Marina thought, where is everybody? She was just about to make her way back into the hall, when she caught sight of four figures running up the road, scattering pedestrians as they went. She let out a sigh of relief, okay the groom himself was still absent, but at least her other friends had made it.

Kate, Danny, Gypsy and Si crowded around her in an out-of-breath flurry of apologies, kisses and hugs before she sent them all in to find seats. Her heart felt lighter knowing they hadn't abandoned her in her hour of need after all.

Kate and Danny ducked into the lobby and began talking animatedly to each other, whilst Gypsy bounded up to Blaine and introduced herself to Vincent. The three of them stood chatting and agreeably posed for a photograph at Duncan's

295

request. Si got a coffee and stood with Stella and his mother before walking outside to join the frazzled looking bride.

"Do you think he's changed his mind?" She asked worriedly, eyes still searching the road for any sign of him.

Si put his arm around her shoulder. "No, he's just running late. He wouldn't have asked you guys to go to all this trouble to not show up."

"Crap! He's so bloody unreliable." She scowled. "I can't believe he went out last night, I knew something like this would happen. What a prick!"

"Ah, true love." He grinned. "It warms the heart."

"Shut up." She dug him in the ribs. "Anyway, talking of true love, where's Tony?"

He rolled his eyes. "He's giving a statement to the police. He'll be along later."

"What?!"

Si nodded. "That's why Gypsy and I were late; I've had the most eventful morning ever. Our lodger has been arrested, and as if that wasn't enough, I've got some family stuff going on that you wouldn't believe."

Marina looked at him concerned. "God, I'm sorry to hear that Si. The family stuff, I hope it's nothing serious."

"I'd rather not talk about it now; I'll fill you in later."

"Sure." She offered him a fag. "What about this business with the lodger?"

"Thanks." He took one and lit it. "Well, apparently he's a big time drug dealer. I think Nadia Olsen, you know the model, is somehow involved. Did you hear she's in hospital?"

She shook her head and shrugged.

"Overdose."

"Oh."

He looked around to make sure no one was eavesdropping. "Someone told me that Blaine was the one who found her. Apparently if he hadn't showed up when he did, Nadia would be dead."

"Oh no! I feel terrible, he didn't need to turn up for my and Dario's half-assed wedding. He should be with her or at home." She looked stricken.

"It's okay honey." Gypsy materialised beside them. "Ida's at the hospital. He wanted to come; besides we needed to talk. It's been a nightmare. Have you seen? We're all over the papers."

Si gave her a hug. "How are you doing babes?"

"I'm fine." She squeezed him back and gave a tired smile. "Have you spoken to your mum about you-know-who yet?"

"Not yet." He silenced her with a look.

Marina interrupted their exchange. "If your mate Ida's not coming then we're only waiting for the groom, the wedding singer and Ash."

"There's quite a turn out isn't there." Si peered into the hall. "Who are all those other people I don't know? Look! Who on earth is that strange looking lady with the floppy hat talking to Mum?"

"No idea." She said distractedly. "They must be friends of Dario's. Jesus, this street's noisy."

Gypsy was frowning, and squinting into the distance. Suddenly she gave a squeal of excitement and raised her arm to point at a large red vehicle coming down the street. It was partially hidden behind a double-decker bus.

"Rina?" She said, laughing. "I think the fire-engine of drag queens you ordered has arrived!"

"You what?"

"Lordy." Si muttered putting his hands to his ears to block out the piercing sound of the siren as it wailed louder. "She's not joking, look Rina... I think it's headed straight here."

X

By the time the fire engine had parked, the best part of the wedding ensemble had spilled outside to witness the spectacular arrival of the groom.

"This is better than Corrie." Si whispered to Gypsy. "I can't believe Tony's going to miss all this."

Marina ran over to where a sheepish looking Dario was getting out of the passenger seat.

297

"Oh thank god! I thought you were gonna miss your own wedding, you fuckwit!"

He hung his head. "I'm sorry. I know I've been a nightmare, please forgive me!"

"Lisa's gonna have your balls for breakfast."

"Would you believe we had to hitch-hike?!"

"What?!"

"I know. It's been the morning from hell, but I'm here now, thank god." He grinned over her shoulder at Gypsy and Si, who both gave him a wave. Duncan Cavendish emerged from the crowd to capture the moment on his camera.

Marina looked annoyed. "But I arranged for the wedding singer to pick you up!" She looked on in amazement as three drag queens started the slow process of disembarking from the vehicle in heels, helped by a handful of firemen. "Where did this lot come from, and where's Ash?"

"The wedding singer *did* pick us up, but her car broke down... so these fine men kindly took us the rest of the way." Dario explained smiling at her as she looked at him uncomprehendingly. "The small, one with streaky hair's Ash, the tall eye-catching one is Gladys Cox-Hardt, the entertainment, and..." he squeezed her hand delightedly. "Wait for it... The one dressed as an eighties Madonna is Mark, *our Mark.*"

Her mouth dropped open. She turned round and shouted to Gypsy and Si. "Guys! It's *Mark.* Mark and Ash are here!"

In a matter of seconds, a busty Mark was surrounded by his astounded friends. Gypsy wanted to feel his boobs. Jeremy, who was having a second wind, wanted to dance; Si wanted to know what the hell he was doing with Dario in a fire truck, and Lisa tried to book him for the pub, arguing this could be the start of a promising new career.

Grinning, Mark introduced Jeff to his friends, enjoying their surprise and approval, not to mention the attention tremendously. Not a bad homecoming all in all. He thought to himself feeling the fireman slide an arm around his corseted waist. He discovered that even the sight of Dario

298

flying into the arms of Vincent didn't bother him now. Well, not much anyway.

Once she had both platform stilettos on terra firma, Gladys Cox-Hardt, eyes focused on some unseen point in the crowd, swept into the throng like the queen she was. Milling guests scattered in her wake, as she made a beeline for Blaine.

The beautiful supermodel stood out like a swan as he watched the proceedings. As Gladys approached he lifted his head up, frowning slightly. His face lit up in delighted recognition, as he shouted out a greeting and ran forward to embrace the drag queen.

From the side-lines Gypsy watched entranced as the two stood face to face, gazing at each other. Both wearing heels, they were approximately the same height, one heavily made up and outrageous in a skin tight PVC dress, inches of makeup and an elaborate hairpiece, the other a natural and exotic beauty in guy-liner and haute couture. Drag queen versus cross-dressing supermodel...

"It can't be..." Blaine gasped one hand on his chest. "JJ... Is that you?"

"Gracie baby!" Gladys shrieked. "I knew it was you the moment I saw you on your first Vogue cover. I'd recognise you anywhere, but I never said I word to anyone. Imagine me, keeping my mouth shut like that?! Look at how hot you got though! And look how far you've come girl; I'm so proud of you!"

The two fell into each other's arms.

Gypsy fished around in her bag producing a tissue for Blaine. He took it blowing her a kiss before dabbing carefully under his damp eyes.

"Hi." She introduced herself to the entertainer with a cheeky grin. "I'm Gypsy but you can call me Faye Kinnett." She stuck out her hand. "Faux queen at your service. I've seen you perform at the Flamingo, you're fab."

Gladys looked down at her, surprised and amused. "Hi yourself. I'm Gladys Cox-Hardt." She smirked. "Drag artiste extraordinaire."

"Nice name."

They shook hands solemnly.

Gypsy looked at her slightly confused. "Have we met somewhere before?"

"I don't think so..."

"Where are my manners? Forgive me. Gladys, Gypsy is a good friend of mine." Blaine explained. "Gypsy, this is my old roomie, JJ. Or... what did you say your drag name is? We knew each other simply years ago." He widened his eyes. "Before the operation, before I became famous. He taught me everything I know about... well, lots of things."

Gypsy raised her eyebrows. "I hear you're performing at the after-party as well. Do you work in London a lot? Coz if you need an agent up here, you should speak to my friend Cathy, she's the best."

None of them noticed the mustached lady in the huge sun-hat edge away having listened to every word whilst scribbling furiously in a spiral notepad.

X

"What's going on?" Kate asked Danny as they made their way through the lobby and out into the open air where assorted guests, celebrities, firemen and drag queens milled around a large fire engine.

"I haven't got a clue." He replied, looking lost.

She linked her arm through his. "Come on, let's go and ask Marina when it's kicking off, maybe I've got time to buy some shoes after all."

When he failed to respond she turned to give him a nudge. However, she noticed he suddenly seemed rooted to the spot, his good-looking head tilted slightly away from her.

"Danny." She tried to propel him down the stairs, but he disentangled his arm from hers without moving.

"Hey? Hello, earth to Danny." It was then that Kate noticed the drag queen standing beside of all people, Gypsy and Blaine Feynard. She was looking right at them, her face a mask of shock.

Similarly, Danny looked like he'd seen a ghost. Following his gaze she was certain he was indeed staring at the eye-catching drag artiste. She looked from one to the other and then slowly back again. It was the identical expressions that were the tip off.

Her jaw dropped open as the undeniable truth dawned on her... Same nose, same face shape. Could those be the same lips and eyes under all that make-up? She gaped, eyes darting back and forth. Fucking hell! She felt a rush of adrenaline. It couldn't be... could it?

Kate took a step back nearly tripping over a rotund lady in a wide-brimmed hat and floral smock. It was hard to tell on account of the hair and costume. Yet the more she looked the surer she was. One was straight and her boyfriend, the other camp as glitter-spray and yet, she raised her hand above her eyes to shield them from the glare of the sun, they were alike as two peas in a pod. She was not the only one to notice the family resemblance. As Danny made his way over, guests parted to let him through their mutterings growing to an audible buzz. Everyone's attention was riveted on the drama unfolding before them. The crowd watched, transfixed, as he strode over to a stunned looking Gladys Cox-Hardt.

Gypsy who was standing next to them watched with bated breath as the drag queen drew herself up to her full height, a sharp retort on her lips. Then something seemed to snap inside of her, she slumped visibly. Her mouth trembled; face collapsing as she burst into noisy sobs. The two hugged clumsily, both in tears.

Gypsy swallowed a lump in her throat at the sight of such an emotional reunion. With a jolt, she realised instantly who Danny had reminded her of. Wow, she thought slipping her hand into Blaine's, if Kate's boyfriend ever felt like doing a spot of female impersonation the two of them would make a spectacular double act. She pursed her lips wondering if she could feature somehow and if Danny could be persuaded to play ball. They could be Gladys and Mia Cox-Hardt, she thought excitedly. With names like that they'd surely be destined for big things.

301

The other guests looked puzzled and unsure of how to proceed. Eventually a few of them started clapping uncertainly, which led to a smattering of applause from the others.

Kate smiled, sniffed and reached into her pocket for a tissue. They'd finally found Julian, she realised... when they weren't even looking. How ironic and wonderful.

Meanwhile, not really understanding what was taking place, Marina started rounding everybody up and ushering them back into the lobby. Although she was relieved that all were now present and correct, she couldn't help but feel a tad disgruntled.

So what if it wasn't a real wedding? Surely as bride she should still get a little more attention?

X

Uncomfortable and dripping with sweat in his disguise, Ronny Fielding stumbled down the steps away from the Town Hall. Casting a backward glance at the double-doors to make sure no one was watching, he tore off his floppy hat and wig and flung them in the nearest bin, heading for his car. He was so focused on piecing together the article in his mind he hardly noticed the odd looks he was getting from passers-by. The wedding would make a great story.

Meanwhile people stared with barely concealed hilarity at his flower print-dress, fake bosoms and court shoes. He remained oblivious to their amusement and to the cat-calls he got from passing traffic.

Once inside the relative privacy and comfort of his car he flipped through his notes critically.

Blaine's Bonkers Wedding Bash!

Today Chalmsworth Town Hall saw Blaine Feynard attend the unconventional and surprisingly star-studded marriage of barrista Dario Kruger, 28, and artist Marina Wells, 30.

Kruger, originally from South Africa and now pulling pints in gay bar 'The Black Cock' arrived at his wedding in a fire engine. Bizarrely, a group of the fire-fighters stayed to support the union. Also in attendance was Blaine's alleged girlfriend, actress Gypsy Wright, keeping the public guessing regarding his sexuality. Other guests included celebrated stylist Vincent Santelli and award-winning photographer Duncan Cavendish.

A reliable source confirmed that an extraordinary after-party was thrown to mark the occasion with drag queen Gladys Cox-Hardt hosting the event. She appeared to be there with her twin brother and is being championed by Blaine as up and coming performer of the year in celeb-land.

Sadly no invitation was forthcoming. It sounds like it would've been one for Insider Magazine to remember!

Ronny sighed, of course what he really wanted was an exclusive with Blaine's actress friend, but to say she hadn't seemed keen was an understatement.

He wondered if he still had time to drive down to the hospital to get the latest on Nadia Olsen's condition, before deciding it could wait until after dinner.

His stomach growled. Luigi's pasta and spicy meatballs was waiting a few blocks away. Licking his lips he decided to stop at his favourite Italian eatery en route. Though knowing his shitty luck, he thought putting the car into gear and reversing, the supermodel would probably snuff it in the meantime. Now that really would be a pisser.

303

Chapter 58. Settling Dust

"Hello stranger." Kate smiled as Si entered the Fraser Buchanan Agency's reception area. "Do you have an appointment?" She teased, looking at her PC.

"It's a fine day when you have to make an appointment to see your own mother!"

He sat down on the imitation leather sofa. "I'm liking what they've done with the place; very chic and it's such a fantastic location. You make a lovely receptionist, darling."

"Thanks. Cathy's in with a client now, she won't be long though. Are you going to wait?"

Si thought about it then nodded. "Yeah, I think she's going to want to hear this."

"Well?" Kate leant forward. "What's up? Or don't you want to divulge?"

"I don't see any reason why not." He settled back into the sofa, eyes twinkling. "I went to see my father today."

"Oh! The fit one you called God?" She got up and poured them both a coffee from the machine.

"Yeah." He winced. "Although obviously I call him Karl or Dad now."

"Well, yes." She added milk and handed him a polystyrene cup. "And how's it going?"

"Thanks." He accepted the drink and took a sip. "It's alright actually. We're taking it very slowly though. Oh and FYI, I only agreed to meet provided we don't discuss the night we met, *ever*." He frowned. "I do want us to have some kind of a relationship, but it'll take some getting used to."

She shrugged. "Yeah, I imagine it's not easy."

"Well, he made a great first impression." He rolled his eyes seeing her expression. "No! I don't mean in the club, you terrible woman! I mean on our first 'getting to know each other' visit he offered to pay for me to go on holiday."

Kate raised one eyebrow. "So you turned him down on principle, right?"

"Er... no, not quite." He admitted reluctantly. "You know how much Tony and I wanted to go on holiday? Well, like an idiot, I spent all my stripping money on a painting for him."

"Aww, bless. You're so in love"

Si grinned soppily. "Yeah, I am, aren't I? Anyway, now we can go to Mykonos."

"Get you, off gallivanting! I would kill for a holiday right now." She sighed.

They lapsed into silence as Jessica Reynolds; star of a popular new soap emerged from a side-door chatting away on her hands-free phone as she went.

"Well, looks like Cathy's available now." Kate said brightly. "Do you want me to buzz through and let her know you're coming or do you wanna surprise her?"

"I'll surprise her." He gave her wink. See ya later, alligator."

As soon as he was gone Kate tried to redirect her attention to a meeting that needed organising. Thoughts of her impending dinner with Danny made it hard to focus. He'd called only an hour ago and told her they needed to talk; words that no woman longs to hear. She had a horrible feeling she was about to get dumped.

X

Unusually, Blaine quite liked hospitals. He'd spent enough time in them, having various operations associated with his transition. Appreciatively he sniffed the faint smell of disinfectant, took in the polished floors, and the sight of doctors, nurses and other medical staff bustling around the corridors; all combined to give him a feeling of comfort and well being. Pottering around the ground floor he browsed in the shops looking at floral arrangements.

Also, he was familiar with this particular Hospital as it was near the in the Gender Identity Clinc, which he'd visited before embarking on the gender realignment process. He vividly recalled turning up for his first appointment. Back then he'd still answered to the name Grace Gillespie. He'd been so young, so full of fear. It seemed like a life time ago.

Blaine settled on a pretty bouquet of yellow roses using his credit card to pay. He was glad Nadia had ended up in a place he instinctively trusted, it reassured him that his friend would be well looked after. Checking the piece of paper in his pocket, and cradling his fragrant purchase in his arms he took the elevator to the fifth floor.

The last time he'd visited, Nadia had been sleeping so he'd sat by her side holding her hand until it was time to go. This time he wanted them to have a talk. It was long overdue; he had a flight to catch that evening and didn't want to leave without tying up some loose ends. His next port of call would be Gypsy, but he refused to think about that yet. He needed to concentrate on Nads.

Due to her celebrity status and the need for privacy, Nadia had been given a private room in the west wing. Peering through the glass panel at the top of the door he saw she already had a guest. He knocked twice before entering.

"Hi!" Ida stood up and walked around the bed to say hello. "I thought I might see you here today, how are you?"

"I'm fine. How are you doing angel." He greeted her warmly giving her a hug and peering over her shoulder to where Nadia lay in bed under crisp white sheets. Her lovely face was pale and pinched looking, with purple smudges under her eyes.

His smile faded. "Ida, could you give us a minute?"

"Sure." She waved at Nadia. "I was just going to get a coffee anyway."

Once they were alone he set about arranging the flowers into a vase on the bedside table, then sat down on the bed and reached for Nadia's free hand, the other being attached to an IV drip suspended above the head-rest.

"I can't believe you've come to visit me." She sounded groggy. "You should hate me. I'm a horrible, awful person B. They told me if you hadn't come home when you did I'd have... well, you saved my life. I don't deserve to live... to have visitors or friends, I'm such a total bitch."

He sighed. "It was you who wrecked my room, wasn't it?"

Nadia closed her eyes and when she opened them they were full of tears.

"Come on Nads. You were in the house alone, the front door was locked and nobody had broken in. I mean it doesn't take a genius. I just want to know why?"

"I can't tell you.... it's too awful." She whimpered her eyes downcast.

"And my private stuff, my photos?" He asked softly, dangerously. "You knew about me being Grace – didn't you?"

She nodded and tears spilled down her face and neck.

"It was you sending me those awful anonymous letters."

"God, I'm really sorry."

"Why, though? I thought we were friends! How could you put me through that?"

She erupted into loud sobs. "I'm sorry! I don't recognise myself anymore. I didn't think I was capable of doing those things to someone I love. But I thought you were going to get the ✡FX contract, and I needed it!" Her shoulders shook; she hiccupped and looked at his disgusted face pleadingly. "That money would've made so much difference to me. I haven't been getting enough work. Everything I've built up seems to be slipping away from me. I've been spending a lot on drugs, I guess... too much. It's all got out of control. I don't know how, suddenly everything I touch seems to turn to shit."

"Yeah, well that tends to happen to addicts." Blaine regarded her coolly. "How did you even know about my past in the first place?"

"My dealer, George, has a boyfriend who recognised you from the gay scene, years ago."

"So he was in on it too?"

"Yeah. He and Raphael tried to dig up dirt about your life before the sex change. He found out you were a stripper and even traced your old flat-mate, this rent boy named Julian."

"Yep JJ; we've actually caught up recently." Blaine replied matter-of-factly. "He's doing fantastic things on the drag circuit now by the way; the boy's a seriously talented performer. But anyway, I digress..." He paused. "He told me he'd been followed while he was living in Brighton. Would that be your doing?"

"Indirectly, I guess. It would've been Raphael. There was a mix up, George thought he'd come across him in London living at a different address and working for an advertising company or something? It got a bit messy."

Blaine allowed himself a tiny smile. "I'll say. You won't believe this, but he has an identical twin. What are the odds of that? It's sounding more like a bad soap opera by the minute. You know that George's been charged. He's going to jail."

"I've spoken to the police, they told me." Nadia sank back into the mattress exhaustedly. "Look, can I ask you one question?"

"What is it?"

"Why didn't you ever tell me you were trans, before all this started? I mean we're best mates."

"Why should I have?" Blaine was exasperated. "Before all this came out I told people strictly on a need to know basis. The beauty of having transitioned is that people see me as who I really am now. Besides, I'm glad I didn't. At least you had to work to find out all my secrets so you could use them against me. I would've been extra pissed off if I'd handed them to you on a plate."

"I don't blame you for hating me." She said in a small voice. "I deserve it."

"Don't be so dramatic. I don't hate you. I'm just really, really bloody mad at you right now."

"Do you think you can ever forgive me?"

"I suppose so. But as to whether I'll ever trust you again, I honestly don't know." He said staring at her sadly. "I forgive you because what you did was low girl, a horrible betrayal... but it wasn't you. The Nads I know and love would never have done those things. I mean sure you have your faults, but disloyalty isn't one of them."

"So what can I do to make it right?"

"I want you to get professional help, stay off the drugs and get yourself sorted out." He squeezed her hand. "You could probably use some counselling. I mean it's a tough old world in the fashion industry. It gets to the best of us."

A tear rolled down Nadia's face. "You're amazing."

"Well, in a way you helped me."

Blaine brushed her long brown hair away from her hollowed out cheeks. "I don't have to live with the constant fear of my secret coming out now, *and* my career is going better than I ever dreamed. You know I'm flying to L.A tonight? Filming for this soap which apparently is like the new, NEW 90210, but edgier – hence moi!"

"I'm happy for you." Nadia managed the first genuine smile he'd seen from her in a long time. "And I really mean that darling. I don't suppose there's any chance of us being house-mates again when you come back to the UK? Or if not, I'd settle for friends."

"We'll see." He hugged her. "Let's give it some time, alright? You've got to get better first."

X

As soon as they'd placed their orders Danny disappeared to the toilet. Kate took a deep breath, then nervously fluffed her hair around her shoulders, removed her jacket and took an enormous gulp of her white wine spritzer. She needed to de-stress. It'd been a busy day at work and she'd spent the entire time obsessing over this evening.

"It smells good in here." She said as he returned, trying to summon up some enthusiasm. "Are you hungry? I'm

309

famished; I only had a salad for lunch... good for the diet." She patted her stomach self-consciously.

Danny filled up her glass for her. "You know me. I can always eat."

Kate sighed. This was hopeless. Pretending nothing was the matter felt contrived and awkward, might as well get straight to the point.

"Look, you said that we needed to talk." She began falteringly. "And I think we should just... What I mean is can we get that part over with now please?"

"Yes, of course." Danny looked solemn and they sat in silence for while.

"I'm going back home, Kate."

"Ah. Okay." She looked at the menu again.

"Did you hear what I just said?"

She sighed. "Yeah, I heard. When are you leaving?"

"Next Monday." He said quietly.

"Well, I suppose we knew all along it wasn't going to be forever. But hey, we had a great time, didn't we?"

"I wish you wouldn't do that!" He sounded angry.

"Do what?"

"Be so goddamn flippant, it irritates the hell out of me. I love you for crying out loud."

She looked away from him. "Then why are you going to live the other side of the country? You could stay here. JJ's moved to London now, so you guys could spend time together. You already have a job. I don't see the problem."

He avoided the question. "JJ's going to share with Ash. Things have really turned around for him, and that's partly thanks to you for helping me find him."

"Did you ever find out why he disappeared in the first place?"

"Apparently he felt like he was living a lie back home, he wanted to be a drag queen and do his own thing. Our parents are kind of conservative, and a bit controlling." Danny took a sip of his drink. "He just went a bit crazy and needed to get away, so he came to London and joined that theatre group.

He just didn't want to be around the family anymore. He felt he couldn't stay there and be himself."

"Then he met up with Blaine Feynard, who was still Grace Gillespie at the time." Kate mused, interested despite the fact that they'd gone off at a tangent.

"Right. Then he got into debt, and tried to pay it off working as a rent boy. He moved to Brighton after he screwed Cordelia over and carried on doing pretty much the same thing there. Then his drag career started to take off."

"Oh my god!" She interrupted banging her hand on the table. "I've just realized James must've known Gladys and thought you were secretly a tranny! No wonder he's been so weird with me."

Danny raised his eyebrows. "I guess that would explain it."

"Do you mind? I mean, is it a big shock finding all this out about your brother?"

He frowned. "Yes and no. I'm not entirely shocked he's got himself in trouble, that's just Julian. As for Gladys Cox-Hardt... Hell, you saw his performance at the wedding party. He's sensational Kate! I felt so proud, I had no idea he'd be so good."

"He looked pretty amazing too. GREAT legs." Kate remarked.

"Anyway, he's paid off his debts now thanks to the money our Aunt left us." He shrugged. "And Cathy and Stella have agreed to manage his career hence the move to London. They'll get him regular acting work too. Plus he's got lots of friend's here in the city now."

"Gypsy adores JJ and says she owes him an eternal debt of gratitude." Kate added. "They're collaborating for a big show at the Pink Flamingo."

He chuckled. "Well I think they're two of a kind. Anyway, it's thanks to her that he talked to your boss and got himself an agent. You'll probably be seeing a fair bit of him at Fraser Buchanan in the future."

311

"Yeah, that's true." Her face fell as she thought of how she could well do without a constant reminder of what she was missing.

"I meant what I said before the wedding, you know?" He'd read her mind.

She regarded him through narrowed eyes. "You want a long distance relationship? Really?"

"It could work." He was looking at her hopefully, but Kate felt her heart sink at the prospect. Didn't they both deserve more than the odd weekend together before the inevitable happened and they drifted apart after a lot of heartache?

"You're going to say no, aren't you?"

He looked so sad and crestfallen that she leaned over and kissed him. "Couldn't you just stay in London?"

"Nah. It's not me, never has been. I want to get back to my old life. It's too hectic here. Everyone's always in a hurry, the crowds are a nightmare, the traffic's hell... and, well the long and short of it is I'm homesick, I suppose."

"I don't know." Kate ruffled his hair and gave him a grin. "I couldn't imagine living anywhere else. All the things you hate, I love! The pace, the fact the city feels so alive, the excitement, the fact there's always a shop open and everything's on your doorstep."

He shrugged glumly. "I suppose that answers the question of whether or not you'd think about coming with me then."

"Oh, Danny! It means so much that you asked. I love you, I really do. But I can't leave London." She took his hands in hers. "Look, I may only have the luxury of your company for... what? A week? Let's enjoy every last minute we have together, starting right now?"

"Okay." He smiled. "Shall we go home? I'm not that hungry anyway."

X

After meeting Blaine in a café near Charing Cross Hospital, Gypsy jumped on a bus toward Putney. She called Si only to discover he was visiting his mum at Fraser Buchanan's offices; however once she'd explained her dilemma he happily agreed to join her at the Black Cock in an hour. Disembarking at Putney Bridge she made her way along the tow-path.

She desperately needed to think. After spending a while staring into the murky depths of the Thames for an answer she wandered over to a riverside café for a solitary cappuccino.

A while later, finishing off the dregs and slowly retracing her steps, she mooched back up to the high street. She shivered in her thin jersey and jeans, already the weather was autumnal. The end of the summer seemed to her to signify the end of an era somehow, but the question of course remained... Should she move on, or stay along for the ride?

By the time she'd walked to the pub, Si was perched on a barstool waiting for her and eating a packet of crisps.

"The drinks are on their way babes, take a pew." He patted the stool next to him.

"Thanks." Gypsy gave him a distracted smile and a peck on the cheek. "How's Cathy?"

"She's fine." Si offered her a crisp. "I told her about seeing Dad, so I think she was pleased about that now that they're new BFF's." He grimaced. "I know, I can't really complain that my parents are getting on too well, but it's all a bit weird. Oh and she's still beside herself with guilt over talking to that reporter at the wedding."

Gypsy shrugged. "It doesn't seem to have done any harm. It's not like it screwed things up for Dario with immigration or anything. They only cared about the celebrity angle! Blaine's used to that anyway. All in all I think the wedding went brilliantly, and business seems to be booming around here." She looked around her. "It's miles busier these days. Although I haven't seen Jeremy for ages, and he's practically part of the furniture."

313

"Oh yeah, he stopped drinking." Si remarked. "He went along to an AA meeting with Jeff, Mark's new bloke and apparently he's doing really well."

"Wow, good for him. And how's it going with Dario and Vincent?"

"Blissfully thank you darling!" Dario sang as he appeared from behind the bar where he'd been pouring their pints. "Look! Do you like the highlights?" He gave them a twirl. "A freebie. One of the fringe benefits of sleeping with your stylist, geddit?"

"Stunning!" She declared.

"You're radiant." Si added cheekily. "Married life obviously agrees with you."

Dario pulled a face and rushed off to serve some more customers clamoring for alcohol.

Si took a swallow of his drink. "Right sweetie. Have you come to a decision? Is it too late for me to throw in my two cents?"

Gypsy nodded slowly.

He regarded her solemnly taking in her expression, before a look of relief spread over his face.

"You're going for it, aren't you?" He prompted.

Another nod.

"Yay!!" He punched the air. "Well, our loss is L.A's gain! When are you going to tell Blaine?"

"I'll phone him after we've had our drinks." Her eyes shone. "I'm so incredibly psyched. My god Si, this is just perfect! I need something to bring in cash when I'm not performing and I've been considering make-up artistry for a while. I learned the basics back at college, and doing femme drag has taught me loads more. I can't believe I'm going to be a make-up artist for THE next big soap. I'll get to meet all the stars; I might even get some acting work while I'm over there."

"So what gave Blaine the idea then?" He asked.

She smiled. "He said he was impressed with the look I gave him that night we went out to the Pink Flamingo. Actually he said he thought I had incredible artistic talent. Of

314

course, he's seen me done up as Faye Kinnett too and he knows I'm qualified."

"That's just awesome. People will be falling over themselves to make use of your skills once word gets around you've got him as a client."

"I know. Look, don't get me wrong, I'm really grateful." Gypsy looked pained. "But this has been a hard decision. Part of me is really sad at the thought of leaving. This is my home. I love living with you and Tony. It's going to be horrible leaving my friends and Jezebel."

"Come on baby, you know I'll be happy to look after the stripy diva. Plus it won't be forever, just nine months or so. That's right isn't it?"

"Yeah, after that who knows, it's quite exciting really." She raised her glass in the air and clinked it against his before taking a swig. "Also, in the future I'll have a second line of work to fall back on. Not that I don't plan on picking up where I'm leaving off with the acting and the drag."

"I should hope not." He grinned. "Everyone's talking about Faye Kinnett since you teamed up with Gladys Cox-Hardt. And as for acting work, you've got mum and Stella representing you so I'd say the skies the limit!"

"It's all looking pretty fantastic, isn't it?"

He nodded agreeably. "Life moves in mysterious ways."

"I mean really Si. Who would've believed it? Six months ago if you'd told me I'd be in the papers, get paid to dress up as a drag queen, have a fling with a supermodel and start a new career in La-la Land, I would've been frankly skeptical. My new take on life is... I don't know, to be open minded. If this summer's taught me anything, it's to expect the unexpected."

"Here, here." Si raised his glass. "I'll drink to that babe. After all I didn't expect to find my father cruising in a gay club."

"Right!" She concurred. "And then there was Marina and Dario's marriage. Who saw that one coming?"

"Certainly not moi." He deadpanned. "Ooh and how about Danny discovering his twin in drag at their wedding?"

315

"As you do." She laughed into her pint.

He was on a roll. "And who would have thought that Vienna Valentine would make it big in the acting world?"

"You what?" Gypsy spluttered, choking on her beer.

"Gotcha!" Si chuckled mischievously. "You should have seen your face sweetie. I gotcha there, I gotcha *good*."

Made in the USA
Charleston, SC
30 May 2012